Contrition

By
Robert E. Hirsch

JournalStone
San Francisco

Copyright ©2012 by Robert Hirsch

All rights reserved. No part of this book may be used or reproduced by any means, graphic, electronic, or mechanical, including photocopying, recording, taping or by any information storage retrieval system without the written permission of the publisher except in the case of brief quotations embodied in critical articles and reviews.

This is a work of fiction. All of the characters, names, incidents, organizations, and dialogue in this novel are either the products of the author's imagination or are used fictitiously.

JournalStone books may be ordered through booksellers or by contacting:

JournalStone
199 State Street
San Mateo, CA 94401
www.journalstone.com

The views expressed in this work are solely those of the authors and do not necessarily reflect the views of the publisher, and the publisher hereby disclaims any responsibility for them.

ISBN: 978-1-936564-40-8   (sc)
ISBN: 978-1-936564-41-5   (hc)
ISBN: 978-1-936564-42-2   (ebook)

Library of Congress Control Number: 2012937963

Printed in the United States of America
JournalStone rev. date: August 24, 2012

Cover Design: Denise Daniel
Cover Art: Philip Renne

Edited By: Dr. Michael R. Collings

Acknowledgements

I wish to acknowledge several people who have shaped both my existence and my fulfillment in life.

I owe my beginning to Kazu Park, my Korean mother who suffered greatly as a young woman at my birth, throughout the Korean war, and upon sending me across the world and not seeing me again until forty years later.

I owe my celebratory mentality to my father, Colonel Peter J. Hirsch, a strong and admirable role model of the highest degree.

And finally, my full adoration and undying allegiance goes to my wife, Melissa, who is the kindest, most generous, and most perceptive human I have ever encountered.

Check out these titles from JournalStone:

Women Scorned
Angela Alsaleem

The Donors
Jeffrey Wilson

The Void
Brett J. Talley

Jokers Club
Gregory Bastianelli

Pazuzu's Girl
Rachel Coles

That Which Should Not Be
Brett J. Talley

Cemetery Club
JG Faherty

Available through your local and online bookseller or at
www.journalstone.com

It is often said that time heals the wound . . . and too often forgotten that nature leaves a scar

so the injury may never be forgotten. The gift of memory has been bestowed upon man not

so much to enable him to celebrate and memorialize his past actions, but to enable him to

work his way through reflection, contrition and redemption . . . and be forgiven for these past

actions.

Chapter One

Brother Placidus slowly wheeled the old Buick along the short span of bayou that separated the campus of Saint Gregory from the northern sprawl of Fishman's Point, where the descendants of French and Yugoslav immigrants lived in weathered shotgun houses painted white and capped with tin roofs. He stopped on the bridge, and as he left the car to open the crusted gate, a Great Blue Heron, standing motionless in the channel's low tide, looked at him with disdain, preened a moment, then lifted effortlessly from the water, its expansive wings beating a muffled rhythm through the air. Drifting along the tops of the marsh grass for a moment, it changed course and suddenly ascended over the treetops, making a wide arc west toward Biloxi.

Fumbling with the lock, Placidus wiped rivulets of perspiration from his forehead with a swipe of the shoulder. "Black clothes," he complained, curse of the religious. With a firm shove of his hand, the crusty gate creaked open and a dozen tiny fiddler crabs boiled out from around the corner posts, clittering their way across wooden slats and disappearing between the cracks.

Brother Placidus was the first to return every August to the deserted campus of Saint Gregory after the July shutdown. As the eldest of the Brothers of the Holy Cross in residence at Saint Gregory, he had been relegated the task of preparing the house and restocking the pantry before the arrival of the others from summer leave.

The Brothers' house was on the historical register and Placidus had spent the greater part of his life there. It was an imposing stone fortress of a structure, two stories with a full attic. It stood alone at the back of the campus, half-obscured by a massive stand of ancient live oaks from whose twisted branches hung great tresses of Spanish moss dangling in fragile clusters that cascaded nearly to the ground. Having survived the forces of nature and man, the house had been standing there in haughty grimness for well over a century, housing the secrets of more than five hundred Brothers of the Holy Cross over the many decades, some more prayerful than others. It was both a holy place and a landmark for five generations of fishermen from Gulf Springs.

But to Placidus the house had become a shade more ominous with each passing season and it required a measure more of courage to reopen it each summer. He used to imagine that he was bringing the old monument back to life, but lately, he seemed to sense that it had a will of its own, and that disturbed him at times. He couldn't remember the exact moment that he began to suspect the existence of something threatening in the old structure, but the fear had now been with him a long time. His anxiety seemed to grow annually, festering there amongst all those other thoughts that went unspoken, feeding silently year after year.

Placidus's old mind was full of such baggage. Overflowing even. Busy hands shove aside such fears. If only he were teaching again, he thought, he wouldn't have time to frighten himself into corners and down rabbit holes. He trudged dutifully to the side entrance. It wasn't until he tried to insert the key that he noticed the door already stood slightly ajar. Upon closer examination he saw that the lock appeared to be scuffed and the door's edge was splintered just below the catch. *Probably young boys or derelicts from Fishman's Point raiding the amply supplied wine cabinet, like last year, and the year before*, he grumbled.

But what if

He froze a moment, straining to hear any sound coming from within. He was met with silence.

Everything's okay. I'll step inside, find the wine gone, call the police and fill out a report. It'll be good to see Peter Toche again anyway, and when we're done with the paperwork, I'll fix some tea and we'll talk about my trip.

He stepped into the kitchen. Several of the cabinet doors stood open and it appeared that someone had, indeed, sorted through and taken some of the canned and dry goods. Next, he shuffled over to the wine cabinet. That door also was open and the contents pilfered. Sighing with irritation, he next examined the chapel and the library but found no trace of tampering. *Better check the upstairs*, he thought, mounting the stairs to the sleeping quarters where he was met with the mustiness of an overly humid summer.

Working his way down the corridor, he briefly peered into each of the sixteen rooms but found nothing. Most were bare and had been unoccupied for years, a fact that testified to Saint Gregory's slow decline from its once elite status as the finest school on the Mississippi Gulf Coast. Placidus missed those busy days when the Brothers were assigned two to a room, when the house was full and the school flourished.

As he neared the west end of the hall, the air became increasingly foul and warm. It occurred to him to go back downstairs and set the air conditioning, but just as he turned, something caught his attention. He glanced up the narrow stairwell that led to the attic and stopped mid-step. The door at the top of the steps stood wide open.

Placidus had seldom been in the attic, especially in recent memory. He avoided it because even since childhood he had dreaded dark, abandoned places, and as he had aged, those ancient fears seemed to have returned one by one. So maybe it was true, the old and infirm become like children again. But what did all that matter now? The attic door was open and it wasn't supposed to be. It was a house rule—Keep that door closed so the hot air of the attic doesn't overwork the compressor or allow the cool air to escape. Close that door so the dust of decades doesn't fill the sleeping quarters.

Close that door because my room is at the bottom of the stairs and the attic frightens me. When the door is open, it's like looking into a dark hole and dark holes

I hear something. It's…

My heart. I'm just frightening myself. Someone just forgot and simply left the door open. Calm down.

But something dreadful happened up there, remember? Or have you forgotten, old fool?

No, he hadn't forgotten, but it hurt to think back on that day, even now. He took a deep breath and squeezed his eyes shut, trying to flush the memory away. But suddenly, he heard a rapid fluttering above, much stronger than the one beating at his temples. A sharp screech followed, then another. Placidus listened, then sighed, relieved. He knew that sound. It was gulls. They must have entered the attic again through that section of fallen siding beneath the eastern peak. He chastised himself for being afraid and for not insisting that Brother Albert repair the damage before the summer departure.

Gulls. That explained the odor. But as he mounted the last steps to the attic, the smell took a turn, becoming fouler than just the musty odor of unused places and bird droppings. Covering his nose and mouth, he stood upon the landing, grimacing, and stared into the attic. It took several moments for his eyes to adjust to the room's cavernous gloom. Pale slabs of dust-filled sunlight filtered through two end vents but the interior remained more obscured than expected.

"The heat," he muttered, "unbearable."

Through the milky light he could see that the floor was strewn with stacks of religious books and school texts, most swollen to bursting from moisture and age. Toward the center stood a dozen or more crates, old music stands, cardboard boxes, and several old suitcases. A life-sized crucifix leaned precariously against a large steamer trunk, facing the door, and for a moment Placidus imagined that Christ's carved, mournful gaze moved from the door to the flooring at the foot of the cross.

Stop it, for God's sake. It's lifeless, carved from wood and painted by man. Darkness plays tricks on old eyes.

But still, it's frightening and desolate. It makes all who see it feel guilty and ashamed.

Then don't look at it. It's always given you the chills. But at least chase the birds off. They're desecrating the statue of Christ. Flush them out.

By now he could see that the gulls were gathered at the far side of the attic near the opening high on the damaged wall, and stooping as he went, he carefully picked his way toward them. Their squawking escalated as he approached. Several rose angrily from their perch on the rafters, flapping their wings to enlarge themselves as if to frighten off this unwelcome intruder. But Placidus was determined to flush them out despite the vein of uncertainty that had been creeping into his bones since climbing the stairwell. He inched forward.

Suddenly, he stepped into an unseen swarm of gulls at the foot of the crucifix and they surged upward, burying him in an eruption of flagellating wings and outstretched claws. Crying out in terror and surprise, he instinctively covered his eyes and face. Then, striking out wildly to ward off the attack, he lost his balance and fell forward, tripping over the base of the crucifix, landing face-to-face on the leaning statue of Christ. He and the large crucifix teetered a moment, then collapsed to the floor in an explosion of noise and dust.

"God forgive me!" Placidus beseeched, shamefully brushing dust from the cheeks of Christ, who only stared grimly ahead, his carved face an eternal mask of agony and sorrow.

The birds, spooked, quickly retreated to the damaged wall. All but one that stood its ground just inches from Placidus's face. It glared at the old man, then dipped its beak and jerked at something fibrous.

Placidus rubbed his eyes, squinting through the haze of unsettled dust. As the bird became more visible, Placidus could determine that it was feeding. He watched a moment; then his breath caught as suddenly the shadowy scene unveiled itself. He blinked twice in horror and disbelief, wishing that he wasn't really in the attic, wishing that he hadn't really fallen on Christ, and that he didn't really see . . .

Shuddering aloud, he pushed himself from the statue of Christ and away from the gull. He tried to rise, looking toward the rafter above for hope, but faltered clumsily, like a candle seeking oxygen. And when he finally gained his feet, the small girl was still there. She lay at the foot of the cross, naked on the attic floor, legs splayed. Her bloodless face gazed dully forward with the same expression of agony and sorrow that Placidus had just witnessed on the crucifix. Her body was splotched with wine-dark stains emanating from even darker punctures that ran the entire length of her torso. And below her navel lay unspeakable horrors.

Trembling, Placidus's hands clapped to his head and his eyelids fluttered limply as his face lifted to the rays of light that penetrated the damaged wall. Quickly he made the sign of the cross, then fumbled for his rosary. His throat filled with vomit. He staggered backward as a man driven by a high wind, senses collapsing. The room began to swirl and the merciless clamor of agitated gulls grew ever louder and nearer. *They're coming after me*, he thought, closing his eyes and shielding his face again. And as they surged forward, the air about him suddenly grew cold. He heard in their screeching, something that was utterly demented, neither of nature nor God's hand.

Fumbling his way about with the desperation of a man blinded, he clumsily backed his way through the dim clutter of crates and boxes, knocking aside stacks of holy books and hymnals, kicking them from his path. He tried to open his eyes but they resisted, afraid of being clawed perhaps, or unwilling to bear witness again to the butchery on the floor. He thought of Saint Michael the Archangel, and strangely, of the Great Blue Heron from the marsh. *If only I could fly*, he thought. He begged to be spared from the gulls, thinking that he would surely descend straight to the fires of Hell if he perished now, thinking how unworthy a servant he had been.

Somehow he reached the landing. Reflexively, he sucked in fresher air, eyes still glued shut, and stepped out into—

—nothing.

Contrition

Screaming, he tumbled down step after step after step, his rosary clutched between now bleeding knuckles.

Paralyzed and semiconscious, he lay there in a heap, lost somewhere between reality and the Dream World. And in this fog, a carousel of images from the past suddenly began to flash before him. Then, just before blacking out, Placidus felt the floorboards creak for a second and sensed a shadow descending the stairs.

Someone . . . He shuddered. *Finally coming to . . . punish me.*

Chapter Two

Father Joseph Broussard rumpled the boy's curled spill of hair and smiled. "After you set the candles in their stands, Jamey, make sure all the kneelers are up," he said. "Then you'll be done. Oh, and your mama wants you to go straight home this evening. Your uncle brought fifty pounds of shrimp over to the house and she needs them de-headed. They're big ones she said. She wants them in the freezer before you go to bed."

The boy wrinkled his nose, warm in the shadow of the priest who had baptized him. At nine years of age, he much preferred the company of Father Joseph Broussard over the chores of his mother. "Fifty pounds?" He frowned, shrugging his angular shoulders comically.

"Afraid so, little man. They had a good haul last night. Weighed in over twenty-eight hundred pounds at Letellier's this morning, so hurry along now, your mama needs you. And don't forget how many hundreds of pounds of shrimp I cleaned for *my* mother, God rest her soul. And I'd give my right arm to be able to help her again, Jamey. Just remember that. One day yours will be gone too, and you'll miss that woman dearly."

"Not if I die first," the boy teased, dodging the swipe of Father Joseph's palm.

"Devil!" the priest wailed, feigning anger. "Get to work and be gone from this place!"

The boy complied, of course, but he was sorry the afternoon had ended. He idolized the Jesuit and cherished these moments spent together. Just shortly after young Jamey's birth, his father had been killed in a boat fire, so he was little more than a brooding face in old photographs to the boy. But Father Joseph Broussard, now *there* was a man, educated and holy, so unlike the boy's boorish uncles and grown cousins.

Jamey already had it in his mind to attend the seminary one day and wear the sacred collar. He would become a Jesuit just like Father Joseph and travel the globe doing God's work, returning from time to time, to share his adventures with those on Fisherman's Point, bringing back little ebony

Contrition

puzzles, exotic brass castings, or leather goods from afar. As the priest turned to leave, the boy watched him wistfully, already eager to help again next Friday.

Father Joseph stepped out from the ornately carved doors of Saint Ann Cathedral and gazed skyward at the great purple smears that hung over the darkening coastline. Shortly they would be turning a deep violet, then black as dusk settled into night. He saw in them the majesty of God's work and the dreams of his own youth, dreams that for the most part had materialized if one ignored a detour here or there.

He had carried the Lord's ministry as an educator and facilitator from the plains of Kenya to the fishing villages of Japan, and a dozen points in between. But it was good to be home again. He had always had it in mind to end his career on the Gulf Coast, and Providence had brought him back to the very doorstep of his youth, frayed perhaps, but hopeful.

He worked his way down the long stand of concrete steps, hastened his way across the Coastal Highway and took a seat on the seawall. The faint pulse of evening breeze felt good against his face, but his black clothes still hung heavy in the humid air. He looked across the bleached span of sand into the darkening waters of the channel and beyond, to Heron Island, an endless scar of spindly pines and sea oats. A campfire flickered there among the dunes and unintelligible voices carried laughter across the water.

Joseph had been coming to the seawall since childhood. Then, of course, he had waded the shallows, gigging flounder or seeking his mother's favorite delicacy, soft-shelled crab.

It was along this very stretch of beach that he rode his grandfather's prize quarter horses, when the Coastal Highway was but a thin ribbon of two-lane blacktop and its drainage system but some engineer's dream. His grandfather had wanted Joseph to take over his well-established and lucrative horse breeding business, but, instead, Joseph chose to attend the seminary.

He pulled off his sports coat and draped it across his knees. Next, he shed his shoes and socks. Then loosening his collar, he dug his toes into the sand, seeking the coolness that waited below the hot surface. He lit a cigarette, and as his face disappeared behind blue wisps of spent tobacco, he heard the prow of a wooden shrimper steadily approaching the nearest channel marker. He loved these wooden vessels and remembered a time when fiberglass and steel hulls were foreign to Gulf Springs and wooden shrimpers still ruled the Sound.

The boat passed the marker, leaving it awash in spume and from the stern an old Yugoslav motioned to him, slowly passing his hand in the traditional fisherman's greeting. Then the boat slipped down the channel and turned south into the Gulf, its diesel engine dissolving with distance into a faint drone. Father Joseph followed that drone, reflecting on his career as a Jesuit. It had been a brilliant one, filled with travel, intrigue, and unfortunately, controversy.

He had seldom failed to fulfill his mission, especially as a younger man, and had established an enviable reputation for mediation and diplomacy. He was multi-lingual, had a grasp of foreign and primitive cultures and was once the confidante of Cardinals Vincento Spada and Paul Fouquet, two of the men most responsible for the reforms decreed by the Second Vatican Council of 1962-65. And to his credit, he still managed to retain the respect and friendship of their greatest adversary, Archbishop Marcel Lefebvre, French-born leader of the traditionalist movement who bitterly opposed the changing trends of Catholicism.

Father Joseph had been censured of late, however, and those glory days were but memories. His fall from favor had been mostly self-inflicted, revolving around foul language and drink, but he blamed the Jesuit hierarchy as well. He had grown weary of the in-fighting and political maneuvering, and their demands were unreasonable at times, causing him to question their motives. The politics of God had become too secular.

But as the pendulum descends, so it rises. He had recently been chosen by the Saint Gregory Search Committee to reverse the decline of their school, the very school from which he himself had graduated. It was at Saint Gregory that he had met young Brother Placidus, the man who had inspired and guided him into the seminary. Brother Placidus had hoped that Joseph Broussard, his strongest Latin student, would become a Brother of Holy Cross. He was not entirely disappointed, however, when his young liege became, instead, a Jesuit.

As he sat there enjoying the stillness of dusk, the clouds began to thicken, and in the distance soft pulses of heat-lightning inflamed the sea's horizon, highlighting a pale moon that now sat just above the pines of Heron Island, casting its warm glow over the channel despite the billowing of storm clouds.

"Dark enough," he said to nobody, content that the traffic to his back was sparse. He reached into the inside pocket of his coat and fished out a flask, unscrewing the cap with meticulous care. Then he bent his head inconspicuously, took a deep swallow, and exhaled. "Damn," he murmured, licking his lips. He took another swig. Then he capped the flask and slipped it away. God, it was good to be home.

Contrition

The diesel drone of another shrimper caught his attention, approaching from the west, but he didn't look up. Instead, he gazed into the water ahead, its gentle moonlit ebb and flow lulling him toward drowsiness. *Saint Gregory*, he thought. He would resurrect the once proud institution or die trying. It would be his last hurrah, his final act of faith.

Damn the Jesuits, he would succeed, if for nothing else then just to spite the order that had shunned him after years of devoted service. And in return the old school, perhaps, would breathe new wind into his own luffing sails. Saint Gregory, like him, was in decay. But they would rise together. Saint Gregory, his final hope. Saint Gregory—

Something suddenly erupted from the water, surfacing in the middle of the channel. It didn't register at first in the dim light, but Joseph managed to cast off his dulled senses, and staring hard at the water's movement, he envisioned a large fish. No, too erratic, he decided.

Leaving the seawall, he took two steps forward and squinted into the meager light. The darkness was deceptive but the thing was still on the surface, struggling. Then a vertical form shot above the thrashing water, disappeared, then rose again. An arm, Joseph realized, alarmed. It's a man, come from nowhere—dead in the path of the oncoming boat. Joseph shot a glance to his right. It was one of the big steel-hulled shrimpers, nearly a hundred feet in length, plowing forward like some monstrous locomotive stuck on a fatal course.

Joseph cried out. Dropping his coat, he ran to the water's edge and waved his arms frantically at the oncoming ship, but its deadly prow continued to slice the black water ahead into frothing halves that fell away in swells.

"Stop! Turn aside!" Joseph screamed. "Man in the water! Stop, damn you!"

From the pilot's seat, the ship's captain saw nothing but the channel marker, its ruby eye directing him forward. Over the roar of his twin diesels he thought he heard the lonely shrill of a night gull to port, hovering low in the channel before the bow. The shrieks grew louder but he ignored them, concentrating instead on the steady squall of his recently overhauled engines.

The man in the water began to scream, suddenly aware of imminent annihilation, and tried to thrash away from the ship's course. But the prow was advancing too quickly. Another few seconds and tons of vessel would crush him, pushing him asprawl into the propeller where he would be shredded like by-catch and cast aside.

"God!" the man in the water cried, filling his lungs with air before diving headlong into the depths with frenzied motions of all four limbs. Eyes closed, heart pounding, he felt the ship rumble over him by inches. Then came the furious pull of its backwash dragging him toward the stern—and the propeller.

Awash in a hell of foam and ocean, he felt his mouth and nostrils filling with brackish seawater, his lungs emptying. Instinctively, he curled into a fetus, covering his face and head, ready to feel the gnashing bite of steel rip him to ribbons. Tightening, he braced for the onslaught, unable to distinguish up from down or life from extinction. He felt the pull, tons of water dragging him backward toward those grinding blades of steel. He was unable to scream, or even utter a prayer because the deafening roar of diesels extinguished the world, and all hope of life itself. *It's over*, he thought, suddenly opening his body, spreading his arms and legs.

Surrender to God and the sea. Return to darkness.

But in that flickering instant, the rushing roll of water beneath the lethal ship caught his exposed torso like an open sail and flung him aside just moments before the churning blades could suck him back. Gasping, he kicked out and surfaced, his lungs filling with water. But then he sank again, his limbs too feeble to hold him up.

I'm drowning.

He opened his eyes and saw only blackness—and felt only his descent. He was dropping like a stone. The water grew colder with each fleeting second, sharp against his bare skin, and all he could hear was the deep burbling of his own breath leaving him and the fading rumble of the ship. He felt icy bubbles bursting upon his forehead, bidding him a cold farewell before themselves ascending to the surface. Suddenly he felt giddy.

The Rapture . . . I'm dying.

His neck went limp, unable to support the weight of his head. Then his arms drifted with the current, flagging to one side, devoid of strength.

Don't fight. It isn't so painful . . .

The bubbles were smaller now, and as his head sank onto his chest, he could feel them escaping in slow sporadic bursts, thumping against a heart he could scarcely feel. It was little more than a tiny blip, pulsating somewhere within a perishing framework of ribs.

I can't feel my body now. I'm left only with my soul, and that too . . .

But he *did* feel something. His bare toes struck sand as his body continued to sink. His knees buckled at first, and the dead weight of his torso drove him deeper into the sand until he was squatting on the channel floor.

Kick out. Kick up!

Contrition

Gathering every ounce of will, tightening every numbed muscle of his dwindling existence, he thrust his feet against the sea floor and sprang upward, hurtling himself toward the surface.

Life. Focus on life.

But with this sudden change of will, rapture fled, and in its place came pain. His lungs began to burn and his head felt on the edge of explosion. And his legs stung as though suddenly pierced by a thousand nettles. He began to scream, but the water muffled his cries and huge bubbles began to burst all about his face as he fought the channel.

Suddenly, he saw a glow. The moon. It was peering down at him through the filmy water, urging him on. And then came a great plashing as he broke the surface. He puked water from his throat and mouth in a frantic struggle to seek air, but felt himself suffocating even more. He floundered about for several seconds, writhing and choking, then collapsed, his entire body paralyzed with exhaustion. He was sinking again.

But then came a hand, grabbing at his hair. And an arm locking about his throat. He felt himself suddenly being dragged under again. Still gagging, he tried to struggle, but his arms and legs were spent.

"I've got you!" a voice cried out. "Don't fight me, dammit! Stay calm or you'll take us both under!" He felt himself floating on the surface and beneath him the struggling of another man, tugging and straining to carry him ashore. And in this final surrender he grew still, gazing skyward at the filtered glow of a white moon, warming him, breathing new life into his limbs and soul.

"P-praise God," he whispered, feeling sheltered in the grips of whoever had been sent to drag him out of the sea. He had twice been spared.

The other man flopped him off his side into knee-deep water. Then, the man began to crawl toward the beach, dragging him along. Finally, in the luminescence of moon and white sand, the two men looked at each other for the first time, both spent and struggling to breathe.

"Damned cigarettes!" Joseph rasped, grabbing at his heart. "I'm too old for this."

"Y-you could have been k-killed!" the younger man wheezed, coughing up water.

"I thought you were gone for sure. The boat, it—"

"Y-you're a *priest*!" the younger man interrupted, his eyes falling on the other's collar.

Joseph was immediately struck by the young man's voice. It was unusually deep and clear, and the quality of that extraordinary tone struck him as nothing short of remarkable. He looked closer at the man he had just dragged from the channel, then blinked, startled. "A-and you're—*naked*!"

The young man looked down at himself, then flushed, cupping his groin with both hands. "I—"

"The channel's a hell of a place to go skinny dipping, son. Judas Priest, what were you thinking?"

"N-no . . . the boat. It must have ripped—"

Joseph eyed him suspiciously. The young man seemed disoriented still, but he *did* appear to be embarrassed about his nudity. Joseph decided to forgive the indiscretion. And that voice, he marveled. Over forty years in confessionals and he had never been so struck. "My coat's over there," he said. "Better cover up before someone sees us from the road. Wouldn't look so good me laying down here in the sand with young, naked Adonis. That's *all* the hell I need right now!"

"Th-thank you, Father." He reached for the coat and pooled it around his waist and hips, tying the sleeves in a loose knot. Then, placing his hands in his lap with the poise of aristocracy, sitting upright, he closed his eyes.

"Are those your friends out there?" Joseph said, pointing to the campfire on Heron Island.

"No. I'm—alone."

"Alone? In the middle of the channel?"

The young man's eyes remained closed. He gave no reply.

Joseph stood, pulling his damp, clinging trousers away from his skin, and noticed the young man making the sign of the cross. And from that single gesture, the old priest felt a faint tug of affection for him, whoever he was. "I swear," he said, shaking his head, "I'd been sitting on the seawall for half an hour watching the water and I didn't see a soul in the channel."

The younger man nodded and finally opened his eyes. "I d-don't know—I mean, I'm not sure . . . "

"You're still clearing your head. Take it easy. And thank your lucky stars. Hell, we could have both drowned, but we're going to enjoy a few more sunrises, eh?"

"*Ad majorem Dei gloriam,*" the young man whispered, his eyes taking on a different light.

"Y-yes," said Joseph, suddenly surprised, "for the greater glory of God. That's the Jesuit motto. How did you know I was a Jesuit?"

"I didn't," said the young man softly, propping his chin in his palms.

Then he slowly blinked at the water, as if coming from far away, exhausted, having survived some terrible ordeal, something even more frightening than the propeller or the cold depths of the sea. "I would like to

Contrition

attend Mass in the morning," he said, "and take communion. But I must give my confession first. Would you hear it, Father?"

The priest nodded. "Now?"

"No, in the morning. I need to pray first. It has been such a—long time . . . and I have much to be thankful for."

The moon was now high above the pines of Heron Island, casting shadow branches across the silvery reflections of the channel. The tide softly lapped the water's edge as the two men sat in utter silence. But it was a comfortable silence. The old Jesuit carefully measured the other's silhouette, as the other in turn measured the night. The red light of the channel marker shone on the young man's pale face, seeming only to heighten that strange trance of his.

They would be friends, Joseph decided, pulling the flask from his coat that covered the naked stranger. But right now he needed a drink and was unwilling to attempt, for the moment at least, to fathom the difference between luck and fate. "*Ad majorem Dei gloriam,*" he whispered, raising the flask to the moon.

Chapter Three

Peter Toche rubbed at the slight swell of belly that only recently had begun to strain against his belt. And though he was one of those rare men who became a shade more handsome than his aging peers with each passing season, especially when he removed his glasses, he imagined that middle age was beginning to extract its toll.

He was a quiet man by nature, educated and thoughtful, overly reflective, some said. Life had dealt him just enough defeats to make him wise, but not so many as to jeopardize integrity. Through his labors as Chief Investigator for the Gulf Springs Police Department, he was highly regarded by law enforcement officers along the entire Mississippi Gulf Coast and had assisted on special cases in nearly every shoe-string city along the meandering coastline. In recent years, he had been called on four times by the D.E.A. and twice by the F.B.I., serving as the catalyst in closing three of those five cases. Nor was he a stranger to the A.T.F. or the Mississippi Bureau of Investigation.

His reputation was based on imaginative and instinctive intuition. He became detached, peers concluded, and his cool self-possession on the hunt was in itself a remarkable thing to observe. Perhaps it was rooted in his twenty-two years of police work in New Orleans before finally returning to the coast. The "killing place," he had called it, where people die over crossed words or a pocket of change. He had seen everything there and learned that death had many faces. There, too, he had learned to neuter emotions and mask thoughts. He had seen crushed skulls, severed throats, and women mutilated beyond recognition, and each of these he had objectively catalogued, tabulated, and filed away as past history.

But sometimes those grisly scenes come back on their own, some more frequently than others, as though burned forever in his consciousness despite strenuous efforts to lay them aside. They crept back while he was sleeping, or idle, to call on him like some unwelcome acquaintance from a past life. He suspected it was merely the walls of time closing in about him, condensing twenty-five years of police work into a small but select gallery of cadavers.

When they came back, he had difficulty remembering whether he had first seen them in New Orleans or on the coast, though he remembered every other detail quite well. Was that possible? Had his thoughts become that disconnected? Was everything behind him truly becoming a blur, and had the world for him truly dwindled to this attic above the living quarters of the Brothers of the Holy Cross where he now stood?

His face revealed nothing. But neutral faces often mask truth, and Peter Toche knew there was a rift opening somewhere within, between his logical side and his instincts. All sorts of black suppositions had begun to cloud his thinking.

It was only last week that he had first stepped into this attic after Placidus's incoherent phone call. "C-come, Peter! Come now!" the old religious man had muttered over and over, in the grips of some unshakable horror that allowed him no other words. And when he arrived at the Brothers' house, he found Placidus bloodied, nerves stripped, pointing at the stairs. "G-go up!" the old man wailed, clutching at his chest as if to keep his heart from imploding. "It's in the attic!"

Pistol in hand, he had left Placidus, crept up the stairs, and shortly thereafter found the small girl. Despite a lifetime of mutilation and madness, a single broken gasp caught in his throat at that moment. In that cry there was something so unexpected and dreadful that he fought to subdue it, as though it signaled the end of his self-possession and objectivity in the face of death.

When that cry had finally dissipated, he looked about quickly, hoping that Placidus hadn't followed him up the stairs. He hadn't. Then, oddly, his eyes darted about the dim chamber to make sure no one else was there to witness his faltering. Yes, he was alone. Except for the girl, and she couldn't have heard because her eardrums had been punctured, her body perforated, her belly opened.

He had sighed heavily then, but as his breath left him, he could feel his courage slinking away, casting not a backwards glance. All of this in two or three seconds. For the first time in decades he stood before a corpse shaken, standing afraid in a lightless place where some human creature had wreaked inhuman havoc upon a small, fragile child.

That was when the worry lines creased his face and the fetid smell of entrails overpowered him. Suddenly, he began to choke on his own breathing, and he involuntarily broke out of the room, stumbling twice, unable to stomach the scene a moment longer.

It hadn't been so much just the blood, the mutilation, or the life-size crucifix where a carved Jesus stood staring at him. It was the air, that rotten, stifling air . . . and his sudden loss of heart in the face of all those factors combined. Damn. Why had he cried out? He berated himself a dozen times as he beat that hasty retreat to the landing, cursing, desperate to plunge backward into time five seconds, no, now ten, then fifteen, to take back that cry of shock and outrage, to pull it out of that putrid air and shove it back down his throat and cap it off forever. But too late.

Now, as he stood at the mouth of the attic for the third time in just as many days, he felt more nerves loosening inside him. But he stepped forward, ushering Brother Patrick Darnell through the door. Brother Patrick was the Provincial of the House, but years ago he had been Peter's classmate at Saint Gregory.

They had been best friends, played football together and chased the same girls. They had remained friends over the decades and had even kept in touch even when Brother Patrick had been sent east, and then to Europe.

Peter wiped his lips with a crumpled rag of handkerchief, then stuffed it back in his pants. "When I retire this one'll stand out, I'm afraid. Hard to figure an act like this. Hell of a lot of sickness involved here." He gazed about the chamber, his magnified eyes swimming behind the lenses with hawkish interest. "Last year that airman from Keesler butchered those two women over in Biloxi. That was bad, but this, *damned* hard to stomach. Little Amanda LaFleur, sweet as they come. Good family, too, especially old Didier, the grandfather. Damn shame, all of it."

Brother Patrick nodded, shielding his eyes from the glaring series of bare hundred-watt bulbs that had been strung by the investigative team. He had been in the attic countless times over the years to cull through the books or to store things. But it seemed naked now, its mystery stripped away, its clutter set aside in tidy stacks along the walls, its center barren and exposed.

This was his first time in the attic since Placidus's terrible discovery, and as his eyes ran the length of the huge chamber, he shook his head ruefully, still finding it difficult to accept that a young girl had been so viciously brutalized just above the room where he prayed before going to sleep each night. "Peter, my God," he said, "*here* of all places on this earth. We're all so stunned. I . . . "

"Everyone knows you close the campus down during July. That Placidus comes back to open it in August. Hell, they closed it when we were kids, too, you know. An isolated place, no witnesses, that part of it fits. It's the rest of it that gets fuzzy. The extent of violence . . . ritualistic as hell. Post-mortem mutilation, a complete absence of conscience from beginning to end. Far beyond simple rape or murder."

Brother Patrick looked at his friend. "*Simple* rape or murder?" he said. "Have the years hardened you to that point? Another example of why you really should return to the Church. We miss you, you know."

Peter felt the reproach. "I was being simplistic. Sorry. I just meant that this is way off kilter, crosses too many boundaries."

Brother Patrick breathed easier despite the thickness of the air. "Absolutely horrible, this whole ordeal. God only knows how much time it will take for the town to heal."

Peter closed his eyes and wiped his forehead. *Time,* he thought, *no, it doesn't always heal*. And it wasn't helping him of late, and he seriously doubted whether it would help Placidus either. Sensitive old Placidus was going to pay a heavy price for bumbling onto the girl's corpse because his heart had thin walls, and thin walls don't hold up for long against the tides of trauma. Peter thought of himself. He could retire soon. A few more years maybe, thanks to his wife's modest inheritance.

Right now he didn't feel much like staring at dead flesh anymore or digging half-decayed remains from secluded places because sometimes those scenes came back. Certain ones more than others. And now, from the attic, another would be added to that unwelcome gallery. He blinked his eyes open with a start, just managing to save his glasses as they slid down his face.

"Pete? You okay?"

Peter cleared his throat and with a knuckle pushed his glasses back to his brows. "Yeah, just wandered off a moment. Happens every now and then. Comes with the territory."

But discouragement darkened his face, unable to conceal itself behind the polished lenses of those owlish glasses, and he could feel that nascent uncertainty taking hold again, leading him into precipitous thinking. He placed his palms together and locked every finger, as if to stop the hemorrhaging going on within his mind.

The two men stared vacantly about and eventually made their way to the center of the attic. Peter pointed to the chalked pattern of a child and shook his head. "This is the position Placidus found her in. Coroner said she'd been lying up here at least five days before Placidus showed up. She was clubbed, beaten, cut all to hell, but we haven't found any weapons up here or on the grounds. And we damn sure don't have a suspect."

Brother Patrick covered his nose and mouth. "I thought the smell would be gone by now." He stared down thoughtfully at the chalk pattern, white dust in a childish scrawl representing what was once a small girl. It appeared that both knees had been broken and the legs twisted away in opposite angles.

"Pitiful, isn't it?" said Peter, fixing his eyes on the chalk pattern, looking beyond it, boring into the wood floor itself. What the eyes don't see, the heart sometimes does, somehow, and his was sending out minute alarms that very instant. He became aware of waves of feelings, silent and unexplained, powerful as the flush of heat against his face.

As he stared at the blood-stained wood, its darkness suddenly made things seem dim and far away, and the entire world telescoped into that blood-stained patch of timber. He wanted very much to crouch and put his ear to the floor, thinking he would hear something in the wood, the creaking tale of what had really happened, perhaps. But he shelved that urge, feeling his friend would think him ridiculous. He would come back another time and listen to the wood and chase other shadows in solitude.

"How long before the smell goes away?" said Brother Patrick. "All those bird droppings only make it worse."

"A while. It's the heat up here, like a damn oven. It decayed her flesh until it was half-cooked. She was disemboweled, too. The first day I came, this place smelled like a slaughterhouse. And then there's all that fecal matter in the corner there."

Brother Patrick frowned. "From the gulls?"

"Well, yes, partly. They came in through that opening in the gable." Peter spat between his shoes, some of the spittle catching his shirt. Then, adjusting his glasses he said, "Human shit too, I'm afraid."

"*Human*? My God, it just gets worse and worse," said Brother Patrick, disgusted.

Peter nodded. "Yeah, afraid so. Seems someone stayed up here for a day or so. We found some empty tuna cans and water bottles over in the corner there. By the way, Placidus *does* know I want to ask him a few more questions, doesn't he?"

"Yes. He's not looking forward to it, though. He's changed these past days. He just isn't right anymore. Never been a more kindly or gentle soul put on this earth, but I'm afraid the shock was too severe. He can't seem to come to grips with this thing."

Peter nodded. "It's upset the whole community. Christ, we've never had to deal with anything like this in Gulf Springs."

Brother Patrick shook his head. "I imagine the worst part for the family is not knowing who or why. For us, too. Lord only knows what effect this'll have on *all* of us."

Peter nodded. "Well, let's go see Placidus. Maybe he can shed a little more light on all this. Didn't get much out of him before, but I've got to keep trying. He's the closest connection we have at the moment."

"He's in the chapel downstairs. Guess I should mention that he's suddenly taken to keeping sacred objects about him. And he carries his Bible everywhere now. And holy cards. He's even wearing a small silver crucifix that was blessed by the Pope. You know, his room was at the foot of the attic stairs, but since that day he found the girl, he won't go near it. He's taken to sleeping on the chapel floor, at the foot of the statue of Saint Michael the Archangel in the rear of the chapel. We've tried to be patient, but he's becoming quite impossible."

"Doesn't seem right, does it? Him of all people to have to find her." Remembering his own weakening and repugnance at finding the girl, he imagined that Placidus's reaction must have been utterly crippling. He pitied the old man. "You know, Pat, when we were kids, one of the Brothers living here killed himself. Hung himself in this very attic, remember?

"Nobody ever figured out why because there was no indication of trouble, no suicide note, nothing. I seem to remember that the man was a very close friend of Placidus, though. And wasn't it Placidus that actually found him hanging from the rafters? No wonder this place gives him the willies. My father was the investigating officer in the case."

"Yeah," said Brother Patrick, "we were in about the seventh grade, our first week at Saint Gregory." Brother Patrick stuffed both hands in his pants pockets before continuing. "Since joining the order I learned that the man's name was Phillip Allison. His death has become part of the history of this house, I'm afraid. And yes, it was Placidus that found him."

It suddenly struck Peter that the odds of one man finding two bodies in the same attic were infinitesimal. And though the circumstances in each case were starkly different, the horror for Placidus must have been the same. He tried to envision finding his own best friend at the end of a rope, then quickly shoved the thought aside. "This Brother Allison, did Placidus ever talk about him?"

"No. During my first residency here I was thoughtless enough to ask him about the incident, but Placidus simply passed it off. Said his friend was suffering a crisis of faith or something equally vague. I don't remember exactly. It was obvious that he didn't want to talk about it.

"Several weeks later, an odd thing occurred. I was in my room one afternoon and I heard footsteps in the attic. I came up the stairs and saw someone standing on a chair reaching up to one of the middle rafters. It was fairly dark but I was pretty sure it was Placidus, and since he never went to the attic alone, I was curious. I didn't make my presence at the landing known, but I remember thinking in a moment of panic, 'My God, he's going to hang himself just like his friend did.' I was just about to rush in when he suddenly stepped down from the chair and moved it against the wall."

"Did he have a rope?"

"No, so I quickly left before he could see me on the landing. I felt pretty silly about it all by then."

"But it *was* Placidus, right?"

"Yes, definitely. And when I saw him coming down the stairs, he looked upset."

"So what was he doing up there?"

"Well, I went up with a flashlight a few hours later when Placidus went into town. I found small woodchips on the floor where the chair had been. I got the chair and stood on it to examine the rafter. He had apparently carved out a small cross. My guess is that's the rafter where Brother Allison hung himself."

Peter was puzzled. "But that would have been almost twenty years or so after his friend committed suicide. Doesn't that strike you as odd?"

"Yes, it did at the time. But I'm only presuming that's what it was all about. Who knows for sure why anybody does anything?" He took a few steps backward and looked overhead. "There"—he pointed—"if you look closely you can still see it. Placidus put it there."

Peter's eyes floated about searching the rafter until he spotted it, mindful that the trivial often had to be examined through a magnifying glass. "I'll be damned," he said. "A final act of friendship maybe?"

"I suppose. Or a final blessing. The church condemns suicide. Maybe it was Placidus' way of asking God to be merciful. But we'll never know. A curtain of silence exists between Placidus and this old place. He's spent more time here than anyone else in the house records, but he seldom speaks of the history. Consequently, we never ask. Who knows what secrets are cloaked by time?

"This thing with Brother Phillip Allison—Placidus has long since put it all behind him. Sure, I suspect he might have an inkling why his best friend chose to exit at the end of a rope, but then maybe not. Perhaps Brother Allison was just running away from the terrors of life. There was a Diocesan Inquiry, you know. It's all on file at the Diocesan Office."

"Yeah, my dad worked the case, but he never talked about it. Did Placidus say anything for the record back then?"

"No, not a word."

Peter shook his head and grunted admiration. "Loyal to the end, eh?"

"Yes. Probably thought he was sparing his friend's dignity. Who knows what kind of problems the man might have had. He drank a bit too much, they say. And it could have even been a woman for that matter.

"There were rumors circulating that he had a fondness for the ladies. Lord, he wouldn't have been the first religious man tempted onto a mattress. We're only men when it comes right down to it. Some remain strong while others weaken . . . like cops or politicians. No matter how ethical we Brothers aspire to be, some just can't escape their humanness."

Peter stared at the bisecting lines carved deep into the overhead rafter, lifting his eyebrows. Maybe he was probing in the wrong hole, but the cross hung directly over the chalky outline of Amanda LaFleur, and this realization loosened something in his chest. He felt his breath stop in his throat for a moment as suddenly another thread fell into place. Or was it only his heart and nerves colluding against him again, throwing him into that uneasy flux of late?

Perhaps, but it was as if this one place in the attic was a dead zone. There it was, simple and withering. A *dying* place. Or no, maybe a *finding* place. The cross made in that rafter twenty years ago had been a monument to a dead friend, but had it also been prophetic, foreshadowing some insidious future occurrence? "Damn," Peter said, shifting his weight forward to the tip of his toes, straining to get a closer look.

"Would you like a chair?"

"Uh, no, no need," said Peter, easing his shoes back. *Maybe I think too much*, he wondered, admonishing himself. Then he ushered that thought away, too, and led Brother Patrick to the landing.

They descended to the ground floor and found Brother Placidus in the rear pew of the small chapel, holding an open Bible, lines red-penciled on both pages.

"Hello, Brother," Peter said gently, squatting beside him like an old friend.

Placidus looked up from his Bible, as though jolted out of his reverie. Brother Patrick moved to his shoulder.

"Brother," said Peter, "I'll try to keep this short. I know—"

"You said that the *last* time you came, and the time before that," the old man grumbled, sharp as vinegar. "How many times are you going to hound me over this business? Are you paying me back for Latin class after all these years?"

Brother Patrick and Peter exchanged a look over his head. "Brother," Peter continued, unruffled, "I know this has been difficult." He touched the old man's elbow deferentially. "When you entered the attic that day, are you positive you didn't hear anything else ? I mean, are you absolutely sure?"

Placidus bristled a moment, uttering nothing. Closing the Bible on his lap, he squeezed it so hard his knuckles paled.

Peter continued , "Was there any other sound besides the gulls coming from inside the attic?"

"Placidus," Brother Patrick whispered, "this is important. Peter's just trying to help."

Placidus remained tight-lipped, but Peter pressed on. "Someone spent some time in the attic with the girl's body, Brother Placidus . . . we're just not sure how long—maybe even right up to when you arrived—maybe hiding in the big trunk or behind the stacks of books. It was awfully dark, you know. Take yourself back. Think *hard*."

Placidus suddenly took on an air of fragility, but then it quickly passed. "I *told* you already," he said with heat. "I didn't hear a thing but the birds squawking. Why won't you believe me? It was just *me* up there, and the girl . . . no one else. Except the statue of Christ—and he was *bleeding*!"

"No, Placidus, there was blood *on* the statue, but the statue itself was *not* bleeding. That's impossible. We suspect that *that* blood came from the suspect—that he might have inadvertently cut himself while mutilating the corpse, and possibly some of his blood dripped onto the crucifix."

Placidus shot an irritated glance at his former student and his face turned pasty. "When I ran out of the attic, I couldn't see, so I fell down the stairs. A pit opened at my feet when I reached the landing and as I was falling, like descending into the portals of Hell, I heard that wail . . . It was *her*, the girl!"

Peter shook his head, confused. "You just said you didn't hear anything except the birds, and now suddenly you tell me you heard a wail or a scream. You never mentioned that before. Why?"

Not a flicker of response.

"*Placidus*," urged Brother Patrick, "you must tell him everything. Without your help, they'll never be able to solve this frightful murder. Please."

Placidus's eyes focused on the detective's in a dark and bitter communion of fear and grief. "It w-was h-her," he stammered, floundering to sound rational. "As I was falling, I heard that dreadful wail and I saw—a shadow?" Placidus felt a cold finger touch his heart and he began to shake.

"A *shadow*?" Peter said, his patience dissolving. "Dammit, you never said anything about a shadow before!"

"Y-yes. I saw it—it followed me down the stairs as I fell. Then it stepped over me as I hit the floor. Then I just . . . blacked out."

Peter's confusion was mounting, but he had no reason to believe that the old man was lying. Not knowing how to ask the question less baldly, he forged ahead. "Did this shadow—*speak* to you?"

Placidus tightened every wrinkle of his face with a twitch of eye-rolling resentment. "*No*, the shadow didn't speak to me! It was the dead girl, the passing of her tormented soul. Or maybe the shadow of Christ, come down off that cross to punish me for *finding* her!"

"Brother," said Peter, his eyes becoming slits , "it was *not* the girl. She was dead. And it was *not* the statue of Christ, that's impossible. Someone else must have been in the attic that day you arrived. The killer, maybe. And he must have been bleeding, which is why there was fresh blood on the statue. I think—"

Placidus threw his hands in the air and began to weep. "No, it was the blood of Christ! *He* was bleeding. From his hands and feet. My God, man, can't you see that!"

Placidus lowered his head into his hands and his shoulders dropped nearly to his lap. He convulsed, trembling in spasms, crying for strength to reinforce the slowly dissolving fabric of his faith. "My *God*, you must believe me. The wounds of Christ were *bleeding!*" He waved the other two men off with a disgusted flap of the hand. "Stigmata! Stigmata!" he hissed, reopening his Bible and burying his face between the pages.

Peter gave Brother Patrick a troubled glance and stood. "Thank you, Brother," he said. "That'll be all for now."

Brother Patrick saw Peter to the door. Before leaving, Peter thanked him for his cooperation and shook his hand. But as the door closed, Peter looked up toward the attic as a sudden coldness began to wash through him. He now felt certain that the murderer had indeed been in the attic that day watching Placidus, for some ungodly reason, five days after the girl had been slain, choosing to leave only after Placidus had bumbled into the attic.

As he walked away, he felt the house behind him, sullenly and deliberately obscuring some unimaginable evil. And when he reached the car, he thought he suddenly heard a ghostly cry coming from the attic vent—the shrill, girlish scream of a young child pleading for the butchery to stop, not knowing that it had only begun.

His shoulders convulsed in an involuntary shiver and he tried to shake the cry aside. But it only grew louder and more urgent. And then, at that same moment, confusing past memories began to pour in so fast

Contrition

and clear that he became momentarily disoriented, not remembering whether he was in Gulf Springs or New Orleans. He shook it off, not wanting to look back at the house, and realized that the cry had not come from the attic at all. It was in his head, and that disturbed him even more.

He shuddered. Sometimes they come back, those scenes, ugly and unwelcome. Some more often than others. And sometimes, if you weren't careful . . . they could drive a man mad.

Chapter Four

Peter Toche and his partner, Dan Wilcox, were penciling and marking with push pins the large wall map of Gulf Springs when Chief James Barhanovich entered their office. "Christ, this damn town has grown." He heard Peter mumble.

"Yeah," said the Chief, "not the same little ville you grew up in, Pete."

Chief Barhanovich was a large man with pronounced and unrefined facial features. His voice was gruff, and his handshake rough, but these coarse mannerisms were deceptive for he was in fact a highly considerate man. More importantly, he was Peter's godfather. And it was James Barhanovich, not Peter's father, who had inspired Peter to join law enforcement.

"Morning, Chief," Peter said, continuing to mark the map. "Yeah, and Jenkins over in City Planning says he's already filed over three hundred housing permits this year and it's just now August."

Barhanovich nodded. "That'll double next year," he said. "More prime property'll be up for sale once the dozers move in next week to clear out the old deserted section of Back Bay . . . the old seafood factory foundations, the Twin Oaks Motel, the whole damn mess. It's just as well that Desporte's old warehouse burned down out there last week 'cause it was gonna get plowed anyway. Waterfront property's gotten too valuable to just sit around and rot anymore."

"Christ, I remember back when Back Bay was the heartbeat of the coast," said Peter. "We're down to two seafood factories now, and they're both on North Bay. Guess you can't stop progress, especially with the casinos moving in. Just didn't think it would all happen so fast."

With the arrival of waterfront gambling, Gulf Springs was indeed thriving, as were all the towns along the Mississippi Gulf Coast. European in heritage and Catholic in faith, the town still thrived in old-

Contrition

world attitudes. These influences were evident in the architecture, family names, religious and civic celebrations, and even a bit yet in the pronunciation and the dialogue of the residents, especially the elderly.

"Day shift's waitin' for you, Pete," Chief Barhanovich said, examining Peter's markings on the wall map. Then he pointed to Peter's unsightly and unkempt desktop. "Christ, Pete, your dad'd shit if he saw that mess! How in hell do you keep track of anything anyhow?"

Peter smiled. "It's all right up here," he said, pointing to his forehead.

"Yeah, I bet, with all those other strange things you keep hidden up there, eh? Anyway, c'mon."

The Gulf Springs Police Department had a hundred and eighteen employees on its rolls, counting clerks and custodians. It operated on a shoestring and rotated on four shifts. In this realm, Chief James Barhanovich was king. What he decided within the confines of GSPD was law, and the opinions of the Mayor, the City Council, or other aspiring town voices mattered little.

Barhanovich was an old-world despot, generous but absolute, cordial but unquestioned. And he absolutely adored Peter Toche, as a man, as a member of his extended family, and above all as a criminal investigator. The acquisition of Peter Toche to GSPD was, for Chief Barhanovich, both a professional coup and a personal triumph.

The two men entered the conference room together, followed by Dan Wilcox. "Listen up, people, and listen close!" Chief Barhanovich called out roughly. "Pete's goin' to give you a quick run-down. And dammit, we want your full attention."

Peter took his position behind the podium. "I've already briefed the other shifts," he said, once satisfied that all eyes were front and center. "Brother Placidus has given us some new information. Seems like someone might have actually been in the attic the day he found Amanda LaFleur."

A chorus of whispers arose, and there was some shifting in the chairs as several officers exchanged surprise. Dan Stewart, a senior investigator, raised his hand. "Placidus swore the place was empty and that he didn't hear anything or see anyone. Hell, it's all in my report. You were right there when he said it, Pete."

"Things have changed, Dan. *Now* Placidus says he saw a shadow and heard a voice as he was tumbling down the stairs. Placidus is half out of his mind right now, but I believe him. I've never in my life seen a man as terrified as he is. Also, you need to be aware that Placidus is convinced that the crucifix in the attic was bleeding." Here he paused. "Keep that under your hat. It's not for public consumption."

"You mean that he saw blood *on* the crucifix and on the floor, same places as we did, right?" asked Jesse Sekul, another investigator.

"No, I mean just what I said. Placidus believes that the statue of Christ was actually bleeding. You know, blood was coming out of the nail wounds."

"Geez!" someone uttered above the sudden burst of side comments. "Here we go off to LaLa Land!" The room erupted into laughter.

"That's enough!" Chief Barhanovich grunted. "Listen up and cut the bullshit."

"Anyway," Peter continued, "I believe the perpetrator might still be in town. If he hung around long enough for Placidus to show up, he must have been waiting for something, or maybe someone. Just a hunch, but let's not rule it out as improbable here. After all, this whole thing's improbable as hell."

"Does that eliminate the drifter theory then?" said a voice in the back.

"No, not completely. But whoever it was had to know the campus was deserted, and that should indicate involvement of someone local. I know we like to think we know our own people and that this town is immune from this sort of thing, but let's not make any assumptions. Yeah, it might still have been a drifter, maybe one that hooked up with someone that knows the town."

"Local or not, this guy'd be shit crazy to hang around after doing something like this," a voice grumbled.

"This guy *is* shit crazy," said Peter to everyone. "Crazy as a damn loon. Bottom line, I think the perpetrator might still be in town, and I'm hoping like hell he's not a damn serial killer. Now so far, the family is clean, and the Brothers were all out of town. Other than that, everyone you meet is a suspect.

"Keep looking, keep listening, and keep digging. Someone out there knows something. Gulf Springs isn't like it used to be, new folks are moving in every day. Lots of new faces out there, and visitors, lots of unknowns. Keep talking to the riff-raff, too, and our other regulars. And don't be afraid to make a stretch, people. Don't be afraid to think the impossible."

"And what about the cult theory, Pete?" a new voice called from the back.

"Not dead either," Peter answered. "Keep an eye on the juveniles and especially the religious kooks. Never omit the overzealous. And one last thing, we've rounded up Willy Turner, Lucas LaTour and Timbo Skremetta—questioned them, released them—but we still haven't found Little Jimmy Dubaz. He's usually camped out around Back Bay, which isn't far from Saint Gregory. Anyway, nobody's seen him for over a week now, ever since Desporte's old warehouse burned down."

"Yeah," Dan Wilcox chimed in, "no mystery there. That little shit-bird probably set the damn place on fire in the first place, and now he's hiding out like the little rat he is."

Peter nodded. "Maybe so. But anything he's ever done, he hasn't been out of sight for long. Keep looking for him. I want him ASAP. Okay, that's it for now, people. I'll keep you posted as things develop. Thank you for your attention, and good hunting."

Chapter Five

Father Joseph heaped a third spoon of sugar into his mug and stirred the syrupy brew with great ceremony. Then he tipped the mug to his mouth, peering over it, and measured his overnight guest in dawn's light. The man was young, yet strangely haggard about the face and eyes. His mop of blondish hair was on the long side, tousled, but possessed a shine that was striking. And though his gaze was dulled by fatigue, his gray eyes possessed a clarity that was almost startling.

"How'd the couch work out last night?" said Joseph.

The guest nodded with gratitude. In a moment of generosity, Joseph had offered him a place to sleep after the near catastrophe in the channel. And though the young man had offered very little information that night at the water's edge, it had become evident to Joseph that the man he had pulled from the water was completely unfamiliar with his surroundings and had no place to go.

"And so," Joseph continued, "you're Catholic, and you're French born. At least we know that much. And you don't have any clothes. Well, I suppose that's a beginning anyway. And your name again?"

The guest pushed his mug aside and drew both palms onto his lap. "Tristan . . . de Saint . . . Germain," he said slowly, with great deliberation, as though pulling the name from a distant place.

Joseph took another sip of coffee, pretending not to notice the slight tremor in his guest's speech. "Your confession this morning, you broke into Latin twice. You did it as naturally as breathing air, never missed a beat. And another thing, you have very little to be forgiven for."

"I have *much* to be forgiven for," said Tristan. "A lifetime squandered, broken vows to my family, my acquaintances, and my God. Misguided loyalties, pretension, false priorities. Much, much to be forgiven for."

Contrition

"We all fail at times," said Joseph thoughtfully, weighing his own past. "No man attains perfection. What I'm saying is that your confession cited no specific sinful deeds or intentions, and failure itself must not be confused with sin."

Tristan shook his head woefully. "Failure in outside things is to be expected, but failure from *within* is a cardinal sin. It is the most heinous act we could ever perform before God's eyes."

Sensing that further disagreement would be futile, Joseph paused thoughtfully. The young man's mind was set, and whatever painful journey had brought him to this present state had been chiseled in stone and could only be worn away with time, not words. "Well, then, just out of curiosity, do you speak any other languages besides French, English, and Latin?"

"Yes, Spanish and Italian. Portuguese. German and Gaelic. Greek."

"Damn." Joseph sighed, never once doubting his young guest because his tone lacked any trace of boastfulness. "How the hell did you manage that?"

Tristan examined Joseph with curious shining eyes and offered a meek smile. "You use odd language at times for a priest. But to answer your question, I have traveled, and I have taught . . . long ago."

"Long ago?" Joseph chuckled. "You can't be a day over twenty-two or three!"

"I am thirty-three. And you, what do you do here, Father?"

"Please, just call me Joseph. We'll drop the title for now. I'm a school administrator. I've just been assigned the principalship of a school here."

"And does that please you?" asked Tristan, both hands still aristocratically poised in his lap.

"Yes, greatly so. This is my birthplace. The locals wanted me back, and the Jesuits, damn their souls, were more than happy to unload my old carcass here." At this, Joseph laughed, but there was no pleasantry in his voice. "So, you've traveled. Where?"

"All over Europe primarily, but I spent quite a bit of time in the Middle East also."

"Oh, really? I've been there myself. *Salaam leium.*"

"Peace be with me? Thank you. After last night in the water, those words have taken on a new significance."

"Dammit. You speak *Arabic,* too?"

"Yes. *Allahu akbar*. God is great. And there is no God but *the* God . . . *La ilaha illa llah*."

The priest's smile broadened. He closed his eyes, marveling again at the richness of tone and texture in the young man's voice. "Ah-ha," Joseph said, "a linguist, an educator, and a philosopher! You said you taught once. Did it suit you?"

"Yes, very much so, but I was called upon to do other things."

"Ever thought about doing it again? Maybe temporarily, I mean."

Tristan looked at him, puzzled.

Joseph continued. "Well, it's just that I happen to be looking for someone to fill in for a few days or so until Brother Corso gets out of the hospital. He's our French teacher and school starts in three days. Might be nice to actually have someone in there that could do more than babysit the students. I could put you on temporarily until Brother Corso is released. If it doesn't work out, I'll have lost nothing. And neither would you from the looks of things."

Nothing could conceal the troubled look that swept over Tristan's face, an expression that evoked sympathy and pity in equal measure. "I don't think—"

"You don't have to decide now," interrupted Joseph, quelling his own personal designs a bit. "Think it over. I'll show you around the school, take you around town. And it just so happens that my neighbor's got a small cottage behind her place. I'd let you stay here but, well, you know how rumors get started. Handsome young man moves in with old priest. I'd never hear the end of it, from the Bishop on down."

Tristan looked away and stretched. "You said you were offering Mass this morning at seven?"

"Yes, it's almost time. The church is just across the street."

"Then let me answer you after Mass. I will pray on the issue." Tristan then rose, holding up the trousers he wore by the belt loops. "Life has been generous to you, Father Joseph." He smiled. "Judging by the waistline of these pants you've loaned me." He then made the sign of the cross and left the table.

* * *

Peter wiped rivulets of perspiration from his forehead with the swipe of a shoulder, then shed his sports coat and tossed it onto the kitchen table.

Contrition

"I'm home, Della," he said, more to himself than to his wife, who could be heard shuffling about in the adjacent laundry room above the whir of the wash cycle and clothes tumbling about in the dryer.

A moment later Della entered the kitchen. She was petite and possessed smooth, dark skin, and even darker eyes and hair. Though she was still attractive for her age, Peter at times wished she could be a bit more demonstrative of gesture and spirit.

"Oh, Peter, didn't hear you come in," she said, leaning upward to kiss his cheek and pat his back. It was one of those dutiful, unsmiling gestures she made each day upon her husband's return. "You get later every evening it seems. Missed you. How'd things go today?"

After so many years of marriage, Peter was not completely uncomfortable with Della's rather mechanical greetings. "Same as yesterday, same as last week," he said. "Still no leads, still no suspects."

"Poor dear." Della sniffed, moving toward the sink. "Oh, Didier LaFleur and Tom Dardar stopped by. You just missed them."

"Oh?" said Peter, disappointed.

"Yeah. Which one of them did you say gave you your first cigarette when you were a kid? Or was it chewing tobacco?"

"Well, it certainly wasn't Didier LaFleur, Della, you should know that. Didier was the *good* one. No, my first cigarette was from Tom Dardar . . . *and* my first cigar, *and* my first chew of tobacco. Old Tom was no role model. He was always egging us boys on, but he was good to us, too."

"I asked them if they'd seen Jimmy Dubaz. They said no, not in a while."

Peter sighed. "Della, you shouldn't have done that."

"Just trying to help, dear," she replied, unaware of Peter's irritation. "Anyway, poor Didier. The old man's just devastated about all this mess with his granddaughter. He looks on the verge of tears whenever he mentions her name."

"Amanda was his life. Her murder was a crushing blow. Don't quite know how *anyone* gets over the death of child."

"It's all so horrible, Peter. I don't even like to think about it. Anyway, he's sure got a lot of faith in you, dear. He went on and on about how you'll be the one to solve this if anyone can. He said—"

"Yeah, yeah, I know." Peter sighed. "I've heard it all a thousand times, from Didier, from the Chief, from everyone. It's a hell of a lot of pressure. And I still have zilch at this point. I feel like a damn rookie."

"Don't be so hard on yourself. Didier LaFleur worships you, and so does the chief. You should be honored. They know you're an exceptional investigator, that's all. Besides—"

"Thanks." Peter groaned, not hearing the rest of her tedious testimonial to his accomplishments since joining law enforcement. She was proud of him, and always reassuring, but her metronomic praise could be bothersome at times. He left the room quietly to seek the refuge of the couch.

Besides, that queer emptiness that had first visited him years ago in New Orleans had begun to stir in his belly again—and he was beginning to feel nauseous. As he rested his head on a cushion, he closed his eyes tightly and exhaled, hoping to chase the sensation away. But it grew instead, coming at him in tiny waves, flowing from his belly up through his heart and on toward his brain, making him want to jump out of his skin. Finally, it subsided, and he breathed easier. Anxiety attack, he fretted, sure of the symptom but unwilling to acknowledge the cause.

These little bouts disturbed Peter, because he was just at that age when health becomes an issue. *Health,* he thought, *so long ignored, so long taken for granted, now a concern.* Worse yet . . . *mental* health. What in life could be more terrifying than the onset of mental illness at his age? And this is what he quietly suspected—the onset of a nervous breakdown. Though he chased this unwelcome trespasser away with the vigor of a man defending his homeland, he ran from it, too—wishing it away, denying it, and pretending that it was high blood pressure, stress, or simply age.

All of this had been thrown upon him unexpectedly one grim afternoon in New Orleans, from nowhere, as he looked down at the face of a nameless little black child who had been brutally bludgeoned to death by her drunken stepfather. All over a pair of shoes she had left in the hallway that caused him to trip and fall.

From that single moment, he had felt strangely alone in life. From that one frightening rush of uncertainty, he had felt an inner and private anxiety—and the sudden need to return home. He fretted over this, and ultimately interpreted this inner collapse as an omen, sensing somehow that evil awaited him in the not-so-distant future—that she was secretly knitting her nest, quietly hatching her brood, like some horrid spider awaiting the opportunity to devour him, his loved ones, and his hometown.

Contrition

The psychiatrist in New Orleans had disagreed. "This is typical," the doctor said. "Anxiety and depression go hand in hand—one feeds the other—and the resulting sense of impending doom is predictable. You fear for yourself or loved ones and goad yourself into foreseeing doomful events at every turn. You dwell on the macabre. I'll prescribe some medication for now. Then we'll run a battery of tests. We—"

Peter thought back on that one and only session with the psychiatrist. *Bullshit*, he had decided. *I'm not talking to a guy that wears a bow tie and sports a flat-top. I'm not depressed and I'm not crazy. Bullshit. I'm just worried. Something inside me is talking to me, that's all. It's happened to me like this my entire life. And I've listened to that voice, and it has served me well. I feel deeper, see deeper, and imagine deeper. It's a gift—a gift that brought me home, a gift that's warning me that something is about to unfold . . . a gift that has been scaring the hell out of me lately.*

Sleep came quickly for Peter that night. It crept over him quietly, shrouding him in a warm and comfortable embrace. He felt himself dropping, spiraling downward into blackness, and rest. And there he lay motionless and at peace for well over three hours beside his wife.

But then he drifted into that strange state of semi-consciousness, that out-of-body detachment that exists somewhere between deep sleep and mental awareness. He felt himself involuntarily twitch twice in rapid succession, then twice more. He was just there, on the edge of awakening, but he felt himself being dragged back again—to that place.

Then suddenly he saw himself standing there, shivering, in that narrow, dimly lit hallway—gazing down at the dead little girl, her angelic black face nearly smiling as if lost in the tranquility of a better life and a better home than the one in which she was slain by her stepfather.

Peter felt chilled. The hair on the nape of his neck stood erect and he felt a rash of gooseflesh coursing lizard-like over the back of his hands and up his forearms. He was afraid. No, terrified—because he knew that in a moment, the girl would speak.

He heard the voice, its soft and girlish tone laughing a bit, as in an infant's sleep. The soft laughter's hypnotic pull mesmerized him. She lay there on her stomach, her cheek flat against the cold and filthy linoleum, her arms sprawled outward. "Peter Tooooocchhheeeee. the voice whispered. "You shouldn't be here." Then a girlish giggle.

Peter shivered again, but was more spellbound than a mouse just before the strike of the serpent.

"Peter Toooccchhheee," the wraith whispered, eyes still closed, cheek still to the floor. "You must gooo hooommmeee."

"H-home?" he managed to stutter though his tongue was frozen and he could feel an icy grip closing about his throat.

"Hhooommmee your father. He is dyyyiiiinngg. Home to your people. They are dyyyiiiinngg, too."

Then her face suddenly moved, and before Peter could catch his breath, she raised her head and her eyes blinked open. Her stare seared the very heart that was about to explode in his chest. "Eeeevviiill is coming home," she whispered, smiling, even though tears had formed in her eyes and had begun to trickle down her soft ebony cheek. "Go now, Peter . . . go now, Peter . . . go . . . "

Her head dropped to the floor again and her eyes closed, and Peter felt himself seized by an utterly mournful sorrow. "W-wake up, little girl!" he heard himself cry out. "Wake up! You're not dead! I'll take you from this place! I'll—"

But the little wraith was truly dead again, and Peter knew that no amount of shouting or pleading would arouse her from her sleep. He began to beat against the wall, cursing the girl's stepfather, cursing the Big Easy, cursing his own helplessness. Harder and harder he beat, with both fists now, until the battering weakened the very sheetrock before him, causing the hallway wall to shatter and crumble—

"P-Peter! My God! Peter! Stop!" someone screamed.

And then he awoke to a frightened and sobbing Della. She pushed away at him with extended arms and out-turned palms, protecting herself.

"D-Della?" he heard himself say. "Is that you?"

"Oh, Peter!" she wailed. "You're hurting me! You were hitting me in your sleep! My God, what is it? You were screaming and rolling around, pounding at me—"

"Oh, Christ," Peter said, exhaling deeply, shaking himself awake. "Oh, damn I'm sorry, Della, I'm so sorry! I must have been . . . I was back there in New Or—"

She flipped on the bedside lamp and sat there on the far edge of the bed, hugging her bent knees with her arms. "Oh, Peter," she whimpered, "it's that dream again, isn't it? It's the little girl. She's back, isn't she?"

Contrition

Peter exhaled again, closed his eyes, then blinked them open. "Yeah," he said apologetically. "Damn, I'm sorry, Della. Maybe I better go to the couch again. I—"

"No, stay here. I don't like it when you're afraid. You just scared me, that's all."

He looked at her a moment, still balled up in her fetal position. *She really is a good woman*, he thought. *I really should show her more appreciation.* But the thought quickly passed because he saw the little girl's face again.

"Good night, Della," he said, laying his head against the pillow.

"Good night, Peter," she replied, flipping off the light and tentatively crawling beneath the covers.

And then he heard another voice, one that Della did not. "Good night, Peeetttteeerrrrr," the soft girlish whisper said, "and sleep well. It has beeeeggggguuuunnnnn . . . "

Chapter Six

Peter looked across the room at his father, Victor Toche, who was sprawled backward in his armchair, easing himself like an old setting hen into the nest of death. The smell of medication thickened the air, and though his father sipped at coffee, the hot liquid brought no color to his pale cheeks. Instead, the brew seemed to only further anesthetize the old man's sleep-dulled senses.

"So," said Peter, "you *do* remember the suicide incident at the Brothers' house?"

"Yeah," his father grunted. "I'm the one that pulled him down from the rope. His name was Allison. He was a little shit-hook of a guy. Couldn't be trusted with kids or women. It was a long time ago, but I'll never forget it."

"I remember you always said something wasn't right about it all. Didn't think much about it back then, but now, well, I'm curious what you meant."

His father shook his head with the involuntary trembling bestowed upon him by the onset of Parkinson's Disease. "Yeah, it's this business with the LaFleur girl, isn't it?"

Peter studied his father a moment, as a man surveys the ruins of war, in wonderment, appalled by the deterioration wreaked by bad health and hard living on this once powerful and inaccessible monument. This man was once frightening to him—imposing and unyielding—an inflexible and brutal law enforcement officer in his prime with a reputation for unflagging doggedness. Not intuitive though, Peter had long since concluded. More like his father once managed his daily police tasks with the methodical plodding of a mill horse that trots around in blinders, unaware of anything but the endless circular path that lay ahead.

"The rope marks around the neck," Victor continued in a rasp, "they started just under the chin and ears, but they went down below the Adam's apple. *Well* below, down into the chest."

"*And?*" Peter said, knowing that his father could never make anything simple. No, not for him, ever.

His father smiled, but the smile didn't set well on his lips—it was false and tremulous. He and his son had never managed well together and the only bond that they had ever shared was Eva Toche, mother to one and wife to the other. As the old man looked upon his son, he thought once again that this creature before him was a huge gap in his life, like one of those great crevices that a storm sometimes carves out of the coast in a single night.

"The rope was small," Victor continued, as though talking to himself, his eyes gazing inward. "Just a cord, really. Should've drawn tight right off, just under the chin and ears. No reason to ride up and down his neck like a damn pogo stick. And his hands, too, palms covered with rope burns. Didn't make sense. If a man wanted to die, hangin's a simple thing. Hell, how many times have you heard of a guy hanging himself in a jail cell—with just a belt or a bed sheet. Boom, bam, nothing to it. It's quick, quiet, no mess, no fuss."

"Well, not always," said Peter. "Sometimes—"

The old man bridled and his shoulders began to shake a little, like a muscle too long under strain. "Yeah, well, you know it all, don't you ? Why the hell'd you ask then?"

"I'm just saying that—"

"Aw, Christ, just spit it out, dammit. You think I'm stupid, Pete. And oh no, you couldn't just listen to me or just nod your head yes. You never trust anyone else's hunches or instincts. No, you're the *almighty* expert. You make me sick. Why the hell'd you even come over, anyway ?" Then he sat up a bit, scowling like an aggravated dog about to snap. He had watched his son's rise within law enforcement with a sad silence rather than paternal pride, much like a ruined man who, through the window pane, watches people feasting at the table of his former home. "Yeah, what the hell would I know, eh, Pete? I only spent a lifetime in the profession."

Overcoming the impulse to snap back, Peter laid his rolled coat aside on the couch and looked downward with filial submissiveness, as though that single gesture might atone for his father's bullishness. But

Peter was not afraid because he had long since shed that fear of his father's wrath.

It had happened one night decades before in high school when as a senior offensive tackle he was getting his head slammed to the turf again and again by an ape of a defensive lineman from Biloxi High. Each time that night, as he had raised his ringing head to the stands, he had glimpsed his father ranting and ridiculing him to neighbors, relatives and classmates. No, that night he had lost his fear.

At game's end, though he was bloodied and broken-nosed, the dam broke and he spoken up to his father, screaming and cursing a lifetime of bitter retorts, avenging every secret embarrassment, unleashing every dread. This he did in front of family, the Brothers of the Holy Cross, and his team. And though he had expected his father to angrily assault him on the very stretcher where he lay, his father had simply stood there, aghast. And since that night, these two had lived on the verge of exchanging blows.

Peter sat there as his father's tirade continued. In a moment he knew his father would launch off into new realms of profanity and disgust. He sat there quietly and uncrossed his legs and pulled at his pants where they were binding him, in the knees and about the crotch, as his father's insolent diatribe became but a distant drone from the bottom of some deep, dark caldron. *Indeed,* Peter thought, *what fine thread had kept us from striking each other all these years?*

Then something heavy turned over in his belly and he felt a slight flush rise at his temples as he realized that the room had suddenly fallen silent. He looked up. The two men stared awkwardly at each other a moment. Then his father's cup dropped stone-like to the floor and he shriveled up in the depths of the easy chair, like a leaf suddenly caught aflame.

Peter quickly sat erect on the edge of the couch and reached over, bracing his father by the shoulders. "Easy, Dad, easy. Just sit back. Can you hear me? I'm right here."

His father's neck slowly curled to one side, but his eyes never left his son. He tried to speak, but unable to shake aside the seizure, he uttered instead a series of incomprehensible, guttural sounds. Peter moved closer and eased his father's head back, and at that very moment, the pitiful expression on his father's blank stare tore at Peter and he felt regret wash through him. *How pointless,* he thought, *to have questioned this old man's opinion.*

Contrition

Then, as suddenly as it had come, the seizure subsided. Victor shivered a moment, then licked his lips and cleared his throat. "Pete," he rasped in a tone both foreign and far off, "let this thing at the Brothers' house alone. Just walk away. Christ, look at me. I'm a mess, man. Hell, I'm worse off than a sick old woman."

Peter sat back, adjusting his glasses. It was as though his father's hostility had somehow simply melted away. Peter wanted to acknowledge this. Instead, he listened.

"I never figured out that hanging in the attic," his father said, his voice clearing a bit. "And that bothered me a long time. Never told you this, but the guy was missing a shoe, it was on the floor. I thought maybe he shook it loose as he was jerking around on the rope, but when I checked that shoe and the one he still had on his foot, the shoestrings were both tied tighter'n a damn clamshell.

"Another thing, the tops of his socks were pulled down, damn near below the ankles. Even if a shoe did slip off somehow, new nylon socks don't slip down like that. Lot of things I couldn't quite figure out, but they rushed me, pushed me into setting it aside. The bishop, he talked to the chief. They didn't like scandal. I found out some things about that Brother Allison during my investigation—he was a little roach, you know . . . about as religious as you or me.

"He was a damn drunk, and he chased the women, even the high school girls. The more I found out, the more displeased the bishop and the chief became. When I told them I thought he had gotten one of the little ninth-grade girls pregnant, they really got on my ass. That's when they got the mayor involved. Best to close the books and move on they all decided. Said it could hurt the school, the Brothers, the Diocese, and the town."

Peter nodded. He understood the politics of scandal and how such a thing could occur, especially in the old days. And he knew that his father had always been, if nothing else, a simple and straightforward enforcer of the law. Political favors and whitewashing were beyond his capacities.

"And all that bothered me," Victor continued. "The more they dogged me, the deeper I dug. There are always little unknowns, dirty little details. And that's what you're digging at now. They knew more than they were telling at the Brothers' house. A wall went up every time I showed up on campus and every time I went up into the attic. Something in my heart whispered that there were secrets to uncover if I just dug deeper."

"Secrets?"

"Yeah. But they stopped me. Made me look foolish. Conspired to make me look obsessed and clownish. The attic, it made me stop, too."

"The attic? How could the att—" Peter stopped mid-phrase, not wanting to again inflame his father.

Lost in his own words, Victor droned on. "Yeah, it was like the attic was working against me, too. You know, I could have eventually been Chief of Police. But they black-balled me, all of 'em. And it stuck, right up to when I finally called it quits and retired. Hell, I should've never got caught up in it. Wasn't worth it. The Devil came after me the day I pulled that little shit-hook from the rafters. I died that day and didn't even know it."

Peter shook his head. "You did the right thing. You—"

"Christ, look at me. I'm pitiful," his father said quietly. "Don't follow my path. You don't eat right. You don't sleep right. Your mind's always off on some damn wild chase . . . has been since the day you were born. You've always been right there, just on the very edge of cracking. But at least you still got a good reputation, so don't screw it up like I did. Let it go."

Peter was unprepared for this. He had no response.

His father continued , "Death is a hurtful business. It eats away at your heart and brain. And this little girl's murder at the Brothers' house, it's worse than anything either one of us has ever seen—and we've seen a lot, too much. But people like us, we always return to the scene—like crows attracted to the smell of death. But we don't have to. Get out, just walk away. This one'll throw you over the edge. Your devil's going to come, too, one day. It's not far off. He's coming . . . "

The cold went out of the old man's eyes and fatigue took its place. Peter searched those tired eyes and he felt the lifetime weight of his father's thwarted ambitions beating at him from the easy chair, despite the softened tone, despite the retreat. Peter's mouth suddenly felt salty and his throat grew dry.

"I can't just walk away," he said. "This one's got me by the throat and it won't let go. It's too personal. I know the LaFleurs. I went to school at Saint Gregory. Brother Pat's my best friend. And this is *my* town. Things like this aren't supposed to happen here. And that little angel, if you had seen her lying there, slaughtered, you'd feel the same as me."

Contrition

"My life's come down to a slow death. When I found that Brother of Holy Cross hanging there, something broke inside me. I heard voices up there, Pete. And that's the day my skin began to crawl. There was a crucifix there—it gave me the willies every time I looked at it . . . like Christ was going to speak and jump to life any second. Is it still there?"

Peter nodded.

"If I listen sometimes at night, I can hear the spikes being driven into that cross—through flesh—driven by a wooden mallet. Have you heard it yet? Have you heard the rope swing against the rafter, like the sway of a hangman's noose?"

"N-no. I don't—"

Something flickered in his father's eyes, and then, as they began slipping shut, he turned, barely, and a hand stole out and touched Peter on the shoulder. How and when dread overcomes a parent, even a poor one, has always been a mystery—but this singular message was clearly telegraphed by the remorseful sigh that issued from Victor's throat as his head slumped backward into the fog of medication.

A ripple of unease ran up Peter's back and he felt creeping into him that unspoken fear men experience when setting out on a doomed expedition—that nervous uncertainty as they take that very first ill-devised step on their slow trek toward annihilation.

"Pete," his father whispered, half asleep, "this one'll throw you over the edge. If you hear the spikes being hammered and the flesh driving into the timber—it's the Devil's work. If you hear voices, get out."

Chapter Seven

The Old French House restaurant sat just next to the Gulf Springs Harbor, and each evening at ten o'clock, it closed its doors. Two hours later the trash had been dumped, the floors mopped, and the kitchen reloaded. Something else routinely occurred also, something that was of interest to Peter Toche on this particular night. At precisely midnight, the lights out back were switched off, and that was when the harbor rats began to emerge and gather.

Like insects of decay, thriving only in the refuge of darkness, they stirred from their hidey-holes beneath the boardwalk or from aboard unoccupied vessels belonging to absentee owners. They made their way to the trash barrels behind the Old French House to forage through the wealth of throw-aways and spoiled goods. And though they were a community of sorts, there was little interaction amongst them. Each was there for his own purpose and acknowledged the others only with watchful distrust.

Flashlight in hand, Peter quietly rounded the restaurant and stood for a moment at the back corner, listening. Then he burst forward, flipping the beam directly on the trash barrels.

"Stop! Police!" he yelled.

The huddle of ragged men churning through the barrels froze for a moment, then instinctively covered their faces and scattered. All but one—an old man who was nearly deaf and in possession of but a single eye. By the time he finally looked up, he found himself alone at the barrels.

"Whozat?" he muttered, shielding his eye from Peter's light. "I ain't doin' nothin'!"

"Peter Toche, police! Just hold it right there!"

"I ain't goin' nowhere, Pete," the old man said. "Hell, you know I'm crippled up!"

Contrition

Peter splashed his beam about the area hoping to spot others, but they had already fled into the blackness and wouldn't be back. The grizzled bum standing before him was Jimmy Dubaz's uncle. Though this man had had many opportunities during his youth, he had turned to drink and vagrancy by the time he was twenty, abandoning family and future in a rapid descent brought on by factors that escaped all those who had known him since birth.

"How're you doing, Willy?" said Peter, dropping his beam to the old man's chest.

"How the hell you *think* I'm doin'?" he said, spitting down at his own shoes.

"I'm looking for your nephew. Thought he might be here with you tonight."

"Jimmy? Hell no. Ain't seen him in months."

Peter was well aware that his own father, Victor, had beaten this man in previous decades and on numerous occasions. For this reason, Willy Dubaz distrusted cops. But he *hated* Victor Toche.

"I don't believe you, Willy. You were seen with him just a week ago over on Back Bay, camped out down by the marsh. Three different people told me that. I'll take you in if I have to."

The old man softened a bit. Even though a trip to jail might mean a mattress and warm food, Willy's memories of mistreatment at the hands of the law were stronger than hunger. "Well, *maybe* I seen him," he grumbled. "My memory just ain't so good anymore."

"We haven't been able to find him. I'm worried. Not like him to just disappear. Maybe something's happened to him—hurt maybe."

Willy Dubaz nodded.

Peter interpreted this as an affirmative reply and inched forward. "You heard about Didier LaFleur's granddaughter, haven't you?" asked Peter, knowing well that Willy Dubaz held old man LaFleur in high regard because of his generosity toward him on many occasions.

"No. What about her?"

"She's dead. Murdered." Then Peter paused a moment. "I'm not my father, Willy. I'm sorry about you and him. I'm not going to hurt anyone. But I need your help."

Peter's gentle manner touched the old man a bit. He looked disturbed as he heard about Didier's LaFleur's granddaughter. "Yeah, I seen him," Willy sighed. "And you're right. He's hurt."

Peter nodded, showing no evidence of triumph. "Go on."

"Ran into him a few days back. He was beat all to hell, bloody, looked terrible. Afraid, too, shiverin' like a wet cat."

"What did he say?"

Willy shrugged. "Not much, just said he was scared. That some crazy guy was out to kill him. Said he was gonna dig a hole and bury himself in it."

"How bad was he hurt?"

"Bad. *Real* bad."

"Did he say anything about a little girl, Willy?"

"Naw, nothin' like that. But he said something strange. Said to say a prayer for him 'cause he needed it."

"A prayer? Hell, that doesn't sound like Jimmy."

The old man shifted his weight to his weak leg and leaned against one of the barrels. "That's all I know. Kin I get back to my dinner now?"

"Yeah," said Peter. "Here, take my light. You'll be able to see better."

"Pete, if you see Didier, tell him I'm awful sorry about his granddaughter. He's a good old shit, you know, eh?"

Peter nodded. "I'll be seeing him in the morning, Willy. I'll let him know."

"And thanks for the light. Just one more thing, Pete. Next time you see your old man, tell him I *still* think he's a mean bastard. He shoulda treated me a little better—and shoulda treated you better, too."

At this Peter smiled, but only to himself. As he walked away, he envisioned a younger Victor Toche thrashing a younger Willy Dubaz, and he felt thankful that his father had never become chief.

The next morning, Peter moved to the small-craft harbor just as dawn began seeping into the dark skies and the file of shrimp boats became visible upon the distant horizon. On the pier behind the Old French House, just where Peter knew they would be, a huddle of old men sat drinking their coffee, heads bent, muttering in broken accents.

They were a feeble lot now, after decades of hoisting nets and stooping over culling tables, or shoveling ice and shucking untold mountains of oysters for pennies a day. In their grizzled expressions were woven the trials of a lifetime of seafaring, splayed lines cutting deep and dark into their unshaven faces. Their weathered eyes bore the look of hardship and testified to the rugged, white-knuckled past of Gulf Springs. Most had begun their careers working masted vessels when flat-

Contrition

bottomed schooners sailed the Sound, before the age of Detroit Diesels and power winches.

Peter loved these men, especially Tom Dardar and Didier LaFleur. They were his childhood idols. He had grown up in their shadow, was raised on their tales of fortune and misfortune, and often envied them, wishing that he could have been part of their era.

In their prime all these old men had been brash, barrel-chested youths, eager to work and eager to scrap, the French against the Yugoslavs. But now they sat together, warm in the company of former adversaries. They sat in a cluster, shoulder to shoulder, enjoying their season of quiet with nothing to do but watch the fleet approach each morning from their roost on the pier where women had no place and children were seldom heard.

As Peter approached them, it saddened him to know that each year this circle of old fishermen dwindled because of age and infirmity. Tom Dardar was there today, though, as was Didier LaFleur, Percy Billiott, Hank Jalanovich, and Vince Skremetta. Even old Joe Kuluz was there despite his waning health, because it was a special morning. The *Dame Royale*, a replica of the turn-of-the-century schooners, was holding her initial sea trials and would be passing by soon.

"Ho there, Pete!" hollered Tom Dardar.

"Hey, Pete!" yelled Hank Jalanovich, followed by a wave from Vince Skremetta and Percy Billiott.

"Say, dare, Pete!" Old Joe Kuluz coughed, sucking on the remnant of a cigarette, unfiltered and yellow. "How's dat dad of yore's?" he wheezed.

Peter smiled, returning the greetings with a wave of acknowledgment. "Hey, men, Mister Tom, Mister Didier."

Joe Kuluz coughed again, then flicked his cigarette butt into the water. "Yeah, ole Victor Toche, now *dat* was one mean bastard in his day," he laughed.

Didier LaFleur nodded. "But a good lawman," he said, standing to shake Peter's hand. "Appreciate all the time you're putting in, Pete. Talked to Della the other day, she says you're hardly ever at home anymore, working on the case, I mean." Then his face saddened. "My son, Albert, he appreciates it, too. It's still tough, though, especially on him."

Didier LaFleur was a massive Frenchman, now stooped and arthritic, but he could still quicken the pulse of the old town queens with a simple tip of the cap or a wink of his great blue eyes. He was the spiritual and conversational leader of the circle.

"It's the least I can do," said Peter, taking a seat on an empty milk crate. "Still no leads, though, I hate to say."

"It'll come. It'll happen, Pete. I've been praying on it. God will set things straight. Just give Him time."

Peter nodded. "Hope so," he answered.

But he was much less confident than the old fishermen. And as he looked over at Didier he marveled that the big Frenchman could still maintain such an immovable stand on his faith in God's will—because it seemed to Peter that God had been unusually cruel to this good man and shown him little mercy throughout his calamitous life. Indeed, as a younger man, Didier had suffered a great deal.

He had lost his first born son, Bernard, to polio when the boy was but ten. And eighteen years after that, he was caught in a storm just west of Horn Island and fighting gale force winds, when he lost his third boat, along with two more sons, Claude and Christopher. After that his wife, Marie, lost heart and slipped into a severe depression that culminated in an overdose of sleeping pills, leaving him alone to raise their youngest son, Albert, who eventually fathered his only grandchild, Amanda. The note Marie had left simply said, "Adieu, Didier . . . Forgive me, I am too sad."

What Peter did not realize, however, was that a hairline crack was finally beginning to fracture Didier LaFleur's once unshakable belief in God—because of the recent death of his granddaughter. It was the most crippling blow he had ever endured. Not because he had loved her any more than his Marie, Bernard, or Christopher, but because he simply could not comprehend the heinous way in which Amanda was murdered. He understood polio's indiscriminate grasp, and the cruelty of the sea, and even suicide . . . but not the deliberate slaughter of one so young and innocent.

Amanda had been the only softness in his coarse, male existence since Marie's death. Beyond the pier, she was his life, his sole source of laughter. His greatest pleasure was to hold her in his lap and tell her about an age long forgotten. And she would laugh, eyes aglitter, at his silliness and puffery about past deeds. "Oh, Granddad!" she would squeal, rolling back those huge blue eyes, mocking his exaggerated

Contrition

mannerisms, especially when he would push out his dentures on the tip of his tongue and waggle them at her.

"Hey," said Tom Dardar, "look, here she comes."

The men followed Dardar's finger down the channel and watched as the *Dame Royale* approached. Her sails billowed to the full, her hull heeled at the perfect angle, silently but swiftly making her way toward them.

"Je-zus Christ," Joe Kuluz wheezed, shuffling about excitedly on his crate. "Goddamn, Didier, look at dat boat. Like a damn ghost. Looks just like *La Marraine*, Didier!"

Didier looked and smiled, because the approaching schooner did indeed resemble his family's once magnificent schooner, *La Marraine*, the former pride of the Mississippi coast. He was but twelve when he, his father and grandfather constructed the wondrous vessel right there on Front Beach. It had been a labor of familial love, and its broad sweeping lines were the envy of every craftsman and boat builder along the Gulf. Graceful as the curve of a woman's bosom, they claimed.

La Marraine had been built for shrimping, but hardly was she launched when she became obsolete, due to the sudden takeover of engined boats by 1916. The LaFleurs quickly converted *La Marraine* for oystering, however, as dredging the shells was not as yet illegal. And each spring they raced her in the Horn Island Schooner Regatta, taking the prize year after year until her untimely destruction when the beautiful schooner was torched by a dirty Yugoslav one night.

In one of the most vicious fights in coastal memory, Didier killed that man bare fisted despite the fact that the culprit drew a filet knife first and stabbed him four times about the neck and chest. Didier never did find out who set his house afire a week after that deadly brawl, but he imagined that it was a relative of the dead Yugoslav.

"Sweet Lord," Didier whispered, nudging Percy Billiott's arm. "Would you look at that! What a boat, eh, Percy?"

Billiott nodded and stood. The others arose too and stood there in awe as the magnificent vessel sailed past. They stood there like old veterans at a Memorial Day parade, still and silent, but stirred within—because the schooner evoked strong memories of a better time.

"The ceremonial launching's tomorrow," said Tom Dardar. "Not sure who's giving the blessing though. Probably the bishop."

"Shit no," said Kuluz. "Dey finally gonna do sometin' right. Father Joey Broussard's gonna bless it. He's back in town, you know, for good dis time, he says."

"Good priest," said Tom Dardar. "Talked to him last night. He's hardened a bit these last years. Glad to be home, though."

"Good," said Kuluz. "Maybe he'll keep God off our back. Dare's another tropical depression forming in the Gulf. Terd one dis season already. But Joey Broussard's always been lucky for us, eh boys?" Then he lit another cigarette and squinted as the plume of smoke went straight into his eyes. "So, Pete," he said, "you boys gonna catch dat bastard what killed little Mandy or not?"

Didier looked over at his old friend and shook his head—leave Peter alone, the gesture said.

"Yeah, we hope to, Mr. Joe," Peter said.

"I heard dat you was lookin' for Little Jimmy Dubaz, Pete. He ain't never been wurt a shit, but you don't tink he was involved, eh?"

"No, don't think so. Hope not, anyway. You haven't seen him around though, have you, Mr. Joe?"

"No," the old man said truthfully.

"It's no big deal," Peter said. "We're questioning everyone. It's just that he's been missing awhile and that's unusual. I'd like to talk to him. Thought maybe he might have seen or heard something that could help us out."

"Good," said Kuluz, shaking his head with satisfaction. "Dat little shit never had no luck in his life—but he wouldn't never hurt nobody, eh, Didier?"

Didier was not listening. He was thinking about his son, Albert, and how the death of little Amanda had crushed him, even more so than himself perhaps. But most of all, Didier was just hoping that God really did exist, and that He would just this once stand up for Didier LaFleur and deliver his granddaughter's murderer into his own hands and not those of Peter Toche or the police.

"Hey, dare, Didier, you okay?" said Joe Kuluz, nudging his friend a bit.

Contrition

"Yeah, yeah, I'm fine." Then Didier grasped Peter's hand and shook it firmly. "Good luck, Pete," he said. "And let me know the second anything turns up, okay?"

"Sure, Mr. Didier," said Peter, "count on it."

Didier waved goodbye, turned toward the Old French House and began walking away.

"Hey, dare, Didier," Joe Kuluz yelled. "You goin' for breakfast? Wait up. I'll go too."

"No," Didier called back without turning his head. "I'm going to Saint Ann Cathedral—to pray."

"For Mandy?" Joe hollered.

"No," Didier said, "for me."

Chapter Eight

Father Joseph knocked on the door a second time. Turning, he put a hand on Tristan's shoulder. "You won't like her, I'm sure," he said. "Hardly anyone does. Crass as she is though, she was my mother's good friend and is about the closest thing to family I have left. Her little cottage out back is vacant at the moment and I'm guessing she won't mind putting you up for a few days, especially if you speak a little French to her. She's French herself and never gets to hear the mother tongue anymore, so that'll please her. But for God's sake, call her *Madame* whenever you address her."

A short, squatty woman opened the door and bowed. "Well, it's about time," she grunted. "And who do you have with you there, Joey? Come on in. Peter beat you to the punch. He's already in the gumbo."

She spoke with an accent, her words coming in cyclic bursts, and she inched forward with each sentence until her forehead was nearly upon the priest's chest. Then she scowled as Tristan stepped forward and presented a hand.

"*Bon soir, Madame. Je m'appelle Tristan de Saint Germain.*" He couldn't help but step back in the face of her obnoxious breath. The smell of old rank female flesh nearly overwhelmed him, but he smiled respectfully.

"*Eh, bien!*" she snapped. "*Un francais, hein? Alors, que voulez-vous, Monsieur?*"

"Father Joseph was kind enough to recommend your cottage. I thought perhaps—"

"*Vous avez une femme?*"

"*Non, Madame.* No wife."

"*N'avez pas d'enfants?*"

"*Non, Madame*, none."

"*Pas de chiens?*"

"No dogs, either. I have very little, really, at the moment at least. *Ces vetements et moi, c'est tout. Je ne suis pas ici longtemps . . . quelques jours, une semaine au maximum.*"

Contrition

"*Oui, je comprends.*" She bristled. "It's done then." She stared into his pale gray eyes and nodded curtly. "You may stay there then until I have the roof fixed in a week or so. I'm cooking, Joey, come in, both of you. You may as well fill a bowl before Peter cleans me out. I'm making a second pot for Joe Kuluz and the men down at the pier. The cottage, it's a mess right now, you know. Was having some work done inside, too, but ran out of money."

They followed her into the kitchen. "Thank you, Madame," said Joseph, taking a seat. He motioned for Tristan to do the same. "Young Tristan is going to fill in for a few days at Saint Gregory. Your cottage is just perfect. I'm glad you approve of him." He winked at Tristan. "We all know how damn particular you can be at times."

She didn't hear a word he was saying. She was too busy surveying the younger man. She hadn't seen a man this handsome in decades. Her eyes raked over the fine features of his face and the graceful flow of his movements. In his frigid eyes she perceived a depth that was both extraordinary and frightening. She stood by the stove stirring the sliced sausage with a wooden spoon, never once turning to look at the skillet. And as the meat hissed, filling the small kitchen with the smoky scent of pork and garlic, Tristan's eyes never left hers. This impressed the old fossil even more.

Peter Toche was sitting catty-corner on the edge of his chair, stooped low over his bowl of gumbo. "Hey, Father Joe. Good to see you again. Really glad you've come back home." He dipped and filled his spoon again, then pursed his lips and blew gently into his bowl. "Damn, this stuff's hot."

Joseph laughed. "Heat hot or spice hot?"

"Both!"

"Pete, this is Tristan."

Peter scooted back and extended his hand without looking up. "Welcome—take a seat."

"You best beware," barked Madame LaFontaine, still looking at the young man. "God save the poor fool that takes on a priest as a friend."

"Easy now," said Joseph, moving to the stove to smell the meat. "You mustn't be so hard on us priests. Especially me, I'm practically your son."

"Ha!" she spat. "Son, my ass. If not for your mother, I'd have nothing to do with you. You're a damn drunk and you know it."

"I'm wounded, Madame!" cried the priest, feigning distress. "You're burning the sausage."

"Then put it in the gumbo!"

He picked up the skillet and poured its contents, grease and all, into the large pot filled with roux, okra, shrimp, onions and seasoning. "Aiee! Handle's hot!" He winced, slamming the skillet back down on the stove.

"So, Monsieur Tristan," she said, ignoring the priest. "You're not another one of those damned seminary dropouts from Coventry, are you?"

"No, Madame. I assure you that—"

"Take no offense," interrupted Peter. "She's an old crab at times and just can't help herself." He made a crab gesture and laughed.

The old woman ignored Peter's attempt at humor. "Can't imagine why a fine-looking young rooster like you would want to hang out with Joey there," she said.

"Now, now, I'm not *that* bad," said Joseph, sucking on a blister.

"The rice is ready, Joey, bring it to the table. And try not to burn yourself this time."

He half-filled each bowl with steaming rice, then ladled a heavy portion of gumbo over the rice and sat down.

"Here, Monsieur," the old woman grunted, shoving a shaker in front of his bowl. It's red salt, my own mix: cayenne, paprika, garlic, sea salt, and black pepper."

"Thank you. The soup smells wonderful."

"Soup!" said Peter. "Did he say soouupp? Oh, no."

"Soup?" Madame LaFontaine sniffed. "This isn't soup. It's gumbo! It's nothing like soup, Monsieur!"

Tristan tasted the gumbo, half a spoon at a time. "Pardon me, Madame. In any case, it is *magnifique. Simplement incroyable.*"

This pleased the old woman immensely. "Good," she said, her voice softening for the first time. The visitor's elegance made her conscious of her loud, vulgar voice, and she suddenly despised her age. "I was once a beauty, Monsieur," she said, disguising her bitterness. "Men fought over me," she cackled. "Eh, Pete? Am I right?"

"Of course, Madame," said Peter, who was still occupied with his gumbo. "And more times than I could count!"

"And *him*," she continued, pointing at the priest, "when he was a teenager, he used to try and look down my blouse or up my skirt! Or at my *ass*, eh, Joey?"

Joseph reddened. "Now, Madame. Yes, you were beautiful, but I assure you that I never—"

Peter began to laugh, but his mouth was full of gumbo and it began to shoot out in explosive little squirts onto the table.

"Pig!" cried Madame LaFontaine, pointing at Peter with an indignant finger. "Now clean up after yourself. That's a new tablecloth!"

"Sorry!" He wiped a sleeve across his mouth and then across the table cloth. "Ah, Father Joe, she caught *you* looking too, eh!"

Contrition

The old woman dismissed him with a flap of her hand. Then she eyed the young man again. Without realizing it she began knotting and twisting the long strands of whitish hair that flowed down her back. "So then, you may as well know, Monsieur, that you will be living behind an old whore."

At this bold and unexpected comment, Peter and Joseph both shot a glance at Tristan, but he gave no response. Instead, he lifted his spoon and ingested another spoon of gumbo.

"You have no answer, no reaction, Monsieur? Hmm, you are a strange one. But I think I could like you a bit. Maybe."

"I certainly hope so," said Tristan, swallowing his fare. He pushed the bowl aside. "An old whore, you said, Madame?"

"Yes," she challenged, leaning over the table. "Joey didn't tell you that? Ha! Just like a damned priest, hiding the dirty laundry. Yes, Monsieur, a whore for over sixty years, and sometimes I still get a knock on the door." She sat back. "Does that surprise you?"

"No, Madame," he replied, his eyes meeting hers in a firm contest of wills. "Whoring does not surprise me. It is an old profession. But you are a wonderful cook, Madame, and I hope, a gracious landlady. I'm looking forward to knowing you better."

The old woman grunted a moment, then cackled aloud. "You're a clever one, Monsieur. I'll have to watch you closely." She ran her finger along the rim of her bowl. "You'll be needing a break from that bunch of dumb geese over at Saint Gregory. Idiots, all but Joey, here. The rest can go to Hell, including the nuns, what's left of them anyway."

"Easy now, Madame," said Joseph, patting her hand.

Tristan smiled at the odd relationship between the old spider and the priest, easily detecting their mutual affection.

"You sound as though you do not approve of the church, Madame," said Tristan.

"Oh, *geez!*" interrupted Peter, "here we go! Father Joe, didn't you *warn* him!"

"I don't!" she snapped, looking at Tristan. "These eyes have seen too much. I had a little one, you know, Monsieur. Antoine, a dear sweet child. He and Joey were great little friends. Two young rascals full of piss and vinegar. But he died. And the way he died, disintegrating week after week. Have you ever seen spinal meningitis? His tiny body shriveling up. His hands took the shape of little birds' feet, and he cried and cried, whimpering out for me to help him, to save him . . . begging for God to take the pain away. He'd fold those tiny little bent fingers and pray. No, Monsieur, no *God* would have allowed a child to suffer like Antoine did, or like I did watching him."

Tristan sat quietly, listening, but Joseph noticed the fingertips of his young acquaintance were beginning to tremble. And though Tristan listened, devoid of visible emotion, the priest guessed that she had somehow touched a nerve. Peter suddenly guessed much the same and began to watch, more curious than before about the young guest. The more venomous Madame LaFontaine's voice grew, the more Tristan's hands shook until, finally, he withdrew them from the table. Peter had witnessed this reaction many times before — it was the faltering induced by guilt.

Madame stuck a finger toward the window. "He's buried in that graveyard next to my house, you know. And I swear I've heard him whimper in the night." Her eyes drew down into slits. "It wasn't right, God making him suffer so long like that," she hissed, her voice containing pain and contempt in equal measure.

"You hear him in the night?" Tristan said, leveling his eyes at her. "That is a sign, Madame. We all hear cries in the night and see faces, especially of children. But we misunderstand their meaning."

Peter's spoon was halfway to his lips, but it stopped suddenly and he set it down. He looked across the table at the young guest and felt something turn in his own chest. Tristan's words had pricked him.

"It may be God speaking to us — through dreams, or visions," Tristan continued, unaware that he had garnered Peter's absolute attention. "Dreams and visions are God's medium. But we pass them off as chance, or coincidence, or sleep's interpretation of things that have already happened or things that we worry *might* happen."

"Or," said Peter, trying to disguise his sudden and very private interest, "maybe simple imagination? Couldn't a dream be simply that, just a dream? You know, just a jumbled, meaningless flow of imagination."

Tristan looked at Peter thoughtfully, then shook his head slowly from side to side. "You — you have that keen look of the perceptive," he said softly. "Yet you don't — embrace the church either, do you?"

It wasn't a question. It was a statement. One that surprised Peter. He picked up his spoon again. "No, not really," he said.

Father Joseph glanced at Tristan. You're on tender ground here, the glance said. — You're a *guest*.

But Tristan continued. "Have you heard voices, too?"

Peter didn't answer. He swallowed another spoon of gumbo, but it didn't settle well, and he suddenly began to feel acid swirling around in his belly. Heartburn, he thought, — but he knew better.

"Have you seen *faces*?" Tristan pressed. "You have that *air* about you."

"Ha!" snorted Madame LaFontaine. "Him? No, he doesn't see or hear anything. He's a cop, you know, just chases people around. But me, yes, I hear my little Antoine's voice—and he's still suffering."

Tristan placed both of his hands on the table again, clasping them as if to pray. A slight flush came over his face. "Are you so sure, Madame, that your little Antoine is not somewhere holy and wonderful right now, this very moment?"

She looked at him, her eyes growing suspicious. "Are you sure you're not a damn priest?" she said spitefully. "Joey, tell him about Didier LaFleur, that praying old fool! Tell him how poor Didier lost his sons and a wife while he was on his knees. Had his boat burned out, and his house set afire. And now a granddaughter he's lost. And still he prays. Can you understand that?"

Peter winced at the comments. He had revered Didier since infancy, and often wished as a child that this great man could have been *his* father. Indeed, Peter wanted very much at this point to step to Didier's defense. But he also wanted very much to hear the young man's reply and knew there was little future in disputing the old woman's views. Quietly, he pushed his glasses further up the bridge of his nose and listened.

Tristan unclasped his hands. "You speak of loss, Madame, with the wisdom of experience. But is it possible that you are a bit afraid—afraid of what has happened inside you? Fear of self is far more frightening than fear of others or fear of circumstances. The true wars of life are waged within our own hearts, Madame—the never-ending war between good and evil, right and wrong. But God has armed us, we mustn't forget the gifts he has bestowed. But rare are those who recognize the gift of perception, the gift of vision, the gift of sensing things that others cannot."

Peter felt the acid moving up into his chest now. He felt foreign things stirring within, strange thoughts unearthing themselves—all through the words of Father Joseph's guest. *He's talking to Madame LaFontaine*, Peter thought, *but dammit, he seems to be directing it all to me.* He began to feel a measure of that familiar nausea and anxiety's unwelcome approach.

"Peter. Peter!" Madame LaFontaine barked. "Are you all right?"

"Y-yeah, just a bit too much pepper and spice," he lied.

Joseph stood and went to the sink. "Here, Pete, I'll get you some water."

"Thanks." Peter sighed, scooting his chair back an inch or so. Then he took a napkin and wiped his forehead. Small droplets of perspiration had begun to bead up just above his eyebrows and about his temples.

"Poor, Peter," Madame chortled. "Never could handle my spices, eh?" Then she turned to Tristan. "You talk a lot, my boy. But you are young. What could you know about life?"

"I understand pain, Madame. And loss."

"Ha!" she jeered. "Not likely. Me, I lost my father when I was seven. My mother, two years later. My uncle took me in. That same uncle bedded me down from the time I was ten, up till the night I stuck an ice pick in his heart five years later. And then I found myself pregnant with that bastard's child. And where was your God, Monsieur? The baby was born and I named him Antoine after my father. I loved that baby despite who his father was, tried to bring him up right. But then he came down with that sickness. Why? What have I, Jacqueline LaFontaine, done to deserve all that? What was my crime?"

"There was no crime, Madame" said Tristan.

"Oh, then what?"

"A test . . . a trial of faith, perhaps."

"Faith? My God! You young ass! Who could—"

"Whoa, Madame!" Joseph interjected, patting her on the shoulder. "Calm down. Tristan, she gets rather upset, I'm afraid, on the topic of God."

Peter looked away, embarrassed for the young man and sad for the old woman.

"I'm sorry, Madame. *S'il vous plait, je m'excuse.* I did not intend to anger you. The world is full of injustice. And yes, you have suffered greatly. But all you have been through, could you just imagine it multiplied tenfold? Or a hundred?"

"So," she spat, "I suppose now you're talking about hellfire? Ha, you're not the first. My boy, I've had priests in my bed before and after their fun, each one saw fit to begin saving my soul. After all that rutting around, they still thought themselves to be priests."

"I'm sure, Madame. After all, priests are but men beneath that black garb. But what if your suffering is but temporary? What if there is a greater reward ahead of you? Or an even greater *penalty*?"

"You're worse than a priest! You're a *convert*, aren't you? Well, I'll not have any more of your damned sermonizing in this house."

"The cottage, Madame?" asked Joseph, hoping that Tristan had not undermined her previous gesture of hospitality. "Could we see it now?"

"Good idea," said Peter, who had been following the escalating discussion with unease.

Though she was angry at the young man, the old woman still felt somehow drawn to him. "Yeah, Joey, the key's in the cookie jar. Take him there, show him around. I'll have to gather a pillow and some sheets. But young man, I'll have no more preaching from you. *Comprends?*"

"*Oui, Madame. Je comprends bien.*"

She scowled, trying to dislike this beautiful man and his stunning presence. She thought she saw in his face a look of pity, but it disappeared and she passed it off as contempt. No matter. This marvelous young man was going to be living within her grasp, and she meant to enjoy him.

"And Joey's window is just across the walk from mine, Monsieur. If I wanted to, I could reach out and slap him awake each morning. The cottage is just as close, so don't think you'll be getting away with anything back there. One slip of trouble and I'll call Pete. He's a cop, better remember that, Monsieur."

"*Oui, Madame. Je comprends.*"

Madame LaFontaine let Joseph and Tristan out the kitchen door, then moved to the closet to gather bedding. Left alone at the table, Peter pushed his bowl aside and closed his eyes, wearied by the verbal duel he had just witnessed. *God* talk always left him feeling uncomfortable. And this young man, he realized, had suddenly left him feeling even more shallow than the emptiness that had invaded his life since finding the little girl in the housing projects of New Orleans.

Chapter Nine

Peter hurried the instant he received the radio call. They had just found Little Jimmy Dubaz hiding out in the long abandoned Twin Pines Motel on Back Bay and were holding him at the station. Only when Peter entered the interrogation room did that quiet surge within his brain begin to temper itself. He shook Wilcox's hand. "Good job, Dan. I was beginning to think we'd lost him for good."

"The dogs found him up under the damn crawl space out at the old Twin Pines. We thought he was dead at first. Had a hell of a time digging him out. He's completely *fried*, Pete."

Peter looked down at the prisoner, who sat staring blankly at the table top, glaze-eyed, muttering gibberish, drumming the table with all ten digits in rapid little bursts as though typing out his thoughts. Peter pitied him immediately.

Jimmy Dubaz was one of those sorry little creatures who was born into life only to be crushed by every weight that the world could impose on him. Penniless at birth, fatherless, ignorant, and spiritless. He had never once generated an original thought in his tiny brain and had never enjoyed a single success. He had earned neither affection nor respect from even the most lowly.

Worse yet, he had never in his entire existence been capable of rejecting trouble's luring invitation. He was simply, from infancy, unable to say no to those who would lead him astray. None of this was to say that Jimmy Dubaz was inherently bad. Indeed, he was merely weak and utterly spineless. And now at age fifty-one he looked to be in his late seventies, and was an absolute drunk.

"Jimmy," Peter said, touching the prisoner's shoulder. "Jimmy, it's me, Pete."

The derelict's fingers stopped drumming and he slowly cranked his head back up and let his eyes rest on the hand that was touching him. "Pete? Ah, good ole Pete. I t-told this goddamn monkey to go straight to Hell." He pointed at Wilcox like a child reporting misdeeds to his teacher. "I ain't t-talkin' to no damn m-monkey, Pete. Git his ugly ass outta' here."

Peter looked down at that filthy, stubbled face. Jimmy's bright little eyes were cracked with red lines that seemed to pulse and flow like tiny rivers. His clothes reeked of urine and wine.

"Tell this monkey to git out, Pete!" said Jimmy, jerking a thumb over his shoulder. "Hit the r-road, man!"

This infuriated Dan Wilcox, but Peter shot his eyes toward the door and flagged him off.

"Little *shit*," Wilcox muttered, leaving. "I'd like to jerk a knot in that stuttering little skull of his."

Peter took a seat, placed both palms flat in his lap, and looked across the table. Then he nodded slowly and gave Jimmy one of those half smiles—that said, "Okay, Jimmy, I'm not going to press you, I'm not going to make you feel ugly, I'm not going to ridicule you because I know none of your life is your fault. No, I'm just going to make you feel comfortable like always, and then you'll start—all on your own, just like—"

"Sc-scared, Pete. He's gonna k-kill me." Little Jimmy shivered then and closed his eyes. "Been after me all week. Nearly got me t-two days back, with that goddamn club of his." Then he raised a finger to his scalp and pushed at his matted hair, loosening crumbles of filth and clotted blood. "Right there," he said, rubbing his head. "B-barely got away."

"Is that why you've been hiding, Jimmy?"

"Y-yeah. Got scared. You know I ain't no kind of fighter, Pete. You know that, don't you?"

"Yeah, Jimmy, I know that." Peter nodded but his half smile slowly evolved into a paternal look of sympathy and forgiveness. "Who's after you, Jimmy? And why? Who are we talking about here?"

"Don't know who. Met him d-down by Desporte's—the night it caught fire."

"The old warehouse? Were you *there* that night?" Peter scratched his chin and his eyes began to squint. "You didn't *set* the fire did you, Jimmy?"

"No. I was sleepin' inside. Had me a little r-room all f-fixed up in the southeast corner. Heard a bunch of noise, like a damn earthquake or something, th-then smelled smoke . . . opened the door. Goddamn f-fire everywhere. I scrambled out a window on the Back Bay side. Whole place was ablaze. Few minutes later I see this fella inside just when the r-roof c-caved in. Damnest thing, looked like he was crawlin' right outta the earth, n-naked as hell, all covered in ashes and embers. He was screamin', on fire, mad as a goddamn b-bear."

"He was on fire?"

Jimmy paused, confused. "Yeah, think so. It all happened so quick. It was like he was comin' outta the gr-ground, half stuck up to his waist. Anyway, I ran over, helped p-pull him out. Big fella, weighed a ton. Burned my hands, my face."

"That was a good thing you did, Jimmy."

"N-no. Shouldna' done it. He's after me now. Gonna kill me, Pete."

"But you helped him, Jimmy. Why would he want to hurt you?" Peter said, feigning a puzzled look, knowing well that amongst derelicts and psychotics, gratitude did not exist. Reason was nonexistent too, because beneath the dark and moldy world of rot, insects feed upon each other without warning and without conscience.

"I f-fed him, too, you know. And gave him some old clothes outta' my b-bag. But he had this funny look in his eyes the whole time. Lookin' around, jumpin' at noises. Starin' at me like I w-was a snitch or somethin'. Gave me the creeps, he did. But I took care of him. Even t-took him up to the Brothers' House. Br-broke in, got some wine and stuff, just like every summer when they're gone."

Peter felt a sudden ripple hit his heart, like a man who's been fishing all day and finally sees the bobber twitch, causing tiny circles to form on the water's surface. He did not want to appear eager, however. "Jimmy, when we're done, I'm going to take you upstairs—I'll have them fix you a plate. It's almost feeding time for the prisoners. I smelled hamburger steak and gravy when I came through. Butter beans and greens, too."

Jimmy's tiny eyes flickered a moment, and he felt saliva loosening within his mouth. "A h-hot meal, Pete? With gr-gravy?"

"Sure. But go on. What about the Brothers' House?"

Jimmy rubbed at his belly, as if it suddenly ached. "We filled an old oyster sack, snuck out and walked back over to the bridge. And just as we was crawlin' over the gate, we see this little g-girl sittin' on the other side. Pretty l-little thing. N-nice, too. She smiled and said hey."

Peter felt a sudden reddening at his temples. "Jimmy, who was it?"

Jimmy sat back and scratched at his belly again. "H-hell, Pete, not s-sure. We was drunk. I seen her somewhere before but, just not sure who—"

"Did she have blond hair, Jimmy, about ten years old or so?"

Jimmy closed his eyes, shifting in his seat. "P-Pete, I'm really hungry, man. C-could I eat a bit now?"

Peter bit his lip, and beneath the table his clenched knuckles began to pale. "Soon, Jimmy, soon," he said, restraining his emotions. "Did she have blond hair, big blue eyes, Jimmy?"

Jimmy nodded, as though suddenly remembering, but the question rattled him because Peter Toche was beginning to press him . . . and he

Contrition

wasn't supposed to do that. He was crossing boundaries here, suddenly. Jimmy's comfort level appeared to dissolve. "Y-yeah," he said reluctantly, "th-that's what she looked like."

"Jimmy, was it Amanda LaFleur? Come on now, help me out, here! You remember big Didier LaFleur, Jimmy. Was it his granddaughter?"

Jimmy squinted, and his fingers suddenly began to drum the table, as he earnestly tried to draw himself back to that day on the bridge. "Y-yeah." He nodded. "I think . . . *m-maybe* so . . . "

Peter exhaled heavily and raised his closed eyes to the ceiling. "Oh, Jimmy, Jiiimmmmmmmyyyyyy . . . Did you hurt her, Jimmy?"

"N-no, Pete. You know I wouldn't do that. But this other fella, all of a sudden he gets mean as all h-hell. Starts growlin' at me to take off. Thumped me on the l-leg with that big stick, told me to get on back to camp. H-hell, Pete, I ran. Like I said, that big bastard gave me the creeps right from the start. Shoulda n-never helped him out."

Peter's head dropped onto his left shoulder, and he sighed, bracing his temples with the opened palms of his hands. Little Jimmy had been *there*, he thought, *right there*, within a hair of saving that child—within a heartbeat of preventing this horrific tragedy.

At that very moment Peter wanted to jump up and choke Jimmy Dubaz. He wanted to strangle the very breath from his stinking, wasted body and then set him ablaze, then hang his corpse before the public for display. But he fought this fantasy back, and wilting from within, he struggled to breathe. He felt his temples flushing purple and the heat forced him to fish his handkerchief from his pocket. "Jesus, Jimmy, that little girl is *dead*, haven't you heard? Dammit, that was Didier LaFleur's granddaughter! Murdered. Butchered! Now dammit, tell me about this man you were with!"

Jimmy shivered and his fingers tapped out a nervous message on the table top. "H-he's gonna k-kill me, Pete."

"*Why*, Jimmy?"

"D-don't know. He's just crazy, man! Somethin's not r-right about him. After he ran me off that day, h-he shows up back in camp after dark. He tore into me with that big stick of his. Wh-whacked across the legs, shoulders, on the h-head. I was bleedin' bad but I g-got away through the marsh. He chased me a long ways but I finally lost him. He was screamin' like a goddamn banshee! I'm sc-scared, Pete."

"What did he look like?"

Jimmy shuddered. "B-big guy—looked Cuban or Mexican or somethin' d-dark, you know ? And *ugly*, Pete."

"Go on, Jimmy, talk. I can help you. I'll keep you safe."

"Didn't h-have no hair on th-that big skull of his. Shaved or bald. And that head of his, bigger'n a damn bushel basket. H-he hurt me, Pete, bad. That's why I been hidin'. He's gonna git me." Jimmy began to shiver again, and this, mixed with his stuttering, made him incomprehensible. Peter knew he was truly frightened, and frightened rabbits dive into holes.

"N-no more, Pete. Ain't g-gonna say no more about him." Then Jimmy folded his arms about his shoulders as though warming himself. "Y-you said you'd feed me."

"Okay, Jimmy, that's enough for now. We'll finish up later after you eat and get cleaned up. Come on."

Peter opened the door and let Jimmy out. Dan Wilcox was waiting outside. "Do any good?" he whispered.

"A little. Not enough. But we have our first lead. Take him up and get him some dinner. Bring him right back down again when he's done."

Wilcox nodded and grabbed Jimmy Dubaz by the waist of his pants. "Come on, you little toad," he snapped.

Jimmy took a few steps then paused. He turned and looked at Peter, and in that gaze, Peter felt a lifetime of loneliness and sheer despair. "I-I'm s-sorry, Pete," Jimmy said, his voice cracking. "I d-didn't know the girl was d-dead. I messed up again, didn't I?"

"No," said Peter, barely able to disguise his contempt. "You've done a good thing today, Jimmy, and I thank you for talking to me."

At this, Jimmy smiled weakly and turned, muttering gibberish again as he accompanied Wilcox up the steep flight of stairs. Peter returned to the table and scribbled a few notes. He was seething inside, but he knew this must subside because Jimmy Dubaz responded to kindness. No amount of anger could loosen his tongue, and there was yet more information he could provide.

Then suddenly from above, Peter heard a clamor and the heavy steps and shouts of a chase. And then came a crashing noise and the echo of cursing on the stairs. He ran out of the interrogation room and out to the stairwell.

"Christ!" Wilcox shouted, "He broke loose and ran! Threw himself over the rail! Pete, is he okay?"

Jimmy lay in a crumpled heap at Peter's feet, his skull split open in two separate places. Blood trickled from his nostrils and his eardrums. There was no movement whatsoever—not even the quiet rhythm of breathing.

"Crazy little bastard!" Wilcox shouted, his face reddening. He joined Peter at the bottom of the stairs and stooped over Jimmy's broken body.

"Dan! My God, what the hell have you *done*!"

Contrition

Wilcox was shaken, and his voice trembled like that of a child who has been falsely accused—a child who was truly innocent in every respect but knew that suspicion would linger and accusations would arise. "Pete, I swear. Didn't do a goddamn thing! Had him by the wrist, but it was sweaty. I let go for a second to wipe my hand off, and he just broke. Took off like a damn race horse. I'm telling you, he just ran and threw himself over the rail." Wilcox pointed to the railing above. "I swear, he took a dive over the rail, head first! Christ, I *told* you he was nuts when we found him under the crawl space. Shit, I'll be filling out reports until Christmas! The Chief's going to have my ass on a pole. You believe me, don't you? Say you know I'm not covering up!"

Peter looked at his partner and slowly nodded. "Yeah, I know you're not that kind of cop. Jimmy was wired, really hyped. Scared to hell and back. I believe you."

Wilcox slumped. "Christ, it all happened so quick. I thought he was okay. Hell, I thought he was starving, wanted to eat. Geez, even the guys on Death Row want to eat!"

Peter stared down at Jimmy's neck. "He *was* on Death Row. We just didn't know it. But *he* did. And he's taken a secret or two with him."

Chapter Ten

Satisfied that dark was beginning to settle in, the large man hurried along the water's edge, hidden amongst the thick sheaths of saw grass that grew in clumps right up to the brackish water line of Back Bay. Soon he turned inland where he parted an especially thick stand of these sheaths and disappeared into a hole—a hole that led him into the long-abandoned and forgotten sewer system that once supported four seafood factories and daily flushed tons of seafood wastewater straight into the bay, well before the days of environmental regulations.

And though he dragged one leg a bit, there was a bitter dignity in his bearing, which was brutal and imposing and warned that he was able to destroy anything or anyone before him—with his will, as well as with his hands. His back was burned and blistered, and he scratched at it over his shoulder and through his shirt, content that the boils and crusting were healing. Pockets of blood, like squid's ink, began to bubble from the wounds as a result of his clawing, but he groaned with relief and dug in harder.

The wind was stronger tonight, he noticed, sitting on his haunches. It would rain and this rain would persist through the night. But he would not be uncomfortable in his tunnel, and he laughed a little, even though his face was swollen with hate—like the venom-filled sac of a watchful spider.

His eyes, barely visible in the half gloom, flickered a moment and his mind raced backward to seek refuge in memories, but there was no comfort there, only bitterness and punishment. So he came back to the tunnel and issued a burst of half-uttered cursing because he was alone and lost in this strange place. But it was good to be free. And he was content to think that the little rat that had helped him escape the fire was off hiding somewhere, battered and half beaten to death. Indeed, was probably dying somewhere in his little hidey-hole. He didn't know this

Contrition

for certain, but somehow he sensed it deep within his own twisted heart, one that felt no warmth for anything living.

Then he stood, holding an old nail, and began scratching against the concrete wall just above where he slept. He drew a primitive figure lying dead just in front of the serpent he had fashioned the night before. The serpent was coiled and its forked tongue slithered out between gaping and curved fangs.

Then, his eyes even brighter with hate, he pressed hard against the damp concrete and etched four long lines emanating from the head of the figure—long hair to signify that the little figure was female. Yes, he thought, immediate fear of extinction *was* the only thing driving him on, so tomorrow he would go in search of the little rat man again, just to make sure he didn't talk to anyone.

"And so, I live another day," he muttered, as the evening sun dropped beneath the bay, enveloping the sewer tunnel in complete blackness. And from the dark bowels of that abandoned sewer, as the moon lifted above Back Bay, the scratching and etching continued all night—heard only by the egrets and night herons as they roosted in the stand of water oaks just above.

Chapter Eleven

Placidus began worrying about nightfall by late afternoon, fretting in anxious solitude. He took a late lunch to avoid the others of the house—to conceal his despondency and spare himself the hushed whispers and sideways glances. As he ate his cold soup, he seemed to lose himself in the previous night's dread. Then, just as the vague, translucent images of that night's dream began to unveil themselves again, he would rattle them into oblivion with an urgent shake of the head, dispelling them.

Things were alright until that day I found the dead girl . . .

He set the spoon down uneasily. Had his long years in the service of God truly led him to this end? A lifetime of devotion and piety scrapped in one grisly moment in the attic? Had he followed this long road of self-denial and austerity only to falter in old age?

You loved that child, Placidus. She was your special angel because you recognized that she was filled with His grace.

But she was a monster there, lying on the floor, her belly open, her eyes staring up at me. She was waiting for me up there. She knew that I was coming to open the house alone. I shouldn't have fallen on the crucifix. Sacrilege! I—

Placidus, she's still there. Hiding from the world, but not from you. She's found you out beneath that black garb of yours and seen into your soul. You're a fake, old Placidus, and every night she'll come after you in your sleep.

Tears began to stream down his rough, unshaven cheeks, welling up in the deep furrows of age. He wept for the girl, remembering the expression of shame and horror that had stared up at him, boring through his heart to the very core of his soul. And he wept for her father and her grandfather. But most of all he wept for himself.

The house, Placidus. It is damned. The voices. You've been hearing them for some time now, as you lay there awake, just before sleep. All those holy men who once slept in your very room long before you came.

Contrition

You try to cover your ears some nights, don't you? What are they accusing you of?

It's age. I'm getting old. Old minds play tricks. They—

Brother Phillip Allison hanged himself in this house, remember, Placidus? Several years after you came here. He befriended you early, and the two of you became very close. He shared your love of Latin and Medieval history. And then you angered him . . . and up the old stairs he went, closing the attic door behind him, vilifying you all the while . . .

. . . When he didn't come back down, you went looking for him—and found him hanging from the rafter, his eyes popping out of that dark little head. You tried to drag him down but failed, remember? You said a prayer over his fresh corpse as he swung there before you, and all the while his froggish eyes were staring down at you. What made him do it, Placidus?

"I was stronger back then," Placidus whispered, blotting the scene from his memory as he slowly shoved himself from the table, unable to stomach the soup. He left the kitchen and went straight to the chapel, throwing himself at the foot of the statue of Saint Michael.

"Holy Michael, Archangel," he implored, "defend us in battle. Be our safeguard against the wickedness and snares of the Devil. May God rebuke him, we humbly pray, and do Thou, Prince of the heavenly host, by the power of God, cast into Hell Satan and all the evil spirits who wander through the world seeking the ruin of souls, Amen."

When the prayer was finished, he crossed himself and went to the rear pew to gather his Bible and rosary. He read the text in earnest, thumbing the beads between sweaty fingers, concentrating on the words before him as though other thoughts might intrude upon this single-minded endeavor. When he was done, it was dark.

He could hear the others shuffling about upstairs in the sleeping quarters. He heard every step, as well as bits of conversation. Laughter. The sound of water pressing through the pipes. The flush of the toilet.

Then suddenly the chapel door opened, startling him. It was Brother Patrick. "Placidus? Didn't see much of you all day. Everything okay?"

"Yes, yes. Just fine," Placidus mumbled, shoving the rosary into his pocket.

"We're about to call it a day. Just wanted to say goodnight. How did things go for you today? Feeling any better?"

"Yes, a little," Placidus lied, wishing Patrick would go away.

"Good. Was thinking you might want to move back upstairs. I—"

"No. I'm fine right here if you don't mind."

"Sure, whatever. By the way, Father Joseph asked about you again today. Said he'd like to come by and see you when you're up to it. You remember him, don't you?"

"Yes, I remember Joseph," Placidus replied patiently. "Good Latin student, credits me with his collar. Tell him to come by, would you?"

"Maybe you'd like to walk over to his office in the morning. I'll go with—"

"No. Ask him to come here. I'm not leaving the chapel."

"Certainly. Well, good night then, Placidus."

Placidus set the Bible aside and moved to the floor where he had fashioned a crude pallet with quilts and pillows. No, not as comfortable as his bed, but it was right beneath the gaze of Saint Michael the Archangel, and far from the attic. And when the nightmare took hold of him again, *she* and the others would pursue him through the attic, clawing at him, tearing at his flesh, but then he would awaken at the foot of Michael and they would immediately disperse, unable and unwilling to penetrate the sanctity of the chapel doors or the sword of Saint Michael with their nightly rampage of terror and extermination.

He pooled the sheets about his neck, his body curled like a fetus, and listened in darkness as the footsteps above faded and silence fell upon the house. Then, shivering, he closed his heavy lids, knowing that the girl would soon be stirring in the attic, creeping out of wherever it was she hid each day.

Soon he was dropping, falling into that black, restless drowse that met him each night like an unwelcome guest, a hated visitor who would torment him until dawn.

When his descent was complete, the blackness gradually began to dissipate and he felt himself standing alone, gazing about, seeing nothing but clouded, unmoving images before him. But then, in the distance, there came a flutter. Then another, louder and closer than the first. Then yet another until soon the air was thick with the thrashing of a hundred gray wings. It was the gulls, gathering. And to the side he heard the slow and deliberate creaking of old wood. It was the steamer trunk . . . opening.

* * *

Peter poked through the burnt rubble of Desporte's Seafood Warehouse with the delicate and meticulous motions of an archaeologist who suspected, after years of toil, that there lay just below the immediate surface a trove of secrets preserved in ancient rock or wood. And though the dilapidated warehouse had stood vacant for nearly eighteen years on this abandoned and overgrown patch of Back Bay waterfront, it hurt him that the old cypress structure had been reduced to a heap of ash and debris. He had always felt an obscure loyalty to things aged and forsaken. It was another peculiarity of his, one that others found curious.

Contrition

Dan Wilcox, on the other hand, was more than content that the warehouse had burned. He saw it as one less rat-infested, derelict-frequented trouble spot that the Gulf Springs Police had to worry about in future years. Even now he wished to be elsewhere, anywhere but this isolated dump of a peninsula standing in the blazing sun. "Geez, Pete," he said, "*what're* we looking for anyway? Arson Squad's already combed the place and didn't find a damn thing."

"Sure they didn't, and didn't look much either. No injuries, no insurance claims, not a damn thing at stake here, so no one cares. But Little Jimmy said he jumped out a window on the southeast corner, right about here I'd say. Had a nest fixed up in a side storeroom. Got out just in time."

Wilcox moved next to Toche and chuckled. "Hell, I still say the little shit *torched* the place—if not on purpose, probably fell asleep with a smoke in his hand."

Peter ignored the remark. Jimmy had said the noise and fire had come from outside his nest. Furthermore, the arson report indicated that the blaze's source of origin was near the rear entrance, which was a good hundred feet from Jimmy's corner room.

"Damn, this just isn't right," said Peter, pushing against a broken chunk of concrete with the tip of his shoe. It appeared that the foundation had burst near the rear entrance, and the break was roughly circular in form as though some horrific force from beneath had punched the slab upward, cracking it, leaving a crater encircled by jagged and dislodged chunks of reinforced concrete.

"What you got, Pete?"

"Fire does a lot of things, but not this." A wrinkle formed between his brows as his eyes probed the crater. "Jimmy said he pulled a man out of the ground as the place collapsed. Had to be right here. Said the guy was screaming and half buried in embers and ash—trapped in the ground, he said."

"And you believe it?" said Wilcox. "Hell, he was half out of his mind, Pete."

But a little warning buzz sounded in Peter's brain and he squatted at the lip of the crater, casting about for possibilities. Yes, perhaps Jimmy had exaggerated, or misperceived, but in every exaggeration there lay a shred of credibility, behind every lie there stands a thread of truth. What if by some bizarre accident of timing or stroke of sheer fortune, a man *did* survive the fiery collapse of huge timbers and tons of asbestos roofing? What if Little Jimmy wasn't drunk or delirious at that moment? What if for once in his pitiful life he had performed a heroic deed. What if—

"What if this hole was made years ago, Pete? I mean, what's to say this happened the night of the fire? Maybe this guy just happened along and in the dark he fell *into* the hole? *That* makes a hell of a lot more sense, doesn't it?"

But Peter's eyes were closed. He was listening intently but not to his partner. Squatting, he stretched his right hand outward, palm down, passing it in slow circles over the crater. Guided by a force outside himself, he gradually created a gulf between reality and imagination. He believed profoundly in the psychology of mood creation and that moods gave rise to sensitized awareness. For him these moods forced aside the self-imposed restrictions of the normal human thought process. They laid bare the sequences of past occurrences, and even in rare cases, prophesied future events. The ability to create these moods and lose himself in them was a gift—his only gift. And at times it seemed a curse as well, but then all things extraordinary are bittersweet.

Peter understood that if one shut out the world, the mind and heart formed a union, and this union gave rise to a formidable force that allowed one to focus on the insignificant and the overlooked. So he cocked his ear to the air where could be heard the winds and voices of supposition—and the power of revelation. His outstretched palm felt that same air, as if fishing for some hushed and secret current that might carry him off to those hidden backwaters where evil and sin bubbled from the ground like poison springs—that secret and filthy pond that his father had spoken of, where all those who witness death and perdition on a frequent basis long to linger.

A flush appeared high on his forehead as he drifted further and further into his own mesmeric state, and perspiration began to roll down his cheeks like tears. And then, in the back of his head, he heard Jimmy Dubaz laughing—because Peter had opened up something deep within himself, a dark and inviting chasm where only the unholy tread, where the naïve and innocent are quickly devoured and cast aside.

Peter winced, and heard the crackle of fire. Then he saw it, the deadly spectacle of an explosive inferno leaping lizard-like up the warehouse walls, onto the rafters and up through the roof. A moment later, waves of heat struck him in the face, forcing him to squint and draw back. Tides of heat washed over him like a burning sea—and somewhere in the distance his father's voice called to him, "Let it alone, Pete. Leave this thing *now*—"

But it was too late. Peter was on that tightrope again, teetering over a great abyss. His heart was surging with expectation, dragging him into the nether realm—kicking him into mental overdrive, opening up within him loose suppositions and wild ravings as to what really happened in this place one fiery night.

Contrition

His breath caught, as if on a thorn, and he gasped, backing away as though the red hot tongues of fire had seared his nostrils and eyes. "Argh!!" he wailed, falling back on his rump. A sudden chill took hold, shook him for a moment—and broke the spell. "Damn!" he whispered, wiping streams of perspiration from his face.

"Pete! Pete? You, okay?" said Wilcox, extending a hand to help him up. This wasn't the first time he had ever witnessed the senior detective chase himself into this hypnotic state of psychosis, but each time seemed more unsettling than the last. Peter Toche had strange notions at times but Wilcox profoundly respected his partner's abilities. He had concluded over the years that Toche possessed a keen intuition and the instincts of a bloodhound. Indeed, this man demonstrated extraordinary insight and somehow managed to burrow deeper and conceptualize on a more abstract plane than any investigator he had ever encountered. "What is it, Pete?"

"Jimmy didn't set the fire, Dan. Something just *blew*, something right here beneath the concrete."

Staggering, Peter raised himself up and shook his head to clear it. In a moment the red spots would clear from his vision. He exhaled, eyes still closed, then sucked the breeze through his nostrils, slowly and hungrily, like a thirst-crazed horse too long gone from the water trough—and this air carried him back.

"Christ, Pete—you scare the shit out of me sometimes, you know?"

"Yeah, I'm okay now. Damn, this place just went off on its own. Bam, just like a firecracker."

"Wh-what? Like a bomb? Or like plastique? What're you saying?"

"Something unexpected happened here the other night, something way out of the ordinary. This place went up in a whiff, it didn't just catch fire and spread. It *blew*."

Wilcox squinted a moment. "Doesn't add up. I mean it—"

"Jimmy said he thought an earthquake hit, but we know it wasn't that. I'm telling you, this place burst wide open—like napalm—the whole place at once."

"Maybe the guy in the hole was an arsonist, and things just blew up in his face."

Peter shook his head with a finality that made Wilcox feel foolish. Then Peter's eyebrows drew down into a scowl. "Hear that? Be *still*, Dan."

"What?"

"In the bushes. We're not alone out here. Move slow, don't be obvious."

Wilcox took the cue and pretended to stretch. Yawning, he partially covered his face with a forearm and scanned the growth from beneath his outstretched arm. From their vantage point several paths beaten hard by fishermen and tramps ambled off into the marsh grass. Then looking deeper, his eyes grazed the tangle of kudzu and green-briar that draped over a small stand of water oaks to the west. And at that very instant, he heard a faint rustle. The tangled foliage at the base of these water oaks moved ever so slightly, closing with the hushed and subtle motion of theatre curtains coming together on a darkened stage.

Wilcox slid a hand inside his sports jacket and unsnapped his shoulder holster. "There, Pete"—he motioned with a tug of his head—"by the trees."

Peter nodded. "Move on the count of three—it's a pretty good distance. And watch the saw grass, it'll rip all hell out of you."

Simultaneously the two men burst into movement. Wilcox, being the younger man, quickly outdistanced his partner. But Peter, with the guile and foresight of a seasoned hunting dog, swept off to the right to intercept in case the trespasser switched direction. Gun drawn, moving as quickly as his frame would allow, he worked his way through the marshy growth with a forearm bent eye-level to protect his face from the ravages of the innocent-looking but deadly reeds that stood between him and the flight of this stranger. Whomever this person was, he had not wanted his presence known and now had absolutely no intentions of being apprehended.

"Stop!" Peter heard Wilcox shout. "Police! Stop, dammit or I'll shoot!"

But just beyond the stand of trees, Wilcox's swift pursuit was immediately hampered by thick clumps of chin-high saw grass. With each frustrating step he heard his pants and jacket snag, then run like a thousand tiny zippers down the length of his polyester suit. Soon he ensnared himself, and while staving off a web of brambles and green-briar thorns, his pistol flipped out into the sea of saw grass that surrounded him. Stumbling forward into a nose dive, he moaned as wicked strands of saw grass began to rip at his face and hands. The tiny barbs cut and pulled at his skin with a cruelty that was both unforgiving and exact, and the raspy sound of his own flesh separating made him so dizzy he cried out.

"Dan! Dan, you okay?" Peter shouted. "Where are you?"

"Over here, Pete! Christ, I'm bleeding all over! Oh man, this shit cuts like razors!"

Peter found him lying asprawl and lifted him from the ground. "Did you get a look at him?"

"Just a little . . . his back mostly. Damn this shit stings, Pete—"

"Boy or man?"

"Too big to be a kid. Big guy. God, he was moving fast, too. Plowed through this damn grass like it was clover."

Peter pulled a handkerchief from his pocket and handed it to his partner. "Here, get your cheeks. They're cut pretty good."

Red, runny lines streaked Wilcox's face and the back of his hands. Each line was razor straight and puckered in parallel ridges of swollen white lips. "How the hell'd he get away so quick—damn, he's *got* to be cut up worse than me."

"Did he have hair, Dan?"

"What?" Wilcox said, nursing a dozen wounds at once.

"Was the guy bald?"

"Hell, I don't know. He was bent down, moving like a damn locomotive. Didn't get a good look at him."

Peter slid his glasses back up the bridge of his nose. "Was he dark, could you tell?"

"Christ, Pete, it was all a blur. He was moving kind of funny though—dragging a foot or something. Hurt maybe. But dammit, he was moving fast."

"He'll be back," Peter said, securing his pistol. "Little Jimmy found him here, and now *we've* found him here. It's the same guy, I'm sure of it. Something's drawing him back, whoever he is—and we need to find out why. Call Dispatch, get some help out here. Even if we don't find this guy, have them scour the marsh for evidence."

"Okay," said Wilcox, licking the back of his hand where tiny droplets of blood were already beginning to desiccate. "But what exactly are they looking for?"

"Something tied to Amanda LaFleur. Anything. Here's where it all began."

Chapter Twelve

Tristan did not sleep that first night in the cottage, nor the second. He had struggled to maintain an air of calm since his arrival, but inwardly he was torn. Exhaustion was beginning to exact its toll, and if he didn't find sleep soon, he would fall prey to the tortuous trail of his past. Still foggy about how he had come to this place, he tried to retrace his steps just prior to nearly drowning in the channel. Had he been aboard a vessel? Fallen overboard? Or more conceivably, deliberately heaved over the side?

Clearly sensing the pursuit of others and remembering his own flight from that hellish and distant place where he had once lost all hope, he did at least aspire to secure some temporary respite by being lost within the obscure sanctuary of this tiny and foreign coastal town.

On the third night it began to rain. From the darkness of his bed he could see Madame LaFontaine bustling about the kitchen. She was a spiteful hag of a woman, but he wished her no harm. It was to Peter Toche's and Father Joseph's credit that they demonstrated the patience and the will to deal with her respectfully and kindly.

Finally, she finished her work in the kitchen and the house went black. Tristan uttered a short prayer for her, and for a tiny instant even envied her, because she would find sleep within minutes. As he lay there in the darkness, he could clearly hear the rain spattering onto the tin roof above. A cleansing wash, he hoped, forcing his eyes shut. He inhaled deeply, then exhaled, as though purging his mind of unwanted images. The process was repeated a dozen times before he finally grew still, to listen to his heart.

To his distress it hadn't slowed a beat. It seemed to pound with even greater desperation, like the advance of some defiant, vengeful army, distant but gaining. And for a moment he saw that army and felt the sharp clatter of weapons and hooves beating against the rocky terrain

Contrition

of a barren land he once knew. At the head of this great force rode a thousand faceless warriors, masked by the shadow of Arabian dust, and behind them marched a never-ending file of grim-faced foot soldiers twenty abreast. Onward the great line slithered, over the twisted path like some aroused serpent, head raised, its endless train disappearing beyond the horizon, speaking not a word but rattling, instead, the instruments of war and destruction.

Startled, Tristan opened his eyes and started up on his elbows, moaning. The army vanished, but he still heard footsteps by the tens of thousands, dissipating into the night—however, it was only the rain. He left his bed. Standing naked, he leaned slowly forward against the windowsill until his forehead pressed against the cold glass. His nostrils fogged the pane, but it quickly cleared as he backed away, unveiling the moon.

Its light was intense though half-draped by silver clouds carved by rain, and it cast a bony aura about the yard. He stared at it for several long minutes, longing to be there on its desolate mountains . . . away from men. Then he turned his eyes away to the wrought iron fence and beyond to the cemetery.

The grave stones were barely visible through the crusted bars and the downpour, partially protected by a canopy of great oaks. But the shadows seemed to fall away, and he felt the cold presence of each stone, awash in a gray world of silence and finality. He said another prayer in Latin and wondered at the irony of so many bodies, some innocent and pure, others vile and corrupt, all moldering there together within an arm's reach of one another.

Suddenly he stiffened, thinking he saw a form moving across the graveyard. It was something pallid and amorphous and seemed to drift through the stones themselves. Blinking, he stared hard a moment, his eyes focusing on nothing. His gaze passed from one stone to the next, but the form was gone. His imagination, he concluded.

He brought a hand up to his eyes and the moonlight to gauge its steadiness. It was shaking the smallest bit. Then he looked out over the roof top of Madame LaFontaine's to the spire of Saint Ann Cathedral, erect and imposing, now bisecting the moon. At that instant the pale form suddenly reappeared, for just a second, swirling about the moonlit spire. But before he was able to make out the shape, it descended onto the roof of the church and vanished like steam.

Unnerved, Tristan was no longer able to control his hands. He brought them up to his face and covered his eyes, his whole body beginning to tremble into slow, twisting knots of pain. In his mind he suddenly heard the weeping of a woman. Then another. They grew louder and louder until he blinked his eyes open, afraid that he would see them right there at his feet, pleading for mercy.

"God, help me," he whispered, fumbling about the floor for his clothes. He shrugged into his shirt and pants and ran from the cottage. Large drops of rain burst against his face as he stumbled forward in bare feet. Wiping rain from his eyes, he advanced with faltering steps, ready to collapse, when a stiff wind propped him up. And in that wind he swore he heard the whisper of his dead brother. Chilled, he grimaced bitterly and drove forward with such intent that he would not have even felt the earth crumbling beneath his feet. Finally he made his way around to the front of the cathedral and fell forward, pushing the great wooden doors open.

He shook his sleeves and passed his palms over his face and hair to rid himself of the rain. Then he focused on the altar, and his eyes met the large crucifix hanging on the north wall. The soft glow of the church's inner sanctum provided warmth, yet somehow heightened his uneasiness. "Christ, I beseech you . . . Christ, I worship you . . . Almighty God be merciful," he muttered, deeply moved by the symbol of universal suffering and redemption hanging there before him on the cross.

Step by step he moved closer until he found himself at the foot of the altar. Tears began to fill his eyes, and he fell prostrate to the floor as he fumbled about his pants and pulled the rosary he had been given by Father Joseph from the pocket. Then, laying it between his face and the floor, he placed its tiny crucifix between his thumb and index finger and began to pray.

Half an hour later, he finished the last decade and, kissing the crucifix, slipped the rosary back into his pocket and stood. He felt stronger now. Much of his anxiety had diminished, and though he still felt a faint tug of fear, he felt more hopeful. But that single remnant of fear crept deeper into his heart until finally, he shuddered, realizing that there was someone in the church. He looked about, his eyes darting from pew to pew until finally they came to rest on the confessional against the east wall. His face suddenly contracted.

No reason to be afraid. Something was there, pulling at him.

He moved toward the confessional. With each step he seemed to walk more lightly, shedding layers of guilt and uncertainty, until soon he was pushing the curtain aside, kneeling. And in that impenetrable darkness, hidden from the world, he found respite from the black despair that had been consuming him. He felt nearly dizzy with joy, disoriented even, and then drowsy, as though the sleep that had eluded him for three days had suddenly descended upon him like some peaceful shroud. Struggling to hold his eyes open for just a moment longer, he clasped his hands to give thanks. Then his head collapsed against the screen and he fell asleep . . .

When he awoke he was in a small stone church somewhere near Rome. An ancient temple, dark and cold, lit only by three tiers of wax candles beside the stone altar, itself crude and damp. Even though he was still inside the confessional and could not see out, he knew this place, and knew that Saint Ann Cathedral was worlds away. He heard the sudden stroke of a great cathedral bell, and then another. With each knell the confessional vibrated, as did the walls of the ancient edifice, and each vibration resounded in his heart and chest. Then silence.

He knelt there in expectation, ear to the darkness. Finally, he heard a grating noise. The confessional screen slid open and he heard the rustle of fine garments on the other side. Then a sigh.

Tristan quickly made the sign of the cross. "*In nomini Patri, et Fili et Spiritus Santus,* Amen," he uttered. "Bless me, Father, for I have sinned."

He quickly gave his confession in Latin, and when he was finished, a voice from the other side of the screen spoke.

"So, my son," it said, in French, rasping each word. "You have seen the Eastern tide?"

"Yes, Holy Father."

"And which direction does that current flow?"

"Against us." Tristan replied. "Truly against Rome, Your Excellence. The Abbasids are routed, and the Seljuks refuse to guarantee passage to the Holy City."

"And Constantinople?" the voice inquired with great patience.

"They plead for your assistance, Sire. They fear the Turks will soon be at their gates."

"And so then, the dove must cross the mountain?"

"Yes, Holy Father."

The rustle of elegant fabric filled the confessional again, and the voice, drawing nearer, continued. "And so, young Tristan, it is truly you?"

"Yes, Father."

"And how has your journey found you ? It has been difficult, I suppose. And you must know that I have missed you these past months, but your mission is vital to Rome. And Christendom. No one saw you enter the city, then?"

"No, Father. My brother and I are camped outside the city with the monks. Though we have been watched since leaving, I was not followed here tonight."

"Excellent. And pass my greetings to your brother, Guillaume. I know he has been of great assistance to you in all this. But now I have another task for you. You will journey west back across the Alps with all the documents and testimonials you have collected. You shall precede me by three months and make arrangements for my entourage. You will call together an assembly of all the clerics and power brokers of France. This assembly will gather in Clermont. I shall designate it the Council of Clermont and we will convene in November. But take care, Tristan. The climate in France has been hostile, and much blood has already effused."

"I understand."

"The journey you have just ended has been the most important of your career, but it pales in comparison to what you are about to do. We are about to call the greatest gathering of all time, excluding the gathering of Christ and his disciples. It could well change the world as we know it. Have you prayed for God's guidance, Tristan?"

"Yes, Father, in all things."

"Then be prepared to double your efforts. And pray that God will guide me in all things that I am about to set in motion."

"I will pray for you."

"Then go with Guillaume, and be safe. May God be with you in all you do. May he speak through your voice and act through your hands. You are my representative, my voice, my conscience. Above all, remember that you are in my heart always, Tristan . . . always, Tristan . . . always, Tristan."

The screen closed abruptly as the voice echoed farewell, fading into silence. Tristan groped at the screen, calling to his confessor, but his efforts were futile. Then, suddenly, a pelting sound began to fill the confessional, gradually at first. The sound grew louder and more

Contrition

encompassing, like furious rain, and then the entire confessional became a constellation of livid, swirling specks, as though bursting into sparks and flame.

Tristan covered his eyes, blinded by the light. "Odo!" he screamed. "Forgive me! I did not mean to be weak!"

Then it grew dark again and he knew he was in Saint Ann Cathedral. Rising, he fled the confessional, his ears ringing with that fateful farewell, "always, Tristan . . . always, Tristan."

He ran from the church out into the black rain. He held his face and arms skyward allowing the heavy drops to burst onto his skin, rinsing his eyes and conscience, purging himself.

"Odo!" he wept. "Guillaume, my brother! This time I will not fail."

His legs collapsed. He fell to the cold pavement and clawed at it as though digging himself a grave. Blood oozed out from under his nails and the tips of his fingers began to shred, but the ground would not give. Finally, he surrendered to exhaustion and closed his eyes as the rain began to pool about him.

Madame LaFontaine found him there asleep at dawn.

Chapter Thirteen

The bulldozers began work on Back Bay just after sunrise. Demolition and clearing of the old shrimp factory foundations, the Twin Oaks Motel, and the remaining outbuildings would take at least the full week, hauling and disposal included. So the operators were in no hurry—except one, the youngest. He was new on the big Caterpillar and liked to push the massive machine to the limit.

The two older men ridiculed him behind his back and took many breaks that morning, complaining to each other that the youngster might damage his equipment. But the young operator didn't, until just before noon when he leveled a small stand of water oaks not far from the ruins of Desporte's warehouse. It was there that his blade struck something. Backing up, he dropped his blade even deeper and accelerated forward at full throttle. The ensuing collision nearly threw him from his seat as the left corner of his blade bit into concrete. Then suddenly, the nose of the Caterpillar dropped and the tail lifted straight into the air. The huge metal treads lost all purchase and began to gyrate wildly, spinning like some out-of-control amusement park ride.

"Shit!" the operator wailed, hanging onto the wheel for life itself, staring down into what seemed a bottomless cavern. Then he began to pray that his machine would hold its place. It was hung somehow, close to collapsing into the huge sewer tunnel below. Finally, he managed to shut the big Cat down and nervously pulled the key from the ignition. "Dammit that was close," he wheezed, collecting himself. Then, just as he was about to jump from the seat, he saw something down in the sewer pipe. "Oh shit!" he said, sucking in his breath with disbelief. "What the—can't be—"

But it was. There it lay, in the depths of that hidden and forgotten sewer system. A corpse.

"Bob! Jake!" the young man yelled, running from his machine, hands flapping about. "Call the cops!"

Contrition

Peter Toche and Dan Wilcox arrived within minutes, along with Chief Barhanovich and two squad cars. "Close off the entrance," said Peter, moving quickly toward the crippled Caterpillar. "Dan, have them run some tape, and no one's allowed in except our people."

Chief Barhanovich braced a hand against the up-ended dozer to support himself and peered down into the hole. "Pete, have Dan get a fire truck out here. We'll need some ladders, too. And have one of those dozer operators tow this thing out of here. Last damn thing we need is it slipping down onto that body, or on us for that matter."

Twenty minutes later, the dozer was cleared and firemen were slipping ladders into the bowels of the sewer. "Come on, Pete," said Barhanovich as he began descending the ladder. "And be careful for Chrissakes."

The dark residue of abandonment covered the surface of the tunnel pipes—filth, algae, and bacteria mottled the walls. The lower arc of floor, where the body lay, was buried in several inches of sand. It was soft and scummy sand mixed with fine sediment, and it lay in a drifted pattern, as if rippled by tiny waves. The body lay facedown in it, limbs sprawled in four directions.

The back of the head was bashed in, and clots of caked blood covered the neck and trailed down onto the sides of the face. And there, just beside the corpse, a dirt-crusted blanket lay half-buried in the earth, like a dead and decaying dog next to its master.

"Any guesses, Pete?" Barhanovich said, kneeling beside the corpse.

"No."

"Anyone been reported missing?"

Peter thought a moment. "No."

"Well, hell, let's take a look." He reached under the face and shifted the body. Instantly little crabs boiled and sputtered out from beneath the corpse, aroused by the movement. "Damn, sure didn't take them long to get started. Give me a hand."

Peter started to bend down, but a part of him remained there, still standing. He wasn't eager to know who this was. His professional instincts called for closure, yes, but this was his town, and he already felt loss pulling at him.

"Come on, Pete, *pull*," Barhanovich huffed.

Peter did. And then, there it was—a familiar face gazing at him through dead eyes. Stunned, Peter's eyes flared a moment and he retreated, refusing to acknowledge what lay before him.

"Goddammit!" Barhanovich swore, stepping back. "Son of a bitch. It's Tom Dardar. Now who in hell would want to hurt old Tom?"

Peter didn't answer because waves of nerves were washing up his spine and over his shoulders onto his chest, raising his chest hairs like prickly spikes of a tiny cactus. His temples began pulsing with blood, thick and worried blood—and at that moment he no longer heard the chief's voice. He heard another voice—that distant voice, sweet and hushed. It was the little girl. He shivered, feeling the hysteria which lay very close to the surface begin to pick its way free. "Your people are dyyyyyiiinnnggg," the tiny voice said. "Your town is dy . . . "

"What?" Peter cried out, as red and white spots began to flash across his field of vision, along with even more pulsing at his temples. "What did you say?"

"Dammit, Pete, quit yelling," Barhanovich snapped. "You scared the hell out of me. I said *a lot of people are dying*. Amanda LaFleur, now Tom Dardar. Hell, poor Tom, he was a good shit. He didn't deserve this."

But the pounding at Peter's temples was so great again that he was unable to answer. "Damn," he whispered, holding his head between the palms of his hands. His face twisted up and he cried out again , "Do you *hear* that, Chief!"

"What? Dammit, why are you yelling? I'm standing right here next to you for God's sake!"

Because I hear *pounding*, Peter started to say—pounding, the sound of an iron spike being driven into wood, cutting through flesh. But he stopped himself just as his father's eyes flickered through his mind. "Sorry, Chief. I just had—"

"You okay, Pete?"

"Y-yeah, fine, just had a moment there," Peter said, reddening about the collar. "Holy God . . . Tom Dardar . . . "

Just then Dan Wilcox descended the ladder. "Who is it, Chief?"

"Tom Dardar," Barhanovich replied, feeling a bit diminished himself.

"Jee-sus," said Wilcox. Then, after gazing down at the gaping head wounds, he nudged Peter. "Here, brought some flashlights. Thought we'd better check out the tunnel. No telling what else is down here. Come on."

Peter wanted to stay. He hadn't even had time to mourn his old mentor's dreadful end. But he knew that with each second next to that corpse, he was becoming more and more unstrung. The dull pounding that was still attacking his temples might soon erode all sense of composure. So he walked away, purging himself of that suffocating dread that had so suddenly unnerved him.

Contrition

They left the chief with the body and moved down the south corridor of the pipe into darkness. Their lights splashed ahead of them and bounced across the walls and overhead. As they spoke, the strange echo of empty places began to trail their voices and footfalls.

They found nothing, until Wilcox suddenly side-stepped something on the ground, nearly knocking Peter over. "Watch it," Wilcox said, pointing his beam at the ground. He focused it on a small mound. "It's—it's—shit?"

"What?" said Peter, aiming his beam to meet Wilcox's.

Wilcox nudged the pile with the tip of his shoe. "It looks like—fresh shit," he said, burying the tip of his shoe in the sand and then pushing it clean. "And look. There's some more." He worked his flashlight about in a grid. "It's all over the damn place. And another blanket."

Peter stooped and lifted the blanket. Unlike the one buried next to Tom Dardar, it was dry. And next to it, a heap of tin cans, some emptied, others still unopened. "Someone's been living down here."

"Damn, you'd think they'd at least shit outside. I mean, what the hell,?"

But Peter's eyes constricted, and he felt that sudden surge of adrenalin that investigators experience when a key turns and the lock falls open. Someone was living down here, just like in the attic. "I was right," he muttered, rubbing his thumb against the inside of his index finger. He rubbed harder with each pass.

"About what?"

Peter moved his light about, his pulse quickening—and then saw the wall, just above the blanket.

"What's that?" said Wilcox. "Looks like—kid graffiti or something."

Peter stared hard at the scrawls and stepped closer. "Oh, much more than that," he muttered, moving his nose to the wall.

Hell, looks like kid scribble to me, Wilcox wanted to say. But the tone of Peter's voice changed his mind, so he just shrugged. Hell, what would I know, the shrug said.

Peter quickly lost himself in the markings, examining each one speculatively. *Simplicity*, he wondered, *or abstraction? Idle passing of time, or menacing symbolism?*

There was a snake, about twenty inches in length, maybe an inch and a half thick. The fangs were curved and extended, striking. And a crude tongue left the mouth, dividing into a fork. Before the snake lay a girl, crudely etched. She was on her back, dead. And next to her lay a man, face down, also dead.

"Oh, Jimmy, Little Jimmy," Peter whispered, forgetting that he was not alone in the tunnel. "You told me he was still in town, hunting you down . . . and I've found his nest, as did old Tom. And he's *still* here—somewhere."

Then he moved beyond the markings, edging his way slowly like a lizard along a wall. Soon he came across a series of lines which were carved more deeply than the etchings. It appeared, if one stretched the imagination, to be two capital M's, one after the other.

"Well, what do you think?" Wilcox said, feeling suddenly alone and useless. "Pete?"

But Peter's only awareness existed just inches from his nose. He adjusted his glasses and puzzled some more. Initials? Code letters? Reflexively, the letter "M" began to cycle quickly through his brain. Mayhem? Murder? Mass murder? More murder?

His finger picked at the letters. Then he scratched his head. The mystery refused to recede, so he turned to his mental rolodex of names, but could not conjure any individuals he knew with "M" as both a first and a last initial. Continuing to edge along the wall, he next came across a series of small shapes, hundreds of them. So many, in fact, that they began at the base of one side of tunnel and continued all the way across, over, and ended at the bottom of the opposite side for at least twenty feet down the tunnel. Each shape appeared rectangular with an arched top, like a single tablet of the Ten Commandments. And inside each of these was etched a cross. Gravestones, Peter concluded. Looking immediately overhead, he next came upon a large crescent shape placed in the exact center of the graveyard.

"Christ Almighty!" Wilcox whistled, spotting his light on the grave stones. "What in the hell? Somebody's lost their damn mind. Who in the hell would have taken the time to do all this?"

Peter did not answer, fortunately, or turn around. If Wilcox could have seen his partner's face surveying the graveyard, he would have seen a withering, ruptured expression that would have curdled his blood because Peter was no longer in the tunnel. He had left this place and entered into that psychic netherworld of backwash and decay, murder and mutilation.

A place where there is no hope for the naïve and where the innocent are slaughtered for no reason other than their random presence. A place that had been reserved, for some inexplicable reason, for only Peter Toche and those rare few who had been gifted with extra sensory capacities.

Standing there frozen at the wall, he could literally feel his hair bristling up the nape of his neck with the anticipation of the weary traveler who had finally come home. In this trance, the fog suddenly parted—and he knew somehow that the graveyard signified that many, many more deaths were imminent. Indeed, the graveyard represented his entire hometown.

Contrition

"Don't suppose Jimmy put this crap on the wall?" said Wilcox, more to remind Peter of his presence than anything.

No reply.

"Did you hear me?" said Wilcox, slapping Peter on the elbow.

"What?"

"I said, suppose Little Jimmy did this? This was probably one of his hideouts, eh?"

"H-mm, possible," Peter mumbled, returning from space. Then he turned around and blinked, slowly, like a frog blinks. And when this occurred Wilcox shriveled a bit inside because Peter's face was unexpectedly pallid and waxen, as though fresh from the embalmer's table.

"Yeah," Peter said, his mouth growing dry. "That might make sense, Dan."

"Yeah," said Wilcox, appalled by Peter's ghostly expression. "Should we keep moving down the pipe?"

Peter's reputation for doggedness had firmly established itself from the first day of his return from New Orleans. Wilcox, therefore, fully expected to be in the sewer system for the remainder of the day, following Peter as he stared and mulled for hours at nothing, lost in that haze that so often overtook him, like now.

"No," said Peter, "I've seen enough for now. Let's get some air."

And air, indeed, was the issue. Peter had gradually felt himself growing faint since coming across the scrawls. Supposition or not, they disturbed him and left him with that sick, infected nausea of the brain and abdomen that causes one to feel weak at the knees and full at the throat. He could endure no more. Anxiety of this nature often leads to misfortune, stampeding men into misjudgment. But anxiety can also accomplish the reverse—subconsciously leading one away from imminent disaster.

Peter turned away and began the trudge back toward light, never once uttering a word or acknowledging his partner who followed. This in itself did not disturb Wilcox because he was accustomed to Peter's sudden onsets of silence. *He's lost in his own strange world again*, thought Wilcox.

More than anything, though, Wilcox was pleased that some color was returning to Peter's face because, for a moment, he had thought Peter dead.

Chapter Fourteen

Business at the Old French House had been brisk since noon because of the previous night's exceptional haul of white shrimp, and the piers were abuzz as boat after boat logged record harvests. Though exhausted and in sore need of sleep, few of the shrimpers had it in mind to go home after unloading and washing down the decks. Instead, they streamed into the old tavern, quickly filling it to capacity. The mood was festively infectious and events quickly escalated into one of those great but unexpected occasions that becomes town lore.

Fishermen chattered in noisy clusters, shouting to be heard above the din, swallowing their beer in weighty gulps and inhaling their smokes in deep breaths, swept away by the tide of success. The girl behind the bar, a fat green-eyed beauty with pendulous breasts, worked the tap with great dexterity, barely slowing to slide the never-ending fountain of tips into her jar, and the old Yugoslav shucking oysters behind the counter hadn't looked up in over an hour.

It was a fine day for shrimpers. A memorable catch. Tuition and clothes for the kids. A new dress for the wife. Women wouldn't be seeing their husbands until well into the night, except those few bitchy strays who would begin showing up at about dusk to drag their men away, unafraid to violate a man's world and unappreciative of the previous night's back-breaking labor.

Even the old-timers were there, drawn by the catch. As the excitement heightened during their dawn coffee, the oldsters broke with regularity and decided to linger into the afternoon. No time for naps. It was a mad moment, for them, and for everyone at the harbor that day.

Didier LaFleur sat in a corner booth with his old friend, Joe Kuluz, nursing his second beer in over an hour. He seldom drank. Only on special occasions and religious feast days, and even then he didn't enjoy it. But Joe Kuluz was having a time. Didier stayed to watch over him as much as anything else.

Contrition

"Goddamn, Didier!" Kuluz spouted, wiping slobber from his chin. "Kin you believe dose shrimp we seen dis mornin'? I ain't seen bugs like dat in years, eh?"

Didier grunted, still amused by Kuluz's heavy Yugoslav accent, even after a lifetime of hearing it. "Like the old times," he replied, watching the younger men's animated exchanges and gestures, wishing he had just half their fire. "Makes me think of the time we broke the scales down at Letellier's."

"Ha! Ah no. Dare's never bin one quite like dat now. But dis, I like dis. The yung men are worked up, the Ole French House is jumpin', and I'll just have me annudder beer."

"Watch it, remember now, you're not the Joe Kuluz of forty years ago you know."

Kuluz reduced the butt of his cigarette to ash with a single suck and crumpled the remnant between his thumb and index finger, flicking it to the floor. "Hey, Julie girl! Bring us two more cold ones. An don't take too long. Us old shits ain't got much time left!" At that he slapped his knee and laughed, choking himself on suds. "Goddamn, Didier, dis is great, eh? Man, I'd like to git my hands on dose tits of hers!"

Didier shrugged, his large shoulders burying half his neck. Then he smiled. Joe's waning health had kept him from the pier on a regular basis anymore, so it was good to see his face red with laughter and too much beer.

The two men were a study in contrast. Didier, massive and muscular, but stooped, still strong and fit as a herd bull. And Joe Kuluz, small and wiry. Erect as a bandy rooster, hyperactive, but far more fragile than eyes could tell. Didier was French, well respected by generations up and down the coastline. He attended mass faithfully and gave more than he could afford both in and out of church. He had even been urged at one time to enter the political arena but preferred instead to represent the fishermen at the piers against the seafood barons and governmental agencies.

But poor Joe Kuluz. Distrusted by many, disliked by most. A lifetime reputation for drinking, whoring, and gambling. He ran whiskey during Prohibition, and had it not been for age, he would undoubtedly be running drugs now with the handful of renegade shrimpers that earned their keep by the bale and the powder, not the net.

Only in old age could two men of such differing grain find affection for each other. The impatience of younger men could never bear the strain. But Didier and Kuluz were brothers in arms who had stood shoulder to shoulder, heart to heart against the forces of life, labor, and the sea. And it was only fitting that that they were sitting together at the Old French House on this fine day. A final hurrah for old Joe Kuluz who would soon never see the piers again. Maybe the old runt, in the back of his thoughts, knew that the good moments left for him were rare indeed. So on this day he sought laughter and companionship with the abandon of a condemned man.

In the midst of this great celebration, barely noticed by most, a group of Louisiana shrimpers filed into the bar. It wasn't uncommon for out-of-state fishermen to water there after dropping anchor during the short season in the Sound. And though there was little camaraderie between the locals and the outsiders, neither was there animosity because the Mississippians would annually take their turn in the waters of Louisiana, Florida, and Texas.

But behind this crew entered a man noticed only by the hawkish eyes of Joe Kuluz. He was massive. Early forties, perhaps. His dark complexion branded him as a man of labor, but what struck Kuluz the most was the man's head, oversized and shaved clean as a pearl. That tremendous skull sat atop three furrows of thickly muscled neck flesh. A heavy black mustache overshadowed his mouth and the yellow ivory within.

The man entered and looked about, his eyes heavy lidded. Old Kuluz thought he detected a limp in the stranger's gait, but that was perhaps owing to the crude walking stick he held in his hand. On closer inspection, it looked to be clubbish. A fat length of dense hardwood, its grain marbled yellow and brown. The top of this imposing stick was bulbous and thickly gnarled, just fitting into the stranger's formidable paw.

As the man gazed about, Kuluz watched him smile with malice. The reptilian smile struck Kuluz, as did the eroded scar that extended down the left side of the man's neck, disappearing into deeply creased furrows.

He leaned on his stick a moment, measuring the crowd, it seemed, then moved to the bar, shouldering his way through the fishermen. The bar was elbow to elbow but at the end, in the midst of several large fellows with a strong facial resemblance, stood an empty stool. He took a seat.

"Aw shit, Didier," said Kuluz pointing at the bar, "dat guy's in the middle of dem Duval brudders. Maybe someone oughtta tell him, eh?"

But before the stranger could even order a beer, the man next to him turned and said, "Stool's taken, bud. My brother's in the pisser. Be right back, he said."

The words weren't said in anger but the message was clear. The stranger, however, ordered a draft. "*My* seat now," he said with an air of quiet contempt.

"Aw shit, Didier," said Kuluz, "imagine dat. A big catch, a big time, and now we gonna see a dance, too."

"I said that stool's taken, mister," said the younger man, louder this time, with enough conviction that some of the shrimpers standing by the bar

Contrition

took notice and inched away. "I think I'd get my fat ass off that chair if I were you."

The large man with the shaved head ran his lip over his teeth and shrugged, turning toward the voice he had previously chosen to ignore. But by then another man had stepped up beside the first. "Look, friend," this one said, "you heard him. Now, I'm Leroy Duval, and this is my brother Jimmy Duval, and that stool you're sittin' on belongs to our brother, Dave Duval. Now you'd best walk."

"Damn yung bastards," snorted Joe Kuluz, elbowing Didier. "Big shits when dey all togeddur, eh?"

Didier shook his head, knowing well that old Joe was hoping push would come to shove.

The shaved one pointed to his walking stick. "Bad leg," he grunted, not giving an inch.

By now the buzz and laughter had turned to whispers as everyone focused on the disputed stool. "Aw shit, here comes dat damn David Duval," whispered Kuluz, straining to get a better look.

The third Duval immediately guessed that something had happened during his absence, and also guessed that his younger brothers were involved. As he approached the bar, his hands turned to fists.

"This big asshole took your seat, Dave," declared the youngest brother, bolstered by the other's arrival.

"Ah, let it be," someone said from across the room. "Leave him alone, for Chrissakes."

A few others mumbled in agreement, but not openly. The Duvals were short-fused and possessed long memories. "Dose stinkin' punks," whispered Kuluz, becoming more and more agitated, automatically siding with the older man.

The man with the great shaved head sized up the three young men, his eyes becoming slits. He was much larger than any one of them, but combined, it would be impossible. For any other man.

"If you want this seat so bad," he said, his voice slow and thick, "then you better move me." Then he grasped his stick by the bulb and stamped it heavily three times against the wood floor, never once moving his eyes as a red flush began to creep up his neck.

The three brothers were momentarily stymied by the stranger's fearless reaction. They were used to bullying. Looking at each other for support, they seemed unsure of what action to take next. But then, as though a signal passed amongst them, they rushed the man, throwing him to the floor.

He flung them off with one quick, hard gesture and gained his feet, bringing the club up over his head, bulbous end out. He took a furious swing, his eyes bright and clear with anger, and a whooshing sound echoed across the room as the club cut forcefully through the air, parting both smoke and the stale smell of beer. But before he could bring the club back, the three jumped him again and he disappeared beneath the flailing arms and legs of the despised clan of brothers like a wild pig under a howling pack of hounds.

Shrimpers scattered, cursing and yelling at the melee, then closed again.

"Ten bucks on the bald man!" someone screamed.

"I'll take it!" someone else countered.

"Fifty on the Duvals! Who'll bite?" another yelled.

"Gotcha' right here!" another cried, fishing out a fist of crumpled tens.

"Hunnert dollars on dat big man!" screamed Joe Kuluz, teetering on his chair to claim a better view.

"Now, dammit, Joe," Didier chided, "settle down. You don't have a hundred dollars to lose today. Get down off that chair before you break a leg!"

"I got yer hunnert, Joe! And fifty more if yer *man* enough!" someone hollered.

"I'm man enough!" Kuluz wheezed, lighting another cigarette, still dancing on his chair.

"Now you've done it, Joe," snorted Didier, totally aggravated.

The big man elbowed his way free again, and when he did, he fired a massive fist dead center into the nose of the oldest brother. The thud was heard throughout the Old French House, sickening some, delighting others. The young man's face collapsed into a pulpy mass of blood and goo, and he teetered about like a drunk for several seconds before regaining his vision.

The youngest brother had managed to grab the stranger's throat from behind. He locked his arm around the man's huge neck to choke him. But the sight of his bloodied brother's face unnerved him, and when he relaxed his grip for just a moment, his intended victim threw an elbow backward into his rib cage.

"Oomph," he wheezed, still hanging off the stranger's back, feet dangling above the floor. He felt the room go black. "C-can't breathe!" he stammered. "H-help me, c-can't breathe!"

The older man showed no mercy. He flung the brother to the ground, kicking the side of his face. Then, backing away in a fitful posture, like a wild beast about to bite, he groped for his stick. And before the last

Contrition

brother could approach him, he leaped forward swinging out blindly like a man possessed. Something snapped like brittle sticks.

Stunned, the last Duval froze, his eyes swimming about in liquid. Slowly, with the twitching of a man too numbed to control his muscles, he raised his fingers and pried his mashed lips apart, spitting out his own crushed teeth. Then came a fountain of blood.

A loud cry went up from the room as fifty shrimpers cheered while another chorus moaned and swore, reaching deep to pay their losses.

"Goddamn, Didier!" cried Kuluz, faint from excitement. "I tink dat big bastard coulda give you a run for yore money back in yore time, eh?"

Didier scratched his temple. He stared into his beer for a moment and said nothing. He was content that the big man won, but there was something in the stranger's naked lack of fear that disturbed him.

Even though the man hadn't picked the fight, he had been merciless and knew from the onset that he would carry the day. The rage in his eyes from the very moment that he had refused to surrender the stool did not convey courage. Certainty, perhaps, but not courage.

"Jeeezuz Christ, Didier," whistled Kuluz, his breath wreaking, "good ting dat big basturd had a stick! I only got a twenty in my pocket. I tot I had more!"

Didier grinned at his friend, and the grin grew to laughter, deep and rich, as a disgusted shrimper counted out fifteen ten dollar bills and shoved them in Kuluz's palm.

"Goddamn, what a d-day!" old drunk Joe stammered, "*what a day!* Only ting what could happen now to make dis day better, Didier, would be to find some pussy, eh?"

Chapter Fifteen

The discovery of Tom Dardar's corpse had a profound effect on Peter. The scribbling on the sewer walls also troubled him. These two factors, tethered to an already mounting level of physical and mental angst since the Amanda LaFleur case had begun, served only to deepen Peter's sense of isolation and withdrawal. For the first time, he began to fathom the unshakable loneliness that Brother Placidus must himself be enduring.

This was a revelation in itself, because Peter found himself trying harder to understand the old man's interpretation of what had actually occurred within the attic that dreadful day he returned to open the campus. Yes, Placidus was old and senile, but senility is a creeping disease that eats into the conscience by degrees, not a condition that suddenly plants itself and takes possession of the brain overnight.

What disturbed Peter the most was Placidus's convictions about the dead girl's wailing soul passing over him as he stumbled down the stairs—and the bleeding stigmata that occurred on the crucifix. Peter's mental wanderings over this unsteady ground invariably led him back to his own demons—in particular, the ghostly wraith who consumed his dreams.

Two days after Tom Dardar's removal from the sewer pipe, Peter felt compelled to begin purging himself of this self-suffocating buildup. Realizing that no one within his circle could grasp even the tiniest measure of his self-spiraling concerns and not wishing to expose his declining mental state, he thought of the young man he had met at Madame LaFontaine's. For some reason, in the realms of human pride and self-preservation, people frequently choose to mask their anxiety from those closest to them and decide instead to seek an exchange with strangers. Such was the case for Peter. He was especially curious about the stranger's interpretation of hearing voices and seeing faces of the dead.

That evening, he entered Saint Ann Cathedral and walked through the foyer that led directly into the church itself. He paused there a moment, peering about. Madame LaFontaine had said that he would find the young man inside, and indeed, there he was, seated alone in the front pew, head bent in prayer.

Peter coughed to make his presence known and moved down the aisle. Then, stopping abruptly, he backtracked, dipped his finger into the small font of holy water, and made the sign of the cross. It was a clumsy gesture, one incurred by respect for decorum more than anything. The water felt cold to his finger and colder yet on his forehead—as though he was unwelcome in this place, a place he had abandoned years ago.

When he reached the front pew, he genuflected before sliding next to Tristan. Tristan's eyes were closed and his lips were moving in silent prayer. After a moment though, he crossed himself, opened his eyes, and nodded, acknowledging the visitor.

"Good evening," said Peter, in that low voice that people use in the presence of an altar.

"To you also," Tristan replied, somewhat surprised. "I couldn't have expected seeing you here tonight. Have you come to offer prayer or light a candle perhaps?"

"No, actually—I came looking for you. Tristan, isn't it? I apologize, but I've forgotten the last name."

"Saint Germain. Tristan de Saint Germain. You are Peter, correct? I remember because Peter was the rock of the Church, and I found it odd that with such a name, you, like Madame, have rejected the Church."

"You *are* a priest, aren't you? Or used to be, at least."

Tristan nodded, not in agreement, but with thought. "You suppose this, I imagine, because of my comments to Madame the other day when we met. I noticed your discomfort."

"You were pretty hard on her, and she on you. But yes, you sounded like a priest."

"Well, if you've come to speak to a priest, you would be better served to speak to Father Joseph. I do not wear a collar." Then he nearly smiled. "But I hardly think that you've come in search of ministering."

"No. Curiosity as much as anything, I suppose. Not sure, really."

Tristan sat erect, folding his arms. "Curiosity about what brought me here, perhaps? It's a good question, but to be honest, I'm not absolutely sure myself. Reason does not drive every movement of man. God leaves room for fate, or coincidence, or impulse. So, at the moment, I suppose that I'm simply wandering."

Peter suddenly felt an awkward connection. "I—well, I suppose we all wander a bit, don't we?"

"Indeed," Tristan said, losing his near smile. "But something disturbs you. I felt it surface at Madame's table the other day. Your concerns run deep, but its ripples are far-reaching. So what brought you here tonight?"

Oh, Madame was right, Peter thought. *This is a clever one, piercing others' veil of self-preservation with the exactness of a surgeon.* "Well—I mean—"

"You asked about dreams the other day. I said you had that air of the perceptive. I suspect that, like me, perhaps you get lost in the solitude and in the night. Does sleep not serve *you* well, either?"

Peter looked down at the kneeler, feeling suddenly exposed. "The other day I, like Madame, thought you might have been a priest. I now wonder whether you are a counselor. You're drawing me out even though I don't—"

"*Want* to be drawn out," Tristan said, completing Peter's thought. Unfolding his arms, he continued , "I have dreams, and they speak to me. I have visions and hear voices, see faces . . . and *they* speak to me also. Everyone experiences this to some extent, but in my case none of it is random or happenstance. I feel that I'm being *directed*. I don't understand it all, but I now accept that it is a *gift* that is bestowed on a special few. So, Peter, do you have the gift also?"

Peter nodded, feeling uncomfortable as heat that began to gather about his collar. "Yes, I—sometimes think so." He paused. "No, I *know* so. But sometimes it's not good. Sometimes it gets confusing."

"Like now?"

"Yeah." And here Peter turned a little red. "I've seen a lot during my career in the way of crime and bloodshed, how people hurt others. I thought I had become immune to it all. But then one day I came across a little girl, dead in her house, killed by her stepfather over nothing. Somehow, for some reason unknown to me, she *got* to me. And still does. She comes back to me . . . in my thoughts, in my sleep. It's—like a haunting."

Tristan sighed. "*Ah, les voix des enfants sont les plus fortes.* The voices of children are the strongest. Not in life, but in death. God

Contrition

balances the scales. These children become a medium, his blessed messengers." He paused for a moment. "And what does she say, this child?"

Peter hesitated, unsure whether to continue. But Tristan's acceptance pushed him forward. "She told me to come home—that my father was dying."

"And is he?"

"Well sort of, he's been on a long decline for years, long before *she* ever got into my head."

"Anything else?"

"She said my people are dying."

"And are they?"

"I—Hell, I don't know. Two murders in town these past weeks. More than we've seen in years. And I was closely connected to both victims in one way or another."

Tristan stared off a moment and seemed to lose himself. "You want to believe this child, don't you? But you can't accept it all. Yet this voice *did* bring you home. But let's not forget guilt, or failure. Sometimes these also create voices in our mind's eye. Guilt and failure force us into profound internal conversations and conflicts that we hide from others. Could *this* explain the voice you keep hearing?"

"No," said Peter, sure of himself for the first time since entering the cathedral. "I live a decent life. I don't cheat on my wife. I work hard and help others. Nothing there to feel guilty about."

"Ah, but so much more is required of you than that. I recognize that you have set God and the Church aside for some reason, but still, I say *listen* to the voice of the child, at least. That voice brought you home. It was a voice too, perhaps that brought me here also. And let us not forget Father Joseph."

"Joseph?"

"He has come home also, after many years. What voice do you suppose brought him back after all his travels, Peter? It's as if someone has called a gathering, and we were meant to be here together in this tiny place, at this particular time. History is dotted with such occurrences, yet they slip by unacknowledged and unrecognized." Tristan's eyes suddenly appeared more lucid and intense. "When a great wheel is set into motion, men like to think they are driving that wheel, but more often than not, it is driven by a higher authority. Sometimes—"

"Okay," said Peter, suddenly feeling himself being somewhat swept away by the persuasions of a clever evangelist. And he didn't like being swept away, either by men or by words, because he was a doubter. He reached out and placed a hand on Tristan's shoulder. "I appreciate your thoughts. Della is waiting for me at home and it's getting late. We'll talk again, I'm sure." Then he edged out of the pew.

As he turned to leave, Tristan lowered the kneeler to the floor and knelt. "I'll pray for you," he said. "I'll pray for your father, and your people—and for myself and for Father Joseph."

When he got home, Peter was much quieter than usual. This did not go unnoticed by Della, and after several unsuccessful attempts to engage him during dinner, she began to clear the table. "You've hardly touched your food," she said quietly. "And you haven't said two words all night."

No response.

"I *did* something today, Peter."

Peter sensed something in her voice and looked up at her.

"I went to see Doctor Switzer today," she continued.

"The optometrist?" Peter said, puzzled.

"No, the other one. The psychiatrist."

Silence.

"Maybe I shouldn't have," said Della, searching Peter for signals. "I've been worried about you lately. I set you an appointment and—"

"Damn." Peter sighed, more from fatigue than aggravation. "Della, you know how I feel about that stuff. Besides, you know damn well I don't like parading my laundry out in public. Christ."

"It's just that I'm concerned. You keep shutting yourself off more each day. You haven't slept in days. I made the appointment for day after tomorrow and—"

"No," said Peter. It was an emphatic "no." It was an "I don't have a problem no," a "now you've crossed a personal boundary and now I'm irritated 'no.'"

It was Della's turn to sigh. She lifted her eyes toward the ceiling, and her hands soon followed. "This can't continue, Peter," she said. "You need help, professional help. Just to get you past this LaFleur business if nothing else."

Peter sat back in his chair and adjusted his glasses. "You've been talking to Dan Wilcox, haven't you?"

Contrition

"Yes. He's worried," she said, shaking her head with apology. "And I am, too. I—"

Peter didn't hear. He had already slipped back into the deep waters of introspection and was, at that very moment, drowning amidst deep-rooted fears that his walls were being stripped away, exposing his gradual deterioration to all those who once respected and admired him. For an instant he saw himself old and haggard, sitting there in his father's death chair, medicated and surrendering. Then he blinked that image away and cradled his forehead in both palms. "I'm just *tired*, Della. Just worn out, that's all. It's just pressure."

Peter sought comfort in these lies, because sometimes if a man lies enough to himself, after a point, he begins to believe his own deceptions. But Della was a wife, and she sought security, not comfort. She missed the old Peter, the sure-footed and detached Peter.

"You're lying to me," she said, showing more heat than he had ever witnessed in their many years together. "Worse yet, you're only fooling yourself."

The words stung him, as did her tone, mostly because she had put her finger on the naked truth—and driven it straight into his heart. He wilted.

"Bad dreams, no sleep, wandering off in the middle of conversations," she said, "those are all symptoms of a bigger problem, even I know that. Doctor Switzer is expecting you. He can help."

"No," Peter said, standing to leave. "I'm not going, and I don't need help. I'm not sick and I'm not crazy." Then he left the room. And though he was awash in the greatest loneliness of his life, he decided to sleep alone rather than endure further discussion with Della.

As he lay down to sleep on the couch, he thought of Tristan sitting alone in prayer in the church pew, of the great gulf that existed between that man's thinking and that of his own wife and peers. Hearing voices, to Tristan, held significance and was not the foreshadowing of mental illness.

Closing his eyes, Peter shivered a moment because Tristan's perceptions were suddenly more comforting right then than those of the accepted wisdom. And as he drifted off to sleep, he saw himself as a little boy—standing in a pew of Saint Ann Cathedral, smiling up at his father, who was smiling back.

Chapter Sixteen

Placidus had prayed for sleep, but he thrashed for hours on the chapel floor, his sheets and pillows flung far from his pallet. He tried to come fully awake, but somehow, the terror again seized his dull senses and dragged him down again, deeper and deeper. He could not struggle free from the grip of his nightmare, and moaning, his throat issued a horrible guttural wail that filled the dark chapel somewhere between sleep and reality.

He was there again, standing alone in the foul stench of the attic, the vision before him vague and clouded, filmy. But through the chalky light, he discerned movement coming through the east wall. A ruffling stream of white and gray entering the attic, its dull strain growing in intensity. It was the gulls, swarming through the hole by the hundreds, by the thousands, filling the east end of the attic in brooding flocks, incensed by his presence.

They landed all about, rocking from one foot to the other, wings half-cocked like angular banners at the ready, prepared to flush forward at the least provocation or trace of flight. Soon they completely covered the floor and rafters, shouldering each other, unwilling to take their gaze from him for even an instant. Thousands of sets of little black eyes, sizing him up impatiently, awaiting the signal to flood onward.

They devour flesh, Placidus.

Jolted, he took a half step backward.

They'll take out your eyes and claw your face. They'll picckkk yoooouuu aaa ppaaaarrrrtttt. Cover your eyes and don't look down . . . do not look down.

He brought his hands and arms to his face, cowering, but determined not to show his absolute terror.

Don't look down, Placidus. You know what's there, don't you?

He cried out and pulled back. But he couldn't keep his eyes from the floor. And in that single blinking glimpse, he saw her, lying on her back, legs splayed, naked and pale as the winter moon, eyes frozen shut in fatal repose.

I said don't look down. Now you've done it! Get out! Run now, you old fool!

Contrition

But his joints locked and he could only shudder, horror quivering the length of his entire spine like a great, frightened centipede skittering for cover.

Okay, okay, Placidus. You missed your chance. You've agitated the birds, though. Just don't wake her up. For God's sake, don't make a sound or she'll open those dead eyes and come for you.

The gulls had begun to shift about, beating their wings with great animation and dropping to kneeling positions. Placidus pleaded in his heart for them to be still, but he knew that the gears had been set in motion. Trembling, he gazed down at his feet, at cold death, and grew even more paralyzed by its terrible beauty. A face so elegant and perfect in every detail. A porcelain doll with tiny purple lips and long, wispy lashes.

I'm okay. Just mustn't disturb her sleep or she'll come after me, like last night and the night before. But I can't run forever. This time maybe they'll get me . . .

They?

Yes, her and . . . the birds. And the man on the crucifix.

Crucifix? Oh my God . . . the crucifix!

Placidus gasped, stunned that he could have forgotten the dark creature spiked to the cross. Again he had forgotten, like every night before until the birds grew restless. The body of Christ was gone and in his place hung an impostor. Someone vile and bestial. A great, surly man with a shaven head, sacrilegious and profane.

A guttural voice suddenly pierced the air, its hoarseness nearly unintelligible. "Pllllaaaaacciidduuussss!" it growled, so loud that many of the gulls flared off the rafter. "Come here, you pitiful old fool! Come get me off this cross now! Now!"

Shut up! Placidus wanted to retort, but he had no voice. He tried to cry out, but his face and lips only contorted, turning his face into a piteous mask of fright and helplessness. "You'll wake her up!" he screamed inwardly, unheard by all but the birds.

The man on the cross snarled and began to struggle against the spikes, squirming and straining like a wounded serpent. Blood spurted from his palms and ankles in tiny fountains with each twist of his body, but his efforts only seemed to grow in intensity. The spurts grew thicker. "Get over here!" he roared, his fury so complete that the crucifix began to rock away from the big trunk against which it leaned. "Get me off this thing now, Brother of Holy Cross!"

He'll wake up the girl! My God, then it'll all start up again! No. Someone help me. Saint Michael!

Suddenly something snapped at his feet. Placidus convulsed and all color left his face. Too late. As though hit by an electrical charge, the girl's eyes surged open. They rattled in their sockets for a moment, then grew deadly still, focusing on Placidus. They were yellow, reptilian, marked with black, vertical slits. And then her fingertips began to move. Slowly at first, but within seconds, her nails were drumming a mad rhythm against the planked floor.

"So it's *yooouuu* again, Placidus," she whispered in a vacant tone, her voice unearthly and filled with contempt. "So, you've come to see me again, eh, naked on this bloody floor. You've been peeping again, you filthy old goat!"

"No! I—"

She cackled, her pitch shrill and full of ridicule. Her swollen, bluish tongue flicked out over violet lips and her mouth twisted into a feral snarl as her cackling grew louder. And then the demon on the crucifix began to cackle, too. And the gulls followed suit. Their mockery filled the attic until the very timbers began to shake, and Placidus was forced to bury his ears to muffle the deafening choir.

Suddenly, the demon on the crucifix screamed with rage, wrenching a spiked, bloody palm from its confinement. "Aiee!" he howled, his pain becoming laughter again. "Ah! That feels bbeetttttteerr! Placidus, wait there. I'll be just another moment!" Then he closed his eyes as an utter look of ecstasy consumed his face while he tore his other palm free and held its gory, black wound outward for Placidus to see. "Stigmata!" he roared. "And now the feet! Stay and watch, Brother. Little girl, don't let him get away!"

Still flat on her back, she shot a small claw toward Placidus, locking her fingers around his ankle. Suddenly feeling this cold embrace, he lurched forward, crying out. He managed to pull himself free and began backing away. The girl quickly rolled over on her belly and began slithering toward him.

"Help me, Placidus!" she wailed. "Take me with you! Get me away from here! Save me this time!" But her eyes were full of mockery.

Got to get out! He'll be off that cross in a moment or two!

Gathering his courage, he turned to run, but there before him, blocking his flight, stood stack after stack of books extending from the floor to the rafters. School books, Bibles, theology books, choir books, all covered with green mold and bird droppings, swollen with moisture and age, coming apart at the bindings. He flung himself headfirst against the piles, striking out against their columned weight, shouldering his way through volume after volume. From above the deafening choir of seagulls filled the cavernous room as they swooped down upon his head and face, pulling at his ears and hair, attacking his hands.

Got to get through these books! These damned books! These goddamned books!

He shuddered, his own profanity shaming him.

God forgive me! Christ forgive me! Oh, Holy Name, I beg your forgiveness! Mea culpa!

He crawled up the disheveled heaps like a fleeing crab, limbs a skitter, but found himself sliding back downward as the books gave way beneath him. Down he slipped, nearer the girl, presenting an open target for the screeching, hovering gulls. But he never slackened. Up the heap he went again, back down, up the heap, back down.

He felt the girl's claws tear at his calf, shredding his trouser leg, and felt the warmth of his own blood. Then suddenly he heard a dull thud and that accursed howl from the beast on the crucifix.

He's off the cross! God save me now!

"Here I cooommmmeeee, Placidus, ready or not!" the demon laughed.

"Here *we* come!" cackled the girl, slithering ever closer, still groping at his legs.

Placidus forced his trembling knees upward again and dug forward with his fingers. The books continued to slide beneath him but he managed to reach the peak. Taking hold of one of the rafters, he tried to pull himself over to the downside of the mountain of books. But the gulls met him, burying him in a cloud of feathered fury so thick with dust and wings that he could barely breathe.

Placidus flailed away, screaming at them, cursing them, damning them until finally he made a clearing and slid headfirst down the voluminous heap to the other side. And when the side of his head struck the floor, he quickly gained his feet, praising God when he saw the attic door flung open as if to assist his escape. He fled toward that opening, his heart full of hope for the first time. It seemed miles away, but he ran with every fiber of strength his old muscles could muster. He heard his own feet stamping heavily against the planks and felt the door drawing nearer. By now the girl and the hellion were atop the heap, coming ever toward him, but he would beat them to the landing.

The opening ahead was a light, a precious luminous salvation. Escape for another night. It grew brighter and nearer, beckoning him, exhorting him. But then, as his jelly legs carried him forward, a vaporous figure appeared in the doorway, suspended from a rope.

I can run through it! It's filmy but I can make it like I did over the books!

There were heavy steps behind him now. And a dragging sound. It was the girl raking herself across the planks, and that vile creature of a man who dared pose as a martyr.

Placidus ran harder, his heart about to burst. He swept away the tears that streamed down his cheeks and began to feel lightheaded. Elated. He began to laugh though his heart was in his throat beating its way upward and out like a quail flushing from the undergrowth.

"I'm going to beat you to the door, you demons!" He laughed madly. "Run, you foul bastard! Crawl faster, you little whore! Come on, catch me if you can! I'm almost there! I'm almost there and then you'll have to deal with the Archangel, damn you! Saint Michael is on the other side and he'll take care of you both!"

But just as he reached the doorway, the vaporish, suspended figure took solid form and Placidus gasped, stopping dead. It was a man, smallish, dressed in black, hanging from a rope. The man's neck was broken and his head slumped limply to one side, resting upon a shoulder. His eyes gazed forward at Placidus, full of shame. They probed into the very flesh of Placidus's heart like spiny, digging fingers in search of something secret and long-hidden.

For just a moment, Placidus forgot the gulls and the girl. He no longer heard the large, bloody-palmed man pounding the floor with heavy feet. For that moment all Placidus saw was the man hanging before him, his eyes frozen, and all Placidus heard was the swing of rope, its hemp fibers squeaking in a slow, deliberate song of repentance.

The man's lips quivered as if to speak, but the rope was too tight. Placidus reached up to him, to loosen it, then stepped away.

"Placidus," the voice gurgled in urgency. "It's me! Take me from this hell. Take me with you. Save me this time. Save your old friend. I beg you—"

But before Placidus could utter a word, the gulls were upon him, and the girl. She wrapped her torso around his legs like a thick snake, and Placidus felt large claws ripping at him from below. Then he felt the cold breath of the demon from the cross, and a massive arm locked about his neck. Still mesmerized by the expression of Brother Phillip Allison's face, Placidus reflexively threw both elbows backward striking his attacker in the belly.

"Aiee!" the demon shrieked, loosening his vise-like grip.

Placidus freed a foot and kicked at the girl, flinging her away. Then, unable to help his friend, he shoved him aside like a pendulum and leaped out onto the landing, the squeak of rope still ringing in his ears. But as he looked down from the landing, there was nothing. No steps, no rail, only a black impenetrable void that led to nowhere.

Contrition

"I won't fall!" he screamed dumbly, hoping for a miracle. But he knew the age of miracles was past, so he jumped out into the blackness, to escape the demons, and the gulls, and the attic, and his—friend.

But as he descended, he began to become even more afraid than before, and in this new terror his arms began to pinwheel wildly, causing his body to twist and tumble. Head over heels, tumbling, reeling, twisting. On and on he fell, helpless, disoriented. Lost.

With a back-snapping jerk, he woke up, flailing about in his sheets, bathed in cold sweat.

Weeping, he struggled to his knees and groped about for Saint Michael. He began to pray, mumbling every prayer he knew, one after another, beseeching God, the apostles, the saints and every blessed soul in Heaven.

Finally, reality crept back through him and the black memory of the nightmare began to dissolve. Slowly unknotting his body, he shook the horror from his soul, like an old dog wringing water from his fur in quick shudders. The gore began to fade, but not the smell. He couldn't shake that, and it lingered in the dark air, filling his nostrils and throat.

He reached over his shoulder to feel his back, then down to touch his calf. No wounds. No blood. He shook his torso, ridding himself of a final shiver, and lay down again, fretful, like a child left alone in a strange house, which is exactly what this place had become. It had once been home, a place of shelter and camaraderie. Now a dark prison of fear and solitude, waiting each night to wreak its havoc on a tired, frightened old Brother of Holy Cross.

He pulled the blankets about his throat and curled into a ball, whimpering. Tearfully, he listened to the eerie creak of timber overhead , praying that dawn would soon free him of the unreasonable terror that had become his nightly companion.

Chapter Seventeen

During the week prior to the opening of school, Father Joseph was immersed in last-minute preparations, speaking engagements, and visits to the Diocesan Office. Registration had gone smoothly, and as hoped, enrollment had increased by just over one hundred students on the strength of Father Joseph's reputation alone. Bishop Logan saw this as a positive sign and went to great lengths to cooperate with the new principal. The Bishop had long considered Saint Gregory a monetary liability and for the first time in years thought the old school might return to fiscal solvency.

He had proposed closing the school three years earlier because it had become a financial drain on his office and the parishes it served. Most of the parish priests were in agreement with the Bishop's proposal, the Irish priests in particular, but the public outcry was so great that the religious community had shelved the idea for another time.

Since his arrival back on the coast, Father Joseph had spoken at every mass, Knights of Columbus meeting, parish bazaar, and bingo game he could fit into his calendar. He proved to be a most persuasive and eloquent speaker, reminding parents of the importance of Catholic education and values in an age of moral corruption. He tapped the business community as well, urging them to support their Catholic heritage and the leadership of tomorrow.

"It is your responsibility as visionaries of the coast to provide tuition assistance to the less fortunate," he said, exhorting them to open their hearts and wallets in the name of Christ and Saint Gregory. "Your parents sacrificed to give you a Catholic education when times were lean," he would say, rolling his eyes dramatically, evoking images of poor fishermen and seafood workers of the past scraping together their meager dollars for tuition payments. "Can we do any less?" he said.

Contrition

He was tireless, weaving humor and guilt in masterful orations to mobilize community pride and support for their alma mater, and his. He revived the defunct Saint Gregory Alumni Association and created the Saint Gregory Action Committee, whose purpose was to raise a pool of volunteers and conduct fund raisers. He rose at dawn and seldom returned to his house before dark, day after day, until he found himself looking forward more and more to those shots of whiskey each evening before retiring.

After especially difficult days, those shots sometimes gravitated toward half a bottle. But he tried to measure his drinking carefully, well aware that he was quite capable of becoming enslaved again. In the back of his mind he remembered the Jesuit hierarchy and his own downfall upon leaving Japan years ago. That had been a difficult time, but he truly wanted to succeed on this current project. Saint Gregory was a part of his youth and owned a special place in his heart. He hoped to repay the old school and had no intentions of letting alcohol foul his efforts.

He had seen little of Tristan since installing him in Madame's cottage and supposed that the young man was acquainting himself with Gulf Springs. The afternoon before registration, Joseph found that he had deceived himself when Madame LaFontaine invited him over for lunch.

The old woman dropped a soft shell crab in batter, rolled it in bread crumbs and laid it in the skillet of boiling grease. As the delicacy crackled and simmered, she looked at Joseph and shook her head. "That Tristan boy, he's really turned out to be an odd one, eh? And Joseph, slice the bread, would you, dear?"

"Odd? Why do you say that?" He looked at her a moment and went to the butcher block. "Mmm, you must have just come from Desporte's. This bread's still warm in the paper."

"You know I won't take stale bread." She flipped the crab in the skillet and the grease bubbled up again. "You haven't noticed him passing under your window and mine well after midnight these past five nights? Every night since you first brought him to my house."

The priest sliced the bread in fat horizontals and piled them on a platter. "Afraid I've been too busy to notice. And besides, what are you doing, spying on him, Madame?"

"Spying? Ha!" She bristled indignantly. "How'd you expect me to sleep with someone creeping around my property like that in the middle of the night?"

"Probably just out for a stroll. Down to the beach, I imagine."

"No, opposite direction. Know where he goes? Straight across the street and into the church. I find that peculiar, don't you? Ha! I'll bet some things are going to come up missing, you just wait."

"Oh, for Pete's sake. Nothing has come up missing."

She flipped the hot crab onto the open face of his bread, then dropped another into the spluttering skillet. "Well, I don't think it's natural for a boy that looks like that to be sneaking into a church at night, that's what I think. And I've told Peter Toche the same thing."

"Sneaking? My Lord, this smells good."

"Here's your mayonnaise. Yes, sneaking. He pulls that door open, real quick like, and steps in like he doesn't want anyone to notice. Yeah, I'd say that's sneak—"

"Argh!" the priest cried, snatching the sandwich from his mouth. "Damn, that's hot!"

"How long have you been eating soft shell crab now, Joseph? Your whole life? And you still burn your mouth every time! Anyway, a few hours later, he comes sneaking back out again, and right back into the cottage. Now I know you like the boy, but don't you find this all a bit peculiar?"

"Well, maybe he's just one to pray at night. Who knows? In any case, I bet he comes out empty handed, right? He's not hauling out the church, is he?"

She ignored the question. "And last night, he comes out of the church and goes straight to the cemetery. The *cemetery*, Joseph. He climbed the gate and disappeared into the dark. But I swear I saw his shadow by the LaFleur plots. Then thirty minutes later he climbed the side fence back into my yard. You don't find that a bit off?" By now the old crone's eyes were bugging from their sockets. "*I do,*" she said.

The priest slowly bit into the sandwich again, gauging its temperature. "This is too good, Madame. It's so good to be home again. I've missed your seafood over the years."

"You like that boy, don't you?"

"I do."

"And that voice . . . I bet you wish you had that voice, eh?"

Joseph nodded. "Hmm, if I had that voice I would be the greatest homilist in the ranks of the Catholic faith. It *is* quite marvelous, isn't it?"

The old woman shrugged. "You best watch him, dear. I'm telling you true, there's something unnatural about that one."

Contrition

"Now, now. I'm sure there's a reason for it all. He's more devout than any young man I've ever met, I'll give him that. I'll ask him about it all in the morning if you like."

She shook her head. "Do what you like. But don't tell him I told you about it. *Comprends*?"

Surprised, Joseph set his sandwich aside and sipped at his glass of white wine. "That's not like you, to avoid anyone or anything. Especially a man. I don't understand."

"You don't have to," she spat. "But I can feel it in my bones. That one's just not quite right, and those are the dangerous ones. When he came climbing over that fence last night, he looked like a ghost. When he got to the top of it, just before jumping down, he looked up at the moon and I swear I thought he was going to howl or something. His eyes looked like two red-hot coals. Hell, I saw that and locked my door. I stuck my pistol under the pillow, too, and there it'll stay."

Joseph laughed, downing his wine in one swig, and then he lit a cigarette. He smoked it, his eyes half-lidded, and looked at her. She was truly getting old, he thought. And though she was nosy, vulgar, and spiteful, he loved her, as one could only love a mother—warts and all. But he had never known her to lie, so he was struck by her uneasiness about the new tenant.

"I could handle another soft shell, Madame, if you don't mind." He rubbed at his belly and leaned back in the chair, stretching. "And another glass of wine, *s'il vous plait*."

She piled the second crab onto bread and flipped it onto Joseph's plate, grunting like a contented sow. "It's good to have you back, Joey. And I'll fix you all the crab you want, but you better watch the wine because we both know how you can get, eh?"

Chapter Eighteen

Eva Toche kissed her husband on the forehead. "I'll be back in a while, Victor," she said. "Just running down to pick up some oysters. I'll fry them up for you tonight. Maybe I'll call and have Peter swing by for dinner with us, too. Just the three of us, like old times."

Victor Toche grunted, and though fried oysters were one of his few remaining pleasures in life, he waved her off. He was lost in his daily crossword puzzle and didn't want to be disturbed. As with everything else, his thought process was becoming scattered and defunct. The morning puzzles were becoming more of a task with each passing day. He knew, too, that his heavy dosage of daily medication betrayed his memory. Nevertheless, he plodded through to prove to himself that at least he could still maintain a minimal vocabulary.

Pressing the pencil against the newspaper propped in his lap, he slowly filled in several letters and completed the word "villa." His letters were squiggly, and the lead of his pencil dull. A moment later he was asleep.

Half an hour later, he did not recognize the shattering of glass and wood. Half asleep, he thought at first it was the soft tinkling of wind chimes. But then there came a crash and the heavy footfalls of an intruder. Before Victor Toche could move, or even rise, a hulking shadow moved across the room and stood over him.

Victor Toche was a large man, but from where he sat, sunk in that easy chair, the stranger appeared to him more formidable than Goliath himself standing before the armies of Saul. But Victor Toche did not shrink back or cry out. He calmly looked at the man before him, measured the spite of his smile, and quickly guessed the purpose of the club-like walking stick slung over his massive shoulder. A lifetime policing the filth of society had, by now, left little room for doubt or false illusions in the face of imminent peril.

"And so," said Victor, "you've broken into my house and caught me here, old and asleep. How cowardly."

The stranger flipped the stick from his shoulder and slapped it against the palm of his right hand. "Cowardly?" he said, his voice full of mockery. Then he pointed to the bottles of medicine stacked one upon the other in a basket on the table next to Victor's chair. "Who are you to speak of cowards, drowned there in your potions and fog, each day waiting to die?"

Victor drew his lips back into nearly a snarl, and his eyes shone bright with quiet rage. "You'll not frighten me. I'll die here and now, but you won't chase me from this life whimpering and pleading like a damn school girl. Do your goddamned damage and be off, you filthy bastard."

The man smiled and behind the smirk; his dark face began to glisten with perspiration. The shine was especially bright on that great, shaved dome that crowned his massive frame. "Do you know who I am, old man?"

Victor sneered and brushed the newspaper from his lap. "No, I don't know who you are, but I know *what* you are. You're everything I despise and have worked against my entire life. You're everything evil in this world. You and your kind cannibalize everything that's decent or good."

"My name is Malik," the man said, his smile suddenly dissolving. "And I've come to end your suffering, old man, like the others in this tiny, God-forsaken town." His face became more waxen. "You should thank me."

"Like the others?" Victor nodded, suddenly connecting dots as a queer look came over his face. "Oh, you *are* the rot and the filth of humanity, aren't you? Spreading your misery like a sickness, infecting the innocent." He paused a moment, appalled, then settled even deeper in his chair. "So there it is, a stranger come to town, an indiscriminate killer. It was you, then, wasn't it, that butchered the little girl!

"Another goddamned demon slinking about, afraid to show yourself in the light. You're not human, are you, you goddamned bastard ? You *couldn't* be to slaughter an innocent child like that. No, you've been sent by the Devil himself to do his filthy work . . . just as he sent your like after me a lifetime ago, in the attic of a holy place, at the foot of a dead man. Only I didn't realize it then. But *you'll* be found out. My *son* will uncover you. He already—"

"My name is Malik, and in my world, the very mention of my name creates chaos and flight. Every man fears me. Your son, you say, will find me out? Then he is dead, too, just like you. He doesn't hear the clock ticking, but he is already out of time if he is looking for me. I will find him first."

Victor ran his tongue over his lips. They were rough and dry. "He's stronger than me, and smarter," he said. "I always thought he was soft—but my son is more driven than I ever imagined, or *you* could ever imagine."

Then, for a fleeting moment, Victor thought of leaping from his nest, believing for one brief moment that he might even overwhelm the stranger. But the ache in his bones instantly refuted that thought, reminding him just how decrepit he truly was. So he simply glared. "Be done with it then, you bastard, and I'll see you in—"

Malik raised the club, and before Victor Toche could finish his sentence, the club met his skull once, twice, a third time. As his head slumped onto his chest, he heard his killer's derisive laughter bidding him farewell. Then the dragging shuffle of parting footsteps and movement out through the smashed window frame.

But as his final breath was leaving him, Victor Toche let his trembling fingers locate the pencil that had fallen between his thighs earlier when he had fallen asleep. Struggling, he raised it to the armrest and pushed its dull point against the white space on the edge of the newspaper that lay there.

Moments later, Malik was weaving his way through several blocks of alleyway leading away from Victor Toche's mangled body. Then he stepped out onto the sidewalks, still moving at a brisk pace—but not so quick as to draw attention. He kept his eyes to the ground and didn't look back, not even once, because he understood that a mere sideways glance could betray one's intentions—or crimes.

But even if someone had perchance observed his unsmiling face, or his limping, fleeing footfalls, they could not have suspected that this man had just committed a brutal murder because there was an aloof calmness about him that would have deceived even the most discerning of witnesses. Even the large club that he carried possessed the appearance of an old-fashioned walking stick, certainly not an instrument of murder.

Contrition

And though Victor Toche was the third person he had executed since arriving to this place, he walked with that unconcerned stride of the anonymous, that confident stride of the criminal who has relocated to another land, leaving behind his guilt, his pursuers, and any trace of intended destination. Indeed, these people here did not know him or suspect him and could not even begin to guess that he was the black beast slinking amongst them, a carnivore feasting in the midst of lambs.

Just a week before, he had sought the isolated refuge of Back Bay, concealing his very existence. But now he moved cautiously between neighborhoods and along the docks. His lair in the sewers had been exposed, and the resulting police activity had temporarily flushed him from that area. But that in itself had reversed Malik's fortunes, and now he moved about more openly, often sleeping in garden sheds or parks. At times he even concealed himself at night among the riggings of shrimp boats, below the hatches in the cargo holds, or engine rooms of the larger iron vessels.

It was good to be out among people during the day, because he had much work to do before leaving this place. There were visits to make. There were names in his head, and faces. He neither understood nor cared about the origin of these names and faces, but simply moved forward—a mission-driven assassin, who blindly followed directives from wherever and whomever. Aware that he had become an instrument of some greater force and entity, he simply had it in mind to survive so he could continue to kill, just as in his previous existence in a place far away and foreign.

That evening, just hours after Victor Toche breathed his final breath, the red sun settled on the Gulf. From the docks it appeared as though the fiery sphere were melting into the water, spreading a scarlet tide of blood outward from itself. And it was from this vantage point that Malik slipped into night, moving between the boat slips, weighing the level of activity or absence thereof aboard each ship. Finally, he came upon a large wooden shrimper named the *Jean-Luc*. He would sleep there, he determined, slipping aboard.

Quietly, he went to the stern and lifted a large wooden hatch that opened down into an ice hold. Crawling in, he pulled the hatch back over his head and disappeared into complete blackness, feeling content that he would sleep well this night.

But even before he could get settled, he heard voices coming down the pier. The voices were boisterous and drunk. Then he heard a balancing act and cursing as heavy footsteps shuffled aboard, just inches above where he lay concealed in the ice hold. Easing himself up on his elbows, Malik reached for his stick and inched toward the hatch. Then gently, he slid it aside just a crack. Now, in the lantern light provided by the men above, he could see.

One of the men fired up a cigarette. "All this shit's got to go," he said, pointing to the culling table and wooden bins that consumed much of the ship's stern. "LeRoy, you and Jimmy take it apart in the mornin'. Strip it all down, but keep the sleds and nets so it looks like we're still rigged for shrimping."

"Damn," said one of the others, crushing his empty beer can and slinging it overboard, "what the hell we gonna' haul this time?"

The first man took a long pull off his cigarette and gazed about the pier. Malik knew that look—the man was scanning about for eavesdroppers. He recognized this man, as well as the others. They were the brothers he had mauled at the Old French House just days earlier, and they still had the bruises and bandages that testified to Malik's ferocious attack.

A malicious smile began to creep up the corners of Malik's mouth as he visualized bursting from his hole and falling upon these drunkards. His jaw tightened and the vessels that ran the course of his thick neck flesh began to sprout as he felt building within him that adrenal flow that causes a cat to make twitching anticipatory movements just before pouncing on unsuspecting prey.

"What the hell we gonna' haul this time?" the second man urged again.

"Dioxin, boys, and other chemical waste. Barrels of it. Three hundred bucks a pop, twenty barrels a load. We'll pick it up over in Pascagoula over the next two nights, run it out to Dog Keys Pass."

"What then?"

"We'll dump it over the side. The current'll wash it out to deep water before dawn."

"Shit," whispered the third brother, "what about the BMR and the Coast Guard? Christ, we could get sent up for life."

"Well, Jimmy boy, how're they gonna' catch us? We'll be in and out before they can blink. Damn outfits in Pascagoula are havin' fits with the EPA, so's the paper mills. Hell, it's a gold mine over there. Beats the shit outta haulin' dope and illegals. C'mon, get started. When we finish up, we'll get some more beer and head back to the house."

Contrition

The more Malik heard their voices, the more he wanted to emerge from his hole. But he swept this desire aside. Patting his stick, he decided to wait. Right now there were other names in his head, and other faces. But these three men, he knew now where to find them, and find them he would, all in good time.

When he did, thought Malik, he would mete out a punishment that was both hellish and final. Not because these men were enemies or because they were the reason for his coming to this town, but for the mere satisfaction of seeing them suffer, because they had stood in his path one day and had dared to raise a hand.

Chapter Nineteen

Peter was sitting at his desk thumbing through notes. He, Wilcox and four others had scoured the Back Bay area for three full days since the discovery of Tom Dardar's body and the strange scrawls in the sewer, and found little other than a handful of hobo camps. As he sat there mulling over his notes, he barely noticed that the phone rang. Nor did he realize that Dan Wilcox answered it and was suddenly turning pale.

"Yeah, he's sitting right here," Wilcox murmured into the mouthpiece. "We'll get over there right away." Wilcox's throat was dry as he looked down at his friend. Searching for words, he reached over and tugged Peter's shoulder. "Pete, your dad. He—"

Peter grunted, but didn't look up. "Yeah, give me a second, tell him I'll be right there."

Wilcox shook his head. "There's been a problem. Pete, he's—*gone*."

"Gone? What the hell does *that* mean?"

Wilcox rubbed at his forehead uneasily, then looked down at the floor as his face continued to blanch. Then he finally spoke again. "Gone. He's dead."

Peter dropped the papers in his hands and as they fluttered haphazardly over the edge of the desk and onto the floor, he felt something jerk at his insides. "What?" he said, only half absorbing the words he had just heard. "Dead?"

"Yeah. Damn, I'm sorry, Pete. That was the chief on the line. He's with your mother. They need you over there right now."

Peter stood, still unable to fathom Wilcox's words. "The chief? What's he doing over there?"

"Your dad. He's been murdered—beat to death, the chief said. Let's go, c'mon."

Peter felt himself go pale, and as he groped about in his pockets for car keys, he felt a palpitation rush through his heart—then another, until they ran in waves.

Contrition

"C'mon, let's get moving. Things are a mess over there and your mom's asking for you."

"Mom? Is she okay? Was she—"

"She's okay, but she found him when she got home. She's upset, losing it. She needs you there."

Wilcox insisted on driving and Peter offered no objection. Within minutes their car fishtailed up the narrow drive, nearly striking one of the squad cars already parked there. Peter jumped from the car and ran to the door. His mother stood there on the porch in the arms of an officer.

"Mom—" Peter whispered.

She looked up, then threw her arms around her son's neck and sobbed. He could feel her small body quaking and shuddering within his grasp. His eyes began to water.

"Go," she wept, pointing into the house. "Go see your father. May God help him, Pete, he's so, so . . . "

Peter released her. Passing her back to the officer, he stepped into the house and found Chief Barhanovich and two other officers circled about his father's easy chair. And in that chair sat his dead father—bruised, battered, soaked in blood. The old man sat there, broken-boned, head slumped onto one shoulder, eyes open.

"My God," Peter whispered, barely able to breathe.

Chief Barhanovich moved aside and ushered Peter closer. "Sorry, Pete. Damn sorry you have to see this. Looks like the same M-O as Tom Dardar. Same head wounds."

Peter shuddered at the sight of his slain father and covered his face with one arm. "What the hell—I mean—God, I can't think straight. I—"

"Easy, Pete," said Chief Barhanovich. "Take it easy. We think he was just sitting there. Someone broke in." He pointed to the demolished window casing and shook his head. "Busted right through there. I'm sure it's the same guy that killed old Tom. Don't know what the hell's going on here in town all of a sudden, but it's way out of hand."

"I know. But why? What started this all!" said Peter.

"No idea. Hell, that's the mystery. We're a peaceful little town. Never had anything even close to this happen here, ever. Another bloody damn assault for absolutely no reason. If it's the guy that was runnin' down Jimmy Dubaz like you think, Jimmy's description was pretty damn vague— big guy, dark, no hair. Doesn't help much. Hell, that could be half the guys down on the piers."

Peter looked at his father again. The two of them had fought since Peter's birth. But this was unspeakable. Suddenly his heart ached again for his mother. Only she had kept them from each other's throat, saving them from one another.

"Pete, I think it happened quick. The guy came in, did his work and left. I know this looks horrible, but your dad was heavily medicated so maybe he didn't suffer. Before he died, though, looks like he tried to scribble something on the edge of the newspaper. Don't know what it means though. Here, take a look."

Barhanovich reached down and picked up the paper from the arm of the chair. Then he pointed to the margin and ran his finger along the illegible scrawl along its edge. It was the scribble of an unsteady, dying hand—a hand that was determined to finish this one task before expiring. Peter strained to decipher the marking.

"Can you make it out?" said Barhanovich. "The first word's *"son"* I think, but can't figure out the rest."

Peter scanned the words, frustrated at first. But then his brows moved closer and he exhaled. "Yeah," he said, "I think I can make it out."

Barhanovich waited a moment but Peter just stood there stone still. "Well, Pete, c'mon—what does it say?"

Peter cleared his throat, and his face drew up into a knot. His hands began to shake slowly. "It says 'son, the devil's come . . . get out.'"

Barhanovich scratched his cheek, then tilted his head and said, "What? Doesn't make sense. Mean anything to you, Pete?"

"No," Peter lied, "not a thing." He set the paper aside. "But I want my mother moved out of here, put in protective custody."

Then he left the room to comfort his mother. But the scribbled words stuck in his head, and even as he gave her a heartfelt hug of condolence, they pricked in him a painful and disturbing connection. His head began to feel as if it were going to explode, as if a noxious sac in his brain were throbbing, threatening to spew forth a dreadful poison that would drive him once and for all over the edge into complete madness.

And then, just as he touched his cheek to his mother's cheek, he felt her whisper in a strange and mournful voice , "Are you finally happy now that Victor is dead? You've wanted this forever. Get yourself to a church, you wicked son, and beg forgiveness."

Stunned, Peter grasped his mother by the shoulders and pushed her away. "What! What did you say, Mom?"

Surprised, she looked up at her son, her eyes still full of tears. "Nothing, Peter. I didn't say anything."

Even though Peter could see that her lips were not moving, and even though he knew that the childish voice he had just heard was not hers, he heard it again. "Wicked son," the voice whispered, "now he's dead and you never once gave him laughter or affection." Then girlish laughter. "Go back to church, Peter, because the Devil is coming—"

The words were like a hammer blow to the head, and Peter's sudden expression of disbelief and urgency upset his mother even more. "Peter! Son! Are you—"

He retreated a step and clasped his hands over his heart. It was thumping madly in deep and irregular spasms, pulsating to the point of bursting. "She's here," he whispered aloud, glancing about, visually reconstructing the delicate facial features of the tiny black angel from his New Orleans nightmare. And then, for just an instant, he thought he saw her standing in the doorway, head tilted, pointing toward the dead Victor in the other room.

"*Who's* here, Peter?" his mother said, shaking at his arm. "Who are you talking about?"

By then Chief Barhanovich had moved to her side, having witnessed Peter's actions from the hallway. "Pete," he said, leading him away from his mother, "I'll finish up here. Go home, get some rest. You've been pushing it too hard lately. And now all this. It's a shock. Go home and I'll swing by later."

"But, I—"

"I *mean* it, Pete. Do it for your mother. Christ, she doesn't need this. She's upset and you're just making it worse."

Barhanovich walked Peter to the car, and though Peter was reluctant to leave his mother, he knew that at this particular moment he had to get away from this house, away from his slain father, and away from the tiny wraith whose prophecies were tightening about his neck like a hangman's noose.

When the Chief rejoined Eva Toche on the porch, he gave her a hug. "Pete'll be all right, Eva."

"I hope so," she said, whimpering a little.

Chief Barhanovich nodded. Then he hugged her again. "And you know something that's a damn shame? Pete loved Victor somewhere deep in his soul. And Victor, somewhere in that strange, hard heart of his, loved Pete—it's sad they just couldn't quite tell each other."

Chapter Twenty

The opening of school was a joyful time for Joseph. And during that initial flurry of greetings, introductions, faculty meetings and assemblies, his spirits and expectations soared to a level that even he found to be dizzying. His smile lit his face, then the faces of others. He busily issued directives, shook hands, hugged youngsters, inspected classrooms, and became so lost in others' dependency on him that Saint Gregory quickly became for him a feast of self-gratification.

How utterly sweet, that honeymoon incurred by the arrival of a highly touted principal at a school in flux. Joseph genuinely loved the laughter and the adolescent chatter that filled and echoed along the halls, those high-pitched and affected conversations, the girlish giggling, the boyish grins.

He scooted about, clucking like a mother hen, mingling with students, teachers and parents with the lofty understanding of the experienced and well-traveled. Indeed, this was his community, and these students were the children of the children of his childhood friends. Saint Gregory was *his* school.

Tristan fared nearly as well. Within days, his clear gray eyes and fine features won the admiration of staff and students alike. Every girl on campus instantly fell in love with him a bit, and the boys, envious at first, all sought his acquaintance and approval. He no longer had about him that dead spirit of fatigue and self-flagellation.

True, from time to time his eyes would inexplicably flare with intensity, and his face revealed inner journeys, but those moments would pass quickly, and it seemed to Joseph that Tristan had truly found his place there. He was so earnest, so uncorrupt an educator and motivator. It seemed a tragedy that Tristan was but temporary help and inconceivable that this beacon of light would shortly be dimmed by the return of the stodgy old Brother Martin Corso, a joyless man who willfully earned the scorn of both students and peers. Worse yet, Brother Corso wore that scorn like a badge of

Contrition

honor, tramping about like a decorated general amongst the bowed and vanquished foe.

"Tristan," said Joseph, as they both stood watching the students stream from the building just after the first Friday dismissal, "I want you to come to the Brothers' House. I'd like you to meet someone, someone I've admired for years. You've heard me speak of Brother Placidus? I've been so busy since my return that I haven't even stopped by to visit him yet. I would like for you to come with me."

"*Altar ipse amicus*," said Tristan nodding. "A friend is another self. I owe you that much. As Placidus is your friend, so will he be mine."

They found Placidus in the chapel, seated upon the edge of the mattress where he lay each night next to Saint Michael. He sat there undressing his feet, rubbing them, pulling the sweaty socks from his toes. Next to him lay an opened Bible, and his gaze, so weary from days of staring at so many verses, seemed dull with exhaustion, as though they could take in nothing more.

Joseph approached, extending his hands to the old religious. "Placidus! Dear Placidus."

Something flickered in the old man's eyes, and his hand stole out to touch Joseph. "Joey?" he said, looking up with joyful uncertainty. "Is that really you?" His joy was nearly like sorrow.

"Yes, yes indeed, Brother. I offer no excuses. I've meant to come by since my arrival back on the coast, but school, well, I—"

"No, no. I understand. So much to be done. So very, very much. But you're here now. I've prayed that you would come. My God, it's good to see you again."

"And I've brought a friend," said Joseph, motioning for the younger man at his side to approach. "This is Tristan, Placidus."

The old religious looked up at Tristan. For a moment he just sat quietly and stared, as though hypnotized, searching the young man's face. Then he reached to the side, picked up the Bible and fluttered the pages. "I was thinking that you would come alone," said Placidus sourly. Then his voice sharpened and his shoulders straightened.

Tristan ignored the rebuff, extended a hand, and took Placidus's in his. "*Ab imo pectore, pax vobiscum*."

The words pricked the old man. And he sagged a bit, softening. "From the bottom of the heart, peace be with me?"

"Yes," replied Tristan, raising a timid hand to Placidus' forehead, which was cold to the touch. "I will leave if you wish, Brother, but Joseph has spoken highly of you. I did not mean to offend."

Placidus looked ashamedly at his Bible, then pressed the covers together, closing it in his lap. "Come, come then," he said. "Be seated, both of you. I apologize. It's just that, well, things—"

"Brother Patrick has explained," said Joseph, seating himself next to Placidus.

At this Placidus bridled, rolling his eyes. "He—*they*, all think I've lost my marbles, Joey. I haven't, not really. Just promise me you won't dismiss me as a crazy old loon like the others have."

Joseph nodded, a half smile creeping up the corners of his mouth, as if keeping a secret. "Ah, Placidus, dear old teacher of mine, inspiration of my youth, confidante. What do I care what the others think, eh?"

"And Peter Toche, he's the worst, Joey. He really thinks I'm lost."

"It's Friday, Placidus. Let's not worry about the world. Instead, let's toast this reunion." He reached into his black sports coat and presented his flask. "I know, I know," he said quickly, deflecting the old man's look of objection, the same look he had deflected for nearly forty-five years.

Placidus rolled his eyes in surrender and uncapped the flask, taking in only a few drops of the fiery spirits. "Joey, Joey," he sighed, contorting his face into a comical grimace. "God help you. You never change. This poison of yours still burns. And it'll still be your undoing."

Then he passed the flask to Tristan, but Tristan declined gracefully. "*Amari aliquid*," Tristan said, "some touch of bitterness!"

"I saw Didier yesterday evening," said Joseph. "He sends his regards."

"Poor Didier," said Placidus, his voice suddenly filling with woe. "If only he knew what little Amanda has become. May God spare him from that, at least, after everything else he has gone through over the years." Then he stared off into a corner.

"Well, he—Placidus?" said Joseph.

"Placidus?" whispered Tristan.

Their voices were but a drone in the distance. The old religious leaned over, resting his head on a shoulder, and hid his face. He knew that soon he would begin to shudder and shake because he had carelessly uttered the girl's name. His eyes would involuntarily water and the tears would come, and his lifelong friend, Joseph Broussard, would join the ranks of those who whispered about the crazy old Brother who had exiled himself to the foot of Saint Michael.

Blushing, he dropped the flask to the blankets and became lost in that profound loneliness of the depressed and the hopeless, wishing that Joseph and the stranger had never come. "She's not dead," he whispered to no one. "She's up there waiting . . . just waiting."

Contrition

Joseph looked puzzled by this, but Tristan quickly folded his palms and, genuflecting, bent his head. "God, Savior of men," he prayed, "help this lost soul. Guide him to the peace he so earnestly seeks. Protect him, Dear Savior, and protect Joseph, and myself. This I pray. Amen."

"Damn, he was fine just a second ago," said Joseph. "It's as though he was here with us, then gone. I didn't know he was this bad off. I should have come sooner."

Tristan patted the old Brother and covered him to the neck with a sheet. "No, Joseph, it would not have mattered."

"But I might have been able to—"

"No," said Tristan firmly. "It's the dreams. They possess him now. He is in another far away world, and I know that world. It is a place beyond friends, or faith, or hope. It is a lonely place where suffering reigns supreme. A dark and impenetrable place. A place that perhaps you know also, Joseph."

Joseph shrugged. "Me?"

"Yes. You . . . me . . . Placidus . . . many others on this earth. Your old friend has simply slipped deeper into the chasm than you or I . . . for the moment, at least. Pity him and pray that we don't join him."

Joseph stood. "Let's leave him in peace, then. Let him sleep."

"There is no peace for him, Joseph, not even here in this chapel. Especially in this chapel. He seeks protection here, but he won't find it."

"What are you saying? You don't even know this man."

"But I do," said Tristan. "Truly, I do. And just as truly, things are becoming more clear to me with each passing day. I was meant to come here with you this day. And even though the old man wanted to speak to you alone, I was guided, just as you were guided back to this place which is your home. Just as your friend, Peter Toche, too, was guided."

Joseph listened, rubbing at his cheek, pulling at his ear, looking confounded. "I . . . You're rambling," he said. "What on earth are you talking about? I came back home because I got lucky and got a job, that's all. They needed someone and I filled the bill. Peter, same thing."

"Don't misinterpret what is so clear. Don't ignore the omens. A great gear has been set in motion, and nothing will stop it, not you, me, or the stars above. Don't you feel it here in this chapel? In this house? In the eyes of this old Brother lying at your feet?"

"No. I don't feel a thing. I just want to get Saint Gregory back on its feet. And want to end my career in one piece."

"*Fiat lux*, Joseph. Let there be light. You want more than that, much, much more than that. Trust one who has journeyed. The clouds have now begun to part for me, because you guided me here to this broken old man. Truly, Joseph, I thank you. *Ab imo pectore.*"

At this Tristan hurried out the chapel door, leaving Joseph beside the statue of Saint Michael. And Joseph, for his part, wanted very much at that instant to take another swig of whiskey, but the Archangel's upraised sword hung just over his head, and the solemn wooden face of that powerful saint seemed to glower at him with a stern and unforgiving gaze.

"Damn," Joseph whispered, looking away with a quickness that could only be interpreted as shame. "Damn."

* * *

Tristan sat on the edge of his bed, gazing through the open window at the full orange moon as it hung over Saint Ann's graveyard, quiet and graceful, like God's shepherd guarding the deceased. Tristan felt a certain comfort in its glow.

He felt more settled now, since meeting the old brother of Holy Cross. In Placidus's suffering, Tristan had witnessed his own hopeless wanderings, and the old man's hopeless state somehow gave him new-found strength. Placidus's misery, for Tristan, had the effect of a stone thrown into a quiet, murky backwater pond, sending out little ripples, loosening the secrets below, stirring things.

Finally he lay down, warm in that patch of moonlight that fell through the window, and the sleep that had escaped him for the past week washed over him as drowsiness slowed his mind to a crawl. There was a blackness at first, that utter sinking of a deep sleep that carries one away from one's life, from the world even, into deep space, floating through the universe.

But this passed and he was in that terrible city again. Voices came, distant at first, rising and falling like the howls of jackals and wolves. He felt the blur of bodies rushing past, shouting, some in retreat, some in chase. Then he saw the women in full flight, holding infants to their breasts, dragging children, screaming. And there was laughter, deep and rich—sadistic.

Suddenly he felt himself begin to move, one foot before the other, a slow walk that turned into a foot race. He saw a man before him, sword raised, towering over two women, who cowered at his feet, sobbing, covering their babies. Tristan cried out, gaining speed, but the sword had already begun its descent and was sweeping downward with the deadly arc of a great pendulum.

Contrition

He could stop it, Tristan thought, there was just enough time—he was almost there—he would throw himself on the women and intercede on their behalf, beg if he had to, struggle even, against that huge, laughing warrior who meant to brutalize them. Yes, he was almost there, when suddenly he heard iron striking stone, as if from a great distance, and he shuddered, dragging himself from the brink.

He sat up in bed. Dogs were barking in the night, calling to each other perhaps or howling their lonely chorus to the moon. He listened a moment. Then, as the fog cleared, he heard the sound of iron striking against stone again. It was the chinking sound made by a stone mason working his will on granite. And it was not in his imagination. It was coming from the graveyard.

Dressing quickly, he moved to the window, and saw movement. A dark, hulking figure was clearly visible stooped over one of the gravestones. The sound continued. Then came the crumbling of hard stone, and at that precise moment, Tristan understood.

"Stop!" he cried, scrambling out the open window with the unthinking, single-minded movement of an aroused spider enraged by the intrusion of some unwelcome presence in his territory. "Stop! You are defiling a Christian grave!"

Startled, the figure stood erect and froze. But before the man could identify the direction of the threat, Tristan hurled himself over the iron fence and was upon him. They both fell to the ground in a heap of tangled limbs, but Tristan quickly felt himself being lifted, then heaved aside. A large hand grabbed him by the neck and shook him about, like one about to wring a goose's neck.

Gasping, Tristan threw both arms back, just catching the intruder across the bridge of his nose with the point of an elbow. The man loosened his grip, and Tristan heard a deep, guttural groan, one that awoke in him a flicker of the past. One that awoke in him both terror and fury in equal measure. One that suddenly evoked an eerie and chilling vision of his dead brother.

"Guillaume!" Tristan screamed, suddenly driven. Turning, he rushed forward, throwing himself on the large shadow of a man that stood before him with the fearlessness of a man possessed. "Sacrilege!" he wailed. "This is God's ground!"

The man caught him in midair with two immense paws, shook him once, and threw him onto a bramble of thorns. Tristan felt their sharp points shred his clothing and pierce his skin. Crying out as the thorns exacted their toll, he tried to disengage himself, but his clothing was caught. Then, looking up, he saw the glint of steel against the moon, just above the shoulders of the hulking stranger.

A sword! This man means to kill me.

But there was no sword. It was a pickaxe, raised against the outline of the moon, and as in his dream, he felt the pendulum about to make its killing descent. He heard that terrible groan, that sound of a man summoning all his strength to administer the final blow. But suddenly, a yard light snapped on and the shrill cry of an old woman rang out. "What the hell is going on out there ? I'll call the police, you sorry bastards! Get out of that cemetery right now!"

The intruder turned toward the light, pausing. Tristan seized that moment and kicked out, striking the man in the knees. The stranger bellowed, tottered a moment, and dropped the pickaxe. Tristan pulled frantically against the rose bush, trying desperately to free himself from its embrace. This caused his pants to rip, but he felt his leg break loose. Jumping up he steadied himself, hoping to give chase, but too late. The stranger was now but a shadow scaling the opposite fence.

* * *

The five men stood amongst the rubble of Amanda LaFleur's headstone in a circle, speaking in low tones, trying to reconstruct the events of the night before. Then, for a time, they were silent again.

Peter studied Tristan's face, and though he felt tiny seeds of doubt spawning from deep within, he pushed them aside because there was something in the young Frenchman that refuted distrust. There was woven into the features of his handsome face traces of goodness and wisdom earned only by the passage through difficult inner journeys. "So," Peter said finally, "you were asleep and the sound of cracking stone woke you?"

Tristan nodded.

"We'll check the pickaxe for prints. Maybe we'll turn up something. But you never got a close look at this man's face?"

"No."

"Could you tell whether he was bald or had a shaved head maybe?"

Tristan shook his head.

"Was he carrying a big club, maybe a big stick or something like that?"

"I don't know," said Tristan, eyes cast to the ground. Reaching down, he fingered the petals of a white, dew-rimmed rose. "He threw me back and I got tangled in the thorns of these rose bushes. Before I could struggle free, he was gone." Then he pointed to the tattered sleeve of his shirt and pushed it up the length of his arm, exposing fine, dark tracks of dried blood. "But I will tell you this. There was something strangely familiar about him, just as there is about this rose."

Father Joseph and Peter exchanged a look over his shoulder. "You're speaking in riddles," Peter said. Then he lifted his eyebrows over the rim of his glasses and blinked into the bright air. "Madame LaFontaine says you spend time in the graveyard, right here by this grave, at night. What's that all about? Is it true?"

"Yes."

"But you didn't even know this girl."

"Not in the sense that you would accept, but, yes, in the sense that she was one who suffered a terrible ordeal, an incomprehensible injustice. Because of that, I do feel that she is a sister, and over there, the tomb of Madame's son. I have spent time there also because of the terrible ordeal that young boy endured."

Nothing could have been more displeasing to Didier LaFleur than the desecration of his granddaughter's grave. He stood beside Peter listening with mute attention. A red flush began to creep up his collar. "I don't understand," he said. That all sounds strange to me. I—"

"Didier, please," said Father Joseph, interceding on behalf of his friend. "Trust me, Tristan means no harm and has done no harm. He simply tried to stop the vandalizing of your Amanda's grave."

Didier grunted, nudging a piece of shattered granite with the tip of his boot, then shoved both hands in his pockets. "I just don't understand why—"

"I know this is difficult for you and Albert," interrupted Joseph, glancing over at Didier's son, "but Tristan is as confused and angered as the rest of us."

Albert LaFleur had not spoken all morning. A large man, though smaller than his father, he was the picture of defeat. His mournful face gave testament to weeks of grief, and as he stared at the damaged headstone, the worst past days of his life seemed enviable now since his daughter's death. He longed for last month when the future was still intact and things were normal.

Didier observed his son with a sad silence, and felt his own soul sinking again, by degrees, into a hole. Albert, of all his sons, had always been the most sensitive and weak in heart and spirit, lacking that fire that once drove his deceased brothers. Albert, in truth, had always made Didier a bit sad, but even more so now.

"The rose," said Peter, gesturing toward Tristan, "you said it's familiar, too?"

Tristan nodded. "My younger brother, Guillaume—his hair was as pale as this flower, pure and white, like his soul."

Another silence fell on the men as the laughter of children passing by on their way to the beach filled the morning air. They carried nets and buckets, scurrying along, lost in idle chatter, unaware of the ugly things in life, or death. "My Grandpa's taking me to Horn Island tonight!" one of them boasted. "We'll be camping out."

"Your brother," said Peter finally, as if seeing a sudden glimpse of some secret, "is that why you spend time here? Because of this rose bush?"

"No, because of the graves. There is a warmth here. This is a blessed place." Tristan stared directly at Peter, and though the polished lens of his spectacles reflected only the morning sun, Tristan perceived a thread of discomfort there.

Indeed, Tristan's remark had caused a fluttering in Peter's mind. "A warmth, you say?" said Peter. "Warm as in heat or warm as in the heart?"

"Heat."

There are secret things in a man's heart, things that could never be adequately explained to others. But Peter felt this very heat, had felt it emanating from the cemetery since his arrival. He had at first thought himself ill, but now, upon hearing Tristan's reply, he suddenly felt something pulling at him from Amanda LaFleur's tomb. Or was he deceiving himself? Perhaps it wasn't the tomb at all. Perhaps it was the attic again. Or the scribbled warning of his dead father.

"I don't feel any heat," Peter lied, looking at the others. "Any of you feel any heat?"

They shook their heads.

But tiny beads of sweat had already begun to form on Peter's forehead, and his physical discomfort was about to betray him. He turned away, pretended to examine the rubble, and pulled out a handkerchief. He gave his head a quick swipe of the cloth and stuffed it back into his pocket. Then he spotted something. Stooping, he brought his face within inches of the largest chunk of broken granite that lay strewn about the grave site and stared at the stone. "I'll be damned," he said.

The others gathered about him. "What is it?" Didier said.

Peter ran his finger along the stone, tracing the outline of several letters that had been scratched into the rock. "M . . . A . . . L . . . " said Peter. "And looks like a mark after that. Maybe the start of another letter or something. Not sure."

Contrition

Tristan crouched beside him and likewise ran his finger along the stone. "It must have been done last night before the headstone was shattered. I would have noticed it before."

"Initials?" asked Didier.

"Maybe," said Peter. "And maybe not. Hard to say." But the scratches were identical in nature to the ones in the sewer pipe, and this sudden connection set off tiny alarms in his brain.

Tristan sounded more certain. "Joseph," he said, "there is something familiar here, like with the rose, like in the sound of the man's agony last night. M-A-L . . . *mal*, in French it means evil, or bad. It comes from the Latin word 'malus' which means evil or bad, or the word 'malum' which is an evil or a harm."

Peter blinked twice in rapid succession, his mind filling. The stone suddenly felt warmer than before, far warmer than merely from the work of the morning sun. He pulled out his handkerchief again and wiped his face, completely absorbed by the heat of this single stone and the grave of Amanda LaFleur. He loosened his tie and slipped his finger up beneath it to unfasten his top shirt button. His cheeks were streaming now, and he felt his armpits dampening the fabric of his shirt and sports jacket. "Blessed place?" he said to himself. "French? Latin? Evil?"

"Didier, Albert," he said, rising, "that'll be all for now. And Joseph, be sure to thank Madame for her input." Then he shook Tristan's hand. "And thank you." As he hurried away, he thought of the primitive serpent scrawled on the sewer wall, and of his father's certainty that the devil had come. He thought of Little Jimmy Dubaz, too, as well as the haunting little wraith from New Orleans.

He recalled Tristan's belief in the power of children's voices and their presence after death. And for the first time in decades, he began to wonder whether there might be any merit to prayer when all else failed— when nothing else made sense, and when there was no other answer.

Chapter Twenty-One

Peter stood in the doorway and surveyed the attic, wincing at the glare flooding out from the bare bulbs strung across the rafters. "Too damn bright," he muttered. Then, loosening the knot of his tie, he undid the top button of his shirt and shrugged out of his sports coat, slipping it over the doorknob. He was tempted to strip off his shoulder holster, too, but his focus shifted to the center of the attic, the dying place, and he quickly dismissed the discomfort of the harness.

Peter didn't really think he would discover any new evidence this trip. Rather, he was after a mood. One that eluded him on previous visits, but had suddenly warmed since the desecration of Amanda LaFleur's grave.

Today, the house was empty because all the Brothers had gone to a weekend retreat in Bay Saint Louis, and Peter was filled with a sense of expectancy. Brother Patrick had even managed to pry Placidus from the house, and this in itself gave Peter great hope because there was something about Placidus's brooding presence that managed to cloud Peter's concentration. But there were other things, too.

From the attic one could hear every conversation below, every door opening and closing, every ring of the phone, and even the flow of water moving through the pipes whenever anyone turned on a faucet or flushed a toilet. None of this would have distracted most investigators, but it seemed these noises and Placidus's presence had conspired to frustrate Peter on each previous trip to the attic. But it wasn't going to happen today. This time he would channel into the right medium and tap into the riddle of this desolate place.

This medium, it was nothing he could discuss with others without being ridiculed. It was something within, germinating in his heart and mind like secret seeds that never surfaced until nurtured by the proper spadework. It was a heightened level of psychic sensitivity more than anything. One that he had always possessed and had caused others to think him odd since childhood.

Contrition

Quite simply, he felt things—secretive things—sensed them all about. At times when he focused with great intensity, he could reach within himself and images would sprout from nowhere. He attributed this to the fact that he had since birth felt joy and sorrow more deeply than others—and loneliness. So from this abysmal well of emotions sprang forth a rare gift, one hidden and kept from those who never sought to scratch beneath the thin veneer of normalcy.

As he had aged, he found himself drifting further and further into his own interior to capitalize on this gift.

"Dammit, should've brought a fan," he complained, stepping into the attic.

He reached sideways and unplugged the string of lights from the black extension cord that snaked its way up the stairs from a second-floor outlet. Suddenly, like the room itself, the mood darkened.

When the child was murdered, he reasoned, there had been no lights. And when Placidus's friend had met his end, there had been no lights—only dust-laden slabs of sunlight slicing through the end vents, like now. If the attic did indeed conceal secrets, as he suspected, they would not reveal themselves under the glare of manufactured light. No, such secrets gravitated to darkness much like those repulsive, many-legged creatures that thrived beneath rocks and rotting wood. And it would be in the gloom that he would root them out.

He pulled the glasses from his face and closed his eyes. Then, rubbing his lids with a pinch of the thumb and index finger, he shut out the world, focusing on nothing for several long minutes until, finally, he felt something loosen within. When that sensation abated, he opened his eyes.

It was the silence that struck him first, utter and vast, more desolate than before. But as he moved toward the center of the attic, sounds began to rise up, faint at first. He heard the squeak of his rubber-soled shoes, the rustle of his trouser legs and the jingling of keys in his pocket. Even the floorboards seemed to amplify their creaking, offering up high and low notes with each advancing footfall.

Oh, it's kicking in now, he thought, satisfied but unsmiling. *I'm really feeling it, coming in from everywhere.* Della's cooking roiled about in his belly and he scratched at it, digging deeper than usual until the irritating grating of his stubby nails against the polyester of his shirt made him stop.

When he reached the outline of the child, a queer feeling of déjà vu suddenly swept through him, confusing him, and for just a failing second, he couldn't remember where he was.

Disoriented, he lowered himself to one knee, palming his forehead with one hand and balancing himself with the other. "Jesus Christ!" he whispered as a psychic flash coursed through him, revealing a series of murdered faces. "It's coming in strong . . . too strong."

Suddenly, Amanda LaFleur's face registered, breaking the spell, and he remembered Placidus. Steadying himself, he stared down at the twisted outline and pressed both palms flat against the floor where he imagined her heart had been. "Come on, little girl, talk to me. Come on, Angel, come out."

His eyes closed and his brows drew together in thought as he grew still, again shutting out all distraction, boring into the blackness.

And that's when the attic came to life.

First, it was the whisper of wind entering the vents. Next, the outside scrape of overhanging branches against the slate roof tiles. Then a furtive sound from the corner, like a mouse skittering across the floor.

Just above, a rafter groaned as wind pressed against the roof, and this caused his heart to flutter as he remembered the cross carved on that very piece of wood and the legacy it left behind.

Shivering, he visualized a dead man dangling overhead from a short length of rope—a small man in black garb, eyes bugged out, body twitching in sporadic bursts, arms and fingertips extended.

But Peter refused to open his eyes or look up because he knew he was looking into the past. That image quickly dissolved as another took its place. Shadows this time, coming up the stairs—one large, one small, struggling.

Squat and still, Peter remained frozen to the floor, palms outstretched as the shadows passed through the attic door, then disappeared. But another image arose, and another. He focused on each, and on anything and everything that came to him from nowhere.

He was sweating now. The images were rolling in faster than he could decipher, but he pushed on, trying to clarify, trying to interpret until, finally, he thought he saw Placidus in the attic again, carving something into a rafter, laughing and singing. And that was when Peter suddenly felt a ripple of malaise crawl up his back and heard the ghost-cry of a child. It was Amanda LaFleur.

Shuddering, he pressed both palms harder against the wood, probing, focusing on her heart, and his. Large blue veins began to sprout on the back of his hands and the tips of his fingernails paled as rivulets of perspiration began to trickle down the sides of his face. His blue shirt darkened down the back and under the arms, and the attic heat suddenly became unbearable as he felt something weak and thready unveiling itself, making its way toward him.

"Come on, little girl," he implored, his voice rising nearly to a shout. "Come on, Angel, come out!" Wiping his beaded upper lip across his shoulder, he tightened his lids to the point of pain and imagined her there with him. "I feel you, Amanda. I think I—"

He lifted a hand from the floor and fluttered it about, grasping air with outstretched fingers, knowing that if he opened his eyes she would disappear. But suddenly a coldness seized him and he went rigid as he sensed another presence, this one real. His eyes popped open and he shrank backward on wobbly knees, his hands covering his head like a cowering dog with forepaws raised. Someone was in the attic watching him. He felt eyes. Not girlish eyes but those of a man.

"Shit!" he wailed, rising clumsily. Instinctively, his hand shot toward his pistol but his fingers couldn't manage the holster snap. "Shit! Come on, dammit!"

Finally, it popped open, but just as his fingers locked around the pistol grip, he sighed, sagging with relief. It was Christ. The crucifix. It was positioned at a slant against the east wall in such a manner that Christ's downcast eyes were staring directly at Peter.

Peter breathed easier and gathered in the panic that had spiraled from nowhere in a single terrifying moment. "Holy Shit," he wheezed, feeling ridiculous. Then he laughed nervously and all thoughts of the girl passed as he approached the cross.

Peter was not at all a religious man. He had been raised Catholic, attended Catholic schools his entire life, and married Catholic, but somewhere among his first dozen murder investigations in New Orleans, he had lost his faith. None of this had set well with his family or friends, especially Brother Patrick.

But now, as he stood at the foot of Christ, he felt a twinge of shame for the first time in years. It passed quickly, however, and he began to examine the carved work with close consideration. The artist had done well. Every detail had been painstakingly sculpted with masterful strokes of the chisel and rasp, and the paint had been feathered on with the most delicate of care.

The hands, palms up, fingers slack, were flawless from the creases of the joints to the tips of the fingernails. The face was mournful but knowing, and Christ's eyes, peering out in prayerful reflection, carried the troubles of the world. The crown of thorns looked ominous and hurtful. Christ's ribs pressed outward against the flesh of his chest and belly, forming a framework of bone strained against skin.

The wounds in Christ's side were authentic enough to cause Peter to bend downward to examine them more closely. No wonder, thought Peter, that old Placidus had been so convinced that the blood drops were real and the statue had truly been bleeding.

Then Peter looked at Christ's forehead and the crown of thorns, concentrating on the three drops of blood painted just below where one of the razor-sharp tips pierced the flesh. The scarlet drops looked so much more real than on previous visits that Peter felt compelled to touch them. Moving closer, he stuck out his index finger and drew it across Christ's forehead. The droplets streaked.

Nothing registered in Peter's mind at first. He looked blankly at the bloody streaks for a second, suddenly caught in that limbo between reality and the surreal that often overwhelms one in a moment of total and unexpected confusion. Then he gasped as the first real terror struck home, like a mallet blow to the head. He jerked his finger back and examined it, trembling. Real blood. Then from nowhere he heard Placidus's woeful voice shatter the silence. "Stigmata!" the voice wailed.

A cry escaped Peter's throat before he was even aware of it, and he was suddenly thrown into the midst of a flashback—he saw himself fleeing the attic that first day when he saw Amanda LaFleur's tortured corpse. Or was it Brother Placidus in flight? Or was it himself fleeing, in the immediate future?

Peter moaned, quickly brushing his fingertip across his shirt to be rid of the blood, but his finger left a red-stained track across his heart and he suddenly knew he was in trouble. That was when he heard the dull, metronomic and distant hammering—of a wooden mallet driving a spike through flesh. He cried out, unable to absorb this terrifying flood of events.

Then there came a stirring from behind the crucifix and Peter heard something foreign that jabbered and muttered in a deep mucous-wet voice, and that was when he realized in the secret courtroom of his heart that he had already been tried, convicted, and sentenced—he would not be leaving this place.

A silhouette began knitting itself together from the shadows behind the likeness of Christ, and Peter turned, hoping that he might yet slink away, but the terror in his belly paralyzed his legs and he teetered in place as though his shoes were nailed to the floor. The muttering continued for a moment; then the voice growled out a burst of filthy language that Peter understood. "God damn you, you little bastard! Say farewell to life!"

A shadow rose up the east wall and someone stepped out from behind the crucifix—a beastly looking half-man of a creature, his face full of spite and malevolence, his skin black and burnt. "You are mine now!" he rasped, a cold glitter filling his eyes. He stepped closer and reached around to scratch at his sloping, misshapen back.

Horrified, Peter started to grasp for his pistol again but hesitated, helpless in the thrall of those serpentine eyes. He tried to cry out, but the

Contrition

words died in the dryness of his throat when he realized he was immeasurably frailer than this man before him. So he just stared, trembling, and it was then his psychic gift kicked in—or was it his curse?—and Peter suddenly saw not a man but a half-man, and this dispirited him even more. His arms dropped to his side. The pistol was useless.

Peter's mind kicked onto another plane, seeing beyond the features of the this half-man, and in this creature's hate-filled eyes he read the stark madness and torment of mankind's dark side racing down the bloody trail of a thousand generations. The half-man began to change by the second, into the Beast. It suddenly seemed darker. Its eyes began to burn violet, then dulled to anthracite. Its tongue lolled out the corner of his mouth, extending grotesquely, and with a lizardly flick, lapped against the bottom lobe of a pointed ear.

Peter's face drained and he felt a hopeless crawl of horror in the pit of his belly as the transformation continued, the Beast before him degenerating into something completely inhuman and unholy. "Peter Toouuuccchhhheee," the voice slurred, "what do your misguided little psychic eyes see? Aren't you glad you have the giiifffttt, my soon-to-be-butchered little hog? You seeeee too much. You think too much. Oh, and if only you believed. You have forsaken, and now will be yourself forsaken!"

The Beast reached a gnarled, wormy hand toward Peter, and Peter groaned with revulsion. The Beast's fingers became scaly, then extended into claws as he took on the appearance of one of those hideous gargoyles perched on haunches atop the parapets of some ancient medieval cathedral. There was a keen look about his eyes and nostrils, as if he was about to feed.

Peter watched dumbly, hoping a miracle might occur or that he would blink and then suddenly awake from his treks into his own mind. Strangely, he even imagined that the wooden Christ might pull himself from the cross and chase this demon back into darkness. But this he knew would not happen because he didn't believe it *could* happen. He had lost his faith years before.

The Beast's claws now seemed long and scabrous and he clittered them about his own neck, the razor nails drawing lines against crusted flesh, flesh that smelled and crunched like the charred hunks of burnt offerings once presented to pagan gods. Then the razors flashed outward and Peter felt a warmness running down his neck. "And so," whispered the Beast, "let the slaughter begin."

Peter thought of his wife, that sweet, agreeable woman he had taken for granted for so many years, and he suddenly pitied her. He had given her so little. He thought of his father, also, and sadly wondered what invisible line was it that had created such a profound gulf between the two of them.

The razors struck again, slicing lower than before, and Peter's hand shot up to pressure-close the wound, but the warmth oozed out between his fingers. He saw himself standing in the hallway of a housing project in New Orleans, staring down at the body of a little girl.

The razors flashed out again, and Peter dropped his hand, trying to focus his eyes, but they were not sharp now. And in their haze he saw himself sitting in a small desk next to Brother Patrick, and there was Placidus, good old Placidus, standing before them at the chalkboard conjugating a verb in Latin.

That image was suddenly blotted away and in its place stood three gravestones. He heard the deep knell of church bells calling worshipers to Sunday service and saw them filing into an ancient cathedral. And he saw himself, standing at a distance, unwilling to follow. Each stroke of that fateful bell resounded in his chest and he began to feel life ebbing out of his dying body.

He half closed his eyes, clinging to any scrap of faith he could muster. But the well was dry, and he could only stand and grunt like a gored pig, not understanding death, salvation, or eternity. And finally, all thoughts ceased and the full weight of his upper body dragged him downward to the floor.

He tried to crawl away but his fingers scrabbled uselessly against the wood. Then he felt something clawing at his legs, dragging him deeper into the attic, and he felt his tenuous grip on consciousness slipping away. The air was thickening with every beat of his waning heart and he began to gasp, like some great, stranded fish breathing its last breath.

Faces flickered before him, like moths fluttering around a light. Children's faces. Then the twisted, distorted faces of people in the throes of great suffering. His blood felt hot now, like lava streaming from his flesh, mixing with the fabric of his clothes, sticking them to his body and to the floor.

"God, help me!" he gasped. "I—"

Then his eyes fell still and a rattle filled his throat as he left life behind . . . and in its place came a rumble, deep and resonant. He saw silhouettes of people, by the tens and hundreds of thousands, fleeing into the dark horizon, falling into great chasms of quaking earth, consumed by white-hot flows of burbling lava.

The screams rose and fell, rose again and fell again, as more and more joined this hellish death parade, like infinite hordes of lemmings leaping to their deaths, trampling over others, scrambling their way over mountains of dead and dying—showing no mercy for the maimed, the children, or the infirm. He cried out, afraid to join the rush, afraid to stay in

Contrition

place. But then the fullness of this horrible vision came after him, pulled him up—he felt his legs moving, and he burst forward, joining the fleeing hordes, his screams mixing with theirs, his horror filling each and every jangled nerve and artery with sheer terror.

It seemed he was flying. Beyond the masses he flowed, over them, hurtling out of control . . . then downward, toward the fire into the lava flow. It seared his skin and he wailed.

"God, save me!" he screamed.

And then everything grew black. Numbness consumed his muscles, but he felt himself spinning as though in a whirlwind—head over heels, around and about, again and again. Finally, he felt himself slam into something solid. The shock of it shook his bones to the marrow, and he felt them snap, all at once.

When he opened his eyes, he looked about and found himself paralyzed, sprawled face down on a cold surface. *Stone*. But there were lines on the surface—long lines, with intermittent smaller lines bisecting the long ones. *Wood*, he thought, still unable to move, or even raise his head.

Half an hour later, Peter slowly lifted himself from the attic floor. Shivering, he looked about. The crucifix stood there as before, solemn and sanctified, and the downcast eyes of Christ gazed at him with a peaceful reverence that made him shiver violently. He looked above, and there was still a cross etched into the rafter, and everything else, too, seemed to be in place. He gazed down at his legs, and immediately saw that there was no blood, no wounds.

"Christ," he whispered, knowing that he had returned from some horrific psychic trip of his own devising. But this time he had taken himself too far. He had pushed himself over the edge, and madness had finally come after him. "Christ," he whispered again, fighting off another chill as it began to creep up his spine. "I'm losing my goddamn mind, full bore and full tilt. It was all just in my—head."

But just at that moment, he looked at the white fabric of his shirt, and froze. Moaning, he then placed his index finger against the shirt and ran it across the scarlet line across his heart.

He swooned and crumpled in a heap at the foot of the cross.

Chapter Twenty-Two

When Peter's eyes opened, he felt entombed. And though he knew he lay in the darkness of the Brothers' attic, there stirred not a breath, and the sepulchral silence was disturbed only by the jangling of his own brain. He could not move. His will said to rise and leave this tomb, but his muscles and nerves had wilted into paralysis. So he lay there, cheek against the floor.

He thought of closing his eyes again, but at that moment there came a soft rustle of clothing and the sound of light breathing. The presence was quite feeble at first. It arose, however, and gradually became undeniable and threatening—and he felt it just next to him. "Who's there?" he asked aloud, startled.

"Welcome back from the dead," said a voice, strong and sure, soothing. "In your delirium you seemed to go mad, but sometimes a fool speaks right. You saw the face of Satan. *Monstrum horrendum.*"

The voice was not foreign. Peter recognized it. "Yes, I think I saw . . . the Devil. He was coming after me," said Peter. "I died today, but I'm still breathing."

"That is because demons and their disciples recognize the power of a superior God. Even *they* take flight when that God raises His hand to protect the worthy."

"What are you doing here?" said Peter, still faint and weak. "How did you—"

"I followed you," replied Tristan with perfect calm. "I recognized you, when we first met, as one that does God's work. The pure blood of principles runs through you. And though you are incorruptible, you are lost . . . but God watches over you still."

Peter heaved a moment, trying to raise his head, but it was as if his cheek were nailed to the floor. "Lost?" he muttered.

"You do not sleep at night. Sleep is for you a chilling haze—no comfort there, only a trail of faces stalked by misfortune and violent ends.

Contrition

Even now your heart suffers, filling itself to bursting with regret and sorrow."

Peter laughed that nervous laughter of the rightly accused. "You read palms, too?" he said. "Ha, what would you know about me?"

"I know that regret remains in you now, in the path of your slain father's absence. Joseph has spoken to me about you and your father. I suppose that you may have loved him, but now you can only divulge your feelings to a tomb. How simple it would have been to shake his hand all those years, or share his loneliness. How simple to flatter, or engage in light and trivial talk. But now you punish yourself because you finally recognize that *his* pride was *your* pride, *his* anger *your* anger."

If a man were to survive a bullet to the heart, he would look as Peter did. He listened to the accusation, open-mouthed. The words penetrated his conscience and forced him to close his eyes in shame.

"You did this to your father, Peter, even though you were blessed with the kindest of hearts, your mother's heart. You did this even though God blessed you with a gift for seeing beyond the scope of others and yet you turned a blind eye to your father. It was you, Peter, who all along kept the battle line drawn, who hoisted the war banner since childhood."

"How can you know these things? Where did you come from, and just who the hell are you, really?"

"*Cela viendra*—that will come. But now, it is time to rise."

"I can't move," Peter stammered. "I—"

"Death is entrance into great light, Peter, and truly you have come back to the light, back from the blackness. Your soul is reborn this day, your spirit breathes again, so stand and live." In the voice was mingled the resolve of a warrior and the gentleness of an abbot.

"I can't move!" Peter wailed. And in his fervor and frustration, he believed himself for a moment. Then he felt something give from within.

"Stand up, Peter. Get up and walk with me. Join me in my struggle before it is too late. A great war has been set into motion in this tiny place and given rise to the sudden and monstrous murders that have descended on this peaceful town. It is not accidental or coincidental. It is all by design. You have been called here, as I have . . . and others."

There are moments when the impossible becomes possible, when one rejects all that is known and suddenly accepts the unimaginable—and this moment suddenly struck Peter with the resounding and reverberating blow of a great cathedral bell. He felt it vibrate in his head, in his chest and in the depths of his belly, and during this singular moment he rejected logic, personal experience, and doubt in the celestial. In their places, he felt that elusive feeling that bonds one to an utter stranger for no apparent reason. In their places he felt an inexplicable devotion for this young man that he had only met weeks ago, this man who had once given rise to uncomfortable suspicions. Truly, in place of doubt, he felt trust and kinship.

And as his muscles limbered and feeling returned to his limbs, he raised himself, first on all fours, then onto two legs. He smiled weakly and touched the blood stain on his chest. "Alive," he mumbled. "I'm still—alive."

* * *

On Sunday morning at 8:30 Mass, the parishioners of Saint Ann Cathedral were quite surprised to find Peter Toche sitting in their midst. But there he sat, next to his wife and the handsome young man who was helping Father Joseph out at Saint Gregory. These same parishioners were further surprised to see Peter actually praying and listening to Father Jamison, new to both the priesthood and the parish, as he awkwardly delivered a nervous homily.

It appeared to all that Peter was genuinely absorbed in the mass. And twice, they noticed, he reached over and affectionately patted his wife on the lap. As if this all wasn't already enough to startle the faithful, several of them later ran into Peter and his wife at the champagne brunch in Sekul's Restaurant. He was offering her a toast, smiling, and she was returning his attentions.

This scene was of course described and repeated by the busybodies of Saint Ann's, embellished with each retelling. And when Peter showed up early for 8:30 Mass that very next Sunday and stood in line for confession, the tongues began to wag even more. He even took communion this time, they said, and put money in the collection basket.

All of this was cause for joy with Brother Patrick and Father Joseph. Both clergymen had always hoped that Peter would become a practicing Catholic again. Now that it had happened, so suddenly and unexpectedly, in fact, that both were unprepared for the extent of his piety. Joseph attributed this to young Tristan somehow. Brother Patrick, however, chalked it up the persistence of his own prayers on Peter's behalf. Neither was incorrect.

In his spare time Peter began to read the Catechism of the Catholic Church and review the Scriptures. He began to work a bit more on his marriage, too, much to the appreciation of Della and her relatives. But most of all, he began to seek out Tristan de Saint Germain. He found there both friendship and solace. Tristan somehow simplified the complex. He was a model of manners and presence. He was, despite his youth, the voice of wisdom and the epitome of humility.

Contrition

That second Sunday after Mass, Peter found him sitting on the seawall across from Saint Ann. "So," Peter said, "talk to me about the power of visions and how they drive you forward."

"I am much like you," Tristan said, staring out toward the water. "I was born thinking too much, delving into holes. The gift grew stronger with age. And then, as I encountered much suffering in the world around me, the gift intensified. Remember, the heart runs in a circle—the more one *witnesses* suffering, the more one suffers—the more one suffers, the more one sees, until at some point the heart swells for others, constantly. Then you shut out much of the world around you.

"This, in turn, forces you inward, which forces you to feel, see, and hear more within the silence that surrounds you. You know this lesson well. Excessive misfortune creates visionaries. I, like you, have benefited from this willingness to see beyond the obvious. Where others see nothing, we see and feel shadows, movement. Isn't it strange that most men can see something, then deny what they just saw? Or excuse it as trickery or imagination? A beast in the fields is more rational than man because the beast does not feel the need to rely on science or reason for every answer in life."

Then Tristan paused a moment and looked directly at Peter. "You also know that many people with this rare gift bray and bridle like a jackass, offending others with a foolish sense of superiority simply because other men cannot fight their own self-imposed blindness. Fortunately, you tend to turn inward and remain silent, not superior, about this advantage. You have grasped what the jackass ignores. Most men do not believe in the supernatural, or in those who do."

Peter nodded. "True. Man refutes the supernatural. And if he doesn't, he is ridiculed and considered strange."

At this remark Tristan looked at Peter and his passing glance was more piercing than a knife. "And *you*," Tristan said, "do *you* accept the supernatural?"

Peter remained silent.

"If I told you who I really am, what I really am, could you accept that, or would you mock me?"

Peter felt a brief discomfort. "Yes. I believe in the supernatural, to an extent I mean. I have experienced it—to a degree."

Tristan looked skyward and followed a flock of gulls as they dropped to the east, then settled in a mass on the shore of Heron Island. "Your vision in the attic, Peter, it was me. I have the capacity to induce visions in others—but only if they are lost, and only if they secretly desire to be found again. That is my gift, that and the knowledge that only God owns this universe."

Peter nodded. "A good gift. One that can change lives. I envy you."

"Ah, but don't. I cannot change lives. I can only serve as a warning and a reminder. And from that point on, those I touch must choose their own path."

Peter smiled and offered his hand to shake. "Anyway, I want to thank you. I was drifting. I felt that I was on the verge of losing my sanity. I don't feel that anymore. I owe you much."

"And I sense that you will touch my life. I feel that you are an ally for what is about to come. Like you, when I came here, I was lost and confused. I felt on the edge of perdition. But now I sense a purpose. I am here by selection, for some reason that is as of yet unclear. But for me a thread of this mystery appears to unravel with each closing day. And you, my friend, in the end . . . may well tilt the balance."

* * *

Didier LaFleur's distaste for hospitals and doctors extended back to his youth. He learned early that they were the harbinger of bad news, pain, or death. And today, it was only his great affection for Joe Kuluz that gave him the will to shuffle down the barren, sterile corridors of the cancer ward at Gulf Springs General.

As he passed several rooms, some with doors ajar, others closed, he heard the whisperings of patients and visitors. From one room he recognized the hushed concern of relatives. Bad news, he supposed. Or final farewells. When he found room 214, he took a deep breath. Then, without knocking, he entered and found Joe Kuluz in bed, on his side, facing toward the window.

"Hey there, Joe, you awake? Got your message so I came right away."

Kuluz cranked his head over a shoulder and grunted. "Come around to dis side of my bed, Didier. I'm too damn tired to roll over."

The old Frenchman complied and slid a chair up to the bed. He hadn't seen Joe since he was admitted to the cancer ward. And when he looked into his ailing friend's gaunt face, his heart dropped. Outwardly, he remained expressionless. "So, how're you doing, Joe? They treating you okay in here?"

"Aw, not too bad," Kuluz said, his voice full of gravel. "Could be better, but I'm doin' awright." Then he pointed to his hairless scalp and closed his eyes. "Started chemo already. Bald as a damn peach, eh? Glad my Annie ain't around to see dis. My hair was what first caught her eye, you know."

Didier nodded. Annie Kuluz had been dead nearly ten years now, and it was a merciful thing that she did not have to be here to see her once vibrant husband. He was barely recognizable in this state of deterioration, and Didier now found it hard to look at him directly.

"My God, Joe, don't they feed you here? You look thin as a rail, boy."

"Goddam cancer's movin' quick," he rasped. "Eatin' me up purty good. Can't keep weight on, can't keep food down. Don't tink it'll be long now. Hope not, anyways. Dis ain't no way to live. Hell, I'm ready to go."

Didier shrugged that sad shrug of the helpless, understanding.

"But I sent for you 'cause I knowed I wouldn't see you again unless I did. Everyone knows how you feel 'bout hospitals. And dyin'. You've seen your share, eh?"

Didier shrugged again, trying to smile. It distressed him to see Joe Kuluz in such condition, and to know that he was now bedridden and would never leave this place.

"I sent for you to say goodbye, Didier. I seen all dem boys from the pier already 'cept Billiot. Dey say he's one ward over. Leukemia. Anyway, I tank you for comin'. I know dis is hard on you."

"It's nothing," said Didier, placing a large hand over the smaller hand of his friend.

"Goddam, we've seen some times togedder, eh?" rasped Kuluz, coughing an old man's cough. "But we wasn't such good friends in dem old days. We was both yung and stoopid back den. But the main reason I called for you, dare's some tings I wanted you to know."

"And what's that, *mon ami*?"

"You remember dat big dumb Juggaslav what burned yore boat, *La Marraine*? Well, he was my cousin."

Didier scratched his throat. "I didn't know that, Joe. Course, we didn't do too much talking back then, the French and the Yugoslavs."

"Well, he shouldna tore up yer crab traps. He was a wurtless basterd at times. But Didier, you shouldna whipped him so bad dat first time when you found out, in front of his whole crew. But dat's not why he *burned La Marraine*. He hated you already, but dat's not why."

"No? Well what, then?"

"You shouldna been messin' with his Marjorie. *Dat's* why he set yore boat on fire."

Didier's face filled with color and surprise. "What ? I never did that, Joe." Then he shook his head. "I swear to you on God's book I never did anything like that."

"No? Den what was you doin' over at dare place when he was gone dat last month? Everyone on the Point knew 'bout it."

"Joe, you know damn well that guy was no kind of fisherman. Croaker had no business even being on a boat cause half the time his wife and kids were starving. My Marie, she made me take money and some of our catch over to his wife . . . and sometimes vegetables from her garden, to help feed the kids. Marie wouldn't go herself because of the bad blood between her family and Croaker's family. You know how bad all that was back then between those people. So she sent me in her place."

Kuluz looked deep into his friend's eyes and sighed. "You swear by God dat's true? You wasn't bangin' Croaker's wife all dat time he was gone?"

"No, Joe, I swear."

"Den goddam, it was all a big mistake. He tot you was pokin' his old lady. 'Course, you wouldna been the first. But dat's why he burnt *La Marraine*. And when you came lookin' for him down at the Old French House dat night, he was already waitin' on you. You didn't know dat, eh?"

"No, not at the time."

"He know'd you was comin', and soon as you walked in the door he pulled out dat big filet knife he had hid behind his back. Every Juggaslav in the place know'd he was gonna kill you dat night. And we was all hopin' he would. Croaker cut you up purty good, eh?"

"Yeah, had me bleeding like a stuck pig. But you know, I never meant to kill Croaker. I just wanted to bruise him up some. Me and my father, we built *La Marraine* from the frame up. And my Grandpapa, too, he worked on her. She was like part of our family and meant a lot to all the LaFleurs and all the other French on the coast. I'm sorry I killed your cousin, but he kept coming at me with that knife."

"I know. And when dat jury said self-defense, we was mad as hell, even doe we knew dey was right. And you know, Didier, I'm sorry Croaker burnt up yore boat. Even back den I was sorry 'cause it was such a fine boat. But dat udder basterd, duh one what burnt down your house a week after you killed Croaker . . . I know who did it, an I'm goin' to tell you now after all dis time."

"You know who?" said Didier. He stared at his old friend. "You've known all these years, Joe, and never said who? Even after we got to be friends?"

"Yeah. First, back den, I was afraid to say. Didn't even tell my Annie. You scared lotta men back den, Didier."

"Yeah, I suppose so."

"Den, later, I wasn't so scared of you, but I still didn't say, even after I got to know you some . . . 'cause I was ashamed."

"Yeah? Why was that?"

Contrition

"Cause dat basterd what burnt down yore house . . . was *me*, Didier."

Didier rubbed his forehead, stunned. "No, *mon ami*, I don't believe. That isn't possible."

Kuluz continued. "Yeah, it was me. 'Cause you killed my cousin. Even doe he mightta had it comin'. Croaker was a liar and a cheat, an he beat his kids and Marjorie. But he was my blood, and he was a Juggaslav, and you was French. *Dat's* why I did it. But I hope you realize, Didier, I did it while you and yore family was away at Mass. I din wanta hurt nobody."

Didier shrugged. "I thank you for that. That was kind."

Kuluz's hand trembled beneath Didier's, and his voice broke. "I ain't a bad man, Didier, an I'm so sorry for all dat now."

"I understand."

"I hope you don't hate me now. Just wanted to clean my plate before I go."

"That was a long time ago, Joe. No, I don't hate you. I couldn't ever hate you after what you tried to do for my two boys."

"Tank you, Didier. You always did have a good heart. Dat's what I like about you. But listen. Now I got it off my chest, dare's sometin else you should know. Remember dat big guy what whipped the Duval brothers' asses down at the Old French House a while back?"

"Yeah, what about him?"

"Well, a coupla nights before I came to the hospital I was at Jacqueline LaFontaine's place."

"Joe, you still seeing her after all these years?"

Kuluz gave a feeble, toothless grin. "Don't tell me you haven't been dare a time or two since you lost your Marie, you old dick head."

Didier frowned. "No, absolutely not."

"Well, she's still purty damn good at what she does. But anyway, when I come out it was past midnight. I left her door and when I pass the cemetery, right dare under dat street light, I see dat big guy comin', carryin' sometin. Looked like a handle was stickin' outta dat top of duh oyster sack he was carryin'. An axe or sledgehammer's in the bag, I was tinkin' at dat time. Well, I pass on by, but when I look back duh sack is gone an he's stopped right dare by the fence. Now, I figure he's dropped dat sack over duh fence, eh?"

"Into the cemetery?"

"Why sure, unless he's a magician an made it just *disappear*. An all dis while he's watchin' me like he wished I'd just move along. Anyway, I turn duh corner like I ain't noticed a ting. Den I count to ten and stick my head back around to see what's up. Imagine my surprise when I see he's gone. Poof. Vanished."

"Are you sure?"

"Hell man, I'm old but I ain't blind. Either he gone up to Jacqueline's door or he went up over dat fence. An I don't tink he was huntin' no old pussy. I din tink too much about it till a few days later when dey put me in dis bed. Pete Barhanovich come up to see me an tole me someone busted up your little Amanda's headstone, eh?"

Didier coughed, clearing his voice, then scratched at his chest. "Doesn't make sense. Must be a thousand head markers in that yard. None of the others were touched. Why would a man do something like that? He doesn't know Amanda, or any of us LaFleurs."

"Maybe so. But if I was you, an I ain't, I'd tink hard 'bout what I just tole you. An he ain't from Louisiana needer. Dem udder shrimpers from dare ain't never seen him. I asked around you know. Anyway, I tot you might like to know 'bout all dat."

"*Oui, mon cher.* I thank you for telling me all this. And about my house, too. I'm glad you burned it down while we were away. That old shack wasn't fit to raise kids in anyway."

Old Kuluz patted his friend's hand and closed his eyes, taking in a deep breath. "If I see your Marie where I'm goin', I'll tell her hello for you, eh?"

"Yes, that would be good."

"An if I don't see her, dat means I'm burnin' in Hell cause everyone knows your Marie went to dat good place. An yore little Amanda, too. If dem two din make it to Heaven, *nobody* did. Now, I'm getting' tired, Didier, so you got to go. Say hey to dem friends of mine out dare for me, okay? An tell Pete to bring me some smokes tomorrow."

"Smokes? But what about the cancer?"

"Ha. Dose goddam lungs are shot to shit already. What the hell, eh?"

Didier nodded yes and stood. "I'll tell him, Joe. And I'll pray for you to get well at Sunday Mass."

"No need to do dat," Kuluz rasped, coughing. "I'll be gone by den. But dare's one more ting." His hand slipped beneath the collar of his hospital shirt and he pulled out a Saint Christopher medal. "Here," he said, handing it to Didier, "dis has been wit me most my life. I want you to take it." Here his eyes grew still and he looked down at the sheets. "I ask for you to take it out to Dog Keys Pass an drop it in *dat* place . . . you know what place. Let it sink down. I want yore boys to have it now. Now, go on."

Didier accepted the medal, gulping heavily, and felt his stomach begin to knot. He wanted to say something affectionate, something final, but his heart filled with unexpected emotion and the words stuck in his throat. He reached out, instead, and clumsily shook Joe Kuluz's hand, and all he could manage was, "Thank you for trying to save my sons out there that day, Joe. It was a good thing you did."

Kuluz shook the great paw without looking up, his hand disappearing into Didier's. He, too, wanted to say something important, something from deep within the heart, but he had never in his life seen Didier weak, and he wanted to remember him as that big, stoic Frenchman that embodied all that he himself had never been and had always wished to be.

Old Kuluz thought that to say much more might cause Didier to falter, just a tiny measure, perhaps, but enough that he might show emotion, and he did not wish to reduce the old Frenchman to that pathetic state.

"An so, Didier," he said, a half smile creeping up the corners of his mouth, and then a little laugh as if he were keeping a secret, "don't forget to tell my girl Jacqueline LaFontaine dat I will miss her, eh?"

Chapter Twenty-Three

By September's end, Father Joseph's mood had begun to slip from the high energy of a new beginning at Saint Gregory into a slumping depression. The honeymoon was dead. Weary of belligerent priests, antagonistic school board members, dissatisfied parents, and complaining faculty, he began to understand the true scope of Saint Gregory's demise. Financial shortfalls, low faculty salaries that attracted only the insipid, and lack of maintenance funds all conspired to ensure failure. The only bright spot was Tristan's presence. Brother Corso was still ill and wouldn't return for yet another month.

Joseph was not quite meeting the community's impossible expectations, as hoped, nor those of the bishop, and he was beginning to see that he had become entangled in a hopeless snare that had been developing over decades. How was it possible, he wondered, for such a fine school to sink to such abysmal depths? He did find some solace, at least, at the table of Madame LaFontaine and in theological discussions with Tristan, but not enough to fight off the bottle.

On this night he sat alone again at his kitchen table in the grips of deep melancholia, remembering his days of travel and missions of substance. Missions that were secretive and schematic, devised and passed down from higher places. Damn those schemes. What had they had to do with God anyway? They were nothing more than the propagation of internal politics. And damn those politics, so cleverly disguised so as to appear spiritual in nature.

Disgusted, he turned the bottle on end and watched the last of that honey-colored fluid trickle into his glass. Then, tipping the glass, he swallowed the whiskey in one dose and belched. He was drunk.

It was a wobbly trek to his bed, but after some difficulty he managed to kiss the mattress. *Damn the bishop anyway*, he thought, his mind awhirl. Damn his miter, and damn his robe. The thought followed

Contrition

him down into darkness as day slipped off him and sleep took its place. "Damn his miter . . . damn his—"

It was a black sleep at first. Dull and lifeless. But without his awareness it gradually grew gray. Then translucent, and he saw a wall. No, he sighed, a cliff. A great, sheer cliff that rose like some interminable rampart, reaching upward to the heavens, its ledge barely visible through the clouded mist that hung heavily over those dizzying heights. And suddenly, he was there on that ledge, trembling at the edge of the great precipice, staring out into the vast emptiness.

"Must look down, but mustn't fall from this height," he whispered. Or *someone* did. There was a shadow next to him. Hooded. It was a monk, pointing down into the bottomless chasm. His lips were moving, but there was no sound. Joseph tried to turn, hoping to see a face, but his motions were dull and lethargic.

"What?" Joseph groaned, his own voice obscure and disconnected.

"Look down, Joossseeeppphhhh," the voice said. The words sounded hollow and quickly lifted into the icy wind that swept across the top of the frightening precipice, and melded into the distance.

"Wh-what?" Joseph said, his voice growing even more lethargic than his movements.

"Look down, Joooosssseeeppphhhh."

Joseph's head slowly rotated as though in the grip of some robotic trance, and his eyes again beheld the craggy walls of the awesome vertical and the distant pit below. Blinking, he heard his breath stop . . . and his heart. And then the wind grew still. The silence was frightful and he suddenly believed himself ill. Then he heard the distant rumble of thunder, soft at first, but approaching, building, washing forward with the crushing fury of an angry tidal wave unleashed by some unknown force from some dark, ungodly place.

And then the thunder was upon them, swallowing them, rattling their insides and loosening the stony edge itself, causing the earth to quake and crumble. Joseph tried to cry out but his throat only uttered silence. Then he tried to reach out to the monk for support, but his arm was heavy as though laden with lead. . . . so he froze instead in helpless wonder. Then finally the thunder subsided and again an eerie silence engulfed the ledge.

Then Joseph thought he heard a laugh. Or a sob. The sound drew near, evolving into a wail. Then another. And suddenly the wall of the cliff below came alive as Joseph saw limbs scratching their way up the crags and fissures, scrabbling for grips, one over the other. Humans, naked and pallid, covered with ash, their bodies festering with pestilence and sores, clawing their way upward with frenetic bursts of motion, getting nowhere.

He stared deeper. Some began to slip, plunging back down into the blackness. But then others quickly took their place and scrambled to defeat that futile, unholy wall. Joseph was now only dimly aware of the apparition beside him, too entranced by the bitter struggle at his feet.

Then the blackness below suddenly became luminous, its deadly shine revealing the gaunt ruins of temples, by the hundreds and thousands. These temples, like the cliff, began to crawl with humanity. Joseph heard weeping and screams of terror. It was the voluminous chorus of perdition and penitence. The figures crawled over each other in their nakedness, shuddering and shrieking to escape the brackish reach of something alien and impenetrable. And then it appeared suddenly that these ghoulish creatures, in mass, began to stare and point at him as he stood at the edge of the precipice. In their lips, he read his own name being uttered by the suffering hordes. "Jooossseppphhh!" they cried. "Jooosssseppphhhh!"

Joseph grew terrified. Rearing his head back, he parted his lifeless lips and listened to himself scream with the complete surety of one who has been damned for eternity. He tried to push the sight of them away by screaming louder, but his throat began to shred and his cry deteriorated into a whimper.

"Joseph," the specter beside him whispered, touching his arm, "these are secret things. The parasites you see below shall be devoured, but the forgiven shall rise from this forsaken place after a time."

The voice was rich and deep. Joseph thought he knew that voice, and he suddenly felt a wave of awe and confusion wash through him. He struggled to turn his head, and ever so slowly he managed to revolve it toward the monk's face. Through the mist he strained to visualize the monk's features.

"These are secret things, Joseph," the monk repeated without emotion, continuing to stare down into the abyss. "You will soon join these tortured souls if you do not put your life in order."

"Tristan . . . is that you?" uttered Joseph, forcing each word from his lips.

The monk turned. "Yes, Joseph, and I share this weighty vision with you as a warning. Your end is not far away, and you are not ready to meet the Maker. You have not yet made peace with yourself. You have forgotten that the Supreme Hour comes to each of us sooner than hoped or expected, haven't you?"

"Is this my end? Are you the—the Angel of Death? Is this Hell?"

"No, my Brother. A much better place than Hell. There is at least hope in this place. You may not see it, but it flowers here, like spring bulbs amidst the barren rocks of Jerusalem. You see faces down there you once knew?"

"Yes," Joseph said darkly. "Faces I had loved . . . and faces I had forgotten. But you—what are you doing here?"

The monk's face became even grimmer and his eyes dropped. "The unholy shall smolder in pathos and anguish. The hopeless are doomed to Hell forever. Remember your vows and pray for forgiveness so you might at least come to this place and not Hell." Then the specter turned and stepped away.

"Don't leave me here!" Joseph cried, turning. "I beg you!" He reached out, groping at air. Then he tried to retreat from the cliff's edge but his legs were locked to the ledge. "Come back! I beg—" He suddenly felt something grab his arm from behind and pull at it.

"Joseph!" a voice cried out. "Joseph! Wake up!"

Joseph's eyes rudely blinked open, and searching for the voice, he pulled his arm free. "What!" he shuddered. "What the *Hell*?"

It was Tristan. "Wake up!" he said, his eyes outlined with concern.

"What is it? What are you doing here? Where am I? I was—"

Still groggy and shaking from the nightmare's clinging torment, the priest looked into Tristan's eyes for an explanation. They were clear with intensity and purpose.

"I've come to tell you two stories, Joseph. And to tell you that, for me, the darkness has finally begun to dissolve."

Joseph rubbed his eyes and sat up on the edge of his bed. Then, looking up at Tristan, he saw a look of perpetual hope and contentment. And as his uninvited guest began to speak in that marvelous deep voice, he could have passed for Michelangelo's sculptured concept of the Archangel, standing there outlined by the window frame, bathed in the light of the moon.

"The first story is about a goat, Joseph. Will you agree, without question, to hear me out?"

Joseph nodded.

"Centuries ago the ancient tribesmen of Afghanistan devised a contest to determine which clans had the finest horsemen. The game was called *Boos cashee* and is practiced to this day in the remote areas of that war-torn land.

"A young goat is beheaded and placed in a neutral zone. When the signal is given, the riders charge forward, and each one strives to stoop over at a full gallop, grab the carcass and dump it in a designated goal. The goat carcass, of course, is usually ripped to shreds, and there are many casualties among the horsemen because, basically, there are no rules of conduct. The end justifies the means."

Joseph shifted on the mattress but listened with interest. "Yes," he conceded, "I am familiar with the game."

"Of course you are. In 1958, Joseph, there was a bloody tribal dispute between two of the fiercer tribes to the south. They rejected official intervention and threatened war. It was proposed by the two opposing chieftains, however, that the matter might be settled by *Boos cashee*, thereby avoiding endless bloodletting and reprisals. And on the agreed day, the greatest known assembly of Afghan gamesmen ever recorded gathered to champion their respective tribe.

"But what is of interest to us here tonight, Joseph, is that there was a young American in attendance. He was the guest of both chieftains, having somehow befriended them the year before. Incredibly, he was designated as the only truly fair and impartial person in attendance, as all others outsiders were barred from witnessing the match. He was to be the sole judge. He was given a cushion between the two chieftains, and it was vowed by all that his decision would be final.

"It is also interesting to note that this young man was there against the direct orders of his superiors. But to continue, after much ceremony and ritual, the signal was given, and four hundred horsemen thundered across the plain, meeting in a bloody, merciless clash of horse flesh and brutality. The young guest's early fascination quickly turned to horror as the mounted mob separated at full gallop, leaving in their dusty wake over a dozen riders who lay trampled to a boneless pulp.

"The chase raged on for nearly an hour as riders darted back and forth, grabbing at the goat's carcass with the fury of men on a holy mission. By then nearly a hundred horsemen lay mangled or dead upon the plain. Finally, unable to witness any further mutilation, the young American jumped from his place, grabbed the nearest horse and whipped it furiously until he was in the midst of the fray.

"The chieftains were stunned, each fearing that the only judge might assist the other tribe. And they feared, too, that the young guest might be killed. They had no way of knowing that his grandfather was a horse breeder born of two previous generations of horse breeders.

"Witnesses later said that the young American rode better than the finest Afghan riders and that he rode with the eyes of a mad man and the screech of the devil. Soon, bloody from head to waist, his skin torn nearly as badly as his clothes, he ripped the carcass from a tribesman and rode at full gallop toward the chieftains. With several hundred confused and enraged Afghans in pursuit, he reined his horse in at the last possible moment and leaped to the ground. Then, jumping between the two chieftains, the goat's hindquarters dangling from his upraised hand, he screamed out in Arabic, "Let the killing end! I claim this goat in the name of Allah and peace!"

Joseph grew uneasy. Small beads of perspiration began to form above his brow and he wiped at them, making the mattress springs squeak with movement. A long moment of silence ensued as the two men looked at each other, each trying to see beyond the other's stare. The priest bit his lip and sighed. "Very interesting. But—"

"Let me finish, Joseph. That was 1958, and to this day the tribesmen talk about that gathering. It has become a legend. They still talk about the young American, dressed in black, who averted certain war with his heroic deed of compassion and faith. The young guest was a priest. *De te fibula* narrator, Joseph. The story is about you.

"You were that priest, and thus began your illustrious career of international mediation. Even your superiors, though displeased, were forced to acknowledge your exceptional heart and ability. Of course, their version was that you cried out in the name of God, not in the name of Allah."

"I hope I can be forgiven that indiscretion," Joseph said.

"Even the Pope heard this story, and you were called to Rome for a private audience."

Joseph reddened a moment, but quickly recovered. "Very impressive, Tristan. Well done. You continue to surprise me time after time. I'm not sure how you've come to know this story. Maybe you have contact somehow with the Jesuit community . . . they're the only ones that could have told you this. It's not anything that I've ever shared publicly, not even here amongst family or friends. So something's amiss here. I've wondered about you ever since that night in the channel.

"I opened my arms and my heart to you, but I've always known deep down that there was something abstract about you, something *very* curious. And I've wrestled with that for weeks now. You are an utter anomaly, a throw back. You are not like anyone I've ever met, and believe me, I've met all types from all over the world. There is something uncommonly good about you, my young friend, but there is also something profound and hidden, something dark."

"There is something profound and hidden about each of us born into this life, Joseph . . . and something dark."

"So, did the Jesuits send you?"

"No."

With each word, Joseph's voice became more accusatory and more confused. Then his nightmare flashed before him a moment, just a flicker, then it vanished, making him twitch. He wanted to lash out, but he was unable to see Tristan's face in the darkness, with only the moon glimmering behind that handsome silhouette. "You were in my dream," he blurted. "How in Hell—"

He didn't finish the sentence. By now his head ached, his mind ached, and his body felt utterly vacant. Licking his lips, he wished for whiskey.

"I am Tristan de Saint Germain," the younger man said calmly. "I came here by utter happenstance, or so I thought initially. I was lost and confused, but time has been working its healing ways on me, and so has the Shepherd. He sent me here. Not to torment you, Joseph, but to help you . . . and to ask for your help.

"I have been given a second chance, a chance to heal, a chance to be forgiven and to forgive myself for I am a sinner, too. My being here, though I do not understand how or why, is my act of contrition. God will shed light my way soon. But until then, please do not stampede yourself into denying me or my arrival here. Not yet, anyway."

"You were in my dream. I saw you and felt you there, in monk's garb, warning me. And then I woke up and you were right there again. How—"

"I was there, yes, in your dream. I was warning you just as you said. But now the dream has faded and I am here by your bedside and I warn you still. There is time yet for you to avoid the suffering of those within your dream."

Joseph rubbed at his eyes with the back of his hand, then inhaled and exhaled deeply, still foggy with confusion. "You warn me still? I'm a priest. I do God's work, or at least I try to do the best I can. So why do you warn me still?"

"Because you are going to Hell for eternity unless you acknowledge God's grace and ask to be forgiven. Time is against you, Joseph, truly against you."

"Hell? *Me*? Ask to be forgiven?"

"I have one more story to tell, Joseph. And when I am done, I will let you weigh my warning. My words will go to your very heart, but perhaps they will light your way. This story is about a bird. The goat was your ascent, but the bird was your fall. There is not a Jesuit alive except you that knows this story. Listen carefully, or live forever in darkness."

"I'm listening," Joseph sighed.

Tristan placed his palms together in prayer a moment. Then, turning his back on Joseph, he faced the moon and began.

"Along the coast of Japan there is a tiny village of cormorant fishermen. It has changed little over the centuries, and the fishermen there use the splendid cormorant, one of God's favored birds, to catch their fish at night by hanging a fire out over the water to attract the trout. By placing a ring around the base of the birds' throats to prevent them from swallowing the larger fish, they labor all night.

"And as you know, these men love and pamper their cormorants much as the ancient Egyptians loved their cats. The people of this village have been fishing thus for over a thousand years and continue to, even though the technique is now obsolete. Like the Afghan tribesmen, these particular Japanese I'm describing live in a time warp. These Japanese, their ways and culture stand protected by the Japanese government. It takes three years to train a cormorant, Joseph. But then you know that, don't you?"

Joseph shrugged, nodding.

"They keep these superb birds in great baskets woven by the women. And in this particular village there was an exquisite young girl. Seventeen, I'd say, and pure as virgin snow. Kind and innocent. Her beauty weakened many a cormorant fisherman, but she remained untouched, her chastity above reproach. But there came a priest. Not so young anymore, but handsome and worldly, speaking other languages and having travelled to places she'd never imagined.

"Their relationship blossomed slowly. An innocent attraction, mainly through the simple sharing of time and conversation. Then a gentle and secret glance here and there, undetected by her father or family, or by the Jesuit superiors. He was sent there on a mission that was initially intended to last less than a year perhaps. But things unraveled and he was given an extension, much to his and her mutual joy."

Father Joseph's eyes began to moisten, and he felt a stab at his heart.

"She nearly led you to denounce your vows, Joseph. In her arms you found the gentleness lacking in your life of priestly duties. Her name was Misao Hirota. You became lovers, unknown to all in the village and the world beyond. Your secret world became one of personal gratification, physical and emotional. She became your release, and you hers, but you were no longer working for the glory of God.

"Her love for you was infinite, and though you pleaded, she would not allow you to leave the priesthood. Which was a wise thing, or you would have actually gone through with your petition to Rome. But she died. In shame. Right there before you and her father.

"Ever the good priest, you administered Extreme Unction immediately after her deathbed conversion to Christianity. And then, holding her dead hand to your tearful face, you converted her father by saying her death was the will of God."

"Please," said Joseph, "say no more."

"I must finish, Joseph. The reason she was shunned by all but her father was her pregnancy. And the reason for her death was childbirth. In a single devastating moment, she clutched your hand before passing, never daring to betray your mutual secret in the presence of her praying father. And in that moment the unborn infant, too, passed. Your *son*, Joseph.

"Shortly afterwards, your mission successfully completed as usual, you were reassigned. But it was a different Joseph Broussard that left that village of cormorant fishermen. And like those great birds, you had a ring around your throat. It has been choking the Godliness out of your miserable soul for decades now. You began to doubt. You began to curse and drink, and the once passionate, God-loving Joseph Broussard began to sink into himself.

Contrition

"You remained a Jesuit. You went about your work as assigned, but spiritlessly. And your lackluster efforts were found out. Gradually, you were given lesser assignments, becoming almost an embarrassment. This descent continued until you were sent here, back to your home where people still unwittingly respected you as both a priest and a man. The Brothers of the Holy Cross even requested you. But look how you've been sliding. Joseph, put your life in order. The parasites shall be devoured, but the forgiven shall rise . . . "

These words struck the priest like a lethal blow to the temple, and he suddenly fell to the floor, tears flowing freely. "Bless me, Father, for I have sinned! My last confession was—"

"There will be time for that, Joseph, but later. Know that your work is every bit as consequential here as anywhere in the world. The Jesuits think they have put you aside. They are overwhelmed by the politics of the world, blind to the great deeds that can be done right here. Get off the floor. I am no higher than you. Worse even. We have been given an opportunity. You a reprieve, and me a second chance. God smiles on us both."

Tristan bent over and grabbed Joseph by the elbows, hugging him, bringing him up. But the priest was too lost in his tears and grief to rise.

"I killed her," he sobbed, "and my son!"

"They were both innocent! I converted the father and killed the daughter and the child! I have carried this secret with me year after year in shame and anger. God forgive me!"

"He will, Joseph, just as I hope he will forgive me."

Tristan put his arm around the old priest and pressed him to his own heart. "We will earn our way again, Joseph. Together. And we have a friend. Peter Toche will join us. He, too, has rediscovered his soul."

Chapter Twenty-Four

Tristan lit the candle and set it between Peter and Joseph. "I brought you here at this hour because this is when I feel her presence the most clearly."

Joseph looked about the cemetery with uncertainty. "I don't think this is wise. Madame LaFontaine might spot us out here. Put the candle out at least."

"No, Joseph," said Tristan, "there is a purpose in this meager light. And there is a purpose in our meeting here over the little girl's grave. I—"

"Didier and Albert wouldn't approve of this," said Joseph. "And now you've dragged me into this. I shouldn't have listened to you."

"Take it easy," said Peter. "What's Madame LaFontaine going to do, call the police? I *am* the police, remember?"

Tristan touched Joseph's shoulder with a gentle gesture and shook his head. "Be calm. There are things you both should know. Things that even I am just beginning to comprehend. But first swear to me that you will both listen with an open heart. I ask nothing more."

Peter nodded readily, but Joseph was less sure. "Okay, but put the candle out," he said.

"No," Tristan replied, pointing to its tiny flame. "This represents light. And as I speak, I want you and Peter to concentrate on its warmth, reaching upward and onward, struggling against the wind. And remember that when light is extinguished, there remains only darkness."

"Very well, then, go on," sighed Joseph.

"Now, Joseph, do you accept the divinity of Christ?"

The old priest nodded, his gaze planted firmly on the candle's flame. "Yes, of course, I'm a priest."

"And Peter, don't you find the divinity of Christ to be a mystery?"

"Yes, it has puzzled me my entire life, I suppose."
"And do you both accept the Holy Trinity?"
They agreed.
"And don't you find that also to be a mystery?"
They nodded again.
"And the sacraments, the Saints, the Resurrection, and a thousand other miracles that represent the cornerstones of our faith, do they not defy reason as well as the realm of human logic? Are all these things not beyond the scope of mortal comprehension? Do they not defy science and reason, and are they not based solely on our faith alone?"

"Yes," said Peter, immersing himself in the twisting dance of the flame.

"Then listen very closely, my friends, and remember the concepts of mystery and faith."

Peter and Joseph blinked in agreement.

Tristan continued. "There once was born in France a child of noble stock, in the Year of Our Lord 1069. He became a priest at the age of fourteen because his mother wished it, and he soon joined the monastery at Cluny—the same monastery that had founded the Cluniac Reform Movement decades earlier. Because of this boy's extraordinary memory and academic skills, he was brought to the attention of Bishop Odo de Lagery who was twenty-seven years his senior.

"This bishop was a man of exceptional talent and perception, and the two quickly forged a profound friendship, a most uncommon bond in that world of ignorance, violence and superstition. Are you still with me?"

Joseph, now sitting cross-legged, nodded, feeling himself, like Peter, entering a near meditative state. He was losing himself to the fire and to the deep, rich lull of Tristan's voice. He vaguely remembered the goat, the cormorant, and standing upon the precipice glimpsing down into the depths of Purgatory. And also, he vaguely remembered pulling Tristan from the channel.

Tristan continued. "I accept the fact that this makes great demands on your faith, but listen and pray. *Fiat lux*—let there be light. Listen and weigh well the end."

Peter and Joseph sat motionless and silent, absorbed.

"The good Bishop Odo de Lagery," said Tristan, "became this boy's mentor and confidante. The boy gave him his confession daily, and the bishop gave him his. The boy grew to be a young man, and as God turned the wheel in that dark and bitter world, Odo de Lagery ascended the heights of the Catholic hierarchy and came to sit upon the very throne of Rome. As he ascended, so he made the young man rise with him.

"Odo de Lagery, the Holy Father, took for his title Pope Urban II and sent for his young liege who was teaching in a seminary in France, appointing him Chief Diplomat of Papal Affairs. More precisely, he became the Holy Father's chief agent in all matters of political and papal secrecy.

"The young prodigy traveled the roads of Europe arranging alliances, conferences, and treaties. He gathered information and kept files on those to be exalted and those to be excommunicated, concentrating on the power brokers of France, Italy, and Germany. He performed every political task imaginable, both inspired and insidious, in the name of propagation of the True Faith. And he answered only to Odo de Lagery, who insisted that this young priest not call him by his papal title, claiming that he, the Pope, needed one voice at least upon this earth to call him Odo, lest he forget his own humble roots or his mortality.

"The young monk was sent to the Holy Land to investigate reports of the abuse and murders of Christian pilgrims en route to Jerusalem. Upon his return, Odo de Lagery became alarmed by his friend's documentation and called for the Council of Clermont to be assembled in France—a council which was arranged by this very same young chief agent.

"Odo de Lagery called for a great Holy War upon the Muslims, a crusade to free the Holy Land from the grips of Islam. And on that fateful day, November twenty-seven in the Year of Our Lord 1095, as he finished his impassioned address, ten thousand knights and clerics arose and spoke as one. *"Dieu le veut*! God wills it!" they cried in unison, raising swords and crosses skyward.

"And as the joyous cheers and clamoring and banging of sword against shield grew to a deafening, thunderous pitch, Odo de Lagery turned to his young monk and passed into his hands a secret scroll outlining what was to be the greatest mission of his brilliant career."

Here Tristan paused, closing his eyes. "That mission, which as fate would have it, was to be the last for the young monk. And both of you should know that the young man who accepted the scroll that day— his name was Tristan de Saint Germain."

Joseph kept his gaze on the candle. "An ancestor?" he asked quietly.

Contrition

"No, Joseph," said Tristan. "I believe it was me. I have imagined it a thousand times, just as I have imagined being born, just as I have imagined dying, just as I have imagined suffering an eternity of hopeless, never-ending winters in that pit of horror known as Purgatory. I have imagined it just as I imagined you dragging me from the water, just as I imagine you sitting across from me now on this sacred plot. Just as I imagined Peter's gift of extraordinary perception and insight, and just as I shared his hellish vision in the attic."

Joseph raised his eyes and as they met those of his young friend, he searched for something in Tristan that might betray pretension. He found nothing.

"I accept," said Tristan, "that this makes great demands on your faith. But remember, *sic itur ad astra*—such is the way to the stars. Great doubt requires even greater faith. My last mission was to accompany that great Crusade and document it. I was placed in charge of Spiritual Affairs and was to report directly to Odo de Lagery upon expedition's end. The Holy Father was kind enough to appoint my younger brother as my personal aide-de-camp.

"Guillaume was his name, young and beautiful, hair and skin as pale as Christmas snowfall, graced by the Holy Spirit, filling all those he touched with hope and inspiration. But poor Guillaume, neither of us had any idea what lay ahead, or how it would end."

At this Tristan paused, his lips trembling, unable to conceal emotion. Peter was touched. "And what became of the mission?" he said.

"What concerns you and Joseph is not so much what happened to me and my brother a thousand years ago, but what faces you now. I have been sent here for a different purpose. Even I didn't understand that at first. My own confusion filled me with doubt and fear at first. I was weak, but God directs us and my strength of purpose now grows day by day.

"I have been sent here to stop a flood of evil that has already begun to rain down on this quiet, unsuspecting place. Just as we were born of the water of woman's womb, I was reborn in the water of the channel the night Joseph fished me out. *Alter ipse amicus* . . . a friend is another self, Joseph, and you were sent to save me from drowning so I could complete my personal endeavor. And you, Peter, God has called upon you, too."

Peter blinked, suddenly feeling inadequate. He moved closer to the candle, propping his face in his palms, rubbing at his cheeks. God calling upon him? Maybe calling upon Father Joseph Broussard, but surely not upon Peter Toche. But the voice across from him was too certain and the eyes too earnest.

"A flood of evil?" said Joseph, his voice barely audible. "What sort of evil?"

"The killing kind. Amanda LaFleur. And Peter has told me about Jimmy Dubaz, Tom Dardar, and his own father. This is just the beginning. I feel that their deaths were contrived by someone not of this life."

Joseph's throat grew dry. "Lord in Heaven. Where are you off to now?"

"I watched it all unfold from the pits of Purgatory," said Tristan. "All of us suffering souls writhing about in anguish and dread, we've watched the violence wreaked upon men by other men, and upon women and children. That's part of the horror, watching the blood fest, knowing that it's all futile and purposeless. Murder, war, theft, envy. All those wicked little screws driven by lust and greed, decade after decade, generation after generation, century after century.

"Therein lies the punishment of Purgatory, along with the damnation and the fear, watching it over and over and over. Such a magnificent world for all within such easy grasp, for me in my time, you in yours, for everyone at any time. But people work against that paradise on Earth and seek their own rewards at the expense of the less fortunate. We have taken a garden, Joseph, all of us, and turned it into a world of scaffolds and prisons, hunger and disease, greed and suffering. And those in Purgatory suffer all the more because those on this earth have lost their way. And to live without faith is even more terrible than the fire."

Joseph swallowed dryly before speaking. "So then, you claim to be sent by—God?"

"There is something very different about him, Joseph," said Peter. "I have sensed something unusual all along. Haven't you felt it?"

"I have been *sent*," said Tristan. "I am here. I once was in the pit, but now I breathe again. Surely it is the forgiveness of God."

"Do you claim to be immortal, then?" said Joseph.

"No, I am purely mortal—and as weak as always. But I was given the gift of perception and vision, much like Peter, though stronger. But thousands have those gifts. Even you, to a certain degree. But as in my time, such gifts go unacknowledged or unrecognized.

"No, I have no supernatural powers, and that's what you're leading to. Cut me and I bleed, hurt me and I weep. Kill me and I die again. Even Jesus was mortal upon this earth and suffered a terrible death. If and when I die, and I surely will just as you and everyone else will, I will possibly return to that horrid place for another thousand years, or two or ten, to pay for my indiscretions and shortfalls.

"And that, my friends, frightens me more than anything you could imagine. Just as the fetus has no hope of comprehending that intricate, complex world outside the womb, you have not one measure of understanding of the horrors and desolation of damnation in Purgatory. And if I fail here I could descend even further, to the depths of Hell itself. And it would be easy for me to lose sight of this, given the same temptations that face any man today. I have the same weaknesses as you both."

Joseph stared into the candle, trying to grasp the breadth of Tristan's words. "Then I can only assume somehow, a thousand years ago, you failed. Am I correct?"

Tristan looked down and nodded, then cast his eyes across the graveyard with naked humility. "Yes, I failed. In many ways. I failed Odo de Lagery, and my brother, Guillaume. I failed in spirit, Joseph, and in my ordeal I became weak with fear and hid in a church while others were being slaughtered. Perhaps, if given another chance, I will do better . . . if I can keep fear in its place."

"And if you succeed?" asked Peter.

"If I succeed, I will taste the fruits of that Blessed Place and gaze upon the face of God. I will shed myself of impurity and join those blessed souls who sit at the foot of the Throne."

"And all of this because of Amanda LaFleur?" said Joseph.

"Yes, in part. And Peter's father and the others. But there is much more yet to come if this murdering hellion is not stopped."

Peter's shoulders contracted. "So then, do you know who killed them, Tristan?"

"From the pit we see but shadows. And though he seemed familiar to me, he was cloaked by the Unholy One. I watched in horror as he tortured and mutilated the innocent girl. Her agony became mine, as did her suffering. But him, I did not see his face, only his brutality. It was the work of a beast, Peter, slowly tearing at the flesh of an unsuspecting child. But somehow, yes, he seemed familiar in his mercilessness. I knew such a man once. He took my life . . . and that of my brother. Such men exist in every world, in every age."

Joseph closed his eyes and sighed heavily. "Then," he said slowly, "she suffered greatly."

"Yes."

"And her last moments on earth were undoubtedly filled with terror and pain. My God, she was so young. She couldn't have understood what was happening or why."

"No, but in one so young and pure, fear and courage are inextricably mixed. And she was courageous through it all. She never forgot God, Joseph, not even as the fiend was ripping her belly open. It was a slow death. He stabbed and hacked, but each wound was deliberately made so as not to be fatal—so he could come and go from the attic.

"She was conscious for hours and all the while he cursed and taunted her as she lay helpless on the floor. And though I have witnessed much suffering over the centuries, her courage went straight to my heart. She endured her ordeal with great faith. Let us hope that when our moment arrives, we can muster such strength."

"The killing, then, you say, has just begun?" said Peter, thinking back on the long rows of gravestones that surrounded the serpent on the sewer walls.

"Yes, and this instrument of Satan is twisted. Those from Hell are wicked from the onset. But with time, as decades melt into centuries, their venom magnifies, they become even more demented until, finally, they lose all semblance of humanity. They truly become demonic, filled with hatred and resentment for all things living and good. They destroy us by destroying the ones we love, to break our hearts and our will."

Peter tried to push Amanda LaFleur from his mind, but the effort was futile. "So, it's a disciple of Satan's we're dealing with," he said suddenly, feeling the final piece of the great puzzle locking into place. That was a cleansing moment for him, one that suddenly justified the long and agonizing trail of mental suffering that he had endured since that day in the housing projects of New Orleans.

"Yes, and he was sent here by the Unholy One," said Tristan. "He is here even now, somewhere, and I believe that it is our purpose to stop him. It was he who desecrated the grave and took your father, Peter. This, I now believe, is my purpose in being sent here. This is my ordeal by fire and it will not be an easy task. But he, like me, has no supernatural powers. He is an inhuman force, but with human limitations. He wants to survive just as I do. And if he dies a human death, he will return to eternal damnation and suffer the dreaded agonies of Hell again. So remember, as he spreads his poison, he will stop at nothing to extend his time in this life."

"And what if he were to change his course?" said Joseph. "All sinners are capable of repentance."

Tristan shook his head. "He has been damned forever, Joseph. *Forever*. And for just cause. Whatever he did in his lifetime, he cannot undo now, or ever. He is damned and may never hope to escape his destiny beyond his short time here. When I find him, when *we* find him, we must see to it that his desecration of God's work comes to an end."

Joseph sat back, unwilling to dwell on how one actually brings such things to an end.

"How will we know him, Tristan?"

"*Domine dirige nos* . . . God will direct us."

"But *how*?" Joseph insisted, more uncertain than ever. "What if we're wrong? My God, we're not infallible. Greater mistakes have been made, I'm sure, even in the name of God."

Tristan reached across and placed his hands palms down over Joseph's. "When he rears his venomous head, we will know." His voice was firm and resolute. "And when that time comes, you must be strong, Joseph, stronger than you can imagine. You must cast aside your intellect, your doubts, and you must stand on faith alone. And Peter, I sense that you understand these things. But will you be strong? Can you kill a man in righteousness, accepting that he is *already* dead? Can you send a demon back to Hell with the power of your hand?"

Peter breathed hard a moment and closed his eyes. In all his years of police work, he had never killed a man with his hands or his firearms—but through his work, his investigation, he had sent many a man to his doom. "Yes, I can kill *this* man," he said. "My father tried to warn me, but I dismissed him as sick and senile. I fought him my whole life, to no purpose. But he knew, just as you know. I owe it to him to see this through, as I owe it to Amanda LaFleur and Tom Dardar."

Chapter Twenty-Five

The old Yugoslav stood behind the counter, head lowered, immersed in the soft dance music playing on the radio concealed at his feet. With a rubber-gloved hand, he steadily picked one oyster after another from the ice-packed crate before him, wedged it open, discarded the top half of the shell, and placed the bottom half on a tray until it was covered with an even dozen. Then he repeated the process until he was satisfied that there were enough full trays stacked one on top of the other to keep the waitress busy.

From time to time he would pause and pick up his beer, drinking with long deliberate gulps, snorting into his mug like an old horse. He had been shucking oysters at the Old French House most of his life, was never in a hurry, and seldom fell behind except during Mardi Gras or the Blessing of the Fleet. From the kitchen could be heard the rattle of dishes and the clash of lids, along with an occasional outburst of voices. The old Yugoslav found contentment in this because he disliked washing pots and pans, much preferring his station at the oyster bar.

He was in a pleasant mood this evening because the public radio network was playing his favorite segment, the Big Band Era. And, too, it was a weeknight so the crowd was sparse. Best of all, the big-breasted waitress was on shift, and watching her lift trays over her head was one of his primary pleasures at this juncture of his life.

In the far corner three fishermen sat, focused on the weather channel. They would be leaving shortly for the Gulf to run long lines for several weeks on one of the big steel-hulled vessels. The forecast wasn't favorable, though, and the eldest, Captain Vince Parker, insisted they linger to catch the full report. On the screen a pudgy broadcaster aimed his pointer at the overblown weather satellite photograph taken nine days earlier that revealed a band of clouds drifting into the Atlantic off the West African coast.

Then the photograph snapped off, replaced by a meteorological chart, and the broadcaster, still pointing, stated that a weather advisory had been issued by the National Hurricane Center. "A rapidly developing tropical depression is expected to move on a curving path to the northwest, possibly reaching the west tip of Cuba," he droned, "and conditions favor intensification of this young storm."

"Hell," said the youngest of the three watching, "that's the fourth damn storm this season already, and every one of ems' petered out before Cuba. *Christ*, Mister Vince, are we gonna sit this one out, too?"

The captain shook his head. "Naw, can't afford to, but it don't hurt to listen. We've missed enough already. We'll keep an ear to the radio, though. If she gets rough we can always run back in."

They listened for several minutes more, finishing their beer, then stood to leave. But as they emptied the corner, the captain turned toward the north window and recognized a friend among the men clustered around the far table. "Hey, Didier!" he called, breaking into a smile.

"I'll be damned. Where've you been? Hadn't seen you around for a while. Why hell, Father Joe, Albert, looks like the whole crew's here, eh?"

Didier stuck a hand in the air, acknowledging the man. "Vince! I hear you're still dragging line out there with the youngsters. Going out tonight?"

"Yeah. There's an advisory out, but it don't look like much. Been a bad season with all the weather coming in and out, but it's all been bluff, no blow." He looked at Joseph and pointed. "Yeah, maybe Father Joe'll say a prayer. That'd keep the Devil off our backs, eh?"

Father Joseph grinned and stuck his hand in the air too. "Vince, haven't seen you at mass lately. Where've you been? We need you there."

"Ha! Need my wallet you mean!" the captain laughed. Then he looked at Didier's son and his merriment fell away. "How're things going with you, Albert?" he said, lowering his voice. "We've missed you on the pier. Been okay?"

Albert LaFleur smiled weakly and nodded yes, but everyone knew better. "Yeah, been okay," he said. "Nothin' to it. I—"

"Good boy!" the captain interrupted, already made uncomfortable by Albert's glum demeanor. The death of a daughter was something Captain Vince Parker had never endured, but he imagined that nothing could be more crippling, and cripples embarrassed him. "Father Joe," he said, moving on, "who'd you drag in here this time? Haven't seen this one before?"

Joseph introduced Tristan, then added, "Saint Gregory is having a draw down next week, Vince. Hundred bucks a shot."

"Won't be here. We're headed out," Parker shrugged.

"Don't have to be present to win," Joseph replied quickly.

"Damn, you're worse than my wife and daughters, Father Joe!" Then he laughed and threw his hands skyward in surrender. "Go see my Michelle in the morning, tell her to write you a check for three hundred. Hell, I'm feeling lucky. Good to see you all!" Then he turned for the door and his companions followed him into the night.

"Good old Parker," Joseph muttered, smiling, "still generous as ever." Then Joseph nudged Tristan and whispered, "Oh, here she comes again. I think she likes you, Tristan. A little too much lipstick, though."

The waitress approached, balancing four trays of oysters in the crook of one arm. She set them about the table, taking great care that Tristan got the best dozen, a maneuver that was missed by no one. Then, smiling at him with the subtlety of a love-struck school girl, she bridled a bit, slinging her hair over one shoulder, and uttered a tittering laugh. "I hope everything's to your liking," she said. "If you need anything, my name's Annie." Then she bowed clumsily and bounced away.

"Oh sweet Heaven," laughed Joseph under his breath, "I think we'll be getting excellent service tonight, huh, Didier?"

Didier sighed heavily and lifted both hands to his chest, forming cups. "Whoo!" he exhaled, rolling his eyes upward until only the whites showed. "What a heifer." Then he jerked a thumb toward Tristan and added, "Geez, these women around here sure approve of this one, eh?"

"I suppose," said Tristan, his blush deepening. "I don't know if I approve of these oysters, though." He stared at the pearly, viscous flesh seated in gritty shells, then frowned.

"Smooth as snot," said Didier, tipping one into his mouth whole. "Try a little hot sauce."

Albert LaFleur quickly placed an oyster on his cracker, spotted it with pepper sauce and lifted it to his mouth. "They're better than they look," he offered politely. Then he turned to his father. "Pop, I'm going back to work. Leaving tomorrow with old Bosarge on the *Fairy Princess*."

"That's good, Bosarge needs the help." Didier nodded, his eyes shining with affection. He had felt Albert's sadness as well as his own since the loss of Amanda. Albert was all he had left in this world now, and he had been greatly distressed by his son's total failure to come to terms with Amanda's death.

Didier's own grief had subsided little since that August day, but he was an old man. Albert, on the other hand, had many years ahead and either had to forge a future for himself or founder the rest of his days. "And the *Fairy Princess* is a fine boat," Didier continued. "I helped Bosarge and his brother build her when you were still in high school." Then Didier looked over at Tristan who had just swallowed his first raw oyster. "Good, eh?"

"Better than expected," said Tristan, forking another onto a cracker. "We are dust and a shadow, Albert, but eternity never ends. I know you are filled with sadness, but do you, *can* you, believe in forever?"

Albert was surprised by the question. "I like to think so," he said, unable to dismiss a cloud of doubt.

Tristan continued, his tone confident and soothing. "It exists. For you, for me, for your little Amanda. Let there be no question in your mind. She suffered, yes, but that has long passed."

Joseph threw Tristan a sharp glance. Ease up, it said.

But there was no resentment in Albert's face, and he lifted his eyes ashamedly at Joseph, a priest he had always admired. "I guess you know I haven't been to Mass since—well, you know."

Joseph lit a cigarette, nodding, and blew a plume of smoke over his shoulder. "Yes, I know. But try to come tomorrow morning before you leave with Bosarge."

Albert sighed and took a drink, then looked away, pulling his cap further over his eyes. "I don't know—we'll see, eh?"

"Come, Albert," said Tristan, "your father will be there. He's hurting, too. Be there for him as well as for yourself."

Albert paused, lowering his head, his eyes glazed with fatigue and surrender. "We'll see. I'll try. That's all I can say. I won't lie to you about it. It's just so damned hard, you know? I can't understand how God could let something like this . . . "

Didier swallowed dryly, his heart in his throat. He wanted very much to reach over and hug his son, but his had never been a touching family, and he had seldom shown emotion with any of his sons, so he said nothing.

The waitress returned, positioning herself so that she was directly facing Tristan. "Everything all right here?" she asked. "We're all looking mighty serious." Her contrived smile managed to lighten the mood, or more so her complete adoration of Tristan. Even Albert was forced to smile.

"I think we're about ready to go," said Joseph with the gravity becoming of a priest. Then he pointed to Tristan. "There is one thing more, however. My young friend was wondering if you're married, only, he's extremely shy."

Tristan shuffled in his seat uncomfortably as a deep shade of red began to flush over his face. The waitress's face lit up and she quickly pulled a pencil from behind her ear and began to scribble something on a napkin.

"Ah," said Joseph, "a telephone number! Now we're getting somewhere."

"I'm *very* single," she said, looking at the priest but addressing the object of her attention.

Tristan smiled weakly, not wanting to offend the girl, but he cut his eyes to Joseph and muttered, "*Advocatus diaboli!*"

This pleased the girl even more for some reason, and, beaming, she collected the half-empty mugs and floated into the kitchen, barely able to contain her delight.

The four men stood to leave, fished in their pockets for tip money and began to file away from the table with Tristan in the lead. Just then, unnoticed by all but the old Yugoslav shucking oysters, a massive, stoop-shouldered man entered the Old French House door. Grunting, he carried his weight on a large burled walking stick as one foot dragged slightly behind the other.

He stepped up to the bar. Easing an elbow on the counter, he slowly raised his other arm and ran a large palm over his shaved crown three times, as if performing a ritual. Then he hoisted his weight onto a bar stool and was about to order a drink when he turned to look about the bar.

At that very moment Tristan happened to look toward the bar, and for a flickering second, it was as if both men had been simultaneously struck by thunder and turned to stone. Jaw sprung ajar, Tristan suddenly sagged a bit and quickly shot a hand to his own throat as if to close a hemorrhaging wound. He stood there holding his neck like a pale, frozen statue, full of dread. But he felt no blood at his throat, only healthy flesh, and his senses suddenly returned as both hands tightened into fists. "Malik!" he bellowed, his voice guttural and inflamed.

The burly man's eyes flared, then darted about like those of a rousted badger instinctively assessing flight or attack. "You!" he snarled, glaring at Tristan.

"Tristan, what is it?" said Joseph, startled.

Tristan broke into a rage, leveling a finger at the bar. "Oh, but God is kind!" he cried out, looking like a wild man. "It's you! Malik the Butcher! The Lame Monster of Medina!"

The man bristled at hearing his name called out in this public place, and seeing that Tristan was among friends, he raised his stick and lashed out at the four of them. He swung again, edging himself off the stool and toward the door. He looked bewildered, like a man who has been exposed at the least expected moment, and though he feared no man before him, it was clear he sought the refuge of anonymity. "You French bastard!" he growled, glaring at Tristan. "Oh, you filthy priest!" he slurred thickly, like a drunk.

Didier, caught off guard by the sudden onset of trouble, thought the remark was directed at Joseph. "Now wait just a damn minute, brother," he said. "What's this all —"

Tristan bolted from his stance and flung himself at Malik, but Malik balled his huge fist and struck a crushing blow to his face. Tristan felt his vision implode with momentary pain and blindness as he collapsed at Didier's feet. Didier, keenly aware that something terrible had passed between these two men, reached down, steadied Tristan, and pulled him to his feet with the ease of a giant lifting a child. Then he leveled his gaze at Malik, and was immediately struck by an inner voice. It was Joe Kuluz talking, reminding him about suspicions of the night

Amanda's grave was desecrated.

"Hold it, Tristan," said Didier.

But Tristan sprang like a coiled snake, and despite the deep gash that split his cheekbone, nearly closing one eye, he mindlessly drove Malik backward to the countertop and onto the stacked trays of freshly shucked oysters. The countertop exploded and beer glasses began to fracture, firing broken glass in every direction. "Holy shit!" the old Yugoslav wailed, retreating to a corner. "Annie, call the cops!"

Tristan had Malik by the throat, driving him farther and farther onto the counter beneath the weight of both their flailing bodies. Splintered glass and oyster shells were slung everywhere, filling the room with deadly missiles. Beneath Malik, jagged shards of glass began to sever shirt fabric, then flesh. As they cut deeper, puncturing him in a dozen places, Malik bellowed hoarsely like some defiant, butchered bull in the throes of slaughter.

It was Joseph who sensed the utter depravity of Malik's wailing. A light of understanding broke on Joseph's face as Malik's primordial roar permeated every nook and corner of the room, and for Joseph, everything suddenly seemed dim and far away except for the struggling man with the shaved head. He saw in Malik's fierce eyes utter corruption and degeneration, and he stood there, mesmerized, as though looking into the portals of Hell, until Malik's flickering gaze met his. Joseph blinked, suddenly terrified and frail.

Then Malik, cursing, bulled his way upward. "You won't send me back!" he snarled, shaking off the shards of glass that had adhered to his flesh. He flung Tristan sprawling into the nearest table. Then he sat up a moment and bellowed again, the muscles of his neck standing out like great purple roots. "I'll kill you, Christian!"

But again Tristan gathered himself and rose like a man possessed. "You murdered my brother!" he shrieked. "By God, as you showed no mercy, I'll have no mercy!" Then he rushed forward again, his hate-filled eyes drawing down into slits.

"No!" cried Joseph. "Tristan, get back!"

Didier stepped forward to block Tristan, knowing that Joseph's young friend was waging a war he could not win. And somewhere from deep within, another voice told him to rush forward, to join the young man in crushing this formidable adversary. But doubt coupled with reason held him back. Perhaps Joe Kuluz had been mistaken about this man. Perhaps his old friend's suspicious nature was only stirring mud again as it has so often in the past. And perhaps this wasn't even the same man Joe had seen by the cemetery.

"Stay back," Didier said, holding out both arms to contain Tristan. "Your eye, you can't see—"

He's getting away!" cried Tristan, delirious with rage. "Joseph, it's him! Stop him! He's the one! Didier, get out of my way!"

Malik sneered, letting his dark eyes settle on Tristan for just a moment. Then, gathering his stick, he brushed Joseph aside with one paw and strode toward the door.

"It's him!" Tristan ranted, struggling to push his way past Didier and Albert. "Joseph, call Peter! Get help now!"

Didier wrapped his arms around Tristan and lifted him from the floor. "No," he said, squeezing firmly, "you're hurt. Let it be."

Tristan squirmed uselessly in a grip he could not hope to break. "Joseph! It's Malik, he's the one! He killed Guillaume! He killed Amanda! He killed *me*, and my—"

Didier's vice-like grip squeezed the words from Tristan's throat, and he dangled there helplessly as Malik kicked the door open and made a wary but hasty exit. Tristan swung out, broke free, and scrambled to the door, but the darkness had swallowed Malik even though his dragging footsteps and the tapping of his stick could be heard in the night.

Joseph ran up behind Tristan, joining him, and at that very instant he too heard the footsteps and the stick. Their fading sound struck a nerve and he felt his heart drop suddenly, as though tethered to some great and mysterious weight from the past, hurling down into darkness.

Tristan sagged with disbelief and wiped blood from his eye. In exasperation he threw his hands to his forehead and looked back at the LaFleurs. "You don't know what you've done. As God is my witness, you don't know what you've done this night." Then he turned to Joseph, defeat deeply etched in his only open eye. "Did you *feel* it, Joseph ? Did you sense the Devil?"

Joseph shrugged apologetically. "I—I'm not—"

Tristan bristled uncontrollably, and every inch of his face filled with seething rage. "Get Peter! I must talk to him—he will believe me. You failed me, Joseph! You were weak! But Peter will be strong enough to bring this to an end."

Chapter Twenty-Six

It was a clear evening, and the moon's luster cast a luminous silver glow about the cemetery. Picking their way through the grave markers, concealed by the shadows of overhanging oaks, Tristan and Peter came to the gravesite of Amanda LaFleur. Her original marker had been removed since being desecrated, and in its place stood a new one.

"It was *him*, Malik," said Tristan, vexed, wiping at his battered, weepy eye. "We could have had him, but Didier was confused and held me back, and Joseph faltered. Together we could have had him."

"Your face looks like hell," said Peter, assessing Tristan's bruised cheek in the dim light. "Damn, looks like he bashed you pretty good."

"It's nothing," said Tristan. "I will survive. If only you could have been with us, Peter. I feel that you would have interceded. The others froze in place, but so be it. One opportunity lost, but another will come. And for that reason, I have brought you here tonight." Then he flattened his palms toward the earth beneath which Amanda LaFleur lay. "I know you feel the power here," he said. "There is a warmth emanating from this tomb. God grants unearthly powers to the places where women of pure hearts have existed because life throws more challenges before them than others. Bernadette of Lourdes was such a woman. But few can draw strength from such places . . . you are one of the fortunate, Peter."

Though the air was humid, Peter began to shiver a bit. It wasn't fear of the graveyard so much as the growing entrancement.

Tristan continued. "The struggle between darkness and light takes place in a thousand abandoned corners of the earth, Peter. It's a conflict between hope and perdition. I now count on you for your strength and your gift. You understand that this great struggle is going on even now, in this very town. That we must find and eliminate Malik is clear, but there is one more thing I must show you. Now, close your eyes and bow your head while I pray for guidance and assistance."

Contrition

Peter complied. But as he listened to Tristan utter a prayer in Latin, he felt his skin begin to prickle—the air was suddenly turning cold.

"Peter," Tristan whispered, not opening his eyes, "it's coming . . . do you sense it?"

"The cold?"

"No, the wind."

"But there *is* no wind, Tristan—it's still as death here."

"No, listen. A vision approaches. But you must believe in its power. Don't open your eyes."

Peter strained to listen. It began gradually, nearly unnoticeable to him at first. But then there was a stirring of the grass, ever so gentle. And then more until the leaves overhead began to whisper, their resonance growing by degree.

"It's coming, Peter. It'll be upon us soon now."

Peter suddenly felt his hair lift, in bursts and heard the low moan of air currents building in the distance, approaching like the steady advance of a ship's prow. Then he felt a blast as his clothing suddenly pressed against him, while above live oak branches began to creak and sway until the air was so thick he could hardly breathe. And then the sand came, whipping tiny grains against his legs until they began to burn, like his face. He fought to open his eyes, becoming fearful, but the tiny crystals fired into his tear ducts and against his eyelids, gluing them shut.

"T-Tristan, I can't—see!"

"Courage, Peter. It will pass."

But instead it grew more intense, the wind bellowing its rage from every direction, deafening the conscience. The sand became glass and Peter felt that he was afire.

"I can barely hold myself up. It'll carry us away!" Peter cried.

"Yes, it will carry us away!" Tristan shouted above the wind. "Take my hand, hold on!"

Peter groped about blindly until he felt his friend's fingers. They clasped hands, fighting the gale together, falling at times to their knees but then pulling each other up.

"My f-face! I have no skin left!" Peter cried, the sand needling his flesh to numbness.

"Faith, Peter! Stand behind me, I'll shield you!"

Peter stooped behind Tristan, finding respite of sorts, but he could hear Tristan's labored breathing and knew that he, too, was taking a fearsome lashing.

"The sand!" Peter yelled, barely hearing himself above nature's roar. "Where's it coming from, the beach?"

"No. The desert."

"What? I can't hear you!"

"The desert! Of Arabia!"

"I can't open my eyes!"

"Soon, Peter. Patience!"

"I-I'll try!" Peter stammered.

But the wind kept growing in velocity, to the point that he felt Tristan's arms fly backwards, flailing him along the ribs and shoulders. Then Peter thought he heard a huge oak separate from the earth, its giant tendrilled roots shredding like paper. Then another.

"It's a—tornado, by God!" Peter screamed. "We've been caught in a damn tornado! Got to find cover!"

Tristan laughed, his song carried off instantaneously by the dreadful wind. "It's—a—vision!" he countered, laughing again, taking in a mouthful of grit.

Suddenly, just as Peter was on the brink of losing it, the winds stopped. The air grew still and the world fell silent.

"Peter, open your eyes now. Behold . . . the desert."

Peter released the back of Tristan's tattered shirt and poked his head around Tristan's shoulder to see, praying that his eyes would indeed open, and they did.

But he was hardly prepared for what he saw. The oaks were gone, as were the gravestones, and the two of them were standing ankle deep in sand. Before them stretched—more sand, an endless expanse of barren dunes, swelling and falling as far as the eyes could wander. In all directions. And above, a blazing red sun so stark that the sky itself could not be defined from the wasteland below.

"My God," Peter rasped, awestruck and disbelieving. "We were— standing in a graveyard just moments ago!"

"This *is* a graveyard, Peter, but in another world and another time. Believe it. Touch the sand, if you like."

Peter touched himself instead. Taking his thumb and his index finger, he squeezed his wrist until the skin paled. Next he slapped his face, hoping perhaps he would wake up and find himself in the darkness of the cemetery.

Then he looked at Tristan and gasped. The once handsome face looked haggard and worn, the cheeks hollow and creased by the lines of extreme age. It was Tristan, and yet not. His hair was as pale as the sand at their feet and hung to his back in a glimmering silver sheen like the great hoary beard that covered his chest. He looked to be centuries old. But the voice was unchanged.

Contrition

"Over that rise, Peter, stands a city. It is the year 1099 and we are in the land of Islam. I prayed in the dungeons of that city before they led me to this very place you see."

"But why has the vision brought us *here*?"

"When the Christian armies left France in the year 1096, as I told you before, I embarked with them as the Pope's agent, with full authority to act as his voice and to document the campaign. My younger brother, Guillaume, was commissioned to assist my efforts. After many hardships and much bloodshed we managed to reach the Holy City. Then more bloodshed until the Crusaders cut their way to the walls of Jerusalem itself.

"On the night of July 14, 1099, I said Mass, issued communion, and blessed the Christian armies. But upon entering the gates of the Holy City that next day, the Christian knights engaged in wholesale slaughter, butchering Jews and Moslems alike. Women and children were not spared from the bloodbath. Infants were torn from their mothers' breasts and hacked to bits, women and small girls were raped and disemboweled, men and boys were castrated before their very families. The streets ran scarlet that day and throughout the night, at the hands of the very men I had blessed and exhorted.

"I was ashamed to be a Christian, Peter. Horrified by their deeds, and by my own loss of courage. Men that I'd known since boyhood turned into beasts, murdering all they could lay their hands on. Temples were ransacked and looted. Homes and people set afire. Innocents tortured and mutilated. It was a world suddenly gone berserk.

"At my very feet two women were carved apart like raw meat by the blades of a dozen Crusaders rabid for blood. And I'll never forget those woeful eyes as those women clung to my knees and feet thinking they might find sanctuary in the shadow of a holy man. I still hear their cries, and I've heard them for a thousand years ringing in my conscience and my grief."

Peter shuddered, not wanting to believe the words. "You couldn't stop it? But you were the Pope's emissary. Surely your position—"

"I was overwhelmed, powerless. My brother tried to intercede but he was beaten bloody and dragged off by knights of the scarlet cross, our own kinsmen. I fled, seeking refuge in a church to pray that the screaming would cease. I hid there, fearing for my own safety. My brother crawled into the church, wounded, cut by a Frenchman's sword about the arms and shoulders. He chastised me and cursed my weakness, then reminded me of my mission to document the expedition.

"He was right, of course, because I had sworn to Pope Urban II, Odo de Lagery, to report back to Rome with a full and truthful account of the Crusades, the conduct of the troops and the status of the Holy City. So thus awakened, with Guillaume's aid, I worked without rest for two days and completed the report, documenting every insidious detail. It was a scathing publication criticizing the entire affair from beginning to end. My brother and I then left Jerusalem with a small armed escort of knights loyal to the Pope."

"But why has the vision brought us here then, rather than Rome?" said Peter.

A slight flush came over Tristan's ancient face, but then disappeared like a gleam. "I never reached Rome, Peter. Several days out of Jerusalem we were captured by a retreating band of Muslim renegades, led by Mahmoud Malik, the Butcher of Medina. But it was an ambush agreed to and set into motion by the Christian barons."

"What? But why?"

"The French noblemen were in a rage over my report. Knowing my intimate relationship with the Pope, they foresaw retribution. Excommunication, most likely, because the good Pope was a man of reform and conscience despite his reputation as the great manipulator of titles and boundaries. And the day we were captured, a Christian knight rode beside Malik as his warriors descended the hill to close the trap. He was a Frenchman from Saint Germain. He was my—uncle."

"But, Tristan, what is *this* place?"

"Malik's army, having already been defeated outside Jerusalem, was in retreat to Medina, his birthplace. Our loyal knights were butchered and fed to the crows, but he reserved Guillaume and me for other purposes because we were men of the cloth. As he fled Jerusalem, he brought us to this place."

"To the city over the dunes?"

"No, to this very place where we stand." Then he raised his eyes to the horizon, squinting, raising a palm to shade his face. "Look there, the dust."

Peter saw a cloud arising from behind a ridge of sand. "Another storm?" he fretted.

"No. Riders."

They waited in silence as the top of the rise lost its pallor, darkened by an army of Moslem warriors. And as they spilled over the dunes, scimitars and banners aglint, they drove down into the valley of sand occupied by Peter and Tristan and stopped, crowding their stallions into a crude circle. Their leader leaped to the sand and strode to the center of the circle, barking orders in Arabic.

"It's Malik," whispered Tristan.

Peter trembled. "My God, he looks—monstrous. Can they see us?"

Contrition

"No, they can't see us. You haven't been conceived yet and I am over there."

Peter didn't understand until he watched a line of prisoners, a hundred or so, being dragged to the center of the circle. Then they were stripped naked, arms bound behind their backs, and forced to kneel in a huddled cluster before Malik. All of the captives appeared to be Arabs but two. One was Tristan de Saint Germain.

"You, Christian, you will be the first to feel the sword!" Malik said, his eyes full of scorn.

Then he moved within inches of the other man and, gripping his scimitar with both hands, he raised it over his head while a thousand warriors cheered. Peter noticed that the man bore a strong resemblance to Tristan.

"Do you denounce your faith and accept Allah as the one God, and Mohammed as his prophet?" screamed Malik. "And me as your Master?"

The young man raised his head defiantly, gray eyes agleam, and spat at his executioner's feet. "Die in Hell, you damned demon!" he snarled with contempt. "My God is watching you this very moment and weighing your actions and He will pass his terrible judgment on you with unforgiving wrath! He will—"

The scimitar suddenly fell with savage force, separating head from shoulder, and the face fell to the sand, eyes still open and defiant even in death. The naked body quivered a moment, then dropped like fallen timber, chest down, next to the head.

Peter felt suddenly ill, his throat filling. He glanced over at Tristan but the old hoary face was expressionless save the tears streaming down his cheeks.

"My brother," Tristan whispered.

Next, Malik stood over young Tristan. "Do you denounce your Pope and the authority of Rome ? Do you accept Allah as the only God, and accept Mohammed as his prophet?"

The young Tristan bent his head in prayer, blessing the soul of his slain brother. Then, he raised his closed eyes to the red sun. "I worship the same God as Islam. I worship the God of Abraham," he said softly.

"Do you accept the teaching of Mohammed?" Malik thundered.

"I accept the God of Abraham as the one true God, but I reject Mohammed. I reject the Koran," he said, his voice growing stronger. Then, as if inspired by the spirit of Abraham himself, he opened his great gray eyes and searched the sky. "Odo!" he screamed, "Jerusalem has fallen! The Turks have been routed. Praise God!"

Malik swung wildly at the young priest, only half severing Tristan's neck. Enraged, he swung again and this second swift blow of the scimitar detached the head completely. Then a thousand cries of "Malik! Malik!" filled the desert air as the head rolled to the side, touching that of his brother, eyes closed.

Peter could bear no more. "Take me away from here! Goddammit! For that declaration of faith you spent ten centuries in Purgatory? There is no justice! There is no mercy!"

"That final declaration of faith kept me from entering the gates of Hell, Peter. The Lord is indeed merciful. It was my cowardice in Jerusalem that earned my suffering. Even though I intended to right some of the wrongs upon reaching Rome, I was weak in the Holy City. I broke my vows and sought refuge in a church while my brother fought on."

"Please, get me away from here—end this vision now."

"No, you must witness a hundred more executions at the hands of Malik's henchmen. And these victims are devout Muslims. That's why they have been brought out here, far from the eyes of the city dwellers so they won't know what is occurring out in the desert."

"Killing his own people? But why?"

"Because Mahmoud Malik is a henchman of Satan, Peter, conceived in sin and destined to be the instrument of evil, both in this world before you now and in the world you inhabit."

The executions began but Peter could not stomach the horror, and the dull thud of steel against neck flesh drove him to the point of nausea. The scimitars grew red, falling again and again for nearly half an hour, and the sand ran scarlet with rivers of streaming blood. Some of the victims cried out for mercy, others uttered prayers to Allah with dignity and bearing.

Finally, the grisly work was done. The horde mounted their horses and followed Malik back over the sandy rise, leaving behind a blood-stained desert strewn with naked corpses and severed heads.

Tristan ran to his brother, leaving Peter behind, and lifted his brother's head to his bosom. "Ah, Guillaume," he wept, "if only all were as stout-hearted and pure as you. I've missed you, brother, these thousand years. How thankful I am that your soul went straight from this place of the dead to the Master."

Peter watched his friend tearfully, his heart sinking to depths he'd never imagined. "God, if you indeed exist, take us away from this wicked hell of a place," he whispered aloud, closing his eyes.

Then he opened them again and suddenly sensed darkness and a gravestone at his feet, and smelled the sudden fragrance of rose petals. There next to him was Tristan, young again, pressing a white rose to his breast.

Contrition

Peter sat down on the grave marker, exhausted but thankful. He looked at Tristan's peaceful face, then shook his head. "So," he said, "Pope Urban never got your documents on the Crusades?"

"No. Nor even word that the Christian knights had taken Jerusalem. He died the same day I did . . . July twenty-ninth of the year 1099."

"And Malik?"

"Killed a week after my death at the hands of fellow Arabs angered by the slaughter of their Muslim brothers on the dunes that fateful day that sent me to Purgatory. He used his faith as an excuse to achieve his own aims, as many do—and was found out, as happens to us all ultimately.

"Now, Peter, you see what lies ahead. You see that that this man is truly an instrument of the Devil."

Tristan then knelt and laid the rose he so tenderly held next to Amanda LaFleur's headstone. "Guillaume, I know your pure soul has encountered this sweet slain angel in Paradise," he whispered. "Please join her now, and pray for your lost brother."

Chapter Twenty-Seven

The Twin Oaks Motel had once been the site of a thriving flesh exchange, frequented by prostitutes, lonely fishermen, and adulterous couples who sought the privacy of Back Bay. It looked more like a row of barracks than a motel, however, even in its heyday. But now, as Peter Toche and Dan Wilcox stood outside its deteriorating office, it looked even worse. Parts of the roof had collapsed, every window pane had been broken, and graffiti lined every inch of its drab, bowed walls. It was another town monument to an era gone by. Chief Barhanovich had lifted the demolition ban on Back Bay, however, and the bulldozers would be back. The old monument would be razed in the morning.

"Here's the K-9 unit," said Wilcox, watching a squad car wind its way up the drive. "And there's the crawl space we pulled Little Jimmy out of." He pointed to a square hole to his left. "Jimmy had the grill in place, had it wired shut."

The squad car pulled alongside the two men and a uniformed officer stepped out. "Hey, guys," the man said, opening a back door. "C'mon, Smoke!" he said. A large German shepherd bolted from the seat and put its nose to the ground immediately, circling the men.

The dog's breathing was loud and the movement of its snout agitated.

The officer's name was Wilbur Guice. He was a small man, quiet most of the time, but he took pride in his dog. The two had spent three years together. They made a good team and shared great affection for each other.

"Wilbur," said Peter, "Dan and I are going to scout the crawl space and the front rooms. I'd like you and Smoke to cover the back. Here's Jimmy's shirt."

Guice took the shirt and held it to the shepherd's nose. The dog whined a moment, buried his nose in the cloth, then squatted on his hindquarters to look up at his master. "Go, Smoke. Go on!" shouted Guice, pointing toward the corner of the ramshackle motel. The dog moved off, nose to the ground. "Damn fine pooch, eh, boys?" he said. "Wish you'd called earlier though, it's almost dark. What'm I looking for anyway?"

"Not sure what," said Wilcox. "Pete's on another of his *chases*. Following something in that head of his, you know?"

Guice understood immediately. "So, Pete, just nose around, eh?" Guice had been stumped more than once by Peter's successes, so he no longer asked for details, just instructions. Then he looked over Peter's shoulder to Wilcox and smiled, as if to say, "Oh boy, here we go again."

Peter caught the glance. "Wilbur, I'm looking for a guy, a big man, name's Malik. I'm following a lead that just came up at the Old French House the other night. Not sure, but we think we might have identified the suspect in our rash of murders. You remember the young guy that's been helping Father Joseph at the school? Spoke to him at length about this Malik, and I think he may have put us on to something."

"Does he know something we don't?" asked Guice.

"Not sure, just following the only damn lead we *got*, Wilbur."

Guice could feel heat in Peter's reply. "Gotcha, Pete. Me and Smoke'll just nose around then. We'll meet back up with you and Dan in about fifteen minutes. Smoke won't last much longer than that. He's pretty high-strung, you know." Soon both he and the dog disappeared around the corner.

Peter got down on all fours and squirmed into the crawl space. "Hand me the flashlight, Dan, and follow me in. I want to go over every inch of this hole. Geez, it's a tight fit under here. Now where exactly was Little Jimmy hiding?"

"Over there," Wilcox grunted, following Peter into the blackness. "Damn, it stinks in here. Smells like Jimmy Dubaz. Over there, Pete. Jimmy dug a hole just against the wall. Miracle I spotted him. Had a hell of a time dragging him out."

Peter moved the light about and spotted the body-length depression. "Looks like he was digging himself a grave or something," he said.

"Yeah, I thought the same thing. Makes you wonder, doesn't it? It's like he knew he was going to die soon. Like he was getting ready.

Say, what all did that Saint Germain guy tell you? Seems like he's got you wound up tighter'n a damn top."

"Oh, not much really," Peter lied, continuing to inch the flashlight beam about the crawl space. "Just told me about some suspicious behavior from a guy he ran into at the Old French House—gave me a name and a description, a little background, that's about it."

"Heard there was a hell of a fight down there a few nights back. They say the little guy was a damn hellcat even though the other guy was twice his size. Guy behind the bar said the big man was the same one that whipped the Duval brothers a while back. Must have been a hell of a rumble down there. Wish I could have—"

"Dan! Would you cool it? I'm trying to concentrate down here, okay?"

Wilcox grew silent, thinking how unusual it was for his partner to be so short-fused. He knew something was bothering Peter,. He had appeared more driven than usual and somewhat out of character ever since taking up with the young Frenchman. After a few minutes, Dan finally spoke again. "Hurry up, Pete, let's get out of here. This place gives me the creeps. I feel like it's full of snakes or critters or something."

Peter placed his hand in the depression and started pushing loose dirt aside. "No, I want to make a close inspection down here."

The light in Peter's hand reflected off the foundation wall and splashed a ghostly light on Peter's profile. Dan Wilcox was not a superstitious man, nor was he easily frightened, but it almost appeared he was peeking into the future, somehow, at Peter, dead.

"Come on, Pete, I'm not shitting you, let's go. Christ, in a minute you're going to close your eyes, you're going to keep feeling around in that hole, and then you're going to go into one of those weird spells of yours and start talking to yourself. I've had it! I want out of here."

At that moment a vicious snarl came from the other side of the foundation wall, followed by the snapping and yelping of an angry dog. Then the snarling of—a man.

Peter instantly recognized the voice from the desert and was immediately overcome by a whirling kaleidoscope of urgent images and emotions. "It—it's *him*!" he wailed, beginning to quake and treble as though he had been hit by the surge of an overwhelming electrical charge.

"Smoke, he's found someone—" said Wilcox. "Come on, Pete, hurry!"

Then they heard the voice of Wilbur Guice, shouting from a good distance away. "Smoke, get' im! Get' im, I'm coming!"

The furious struggle on the other side of the wall continued. Peter could hear cursing and howling, fangs snapping, and the sound of fists striking fur and bone.

Wilcox scrambled backward on all fours, speeding up his movement out of the hole. "Shit!" he yelled, suddenly cracking his backbone against a floor joist.

Peter, too, was making a rapid backward retreat out of the crawl space. So much so that he ran into Wilcox, bowling him to the side. "Shoot him!" Peter suddenly screamed, hoping Guice could hear him through the wall. "Dammit, Wilbur, shoot! Kill that bastard before he gets away!"

Stunned, Wilcox lifted his eyes at Peter in complete dismay. "Christ, Pete," he yelled, "it might be a damned kid out there or something! Guice, don't shoot, don't shoot!"

"It's *him*!" Peter screamed. "It's Malik! Wilbur, *shoot* for God's sake!"

"Stop it, Pete! Goddammit, stop it! What the hell's gotten into you?"

Then, in the midst of their bickering, the noise beyond the wall abruptly halted. "Damn!" Peter whispered, backing his rump out of the crawl space opening. He reached in and jerked Wilcox out with an impatient tug.

They both stood and ran around the end of the Twin Pines, the flashlight slashing high and low beams of light over the ground and against the walls.

"Dan! Pete!" Guice shouted hoarsely. "Give me a hand, quick!" When they reached Guice, he was sitting on the ground, holding his dog in his lap.

"He's dead! Smoke's—dead," he said, ruefully brushing his palms over and over between the hound's ears. "Ribs are crushed—whole body's crushed flat—can't believe it. Don't know a man alive could do this." Then he looked up into the beam of the flashlight Peter held. He said nothing, just stared into the beam with that sad gaze of the bereaved.

"It's him!" said Peter pointing into the darkness. "It's the Devil's messenger! Do you hear me, Dan? Tristan was right, and my father, too."

But Wilcox was not listening. That ghostly image of Peter under the crawl space had disturbed him deeply, and still did, as did Peter's frantic plea to shoot into the dark, possibly killing an innocent person.

Then, at that very moment, as Wilbur Guice caressed his dead dog's snout and Peter stood trembling with the fury of a man gone over the edge, Wilcox heard the banshee wail of a night loon in the distance just beyond the salt marsh—and suddenly his skin was crawled. "My God," he whispered to no one, "this can't really be happening . . . what the hell's going on here?"

* * *

The funeral of Joe Kuluz was a sad affair. Not because of mourning relatives and pews full of grief stricken friends, but because of the lack of both. The funeral was sparsely attended. Embarrassingly so. Father Joseph, as requested during his last hospital visit to the old renegade, said the mass and delivered the eulogy. The bishop was displeased with these arrangements because Joe Kuluz had not stepped into a church in over fifty years. "That man does not deserve a church burial," he had decreed.

The pews were empty except for six men in the front row, five old Yugoslavs and Didier LaFleur—just enough to carry the casket. Tristan attended the service also, but chose to remain in the rear of the church. He was deeply absorbed in prayer for the old fisherman, guessing that Joe Kuluz had by now entered a world far less forgiving than the one he had known for over seventy years in Gulf Springs.

So, after a lifetime of hard labor and hard living, old Joe Kuluz departed life mourned by a mere handful of acquaintances. He and his Annie had had no children. Had Annie Kuluz still been living, St. Ann's Cathedral would have undoubtedly been filled with attendees mourning her loss of a husband. But she had long since been laid away, and her surviving friends and relatives saw little in Joe to warrant attending mass on a Tuesday morning.

As Father Joseph administered communion, the door of the church opened. Someone stood there a moment looking toward the casket, then left hurriedly. Joseph thought for a second that it might have been Madame LaFontaine, but he saw little more than a silhouette, a dark figure outlined by the bright burst of glaring sunlight flooding into the doorway.

The quick gesture that shadow had made appeared to be the sign of the cross, but surely it was more imagination at work than anything else, he decided. Besides, Madame LaFontaine held only disdain for the church.

After Mass some final words were said at the cemetery and the casket was lowered into the earth. The small party then split up, but as Tristan and Joseph walked the short distance to Joseph's house, Didier LaFleur approached them from behind. "Thank you for saying the Mass, Father Joe," he said. "I heard the bishop wasn't too happy about it."

"Oh," Joseph said shaking his head, "some of the parish priests complained to him, but you know, they're not from here. Joe was a good man deep down. Just didn't do church."

Tristan shook Didier's hand, impressed by its size and firmness. "I prayed for him today," Tristan said. "I didn't know him but Joseph has told me stories. He'll need our prayers."

"Yeah, I'm sure," agreed Didier. "Poor old Slav. He never could quite put things right, but he had a good heart under all that crust." Then Didier tilted his head to get a closer look at Tristan. "How's the eye? That big guy got you pretty good the other night."

"It's fine. It hurts, but nothing fatal. Perhaps your friend's heart will be his salvation. Nevertheless, I want you to know that I shall pray for him all week."

"Better make it all month," said Joseph, "he's crossed a line or two, eh, Didier?"

Didier nodded, scratching at his neck. "He left me something. Joe asked if I'd drop it in the Gulf for him after he was buried. Out there by Dog Keys Pass."

"Oh, what is it?" asked Joseph.

Didier fished into his pocket and pulled out a Saint Christopher medal. It was heavily tarnished. "He wore this all his life." Didier smiled. "A gift from his momma when he was ten. He said it saved him many a time. He was with me when my boat went down, you know."

"Ha! Which time?" Joseph laughed. "You've lost a damn fleet over your lifetime."

"The last time . . . when I lost my boys."

"Oh, I see," said Joseph, suddenly feeling awkward. "I didn't mean to make light, Didier. I'm sorry."

"I understand," said the old fisherman. "Yeah, Joe was with us that day. He tried to save my boys, but the current was too much. He nearly drowned, too, trying to drag them in right after he dragged me to shore. How that little runt managed to save my big carcass I'll never know. He claims Saint Christopher carried him that day."

Joseph squinted, trying to recollect the story. "That was just off the west tip of Horn Island, wasn't it?"

"Yeah, Dog Keys Pass. We were less than two hundred yards from shore when the bottom dropped. We'd have been okay, but you know how that current runs through there. Didn't have a prayer, really."

"But the medal?" asked Joseph. "Why did he want it thrown in the Pass?"

"That's where I lost my boys. Joe said he wanted to give the medal back to the sea, to help my boys."

"To help them?" said Joseph.

"Yes," said Tristan with surety. "To *bless* Mister LaFleur's sons."

Didier scratched his chin, puzzled. "Yeah, those were his exact words—to bless the boys."

"I see," said Joseph. "Makes you wonder, doesn't it? Joe thinking of something like that just before passing away."

"Not so strange," said Tristan. "Men's thoughts usually turn to God in the end, if given time to think. Even after a lifetime of denial."

Didier laughed. "I'm beginning to like this boy, Father Joseph! Clever as a crow, eh?"

"So when are you going to dispose of the medal?" said Joseph.

"Tomorrow morning. Dawn, because that's when the boat went down. The reason I stopped you, I was wondering if maybe you'd come with me, Father Joe, maybe give a blessing. We'll take the *Miss Marie*. Pete Toche is coming, too. Funny thing, he says the chief was making him take a few days off. Anyway, Pete was friends with my boys since the cradle."

"Whoa there," said Joseph. "I thought the *Miss Marie* was in mothballs. I'm not too sure I want to—"

"She still floats, and the engine's fine. We'll go straight out, straight back. And Tristan can come too if he wants."

"You still know how to pilot a shrimper?" said Joseph.

"Nothing to it. Just like walking."

"I don't swim," Tristan said, pausing. "But since you say the boat floats, I'd be happy to go."

"Okay," said Joseph, "it's a foursome then. What time?"

"Five-thirty," said Didier, turning for his car.

Contrition

As Joseph and Tristan passed Madame LaFontaine's, they saw her sitting on her porch swing. "Hey, Madame!" Joseph yelled. "Was that you that stepped into the church this morning?"

She wiped something from her eye and spat over the railing. "Don't be such a damn fool, Joey Broussard!" she snapped. "You know I won't set foot in a church!"

"Jesus," Joseph muttered. "What's wrong with *her* this morning?"

"Joe Kuluz, I'd say," said Tristan. "I was sitting in the back of the church. Yes, that was her."

Chapter Twenty-Eight

An hour after dark the *Jean-Luc* traveled several miles up the Pascagoula River and slipped into the mouth of a concealed cove. Even though the task before them was both clandestine and filled with risk, the Duval brothers had been drinking heavily since mid-afternoon. Their kind seldom concerned themselves with the possibility of consequences or with being apprehended. After a lifetime of fraternal criminal activity, theirs was a world of confident and unpunished malfeasance.

"Back her in, LeRoy, ass to the pier," shouted David Duval, the eldest and dominant brother, pointing at a large dock with the beam of his flashlight. His voice was barely audible over the loud drone of the *Jean-Luc*'s twin motors.

Two minutes later, they tied to pilings and stepped aground. A small nervous man awaited them. "Bout damn time," he growled. Then he stuffed his fist in his pocket and withdrew a wad of hundred dollar bills. "Five thousand," he said. "Now let's get rollin' so's I can get the hell outta here."

"Take it easy, Hooks," said David Duval, smirking at his brothers. "It's all under control, you nervous little shit. Got it on your flatbed?"

"Yeah, right over there."

"Then back it up to the pier, tail end to my tail end."

"How the hell we gonna unload? Damn barrels weigh a ton apiece."

"Power winches, Hooks, we're all rigged up. Now get movin'. We'll take it from here."

Two hours later the *Jean-Luc* was loaded and motoring south out of the mouth of the Pascagoula River. Then the vessel turned west toward Horn Island and Dog Keys Pass. It moved slowly and rode perilously low to the water under the strain of great weight.

Contrition

"Shit," said Jimmy Duval, "we ain't gonna make it, David."

"Aw quit worryin'," said the eldest. "Christ, you're worse at whinin' than Hooks. We're almost there."

Within the hour they entered the channel just off the west tip of Horn Island and began dumping their cargo. One by one they winched each barrel onto a makeshift saddle, popped the lid, and swung the barrel out over the transom, tipping it over into the sea. Upon completion of this process, each barrel was then released into the water and tipped so as to force it to sink.

Two hours later, David Duval slumped onto an ice chest and wiped his forehead with a sweaty palm. He was spent. The labor had worn him out, but it was the alcohol that had accelerated his fatigue. His two brothers slung their gloves onto the deck and threw their rumps onto the boat's railing. "Let's have another beer," one of them said.

At the precise moment these words were spoken, the hatch to the ice hold of the *Jean-Luc* exploded upward. And before the unsuspecting brothers could fathom what had just occurred or recognize the large man who vaulted from the depths, he was upon them with the murderous rage of a sociopath. In one hand he wielded a great stick and in the other a rusted machete that had been stashed below by the brothers themselves.

As he struck and hacked and grappled, the madman bellowed and cursed, drowning out the bloodcurdling screams of his victims and even the loud rumble of the Detroit Diesels below.

All of this bloodletting, this butchery in the night, went unheard and unwitnessed because the world of people was nestled fourteen miles to the north—tucked away on the mainland, sleeping along the quiet edge water of Gulf Springs.

Chapter Twenty-Nine

Didier LaFleur and Peter Toche were at the pier before dawn as promised, and the *Miss Marie* sat sputtering at low idle, blue smoke billowing from around the exposed motor. As Joseph eyed the old shrimp boat squatting in the harbor, her curved prow splintered and scarred, he grew concerned about the old vessel's ability to motor out to the barrier islands.

"You sure this thing's seaworthy?" he yelled, trying to outcry the heaving engine.

"Fit as ever," Didier replied. "Just a bit tired, like me. Come on aboard. Be careful, Tristan, the deck's wet, so step easy."

"A beautiful old boat, Didier," Tristan said, smiling. "And a wondrous morning, too. Good morning, Peter!"

Peter was coiling a length of rope just aft of the cabin. He was wearing khaki shorts and a red T-shirt. Tristan had never seen him dressed so casually, but despite his apparel, Peter appeared morose. "Hey, men." He nodded.

Joseph immediately began inspecting the yards of crusty, peeling paint and the corroded rigging. "Yeah, Didier, a beautiful old boat," he muttered. "Where the hell are the life jackets?"

"Down below the cabin I think," said Didier. "Under the port berth last time I looked, but it's been quite a while."

Joseph glanced at the radio mount just above the wheel. "No radio?"

"Pete," Didier interrupted, "could you undo the lines for me? We're ready to shove off."

They left in the dark, following an eastbound line of channel markers that ran the length of Heron Island and led out into the mouth of the bay. Then, cutting due south, they motored out into the Sound, picking up another series of markers that directed them toward Horn Island.

Gradually, as dawn began to seep into the sky, the darkness subsided and the sea turned from black to stone gray. It was a flat sea, broken only by the wake of the *Miss Marie* as it crawled south toward the island, which was as yet nothing more than a break on the gray horizon where it merged with the sky. But as the sun began to climb, the mist began to burn off and the water gradually melded to a dark green. Then became translucent.

"Be there in another thirty minutes," Didier said. "It's a snail's pace but I don't want to push the old boat too hard. It's a good morning for going slow, eh? Hard to believe it stormed last night. Water's usually more stirred up after a big rain like that."

"Haven't seen it this flat in years," said Peter, his mood lightening upon seeing Father Joseph standing there holding firmly to the life jacket that was now secured about his torso. Then Peter laughed. "Worried about something?" he said.

"Yeah, this damn boat's a wreck," said Joseph. "It'll be a miracle if we don't sink!"

"Unbelievably beautiful," Tristan said to Peter, his eyes wandering across the endless mirror that lay ahead of them. "Makes one understand the call of the sea over the ages."

"Absolutely," Peter replied. "If I hadn't gone into law enforcement, I'd have gone to sea like my uncles. It's a hard life, though."

"No harder than what you do now," said Tristan. "I know your heart is heavy with all that your work brings your way."

"Yeah . . . you're right. Chief made me sit out a few days after that incident out on Back Bay the other night. Said my partner's worried about me losing it. They think I've become obsessed. Same thing happened to my father years ago." Then he lowered his voice. "Tristan, I thought we *had* him. I'm sure it was him, Malik."

"Patience, Peter. Patience. We'll find him soon. I can feel it. But please know that I thank you for your faith. I believe that Joseph still has his doubts. I—"

"What are two talking about over there?' said Joseph, yelling over the motor and moving closer.

Peter was about to fabricate an excuse, but just then a black fin cut the surface, its sheen radiant in the morning light. Then another surfaced, more playful than the first. Within seconds the vessel was surrounded by a pod of dolphins, their graceful forms bounding ahead, rising and falling rhythmically before the soft swell of the old ship's prow.

"A good sign," said Didier. "Means we'll make it out and back in one piece. And I don't really think that life jacket's necessary, Father Joe. One usually only puts those on when a bad squall hits, not on a morning like this. Whatever happened to that young Joey Broussard with the big balls, eh?"

"He had them snipped, obviously," said the priest. "They were getting too heavy, you know. Anyway, why don't you just steer the boat?"

The old Frenchman broke into laughter. We all get snipped sooner or later, somehow or the other," he said, looking at Tristan. "And it's a good thing or we'd all be like Joe Kuluz." Then he dug in his pocket and extended his palm. "Here," he said, extending the Saint Christopher medal, "I think Joe would appreciate a young man doing the honors. And me, I know there is something good about you, so I would be honored, too."

Tristan accepted, closing his fingers about the chain and medallion tightly. "*Merci*," he said, humbled. Then he placed his fingers to his eye and kneaded the tender flesh of his still-bruised upper cheek.

"Yeah, I miss old Joe," Didier continued. "He was a good man. There's been a lot worse, I know that. How's that eye? Still giving you trouble?"

"These deck boards are sagging," said Joseph suddenly, stamping at the flooring of the boat.

"Keep that up and you'll punch a hole right through the dry rot!" cautioned Didier. Then he turned back around and said in a low voice, "That big man at the Old French House the other night, he really set you afire, didn't he? I thought I heard you yell something about your brother. You *know* that man?" Didier saw Tristan's jaw tighten. "Who is he to you?"

Tristan looked out over the water and tried to close his wounded eye, but the maneuver was too painful. "That man," he said, "is not a man, but a monster. He killed my brother, and many, many others. And as surely as I stand before you, I believe that he is the one who killed your granddaughter."

Didier looked directly at the younger man, and something momentarily looked back at him out of Tristan's eye—but when Didier

Contrition

looked again, it wasn't there. "Old Kuluz told me he thought that he had seen that big guy by the cemetery the night my Mandy's headstone got busted up. Joe and I saw him get into it with the Duval boys down at the Old French House about a week or so before that. Joe swears it was the same guy."

Tristan turned and felt a tiny surge of corroboration race through him. He summoned Peter, who had been listening to the entire conversation, to come closer. "Didier, Peter knows what I am about to tell you already, and so does Joseph.

"Since I saw that man and tried to stop him that night, I have known that it was he who killed your granddaughter and all the others here in this peaceful place. It was he who smashed the gravestone. Do you remember the letters that were etched into one of the remnants, Didier? The letters were M-A-L, and there was a mark behind them, as if another letter was about to be formed in the stone. Do you remember this?"

Didier nodded. "Yes, the word was French for *evil*."

"No, no, most assuredly not," said Tristan with finality. "I understood what it signified right after that monster escaped me and fled that night. Didier, his name is Malik, and I interrupted him as he was performing his wickedness in the graveyard. His name is Malik and he was inscribing his name on the stone."

Didier cupped his forehead with a huge palm and began to rub. Then he looked at Peter who gave him in return a knowing nod.

"He is the one," Tristan continued. "He killed your Amanda."

"But why? He's not even from here. He didn't even know her. How could—"

"Didier," said Peter, "Tristan is not suggesting some wild supposition here."

"You—believe this?" said Didier, surprised.

"Yes I do," said Peter. "As difficult as it may be to absorb, I believe every word of what he has said. Tristan knows things we could never hope to understand. I've been chasing that man for over a month without even knowing who he was, but Tristan has cleared the mystery. Tristan and Malik are old enemies from another place, I'll leave it at that. You've known me my entire life, Didier. You know I wouldn't lie to you about this."

Didier then looked at Father Joseph. "Father Joe, do you—"

"Yes, I do now . . . I didn't before."

Didier took a breath, then shook his head. "You're lucky he didn't kill you that night. A frightened man is dangerous. And you may be scrappy, Tristan, but I don't think it was you he was afraid of."

"He was afraid of being found out," said Tristan. "That's why he ran. I wish you had not stopped me. He has killed and will kill again and again—until he is stopped for good."

Silence fell around the group as they stood there motionless for several seconds, simply staring at each other with that odd look that befalls those who have just shared their innermost secrets. But then Joseph looked out onto the water, and suddenly pointed. "Look," he said, "dead fish ahead."

Didier peered from behind the wheel. "Ah, probably left over from last night. Some shrimper cleaning his nets of trash fish. It's nothing." He gazed down into the water, however, and soon became puzzled. "Hmm, looks like white trout . . . Now that doesn't seem right."

As the *Miss Marie* plodded ahead, nearing the Dog Keys Pass, the number of dead fish gradually increased from several dozen or so to hundreds. The air turned rancid, as did the water, until soon the sea was covered with a film of oily rainbows. Didier dropped the engine speed to an even slower crawl, and leaning over the starboard rail, scooped his fingers in the water. Then, returning to the wheel, he brought his fingers to his nostrils and sniffed.

"Whew!" he gagged. "Something's bad here."

"What is it?" said Peter. "Oil?"

"Naw, too thin," Didier replied, running his hand across his shirt. "Something else. Never smelled anything like this before. But it doesn't belong in the Gulf, I'll tell you that for sure."

The dead trout grew even thicker and Joseph moved to the bow, shading his eyes from the glare. His concern quickly dissolved into bewilderment. "Jesus!" He whistled. "Didier, Peter, move up, you better look at this."

Didier cut the engine and they all met at the bow. Didier sighed and Peter clapped his forehead in disbelief. Before them on the water lay a great white lake of dead trout, their gas-bloated bellies crowding each other in a congealing mass of death and stagnation. An endless sea of pale fish eyes staring blankly at the sky, carcasses stiff and lifeless. It was a wasteland of scaly flesh, already covered with hordes of feasting flies and scavenging sea birds that scurried across the dead as though uncertain where to feed or what to devour. And this horrid accumulation extended nearly as far as the eye could see.

"Never seen a fish kill like this," murmured Didier, drawing the back of his hand across his lips. Something's awful wrong here. Look there, the birds . . . Looks like something's wrong with some of them too—they're falling over, dying. Something's poisoned the water."

The current of Dog Keys Pass began to ease the *Miss Marie* into the mass, enveloping it. And as the four stared down into the floor of fish eyes, suddenly two larger eyes appeared.

Joseph peered deeper and then swooned, nearly slipping over the rail. "A face!" he cried. "My God, it's a face!"

Didier grabbed the priest with a jerk and pulled him from the railing. Then, moving beside Peter and Tristan, he looked down into the mass of dead fish. It took a moment for the scene to register, but then it hit home. Tristan looked away, unwilling to linger at the sight in the water. But Peter knelt and reached. With both hands he wrenched the head by the hair, expecting the weight of the submerged torso to follow, but toppled backward from the unexpected lack of resistance. Startled, flat on his back, he lifted his face to see on his chest, still in his grasp, a severed head, its eyes glaring mutely into his. In revulsion, he moaned and shoved the thing away, scrambling to gain his feet.

Joseph began to vomit over the edge of the boat and Tristan, the only one in control of his senses at that instant, stepped heavily on the head to keep it from rolling toward the priest. Then, grimly, he lifted it by the hair with his left hand and held it up, crossing himself with the right, Saint Christopher medal still in hand. "Do you know this man?" he said coldly, looking at the others.

"Yes—I baptized him," Joseph coughed.

Peter wiped his mouth with an arm and nodded. "It's David Duval," he said. "He's . . . Damn, what the hell's—"

"He's been murdered," said Tristan. "Look at the cut."

"Could be a boat propeller," Didier added quickly. "It's happened before."

"No," said Tristan. "As sure as we stand on this boat, this man has been executed."

"Look," Peter said, pointing toward Horn Island. "A boat."

Didier scanned the shore, and there lolling about in the low surf of Dog Keys Pass, grounded, sat the half-charred hull of the *Jean-Luc*.

"Belongs to the Duval brothers," Didier mumbled, recognizing the rigging. "Better take a look."

Tristan set the head in a bucket and held up the Saint Christopher medal. "Didier, what about this?"

"Fling it," Didier said, "here and now."

"But the fish—"

"When I come about, drop it behind the prop, it'll make a clearing. This is where Joe Kuluz wanted it. This is where my sons went down."

Didier cranked the engine and immediately the prop began to chop dead fish flesh from the stern. As the surface cleared, Tristan dropped the medal and chain into the sea.

"I wanted to say a short prayer for Joe and the boys," Didier pointed out, "but right now we've got to get to the *Jean-Luc*. There's two more Duvals out here somewhere." He wheeled the *Miss Marie* about and worked his way slowly toward the tip of Horn Island, careful not to bog down in the fish fill. "We'll have to anchor off the shore," he added. "*Miss Marie*'s got a deeper vee than usual, she was built to go further out than the Sound. And, Father Joe, we'll have to wallow in trout to get to the *Jean-Luc*. You can stay aboard if you like. Pete and I'll handle this."

"No," said the priest uneasily. "I'm coming."

Peter leaned over the bow, scanning the surface for other corpses. "Tristan," he said, "keep an eye out. If one's dead, the others are dead. They always stuck together." Then he looked at Tristan grimly. "More dead—just as you said."

As they neared the beach, Didier threw the engine in reverse, bringing the old vessel to a gentle stop. "Drop anchor, Pete." Then he dropped into the muck feet first, landing neck deep in fish flesh. "Damn, should've come in a little farther!"

The others quickly dropped over the side and pushed their way toward Didier.

"Stay near, Joseph," said Tristan, "Remember, I don't swim."

Raising their arms over their heads, they trudged forward, their bodies parting the fish-littered surface. "The smell!" said Joseph, again nearing the point of illness.

Suddenly, several feet away the surface stirred and the swell of trout gently rose an inch or two, then dropped."

"Damn," said Peter.

Contrition

The swell rose again, then broke, exploding into a fountain of water and fish parts. Then a black fin, vertical and cutting.

"Shark," Didier called, his tone calm. "Should've guessed they'd moved in by now. Don't panic, not a damn thing we can do but keep moving. Father Joe, don't go soft on me now, just keep walking."

But it was Tristan who shuddered, realizing that he could well meet his end here and now, before completing his task, before finding Malik again. He froze.

"Go, Tristan." Joseph prompted, pushing against his shoulders.

Tristan took a step forward but froze again as the fin dipped below the surface. And suddenly, he felt the return of those unwelcome tremors that owned him those first weeks of his arrival, and his courage fled.

"Tristan," whispered Joseph, sensing his friend's sudden loss of confidence, "are you all right?"

"It—it's Malik," Tristan said, forcing deep breaths to calm himself. "I feel his hand in this. His presence is here in this poisoned water, in these dead fish, in that severed head." With each word he trembled more. "I must not weaken now, Joseph, not now."

"Tristan, are you afraid? You are stronger than all of us. Just keep moving."

"Afraid to the bone, Joseph. Surely God Our Father would not have us meet our end before our work is done."

Didier turned, not comprehending their whispers, and saw that the young man who had so coolly held David Duval's head and placed it in the bucket was going pale. "Tristan," he commanded, "take my shirt tail, son, and hold on. It's getting shallower now."

The shark circled lazily, at times snapping and rolling. Then the fin moved within several inches of the men and slowly tilted. The shark's head slowly raised, its eyes dull black, its jaws a cavern of jagged knives. Tristan's entire body shook.

Didier quickly reached back and grabbed him, pulling him upon the shore. Then, without hesitation, his huge hand grasped Joseph by the arm, dragging him up in one swift motion. Peter made it on his own. He crawled onto the beach just as the shark yawned lazily and slipped beneath the surface.

"Guess he's had his fill." Didier shrugged. "Come on, the *Jean-Luc*."

Tristan and Joseph exhaled in unison and followed Peter and Didier's path, wondering how they were going to get back on the *Miss Marie*, which now appeared miles away. The *Jean-Luc* was tilted to starboard, its rudder hopelessly buried in the sand. They could see that the stern had caught fire, but the bow and cabin were reasonably intact.

They edged around the stern and were instantly met by a gruesome scene. A corpse lay belly down on the deck, its entire length charred beyond recognition. Charcoal shoulders extended into black arms, propped at the elbows, which were bent as if crawling to safety—or praying.

Another corpse, scorched as badly as the first, lay on its back just below the wheel, its arms also bent at the elbows, but reaching skyward. The two bodies lay in frozen motion like lignite sculptures fashioned by some mad craftsman, their mouths open in lurid contortions, eye sockets hollow and dark. Agony was woven into every crusty fiber of burned face flesh, and, but for the flies, one could nearly hear their silent screams.

"Jimmy and LeRoy," said Didier limply. "God only knows what went on here last night."

"Mass murder," Peter mumbled, "that's what went on, pure and simple. Tristan was right . . . These men were all executed. Look at the slash marks all over the arms and torsos. Hacked to death, then set on fire."

They didn't bother to board the *Jean-Luc*, whether through lack of strength or lack of will. Instead, they simply stood at the tide line, distraught and spent, not even offering conversation. Each had his own thoughts on the morning's horror, and the Saint Christopher medal seemed insignificant in light of the fish kill and the slain Duvals—to all except Tristan. Something stirred within, and he believed they were all four led to Dog Keys Pass this very morning by the medal, and by Joe Kuluz.

"Our existence and mortality are feeble indeed," he offered. "The shark was sent to remind me, as were these slain men. I tell you, Mahmoud Malik has engineered this destruction. Didier, you said that Malik fought these men at the Old French House, so I now say that he sought them out. Since that night of their fight, Malik knew that he would come after them.

"Vengeance is a poison, and he is like a bloated spider spilling venom in his wake. Just as I am looking for him, he is seeking me." The

Contrition

three men took a seat in the sand, but Tristan remained erect and felt an odd and sudden chill in the hot morning sun—an uneasiness beyond the fish kill and the *Jean-Luc*. He closed his eyes a moment to listen to the wind, then, as if jolted by a strong current, he blinked, returning from far away.

"Tristan?" Peter said. "Are you okay?"

"A storm," Tristan muttered, his voice suddenly dull and thick.

"What's that?" Joseph asked.

Tristan's eyes fluttered, then opened wide. "A storm, a great wall of water . . ."

Didier glanced skyward, then gave the others a sideways glance. "Maybe the shock of all this, I think. Sky's clear as glass."

Peter nodded, concealing his concern. "You're right," he whispered, mostly to himself, "but Tristan's gift is greater than mine, and that, at times, is more frightening than what lies aboard that burnt ship."

Chapter Thirty

The sky grew even blacker as dusk approached and great masses of threatening clouds billowed in and out until all semblance of day had been blotted into extinction. Distant rumblings of thunder drew nearer, and finally, a jagged fork of lightning pierced through black-bellied clouds, signaling the arrival of the downpour that had been building since noon.

A blowing rain swept onto the coast, causing boats to bob and shift in their foamy slips, straining against the ropes that confined them, pulling at pilings and cleats in a tireless effort to break free. But the ropes held fast even as the winds grew, and the sea heaved sullen white surf against the beach front and the small-craft harbor.

Inside the Brothers' house, Brother Patrick entered the chapel and approached Placidus with the impatience of a man whose tolerance had reached its threshold. "Placidus," he said, "it's the bishop's dinner and he expects all of us to be there. Come on now, it'll do you good to socialize a bit."

"No," Placidus snapped, "I'm not going and that's that. End of discussion! Just let me be."

"You've become impossible, Placidus. You can't go on like this, you know. You're driving yourself nuts. You won't discuss what's eating at you, you refuse counseling. You've become a shut-in. You've thrown the whole house in turmoil. I'll have to put my foot down soon. It's just a matter of time, you know. I hate the thought, but I'll request that you be sent from this house if I need to."

At this Placidus withered a bit. He feared the attic, like a child who fears dark places in his own house, but that very child would never consider leaving home. And so it was with Placidus. He was tethered to this place by something that even he was incapable of understanding.

Contrition

"No, please," he said, his determination softening. "You wouldn't chase me off. You couldn't—"

"It's something you better think about. Yes, I'll sign a grievance if need be."

"Please, not that, Patrick! It's just that it's—storming out. Don't make me go out in this weather on a night like this."

Patrick placed his fists on his hips and shook his head with a sigh. It pained him to threaten the old man. "Well, maybe so. But I don't feel right leaving you here alone. Maybe I should stay, too, let the others go on."

"No, that's not necessary. I'm not a child. I'll be fine. And—I'll consider counseling. I don't think it'll do a bit of good, but if you insist, I'll look into it, okay?"

"Very well, then," Patrick said, satisfied that his threat had at least cracked the old man's stance a notch. "I'll tell the bishop you're not feeling well. That's not quite a lie, I guess. But I'll hold you to your word about getting help. Anything to lift you out of this hole that you have dug for yourself."

As the Brothers left, Placidus felt a twinge of guilt. He knew that he had been drifting further and further into his own interior blackness, but he suffered from a sorrow that was so deeply rooted that he doubted whether he would ever see the light of day again.

Though he had always enjoyed the bishop's annual dinner in years past, his reason for refusing this time was not a simple matter of agoraphobia, but also a matter of personal dignity. His life had become a series of small humiliations heaped one upon the other. The others in the house had begun to treat him like an old invalid, mentally incompetent and senile. They didn't understand that his problems lie elsewhere, in the realm of dread and uncertainty.

He longed for the summer when things were still right, when his thoughts were reasonable and he wasn't afraid. And each night since that dreadful day he had prayed silently and fervently that he might shake the terror that had driven him into isolation—the terror that had unearthed in him something that had long been buried.

He went to the refrigerator and rummaged about the racks, finally dragging out a plate of leftover cold cuts. The others would soon be eating rib-eyes drowned in mushrooms and Hollandaise sauce, the bishop's favorite fare.

It wasn't until he sat down at the table that the utter silence of the house became noticeable. Then, the refrigerator motor shut down, creating an even deeper quiet. Placidus dragged his fork across the cold cuts, slicing them into neat little squares, and as his knife and fork clinked against the plate, he heard the wind come up, pressing against the window.

Somehow, this caused a grotesque image to arise in his mind, and he expected to see a young girl's bloody, bludgeoned face pressed against the glass, peering in at him. Sensing the onset of hysteria, he looked away from the window and sought refuge in the plate, fighting off the dim terror that was creeping into his old bones.

I won't look at the window . . . even though no one's there.

My God, what am I afraid of? She's dead. Gone. I don't believe in ghosts.

The refrigerator motor clicked back on again and the noise comforted Placidus. Then he began to listen to the rain pound against the slate roof tiles, and the rhythm suddenly reminded him of a childhood song, and he began to hum it. But then a ridiculous thought occurred to him. What if someone was truly out there, standing in the downpour, watching him eat? Not a girl, necessarily, but someone.

He hesitantly glanced at the window but saw only his reflection.

I can't see out—but they can see in.

He leaned back in his chair and reached over to flip out the light, momentarily finding comfort in the darkness. But the storm outside filled the kitchen with bursts of light and he felt exposed again, and this forced his thoughts back to the attic. And just at that moment, above the sound of thunder and his own nervous humming, a noise came from above. A soft scrape that died even as it began.

Then it came again, and Placidus sagged, dispirited, as he felt the weight of dread dragging him down like a man drowning in a deep, bottomless pool. He cocked his head as he sank, listening, concern creasing his face.

Then came steps on the stairs, light, catlike, and it seemed he heard bare feet descending the stairway. But he knew sound carries in an empty place and he hoped that was the explanation, knowing well that it wasn't.

It occurred to him that he might run from the house, but his legs were old and arthritic, and if someone was there, coming for him, he had no hope of escape. He placed his face in his hands and began to cry softly, aware that he was on a track as preordained as birth and death itself, unable to stop, unable to alter course or speed. A cold terror began to spiral up his back, reminding him that this was not a dream, telling him that he could not chase it all away by opening his eyes at the foot of Saint Michael.

Then something reached down with icy hands and pulled him up from his chair, away from the table. Up toward the stairwell. And there, at the bottom of the stairs, he heard laughter, girlish and faint. He looked up and saw a vague silhouette standing at the top of the stairs, and a frustrated cry burst from him as the figure slowly descended.

It was her. Amanda LaFleur. Dead again, but moving somehow.

As she drew close to him, a sourceless light flickered about her face. Sweeping her white gown aside, she stopped mid-step, and her long hair, rippling silkily, fanned out from around her head, sending baby-fine wisps across her pale, delicate face. Terror flooded Placidus and he drew back for a moment. There was an air of fragility about her, but something else, too. And as her gown belled gracefully about her ankles, her eyes shone with the brilliance of hope—but that deadly shine . . .

She's back from the dead.

She's come back to take me with her.

Placidus gazed at those eyes, mesmerized, lost in their thrall. And then her luminous, moon-white face seemed to smile.

What's behind that pale, beautiful face?

How will she end my life?

"Plllaaaccciiiddduuusss," she whispered, her soft voice chilling his flesh. "Come to me—up the sstttaaaiiirrrrsss."

He heard a groan and knew that he had made the sound, and he felt the first stirrings of surrender. She stood there on the steps, as on a scaffold, beckoning him upward, and he was powerless to resist the call.

"Plllaaaaccciidduuss" she urged softly, "come up."

He felt a cry rising in his throat but, uttering no word, he mounted one step, stopping to search her waxen, pallid face. He saw much there that frightened him yet, somehow, that also offered a thread of hope.

"Placidus, don't be afraid. I haven't come to huurrrrttt you," she whispered, her voice hollow and distant.

He mounted another step. Then another, until soon he was standing before her, his face level with her shoulders. Mouth agape, heart pounding frantically, he stood there in her light and caught a glimpse of something shiny in her small hand. A crab knife.

His face gnarled up like a twisted root, a picture of horror in the face of death, his own. But he did not cry out. He stood there in her brilliance, certain that she would slit his jugular in one swift slash. As she raised the blade, he could already feel his own warm blood emptying from his neck, washing the life from his long dead soul.

But good, he thought. *My misery will end here, this very moment.*
Let it come, then. Slice my throat, little angel.
End this hell of mine and let me go on to another.

She raised the knife over her head, and as her eyes grew even more brilliant, he closed his. But then she opened her palm and the knife fell stone-like from her fingers, bouncing heavily against the wooden stairs. The noise startled Placidus, and when he opened his eyes, she bent gently, touching his forehead with her lips. It was a chaste kiss, and in its sincerity Placidus felt a sudden warmth. The girl seemed to blush, color nearly returning to her pale face.

She then dropped the top of her gown and a small hand stole out, taking his wrinkled one, pressing it against the dark, discolored stains that ruptured the soft skin of her torso. He touched one of her wounds lightly, then drew back as if she was on fire.

"Don't be afraid Placidus," she murmured, seeking his hand again. "Feel my suffering. Touch my wounds."

A deep shame brought a hot flush to his cheeks, burning him to the core, but he meekly allowed her to move his hands about her body. He was so touched by these cuts, so consumed with sorrow, that he began to weep gently, clinging to her like a drowning man to timber in a turbulent sea. He looked up at her, then dropped his eyes, unable to stare at such purity and innocence.

She cast her eyes down on him, lifted a small hand and ran it softly over his balding crown, aware of his profound loneliness. "LLuuuccciiifffuuurrr has worked his will on you," she whispered. "He has forced his wicked visions into your heart so that when you sleep at night, they come alive and torment you. You haven't been well since that day of the—rope. And worse yet, when you found me, it was to become your physical and spiritual destruction. You are near that final point now, sweet Placidus, but I've come to help you."

"But my dreams. In my dreams you—"

"He has twisted the truth. I am not the girl of your nightmares. He has used my image to destroy your faith. So beware, Placidus, you must bathe yourself in the blessed water. Come alive again. God forgives all who seek forgiveness, but not those who remain silent. You must plead for mercy, Placidus, because your time is nearly gone. You must let the truth release you. Contrition, Placidus, will be your only salvation."

The old religious man began to sob, his chest convulsing against her. He leaned over to kiss her cheek . . . and instead heard himself whisper, "So then—you know."

"Yes, Placidus, I know, as do all those souls in that blessed Place. But there is time. Seek forgiveness and cleanse yourself. Shed your grief."

They stood there together holding each other quietly, he weeping, her caressing, until finally the light about her face began to dim. "Reach down, Placidus, and take the knife. Take it to the attic. Hang it there in a secret place. It will taste blood again, healing blood, the blood of salvation."

Trembling, Placidus stooped to retrieve the weapon. When he looked up, he was alone in the blackness of the stairwell. But he felt the handle of the crab knife in his palm, and with the unquestioning obedience of an old dog, he trudged to the attic, flipped on the lights, and found a nail protruding crookedly from one of the framing timbers toward the rear of the attic.

The knife handle had been drilled, and from this tiny hole hung a string which had been neatly looped, tied and snipped. Slipping this over the nail, he turned to leave, calmer somehow.

Chapter Thirty-One

Jacqueline LaFontaine was already in a foul mood when she heard the knock on her door. She had just wasted the better part of the last half hour stirring roux for her gumbo, only to notice too late that tiny black specks were bubbling to the top of the reddish brew. "Dammit," she said, "burnt after all that! Who's *there*!"

The knock came again. Irritated, she removed the smoking skillet from the stove and flipped the wooden spoon into the sink. "I'm coming," she huffed, moving to open the door.

"LaFontaine?"

"Well, what is it?" she barked, giving the big man a sharp and impatient stare.

"Something for you," the man said, pointing to a large chest strapped to a two wheeled dolly. "If you are Madame LaFontaine, that is."

She studied the box for a moment, suddenly aware of the stranger's strong smell. "I didn't order anything," she said. "Who sent it?"

"From a friend," he grunted with the serious expressionless of a man who did not enjoy performing favors.

"Ha! I only have two friends left on this earth, Peter Toche and Joey Broussard—the rest are dead."

The huge stranger lifted his hat with the flick of a finger, exposing dark, sullen eyes that seemed to mock the old woman. "Well, this is from one of those dead friends," he said.

Jacqueline LaFontaine's lips drew back in a humorless grin and she gave a sweeping gesture with her right hand. She was experiencing the beginning of contempt and already despised this man for his manner. "And who the hell would *that* be?"

"An old man. Said you would know what to do with it. Said there was something special in this trunk—something to keep you company. His name was Joe Kuluz. He was an old fisherman."

At this, the old woman's face contracted a moment, then involuntarily softened. In her heart she felt a pang, a surging joy, and she reached back in her mind for the face of Joe Kuluz, and his touch. "Joe?" she said, her lip trembling a bit.

"Yeah, but I don't have all damn day. Mind if I bring it in? I've got other things to do, you know."

She didn't like the man's tone, and though a tiny warning buzz did sound in her brain, it wasn't loud enough because the stranger had managed to unearth in her a mountain of emotions that she had tried to bury since Joe Kuluz's funeral. She pushed the screen door aside and ushered him in.

"Damn heavy," he said, removing his hat to mop aside the beads of perspiration from just below the crease left by it. The rest of his head was shaven and dry.

"Well, come on in then, get it off the dolly and be on your way."

The man looked at her sharply. "Joe Kuluz said I was to be there when you opened the trunk," he insisted.

The old woman's eyes narrowed and her face drew up into a scowl. She threw both fists to her hips. "Just who the hell are you, mister, and where did you know Joe Kuluz from?"

He swept the question aside. "Look, I didn't come here to bitch and argue with you. I simply—"

"What's your name? I haven't seen you around here before, not ever. And what are you to Joe Kuluz?"

"The boats," he snapped. "Used to work with him a long time ago. So what's it going to be, lady? Do we open it together, or do I take the trunk and leave?"

"Very well, then," she said heatedly, "open it."

He loosened the straps and with great effort pushed the chest upright. He fished a key from his pocket and slipped it into the padlock. "There," he said, nearly smiling, "open it."

She let out her breath gently, pressing down her contempt for the stranger. She removed the padlock, dropping it to the floor, and lifted the lid back on its hinges. She stared a moment, as if puzzled, then stepped back as a wave of revulsion struck her and the horror in the box suddenly registered in her aging, unprepared mind. Her hands flew to her face like startled birds sent aflutter, and a slow, rasping moan escaped her throat.

Just as suddenly, the stranger grabbed her about the neck and picked her up, shoving her face nearer the chest, forcing her to look down into it. "Do you recognize him, whore!"

She wanted to scream but his fingers were locked about her throat in a crushing vice that caused her to gurgle helplessly. Though her breath was leaving her and she felt a fainting dizziness edged with red and white spots, she thrashed out with the instinctive fear and fierceness of a cornered rat because she understood instantly that this hulking stranger had meant all along to kill her.

Throwing her right arm over her shoulder, she reached back and raked her nails across his eye, again and again.

"Aiee!" he shrieked, not prepared for a fight. "Damn you!"

The grip on her throat loosened a notch, and she let loose a burst of profanity. Then, though her feet dangled half a foot from the floor, she kicked backward and upward, hoping to strike a kneecap or his crotch.

This only infuriated her assailant, and he locked his fingers tight again and began to shake her, swinging her about from left to right like a metronome, choking the life from her.

Madame LaFontaine suddenly went limp. And though there was still some fight in her bitter, hateful old bones, she fell limp purposefully, as if to cooperate with her executioner.

Malik squeezed harder, until his fingers began to pale and he heard something snap. "There, you whore, join the old fisherman!"

She closed her eyes a final time and tried to erase the face of Joe Kuluz gazing up at her from inside the chest with the blank look of the embalmed. He lay there, stuffed in the chest, gazing upward but with closed and dead eyes, hands folded over his stomach. "Joe!" she screamed. "Joe! He's dug you up from the dead!"

As her eyes squeezed tightly shut, forever, she saw not the dead face of Joe Kuluz, but his smiling and mischievous face, a face weathered by the sea and the wind and difficult times—a face full of gentle meaning for a worn, bitter woman who had enjoyed little during her empty existence on this earth.

Kill me, you foul bastard, she thought, already forgetting the face of the intruder. *I'm ready so make it quick.*

* * *

Contrition

Peter entered the chapel of the Brothers' house and found Placidus prostrate before the altar. He took a seat in the rear pew to wait for Placidus to finish his prayers. As he watched the old religious man before him, he thought back to his adolescent years in Placidus's Latin class. Placidus had been a good instructor, caring and sensitive. And even though Placidus had been the butt of many student jokes back then, the serious academic students always gravitated toward him.

Placidus had had a quiet grimness about him, one that he usually shielded with unnecessarily polite smiles. This grimness had always been attributed to his deep faith in the Almighty, and those who knew him saw nothing out of place. Simply a cautious secretiveness, they claimed. But now, as Peter observed his former teacher before the altar, Peter wondered about that wall of silence that Placidus had so carefully erected decades ago.

After several minutes, Placidus made his way up from the floor, crossed himself and moved to the pew Peter occupied. He looked haggard and unkempt. The rough stubble covering his pink face was uncharacteristic, and Peter guessed that all pretense of personal hygiene and grooming had ceased weeks before.

"And so," Peter smiled, "what can I do for you today, Brother? Brother Patrick says you've been feeling a bit worse than usual, so I was a bit surprised to hear that you wanted to see me. He wants to take you to see Doctor Wainwright later today, you know."

Placidus rubbed his eyes with a thumb and middle finger, pinching them together then spreading them apart. "Ah, Peter." He sighed. "I'm afraid a doctor could do little to help this tired old soul. That's why I've asked you to come by. I'm worn to the nubs. I see now that there is only one hope for me, only one path to take now. I must bare myself—to the world."

Peter fixed his eyes on Placidus and cleared his throat, hiding the discomfort that suddenly crept into his head. "Certainly," he said.

There was a queer moment of silence. Placidus started to speak twice, but faltered. Then, flushing deeply, he began to spill words out in a burst. "A dark, hidden scum has covered my soul for—over forty years, and I mean to clear it away. I must. I beg your patience and understanding. Stand by me now. You are my friend, but I speak to you now as one who must reveal past sins. I am a—*criminal*."

Peter closed his eyes and covered his face with an outstretched palm. Somewhere deep within he felt his heart go limp, as if confronted by a great event, one that once released, could never be retracted. Placidus quietly continued, content that Peter was not looking at him and happier still that he himself was about to rip through that wall of guilt and self-hate that had confined him to a private hell for the better portion of his adult life.

"When I first came to this house," Placidus began, "I was young and naïve, but I did truly believe in doing God's work. And still do—I think. I was full of hope and sacred intentions. The world was mine to set right, the children of God mine to shepherd. May God forgive us our detours. Then, into this blissful, blessed world of mine came . . . a friend.

"Upon his arrival to this campus, this young Bother was assigned to share my room. The house was full back then. We were doubled and tripled up. The school was a hive of activity. Oh, Peter, those were good days and I miss them dearly.

"His name was Phillip Allison. He befriended me from the start. We both taught Latin, enjoyed classical music, and were budding young theologians who had published papers on the Renaissance. We would stay up nights and debate the historical evolution of the Church, or the downfall of tradition and the upsurge of secularism.

"I found in him the brother I never had, the friend I had so longed for since childhood. I was always timid as a child, you know, Peter. Afraid, I suppose. Making friends for me was impossible because idle chatter and small talk came hard for me and I was forever too embarrassed to even introduce myself. I always felt clumsy.

"But Brother Allison was my opposite. He was handsome, outgoing, popular amongst peers, loved by superiors, envied and admired by subordinates. He took me under his wing, forgave me my shyness, overlooked my lack of social cleverness.

"But he was one of those cunning creatures who from birth weighs and measures the world around him. He was a flatterer, a politician, and above all, a sneak. He could shake your hand and win your eternal loyalty with that engaging smile and wit, then verbally disembowel you the second your back was turned. He could lie to your very face and somehow manage to make you feel guilty for doubting his word. All these things I watched him perform with perfect ease.

"But he had two weaknesses. He couldn't walk away from whiskey, and he had an eye for women. And though he managed to keep his intentions in check much of the time, he would slip, and it wasn't just women. He liked high school girls most, and had his way with several over his first three years at Saint Gregory.

"I knew about each and every one of these conquests. He delighted in telling me, *only* me, because he knew I adored him and forgave him anything. Above all, he knew I was a coward, too. To be sure, I advised him to stop these practices, but he persisted. I pretended to be horrified, of course, but soon found myself gradually becoming titillated by his graphic, detailed descriptions.

"Then, over the years—and this shames me, Peter—I found myself becoming . . . jealous . . . of the girls. I began to wish for his affections more and more, but he focused on his seductions of the young ladies. I began to resent them

"But I never let on. God, the very thought of physical affection with my friend Phillip Allison shamed me to the core. I prayed on the matter. But in my mind images would arise, me and him together, touching, caressing. Embracing."

Peter moved his palm from his eyes and raised his head slowly. When his gaze met that of Placidus, Placidus did not look away. "Br-Brother Placidus," Peter stammered, "I—"

"Not a word, Peter. Let me finish. I'm so close now, finally. One night he came in drunk. It was late and he had sneaked up the fire escape. He stumbled into our room and I could smell the heavy aroma of whiskey and cheap perfume mixed with his own musk. He had been 'plowing the furrow' as he liked to put it. That night, this angered me.

"He launched into a laughing, drunken tirade about the softness of some fifteen-year-old girl's breasts and thighs. And then, as he stripped for bed, he pulled his underwear off and stood before me, exposing himself. Then, in his drunkenness, he said to me, 'Don't be mad at me, you big queer. If you were a woman, I'd give you some of this, but you're not, so you'll only get to dream about it!' This hurt me, Peter. It crushed me.

"I don't know what came over me, but I jumped from my bed and slapped him. Then I grabbed his privates. It happened so fast, and he was so drunk, he began to laugh. I was afraid he would wake the house. In my panic and anger, I threw him to the bed and covered his head with a pillow. My hands were still on his privates . . . I—"

"Brother Placidus," Peter interrupted, seeing that the Brother had turned nearly purple with shame, "you don't have to go on."

"And I—I began to touch him with both hands. I sat on his head to hold him down. I started to beat at him and abuse him. It happened so fast, as if my whole life of rejection and humiliation revolted all at once. I turned him over on his belly, choking him, and I—pulled down my pajamas. I spread his legs and—"

Peter shifted uneasily in the pew and turned away, unwilling to watch Placidus's utter humiliation.

"I—violated him that night, Peter, over and over. I couldn't stop. I hated him so much, and wanted him, too. He began to cry, like a child, but I felt so strong, and I felt no pity for him. In his drunken state, he finally passed out.

"When he woke up that next morning, he jumped up from the bed. He was hung over badly, but he remembered what happened, and, reconstructing the details, he went into a rage. Ranting one minute, then shame and silence, then violent outbursts of cursing and threats. He began to throw up then. I went to help him but he shoved me away and fled the room.

"That afternoon he asked the Provincial to assign him to another room. This he did with great insistence but without explanation. From that moment, he refused to speak to me or acknowledge my existence. He felt violated and angry, but *he* was a coward, too, I learned. He never breathed a word of that night to another soul because he was not accustomed to shame and refused to invite scandal upon himself or be the topic of gossip.

"Three weeks later he went to the attic. I saw him go and knew he had a rope in his hand. I didn't think much about it until a few minutes later when I heard a noise. Then it hit me. This crazy little man, this hypocritical coward meant to end his misery. I ran up the stairs and there he was, hanging from a rafter.

"But between the time he kicked the chair out from beneath his feet and the time the rope closed about his neck, he had yet another change of heart and decided he didn't really want to die. His hands were grabbing the rope above and he was trying to pull himself up. 'Placidus!' he cried. 'Save me!'

"I ran to him with every intention of hoisting him up, hoping he could monkey his way back up to the rafter, but as I pushed upward, grabbing him, I saw a note taped to his chest. 'Punish Placidus . . . he has violated God's law and me through rape,' the note said.

"He was still squirming and trying to wriggle his way up the rope, and I was still trying to hoist him up. But, Peter, that note made something snap inside me, coward that I am, coward that I have always been. I suddenly saw myself entangled in a scandal, driven from the order of the Holy Cross, shunned.

"I tore the note from his chest and stepped back. But he was almost to the rafter. He had one hand on it and the other just inches away. So then, Peter, oh Peter—I did a *horrible* thing. May God forgive me! I threw myself at Phillip Allison and pulled him down grabbing at his legs, letting the rope choke his dying words from his breath. 'Save me, Placidus,' he cried, dying. But I didn't, Peter. I killed him, to save myself. I took the note. I fled. I burned it, then pretended to find him dead in the attic a few minutes later. May God rest his scummy soul, Peter—and mine."

Peter's head slumped nearly to his lap. He wanted to say something, anything, but his groping mind found nothing, so he sat there dumbfounded, silent for several impossibly long minutes. Then finally he spoke. "Brother, it's a horrible burden you've carried all these years, and you have paid tenfold. I can't begin to fathom how torn you have been, secretly holding onto this, *grappling* with it. I—"

"Arrest me, Peter," the old religious muttered. He extended his wrists forward in an awkward gesture to be cuffed. "I can no longer live with myself."

Peter took a long and reflective look at Placidus. He stared into his eyes, beyond the tears, beyond the fatigue and desolation, into his conscience. Then he nodded, "Yes, Brother Placidus, I will take you in because you killed a man. A roach of a man, maybe, but a man nevertheless. But I won't take you in now. You've turned me on end with this story. I need time to absorb this. I . . . "

Placidus dropped his head and sighed. "You don't understand. I had a visitor the other night. She told me to shed my deceit. She told me to cleanse my hands. I must finally atone for my grievous sin, and I must do so immediately, Peter."

"A visitor?"

"It was a girl. Amanda LaFleur. She was an angel, Peter. I touched her wounds."

Peter immediately pitied the old man even more than before. *Delusions,* he thought, yet there was something so profound and calm in

Placidus's expression that Peter weighed the comment instead of shoving it aside. "Amanda? She came to you?"

"Yes—beautiful and alive. Full of grace. She said God forgives. But I know I must pay the cost if I am to be forgiven."

Peter slid closer to Placidus, and placed his hand behind Placidus's neck, affectionately. "My father, he suspected things, you know. He knew there was something more than a suicide in the attic."

Placidus nodded. "Yes, poor Victor. He was more clever than you knew, Peter. He could read a man's eyes. He kept coming back to the house again and again, kept probing. He dug up Brother Allison's indiscretions. He talked to the girls. But all this caused alarm with our Provincial and the bishop. They spoke to the mayor and the Chief of Police—silenced him."

"My father, there was more to him than I suspected. I could have done better by him."

"Indeed, Peter. When you were born he was so very proud. He adored you, but from the moment you could talk, it seemed you shunned him and pushed him away. You were a strange child, so sensitive and caring, yet you seemed to push your father away at every opportunity. You forced him to begin hating you by adolescence and into your adulthood. It was you, not him. You were not an easy son."

Peter looked down and nodded. "Yeah, maybe so," he said. "I was busy looking at him—I should have been looking at myself."

"Thank you for coming here today, Peter. I will wait for your instructions, then. I will not run or hide. I will be right here. Please know that I feel a great weight has been lifted from my neck by baring my crime to you." Then he withdrew his hand and placed it across his heart. "And yet," he calmly said, "I feel that someone, or something hideous, is coming after me. I feel a dread."

"Yes," said Peter with equal calm, "I feel it coming, too, for *both* of us, and others that are dear to us."

* * *

Dawn cast an eerie, pallid light over the Gulf as winds and rain heralded nature's rebellion. The whisper of the tide became a rushing flood and the wind a moan, sending a greenish-black wash of ocean surging over the barrier islands, flattening dunes and snapping pines under the crush of tons of swirling sea.

Contrition

Most of the fishing fleet had moved inland, up the channels and bayous to weather the storm, but some had pressed the clock, choosing to run their nets and long-lines until the eleventh hour. They had been frustrated that the season's previous storms had shortened their fishing season and gambled that this storm, like its predecessors, would fizzle into nothing.

But now those little ships heaved through a backwash of thundering surf whose spume rose like towering walls of mist in the strange light of a hidden sun. Their compasses pointed north to the coast as sea-buffeted captains fought their wheels to stay their courses. Their ships would rise like tiny corks up the rolling mountains of surf, teeter perilously upon wind driven crests, then disappear, dropping into great chasms of boiling sea.

Timbers groaned and bent as the vessels wallowed in bottomless wave troughs, then strained even more as the ships shot skyward under the forward rush of massive swells. Radios crackled with exchanges and distress calls. The voices were urgent but controlled—voices of men facing impending doom yet refusing to acknowledge panic.

Forward the file of fishermen surged, fighting off imminent annihilation with that peculiar courage that only seasoned men of the sea can summon. These men had survived a lifetime of storm-driven weather, but this, they sensed, was something beyond past experience. They were riding the very edge of extinction, pushed by gale-force winds, driven by an erupting sea. They began to think of their wives and children. They clung to whatever they could grasp, some even lashing themselves to rigging as walls of billowing water washed over the stern, throwing everything forward, flooding the decks.

Just south of Dog Keys Pass the *Fairy Princess*, a sixty-foot shrimper of thirty seasons, went down in the gale. A huge wave smashed over the transom, ripping the hull apart and filling the cabin with water. Every man aboard was washed over the bow except the captain, known as old Bosarge, and he was flung into the wheel with such velocity that his skull cracked, killing him instantly. Slumped into the wheel, his arms entangled among the spokes, he went under with the boat he himself had built as a younger man with his brother and Didier LaFleur.

Just to starboard ran the *Miss Julie*. Her captain, Tookey Marvar, spat tobacco between his shoes and cursed as he watched the *Fairy Princess* disappear into the blackness. He quickly surveyed the water and saw three men clinging to a shattered fragment of hull. One of the men was his brother-in-law. Marvar spat again, mopped dribbling tobacco from his grizzled chin with a forearm, and saw the faces of his now-widowed sister and her three daughters.

Then, in a moment of supreme selflessness, he spun the wheel sharply to bring his boat about in an attempt to collect the three survivors. The effort was futile, however, and his courage was quickly punished. As the *Miss Julie* turned, it was broadsided by a thundering wall of surf and foam, and the boat went on its side, then turned turtle. Every man aboard was either crushed or caught beneath the hull and drowned in seconds.

Behind the *Miss Julie* came the *Gulf Tide*, the largest wooden vessel of the fleet. Captain Jojo Skremetta had witnessed the catastrophe and he was fighting to keep his ship off the wallowing wreckage of the *Miss Julie*. He scanned the seething water for survivors but saw nothing. Then, clear of the wreckage, he heard a faint cry in the wind and looked to port where he spotted the men who had been washed overboard from the *Fairy Princess*—but there were only two, hanging desperately to an ice chest bobbing wildly in the boiling wash.

Captain Skremetta tried heroically to ride the surf toward them, but his boat rolled nearly to its side and he was almost thrown from the wheel as tons of sea washed over the deck. Clinging to the wheel with outstretched arms, his fingers locking, he grimaced as cold sea water flushed over him, then into his eyes and mouth. He felt himself being dragged. On and on the water came, pulling, tearing at his grip until, out of breath, about to release himself, the *Gulf Tide* somehow righted itself.

Wiping his face and regaining his stance at the wheel, Skremetta turned his boat away from the two men in the water. He shrugged at them helplessly. Though he could not bear the idea of leaving them, neither could he sacrifice his boat and entire crew in a suicidal rescue. The two men stared at him, shocked. Then compassion swept over their weary faces. They understood.

Skremetta raised a fist to the rain and screamed, but his rage went unheard above the sound and fury of the storm. His crew, to a man, turned away as their captain cursed, and they prayed that they would not meet the same fate as the men in the water. They prayed for a miracle, that the two men might survive. But even as they implored God, one of the men in the water lost his grip. He waved his arm in a bleak farewell, saluted his friend, Captain Skremetta, then released the clip to his life jacket and pulled it off, flinging it to the sky. Then, grimacing weakly, he opened his mouth and began sucking in the briny sea.

"No!" cried Captain Skremetta, pleading to his friend not to surrender. "No! Damn you, Albert! No!"

But the man's head disappeared, and Skremetta slumped helplessly over the wheel, covering his eyes with his forearm as if to dispel his grief. It was simple enough, but crushing. His friend had lost his will to live. Not on this stormy day, but weeks before when his daughter's mutilated body was discovered in the attic on the grounds of Saint Gregory.

Jojo Skremetta straightened himself at the wheel and grew still, taking on the rigid appearance of a stone sculpture. There was little time for grief and it was entirely up to him whether his crew would live through the day. He set a determined course north and bitterly swore to himself that *he* would not be the one to tell Didier LaFleur that he had now lost the last living member of his family.

Chapter Thirty-Two

White spray erupted onto and over the seawall, spilling in foamy swirls onto the Intercoastal Highway. Huge live oaks began to bow and heave to the storm, their roots freed from the earth by prying wind. Rain fell in slicing, diagonal sheets, and from Fisherman's Point the gray horizon melded into the dark, frothing sea, making sky and water indistinguishable.

Coast dwellers began obeying impulses of survival that registered only faintly in their minds. And though a sense of hurry crept into them by mid-afternoon, they felt they were performing the sequences of a familiar drill rather than preparing for possible doom. Glass was taped, windows boarded, water stored, batteries and canned goods gathered, important documents and family photo albums secured, cash withdrawn from banks, and generators serviced.

They went about these tasks cheerfully, neighbor helping neighbor, families and friends gathering at common houses. The hurricane was spoken of with caution but not terror, because they supposed that though this great storm might be costly and bothersome, it was an inconvenience more than a threat.

Many would go without power or running water for several days after the hurricane's departure, and there would be much cleaning up to do afterwards. There had been little loss of life related to the numerous storms over the decades since Hurricane Camille wreaked its havoc in 1969 on an unsuspecting Gulf Coast. Camille had far exceeded original expectations, and in her wake, she had left a legacy by which storms would be measured for generations to come.

Saint Ann Cathedral, like the rest of Fisherman's Point, stood on a rise just north of the highway that looked down on the beach, Heron Island and the Gulf. The sea had only once violated that rise, in 1969 when Camille smashed ashore, sending her thundering thirty-foot wall of water over the highway and up the hill, washing away seafood factories, houses, and churches, and drowning victims by the dozens.

And though Camille was spoken of with great reverence, time has a way of softening dread over the years. Consequently, when evacuation orders were issued, many of the Gulf residents ignored them, stubbornly refusing to leave their homes and personal possessions. Along the entire length of the Mississippi Coast, there were no more stubborn, self-reliant people than those from Fisherman's Point.

So even as the wind grew from a whistle to a howl, and the rain grew from a downpour to a flood, and the sea swirled about with increasing anger, residents refused to leave. They chose, instead, to work in the blinding rain and wind, moving about the gloom in the circles of their lantern lights, making last ditch efforts to fortify their homes as the meager light of dusk began to fade to black. If they had seen what was already occurring along the water's edge, however, they might have chosen to abandon their futile efforts and head north.

The Old French House had lost half of its roof by late afternoon, and the pummeling storm tide had begun to undermine the outbuildings and the pier. Most of the boats in the harbor had moved to the safety of the bayous, but five had been left, and they had each been hurtled upon the now disintegrating wharfs. And everywhere debris and flood wood littered the harbor, rising and falling with the waves.

By dusk the sea had risen another eighteen feet and began sending great waves reeling into the yards and gardens of the first bank of houses of Fisherman's Point. Fences and sheds collapsed like kindling and washed away on debris-littered waves. Surges were lapping at the foundations of the houses, scooping out scars of earth with watery claws.

For the first time, those who had refused to evacuate began to doubt the wisdom of staying behind. Families huddled together against the south walls of their tiny wood-frame homes, and as darkness approached, they lit candles and lanterns and ate quietly from cans, wondering if this storm would be as disastrous as Camille in 1969. Surely not, they agreed. But as night progressed, and the rain, hail, and wind battered their nests with relentless fury, the specter of Camille loomed ever larger.

The men left the floor every now and then to peer out of opened doors at the blackness and listen to the sound of things crashing in the night—trees splitting, the crescendo of wind, the staccato crack of a million lethal missiles, and the dull thunder of tightly closed buildings imploding.

As the killer right-front quadrant of the hurricane approached, they could see the bluish blazing and violet arcing of exploding electrical transformers flashing in the darkness. At times they heard voices in the street, the skitter of footsteps, strange knockings at the door, shouts, front porches coming apart, sirens, and always—the howl of that meteorological monster of the sea.

They had stayed on Fisherman's Point because their neighbors stayed. Courage in numbers—it was an infectious concept. But now, it was each family on its own, alone, isolated. The world and life itself had become that lantern-lit circle in the south corner of the house, sitting atop blankets and mattresses, hoping the water would not continue to rise, hoping there wouldn't be another thirty-foot tidal wave, wondering about fathers and brothers who hadn't come in the day before with the rest of the fleet. Where could they be? Had they taken refuge elsewhere?

And as the water began to seep under the door, they began to wonder again why they had stayed. And finally, they began to pray.

* * *

A thousand noises fractured the night as Joseph and Tristan sat huddled on the floor of Joseph's cramped hallway, lost in the flickering dance of a yellow candle. They sat there silently, half in and half out of the pale circle of light thrown out by the tiny flame. Each man was visible to the other up to the neck, while eyes and face remained obscure, as if by design, to conceal the apprehension that had begun to etch itself into the expression of each.

A funereal quiet had fallen between them as they listened to the thunderous eruptions of sound outside, things collapsing, things ripping free, things disintegrating. At times the sounds would dissipate, leaving only the sharp rattling of the rain and hail against the tin roof. But then sudden gusts of wind would sweep against the house again and they could hear explosions in sporadic bursts, some crackling sharply in close proximity, others muffled by distance.

Joseph tried to shut out these sounds, in order to listen more closely to something that was much less acute but more constant. Closing his eyes, he focused south, and somewhere between the crackle of thunder and the whistle of gale force winds, somewhere beneath the steady destruction of man-made structures, he could hear the sea, rising, swelling forward, careening up the rise toward Saint Ann Cathedral and Fisherman's Point.

"Shit," he murmured softly.

"What is it?" said Tristan, leaning into the circle of light so his face was illuminated for the first time since dusk.

"The water," said Joseph, as lines of strain began to crease his face. "She's coming up fast. I wasn't counting on that. Nobody was. This is going to be worse than expected."

Tristan cupped his chin. "Should we leave then?"

Joseph sighed heavily. "Too risky now. Sounds like a damn firing range out there, things flying around everywhere. We could easily get killed out in the open." Then he shook his head. "Wish I knew where the hell Madame LaFontaine was. Just not like her to simply disappear like this. Haven't seen her for two days now."

"The storm, maybe she left?"

"Her? Never. Besides, she doesn't have any family anywhere—nowhere to evacuate to."

Tristan nodded, then said, "But what about the water, Joseph?"

"Yeah, the water. We'll wait it out . . . maybe it's peaked, who knows?"

Tristan stared at the candle a moment and shifted position. "Madame LaFontaine—you still think she will show up, don't you?"

"Yes, damn her," said Joseph. "Doesn't make sense. No note, nothing. She's out and about somewhere. I can feel it."

"But if she has no one, where would she go?"

Before Joseph could answer, heavy footsteps bounded and splashed up the porch, followed by a loud banging against the door. "Joseph! Open up! Are you there!"

"It's Peter," said Joseph, quickly rising and moving to the door. "Come in!"

Peter stepped in and the wind slammed the door behind him. "Geez!" he whistled, shining his flashlight about the room. He was dripping wet.

"Damn, it's a mess out there." As he said this, he folded his glasses, tucked them away in a pocket and began to shake himself dry, like dog would after a short swim in the lake.

"Got word from the Coast Guard earlier about the long-line fleet—half of them finally made it in several hours ago."

"Half?" said Joseph. "Where's the rest?"

Peter pressed the palm of his hand flat against his hair and squeegeed it from front to back, then shook his head. "Lost, went down . . . the *Miss Julie*, the *Reverie*, the *Pursuit*, the *Fairy Princess*."

Tristan lowered his head and made the sign of the cross.

Joseph sighed heavily, slowly absorbing the grim news. "The *Fairy Princess*? Old Bosarge and his crew?" Then he thought a moment and wilted. "Albert LaFleur was on that ship."

"*Gone*—drowned . . . " said Peter.

"Oh my God," said Joseph. "Poor Didier. How much more can a man lose in this life? Does he know yet?"

"Yeah, I was the one that gave him the news—left him just an hour ago."

"How was he?" said Tristan, finally looking up.

"Not well—he *buckled*, went down on a knee. I had to help him up."

"So where is he now?" said Joseph, still shaking his head with sorrow.

"After he finally got up, he said there was work to do, said he was going to take the *Miss Marie* up the marsh behind Saint Gregory and help some of the old people get out, like he did during Camille. Lots of injuries all up and down the coast already tonight. Ambulances and squad cars are running the roads like army ants. Many dead reported down in Pass Christian and Long Beach. Biloxi and Gulfport have had casualties, too. It's going to get worse, landfall's just hours away." Then he paused a moment. "Where's Madame? Thought she'd be here with you."

"Don't know." Joseph shrugged.

"What?"

"We couldn't find her anywhere," said Tristan. "I think maybe she left, but Joseph—"

"No, she never evacuates, never has, never will," said Peter. "Well, I'll be damned. Anyway, time's running out. Seawater's already on the porch and coming up fast. We've got to go."

Joseph palmed his mouth, vexed, and exhaled through spread fingers. "Maybe it's a good thing she's not here. Maybe someone dragged her to a shelter or something."

"I understand your concern," said Tristan. "But I must be honest at this point. I feel something urging us away from this place, Joseph.

Contrition

And true, if God means for us to die here this night, then so be it—but I do not feel that that is his intention. I feel like a rabbit trapped in a hole here. We should leave."

Joseph shrugged, raising his shoulders to his ears, and sighed with the weariness of a man who has made a poor decision and has just begun to weigh the consequences. "Okay," he said.

But suddenly the small house cracked loudly and shifted as a ripping sound shook the rafters, peeling sheets of tin roofing away in rolls, exposing the three men to a deluge of rain and hailstones.

"Get down!" Peter cried.

"Jesus!" Joseph yelled, startled, stumbling in a burst of blind motion over Tristan who was still seated. Tristan, too, was startled, and instinct drove him, crawling backward like a rousted crab, carrying Joseph on his belly. "Got to get out of here!" Joseph shouted. "We're getting soaked and the water's coming in the doorway!"

Peter began to laugh at their comic posture, sure that they looked like some prehistoric insect scooting down the hall, connected as if by some bizarre twist of nature. But humor quickly fled in the face of destruction. When they found their feet, they quickly discovered that the water was now well above their ankles. All three quickly made their way out to the porch.

The foundation of the house was completely surrounded by seawater. Peter stepped down, and as his legs disappeared in the brine, he stood there a moment, the water about his calves and thighs. Then, shielding his head and eyes from the rain, he looked out toward what was once the beach. "Come on," he said finally, satisfied that the sea would rise even more before receding. "Madame's foundation is a good three feet higher than Joseph's. "Quick!"

Tristan and Joseph obediently sloshed into the water and waded behind Peter to Madame LaFontaine's porch which was still well above water level. As they entered the kitchen, the beam of Peter's flashlight splashed off the walls, throwing a pale luminescence about the room which allowed him to appraise the furnishings.

"If the water comes in," said Peter motioning to the corner, "you two get on the buffet, I'll take the table."

"Will it stop there?" asked Tristan.

"Can't imagine it'd keep coming much higher. Water didn't even come in the house during Camille. If it does, though, we won't want to get trapped in the attic so we'll just have to swim out, keep heading north."

"We'll trust your judgment, Peter," said Tristan. Then there came a calmness in Tristan's voice that both puzzled and reassured Peter. "There will be much to do after the storm. The dead, the suffering." Then he took a seat and closed his eyes, covering them with a palm, and his lips began to move as if speaking to someone. After several moments he stopped and looked at Joseph. "I pray for them, Joseph. There will be many, many dead tonight, and most will not be ready for judgment."

Joseph nodded. "Like Madame. Something has happened. I keep thinking she will show up, but in my heart I feel that something bad has occurred. Am I foolish to even hope now?"

Tristan shrugged with uncertainty. "*Dum spiro, spero*—while I breathe, I hope. Hope is what keeps man crawling forward through the darkness, century after century, age after age. It is quite possible that she has encountered what we will all encounter. If that is the case, then she has never made her peace with God. She has suffered in this life, yes, but she does not begin to understand the true nature of suffering. She will suffer tenfold in the next life, and the loss of a child will seem but a droplet in the sea of despair. But there is always hope, Joseph, when all else fails. Perhaps we will find her yet."

* * *

As Tristan talked, water began seeping along the baseboards like tiny sand-filled bubbles rising from a freshly unearthed spring, slowly at first. The suddenly, it came spraying up like a giant fountain through the floor-furnace grate and from beneath the kitchen door.

"Christ!" said Peter. "She's coming in fast! Get up on the furniture!"

There was no mistaking the alarm and urgency in Peter's voice as he mounted the table and ushered the others onto the buffet top. Then he flipped his flashlight on and watched as water swirled around the furniture legs, submerging them, visibly working its way up the walls, filling the house.

But what the men could not see was the effect of tons of invading sea on the foundation below. Gushing forward in relentless, heaving waves of broken foam lines, the water quickly filled the crawlspace beneath the house, and as it rose, it stripped the screws that held the large floor furnace grate in position. The grate rose on this tide and fell away. And from the earth below the crawlspace, two dark forms stiffly rose out of the earth, like inflated, perpendicular balloons, and were pushed upward, forced through the opening and up into the kitchen.

Peter, standing atop the table, was moving his flashlight about the length of the kitchen, appraising the wisdom of flight, when the luminous cylinder of his light grazed across something large and dark floating next to the table, bumping it. He bent over and kicked at it lightly with the toe of his shoe. It was solid. "Tristan, lean over and give me a hand here," he said.

At that very moment another form surfaced, bumping into the first. Peter dug for his glasses, slipped them over his nose, then dabbed his hand in the black water. Reaching out, he pulled at the first object. It bobbed under his touch, then rose another inch or two under the swell of the rising sea, and Peter could distinguish white fibers like those on the end of a mop, fanning out and rippling in that filthy current. Leaning forward, he pulled at the fibers, spun the object about, and then, gazing downward, tried to determine what it was he was fishing out of the water. It was difficult through his foggy glasses.

But then a light of understanding briefly broke upon his face. Then confusion again. Then dismay as he felt himself go cold from the roots of his hair to the tips of his fingers. Gasping, he went rigid as a stick, then dissolved as if a spring somewhere within had suddenly snapped free, collapsing his arms to his side. He slumped forward, nearly losing his balance, and himself.

Tristan, seeing only Peter's back, heard a deep shuddering breath. "Peter? What is it?"

There was no reply. Peter, on one knee, trembling, covered his eyes. Tristan stepped from the buffet top onto the table and moved next to him. The combined weight of the two men was more than the table could bear, however, and the spindly legs began to rock. Tristan steadied himself, then peered over Peter's shoulder, focusing his light onto the shape that was by now floating nearly parallel to the table top. He instantly understood Peter's reaction.

There was Jacqueline LaFontaine, floating face up, her face more pale than winter's moon, her eyes vacant and dull. Next to her floated Joe Kuluz, and in death together, both were more ghostly even than in life, their faces barely recognizable.

"Joseph, it's Madame," whispered Peter, "and Joe Kuluz."

Joseph had been watching Tristan's actions and had already recognized what was occurring. "My God!" he cried. "Madame, my poor old Jacqueline!" The words tumbled out in a passion and his voice rang with pain and confusion as the two corpses bobbed about in the half gloom of the flashlight, bumping against each other like buoys in the rising water, as if tethered for eternity by some wretched, ill-conceived cord hidden below the surface.

There was in the tone in which Joseph pronounced the old woman's name a melancholy so solemn and quiet that Tristan began to tremble. Then Joseph cried that mournful laugh of the bereaved and reached out to draw Madame LaFontaine's face toward him. Kneeling to a crouch, he lifted her cold head and cradled it in his palms, and with a sort of veneration mingled with despair he raised his eyes, whose tears could not be seen in the darkness, and moaned.

Tristan crossed himself, feeling Joseph's anguish, aware that the crushing weight of God's impersonal justice was blotting out a lifetime of sentiment and love in the old priest. The whole interior of that soul was crumbling, because in that floating carcass, Joseph saw a surrogate mother and mourned, disbelieving. Peter, too, was mourning. But Tristan's vision transcended their earthly bonds of filial devotion, and Tristan saw damnation, bloated with only venom and bitterness. He suddenly felt the need to be away from this watery tomb.

"Peter," he whispered, "It's Malik. This is his work. We must leave. There is nothing to do here. She is gone and judgment has been passed." Then he reached over and touched Joseph's shoulders. They heaved a bit with weeping, and though Tristan felt both tearful for and tender toward the priest, he knew that he could only be outwardly strong if they were to survive. "I know you loved her, Joseph, but she is now but a distant shadow of your youth, a past shelter, but a false refuge. Her expression is not a peaceful one, nor is Joe Kuluz's. Theirs are the faces of the lost. We must leave."

Joseph felt the stirrings of anger and the tug of mortal love against spiritual faith. He could not bear the thought of abandoning this woman who had nurtured and comforted him over the long decades of his dubious treks in life. How could he leave her? How could he . . .

"Come on," said Peter. "Tristan's right. We've got to move, *now*."

Joseph let Madame LaFontaine's head slip back into the water, with resignation, entering that calm of despair that numbs the consciousness when anger at last subsides in the wake of futility and loss of hope. "We'll have to swim our way out, like Peter said," Joseph whispered, pulling each word from the depths of his knotted stomach, swallowing, as if his words left a bitter aftertaste. "Better head toward downtown. That's the highest elevation. If the sea rises any higher than that, we're lost. The whole town'll be lost."

"Remember, I don't swim," said Tristan.

"We'll help you," said Peter.

Joseph turned from the floating corpses. "Both of them were good in their own ways. It hurts to think that God would turn them away."

"God turns no one away," said Tristan. "You hurt inside now, but don't turn from the light, Joseph, as they did. It was their decision, not His. Such is the cost of free will. A terrible price for some, an eternal reward for others. *Sic itur ad astra*—such is the way to the stars. Now let's go."

"Let's hope the current doesn't drag us out," said Peter. "If it's still coming in we'll have to fight the cross currents, but it can be done. But if the water starts receding while we're in it, there'll be no hope." He stripped off his jacket and undid his shoulder holster, placing it on the table. "No need for this anymore. Father Joseph, off with your jacket and collar, better lighten the load. It's going to be a damn hard swim."

He slid off the table, pushing the corpses aside, and inched into the water until he felt the floor. He motioned for the others to follow as he waded toward the door. "Damn, door's stuck—too much water holding it in place. Quick! To the window." He groped about the water until he felt a chair. Then, raising it above his head, he moved to the window and threw the chair against it, showering glass about the room and outside in a rain of jagged splinters. He mounted the sill and hung there by holding onto opposite sides of the frame. He gazed out at the heavy encroaching sea, swirling about the house, which was now gurgling beneath the foundation. "Damn," he whispered.

"I'm ready, Peter," Tristan urged. "This house will soon be a wallowing shipwreck, and our coffin. My life is in your hands."

Staring out into the blackness, Peter briefly thought of Della, then entered the water as a serpent glides into a hole, dragging Tristan behind him. Joseph quickly followed.

Chapter Thirty-Three

They squirmed into the cold water like muskrats and pulled themselves along, only their eyes and noses above the surface. Tristan had hoped to touch bottom but found none. The sea was well above their heads and there would be no wading their way out. Frightened, he clung to Peter. It was going to be a hard swim, in a lashing rain, struggling against the heave and pull of currents and swells.

Against the dim red glare of a distant fire, the tops of houses could be distinguished; some of them had been pushed off their foundations by the rising tide and were slumping at angles. Their ghostly silhouettes were distorted by rain and obscurity, and their silence was appalling, like once living structures now defunct, broken-backed and dying.

But these perishing shells and the distant fire served as a beacon north, and the three men followed them, struggling against their own weight, struggling against the image of Jacqueline LaFontaine and Joe Kuluz. They would have prayed, perhaps, but their faith was lost in the immensity of nature's wrath, and like frightened children standing before the angry father, anticipating a most terrible and violent punishment, they sought only escape.

Then, out of the dark howling wind came a small voice, crying. A sudden flash of lightening revealed a baby floating on wreckage just feet away. Peter, with Tristan in tow, struggled to reach out but another flash revealed the mother, dead, still clinging to the wreckage with arms outstretched toward the infant, and this momentarily caused Peter to stop cold. Then he reached out again, but this caused his grip on Tristan to slip.

Tristan witnessed the scene, too, and felt great pity, but then, horrified, realized that Peter no longer had a hold on him and there came a moment when the instinct of self-preservation raised a howl and the animal reappeared in him. He thrashed about, grasping at the dark for Peter in a panic of kicking limbs and deep breaths. He felt the immense awakening of selfishness, and it suddenly shamed him. "Go for the child!" he cried, his mouth filling with sea. "Save the child, Peter!"

Peter, who was aware that he had released Tristan, suddenly froze, paralyzed by the dreadful choice. He lost sight of both Tristan and the infant in the darkness but another flash of lightening revealed Tristan's head slipping beneath the surface. Peter, torn, went for the child. But the wind and the current swept the wreckage aside, and Peter heard the infant's wail dissolve into the night, beyond any hope of retrieval.

Cursing, Peter turned and dove below the surface where Tristan had gone down and grabbed about blindly, hoping to feel something, or anything. But there was only the water. Surging upward, he broke the surface. "Joseph!" he cried out, "Tristan's down! Help!" Then he gulped air and went down again, kicking about wildly, groping. Suddenly he felt an arm, and in a joyous dance of heart and limbs, he dragged Tristan to the surface.

"The child!" spluttered Tristan, expelling water from his mouth and nose. "Did you save the child?"

"Be still, you'll take us both down! No, the child's—*gone.*"

"Go after him!" Tristan cried, breaking away from Peter's hold. "Leave me and go! There's—"

"He's *gone!*" Peter shouted angrily, reaching for Tristan's collar. "Dammit, he's gone. I couldn't even see which way he went! He's lost! We've got to move on."

Tristan shivered, suddenly remembering the horror of the pit, the suffering, the lost souls and despair. And as they struggled north in the fluttering storm light, he vowed to himself that he would not doubt God's will or grow weak. He prayed for the infant, fretted for him, begging God to be merciful, and found a small measure of comfort.

But he felt chilled by something in all this, too, as if directed forward from this imminent extinction toward another future danger, some unthinkable confrontation with eternity. And seen through the magnifying distortion of darkness, the destruction and death that swirled about him seemed but a backdrop to God's ultimate intention for a young Cluniac monk who ten centuries before had somehow, somewhere, lost the vision of his youth.

Some other voice from deep within spoke to him then, a voice which could have been his conscience, or Odo de Lagery, or Guillaume de Saint Germain, or simply the cold-driven rain that was banging in his head. He began to feel fretful as he listened to the wind. Then a jagged hand of lightning broke through the belly of black clouds overhead, each finger casting out a bluish light that hung there in the air, illuminating everything below like the bursting of an unexpected flare.

The child that was floating aboard the wreckage was revealed again. But this time the lost infant appeared older by several years, and he was standing, bathed in that bluish light, smiling, pointing north. In that instant Tristan recognized the snowy-headed child. It was—himself, as a boy. And suddenly the dead woman, still slumped over the edge of the wreckage, raised her head and gazed at him. It was his mother. She raised a bony finger, and like the child, pointed north, not for refuge, but for . . .

Tristan's eyes filled with a strange and dismal light as he looked with almost religious awe at the apparition before him, and there occurred in his heart one of those silences that occurs only in the presence of wonders, as the thunder seemed to fall away and the wind no longer howled. But the moment passed and the lightning dissolved, leaving Tristan in blackness, heralding the return of the storm's noisy wrath.

"Peter," Tristan whispered, clinging tightly to his friend who was still plowing blindly forward in the froth, "did you see?"

Peter heard nothing, saw nothing, and felt nothing but the drive to keep swimming northward. Tristan whispered his question again but his words were lost in thunder, and Tristan was left wondering whether he had seen an illusion, or Providence appearing in the guise of a vision. And when lightning struck again, the wreckage and the boy were gone, like the mother. On the surface there could not even be seen that quivering and trembling caused by a sinking object, or those obscure concentric circles that announce that something has been lost to the water below.

Peter continued to paddle with Tristan in tow, deafened by thunder, his face needled to numbness by rain. As he labored in the swirling liquid, he began to fall prey to the seesaw of his thoughts. Would they make it? Would the water suddenly begin to recede, washing away all hope of survival?

Contrition

Joseph was tiring and also felt himself falling prey to the seesaw of his thoughts. He began to grapple with his conscience, desperately wrestling against it. He felt derailed, uprooted, and his reflections grew darker and more terrible as he again sensed the face of Jacqueline LaFontaine. Would God truly predestine such a tragic ending? For what purpose? To what end?

But somehow his wavering, disjointed thoughts found solidarity as he looked ahead and saw Peter's struggle to save Tristan from the sea. His own doubts and confusion seemed to crumble away because of Peter's courage and Tristan's singular, quixotic quest. "Of the water we are born," Tristan had said, "expelled from woman's womb. And of the water we are *reborn*, a baptism of cleansing water and the salt of our tears."

As Joseph remembered these words, the immediacy of death seemed to fade, and there occurred in him one of those peculiar moments of utter transference, and he imagined himself for a moment swimming in the Sea of Japan, calling to the beautiful young Misao Hirota, whose dark almond eyes laughed in the warmth of love and adoration. She was calling to him, but her voice was so dull and faint it seemed to come from the other side of an abyss and the memory grew misty and indistinct, like all his mental wrestling, and he was back in the cold waters of the storm, struggling to survive.

Lightning briefly lit the night a final time, and then the curtain of obscurity fell back over them as the dark swallowed them up. Peter had a hold on Tristan by the collar, as one would grip a beast of burden by the harness, and, tugging him along after him, continued to ply the water ahead.

Neither man spoke but they could hear and feel each other splashing in the black tide, each giving strength to the other. Tristan, who could not swim, received from Peter the hope of surviving this worldly storm in order to meet an unearthly one, one that he somehow knew awaited him before dawn. And Peter, who could not see clearly through what had been set upon him this night, reaped from Tristan gleams of hope and truth to fill in his clouded reasoning and shore up his faith.

Tangled together in this gloomy web of death, they prayed as they labored, their lips moving rapidly as if heavily immersed in some profound, urgent inner dialogue. But finally Peter began to grow weary. Sinking deeper, he threw his face back, raising his head as if to drink air, and his face, in the obscurity, took on the appearance of a pale mask floating in the darkness.

And suddenly, for no apparent reason, only dimly aware of the weight of Tristan's drooping head across his shoulder, he could feel in the darkness the appalling spider. Even as his legs sank and his toes touched the solidity of pavement below, allowing him to stand chest deep in the flood, he felt the closing entanglement of some hidden, dreadful trap weaving its way about their escape from the sea . . . not in the water, but in what was about to begin.

* * *

Peter mopped his face with a soaked sleeve and dragged Tristan from the water, stumbling twice. The effort had exhausted him. He lay sprawled on his belly, breathing heavily, his cheek flattened against the cold pavement.

Patches of light fell from nearby windows and lanterns, and on the wind drifted sporadic voices, cries of women and children, men bellowing instructions. Peter could hear the occasional drum of footsteps. And though the cutting rain scythed about in gusting horizontal sheets, people were gathering in somber groups, coming and going, exchanging news, helping each other, staring into the black sky or listening to the sea, then hurrying away in search of friends and family.

The fraternity of strangers born of great peril was forming. Amidst utter confusion they were beginning to gel and were soon ushering each other northward to seek shelter in the nearby buildings of the old business district which stood elevated above the flood. These were old buildings of stone and concrete that could withstand the hurricane-force winds sweeping coastward and the reeling destruction of spin-off tornados that had begun to drop from massive swirls of black night sky. But before Peter could stand, the streets fell silent again, suddenly deserted.

Tristan sat up, embracing Peter. "Thank you, my friend. Where did you find the strength?"

Peter stood, rooted straight as a poker, observing the sudden silence of the houses, lost in the funereal repose of deserted streets. "Damn, look at all this wreckage. This could end up dwarfing Camille."

"I dread the dawn," huffed Joseph, dragging himself beside the others. "We'll be counting the dead."

A bar of light swung across from the east, crisscrossing about, and they suddenly heard footsteps as the light bounced off the empty houses. Then the rip of plywood being torn from the windows.

"Damn them!" Peter said softly, lifting Tristan with an urgent tug. "It's the ghouls and looters. They've already begun. They'll have guns. We should move on. We can't stop them. There'll be no law until morning. Come on."

There were several voices now, barking instructions with the hushed growl of secrecy. The beam of light drew closer, bouncing into the sky and into the houses, peering into black holes. "The bedrooms only," a voice muttered. "Be quick, cash and jewelry, nothing else!"

Stooping to keep a low profile, Peter led Tristan and Joseph away from the voices and took them on a circuitous route into the business district. The rain had softened and the wind was less steady now, coming only in periodic but murderous gusts that swept away anything loose or free standing.

Soon they found people again. Men in doorways, blocking their families inside. Behind them, children peeked out into the streets, secure in the shadows of their fathers, but cautious, too. An infant wailed from within one of the store fronts, and then the comforting cluck of a mother followed by a lullaby.

As the three friends passed one of these doorways, a hand reached out. "Joseph! Peter! Thank God you're alright." It was Brother Patrick. He stepped out onto the sidewalk holding a lantern that hissed of white gas but put out a welcome warmth.

"Patrick! What are you doing here? Why aren't you at the shelter?" said Joseph.

"Not enough time. The marsh behind the school, the water was rising too quickly. We thought we better head downtown for the high ground."

"So all of you are here, then?"

Patrick frowned, shrugging. "All but Placidus."

"Placidus?"

"He lost it, Joseph. When I gave the order to leave, he refused. He cursed us, then ran to the attic. He had a broomstick in one hand and a rolling pin in the other. Went completely berserk, fought us off at the landing. Struck me on the shoulders and broke Brother Albert's nose."

Peter shook his head. "What in hell's name was—"

"Said he wasn't leaving. Said he was staying there with little Amanda. He's lost his mind completely, I'm afraid."

"Amanda LaFleur?" said Tristan, moving beside Peter. "Was *she* there?"

Patrick looked questioningly at Tristan. Then he looked at Peter and Joseph, as if to seek help. "She's *dead*. You know that. She was—"

"But did Placidus *say* that she was there?" Peter pressed with unmistakable urgency.

"Yes," Patrick said, "he said she was in the attic waiting for him."

"Damn," Peter whispered.

"We must go there," said Tristan. "Malik will be there. He means to kill Placidus."

"Malik?" said Patrick, his confusion deepening. "What are you talking about? For God's sake, Joseph, what's going on here?"

"Joseph, you better stay," said Tristan. Peter, we must go immediately. It may already be too late."

Patrick gave a dismal shake of the head. "You'll never make it. The bridge is flooded by now. We just barely got out ourselves. If Placidus stays in the attic he might ride it out. And Didier might be able to get to him, too."

"Didier?" said Peter.

"Yes, as we were evacuating across the north bride, he came by on the *Miss Marie* on his way to the marsh. We told him about Placidus. He said he would try to drag him out if he could maneuver the rise behind the school."

"We'll go regardless," Peter sighed, knowing that Tristan's immovable certainty left no options.

"Power lines are down everywhere," Patrick warned. "Oak trees, too, by the hundreds. I don't think you should go, Peter."

"No, it's done," said Peter. "I couldn't stop Tristan with a bulldozer, and he'll need me. Hell, he can't swim. Father Joe, stay and help Patrick and the others—there'll be a lot to do by morning."

"Then we'll pray for you," said Brother Patrick. "And here, take the lantern."

"Thanks." Peter accepted the lantern but his smile was both weak and false because he suddenly felt the advance of something inexpressibly tragic and final. He felt it in his heart and in the dull banging of the distant wind-loosened shutter across the street. He felt it in the earth below, whispering under the beat of the slow rain. But most

Contrition

of all he saw it in Tristan's peaceful gaze, where a new light suddenly shone, a light at once entrancing and terrible.

This caused Peter, for just a moment, to doubt the wisdom of heading back out into the stormy night. Once they set course north, he sensed, a train of mysterious forces was about to collide and unravel, and he would have no control whatsoever over the outcome. He looked at Tristan a final time, then turned.

"Okay, Tristan," he said, "follow me."

Chapter Thirty-Four

Within minutes Tristan and Peter were out of the business district, and, as the elevation dropped, their pace slackened. Soon they were up to their calves in water again, shielding their faces from the rain. But it was Tristan that led the way, and one would have thought him a phantom as he picked his way through debris and over felled oaks. With priestly inflexibility, he pressed forward through the shadowy, ill-defined wreckage of what was once a neighborhood.

As they traveled, a great gulf opened between the two men. Peter grew red with exhaustion, lost in all sorts of apprehensions about where he stood in what was about to begin. A small but constant tremor had taken over his body, and he felt flushed as the salt of perspiration filled the creases of his face, washing down in rivulets to his neck and shoulders.

"*Hora fugit,*" urged Tristan, nearly dragging his friend, urged on by that invisible force that drags men toward annihilation, happily and without reservation. He had grown pallid with a waxy whiteness, and his eyes glittered in the lantern's pale light. His lips moved as if he were speaking to somebody, his face grim, his motions hurried as if he were administering last rites, as if he were racing to beat Satan to that final moment of a dying man's consciousness.

In places their footing disappeared and the water deepened, and only then would Tristan cry out for Peter, and only then did Peter become strong again, his purpose clear. Peter would grab him, drag him through the deep water, and prop him up as he found a footing again. Then he would slip into apprehension as Tristan's confidence resurfaced, forcing them onward.

And finally, after more than an hour of impossible travel, they swam the channel onto the campus of Saint Gregory and found

Contrition

themselves wading in knee-deep brackishness, approaching the Brother's house.

"Give me the lantern," said Tristan, a pontifical and warrior-like expression creeping over his face. He stepped into the doorway and moved up the stairs. Crossing himself, he whispered to no one, "We are dust and a shadow, Lord."

Chapter Thirty-Five

The door above them stood open and from within came a soft glow. Peter heard a sudden creaking of the floorboards that betrayed movement and immediately imagined that it had to be Placidus moving about. But there was another creaking too, like that of a pendulum. *Rope against timber,* thought Peter, struck dumb by the words of his dead father.

They entered the attic. Tristan took several steps, then froze, his gaze as impenetrable as granite, and Peter could not tell which was more inspiring, Tristan's pallor or his serenity as he measured the attic.

There hung Placidus, from the rafter, swinging softly by the neck. The metronomic sway of the rope was hypnotic. It paralyzed Peter for a moment, but then he caught his breath, trembling, and cried out, "Placidus!"

But Placidus could not reply. He was dead. He hung there, his neck crooked to one side like a bird, broken-necked. His eyes protruded from their sockets in a grotesque mask of agony, his lips were swollen blue, and his face was twisted like a root, frozen in the final throes of staving off strangulation, gasping for that final breath of precious air.

Peter sagged, unwilling to absorb the scene. He felt as though he were staring at something unreal, through the haze of wine. Something ill-defined or imagined. Then a form emerged from the blackness of Placidus's shadow, from against the back wall.

Peter's eyes slipped past Placidus and settled on a huge man, a creature of some dark origin that he had been seeking for weeks now—a creature that had been brewing his poison over centuries of winters, in the pits of despair and anguish, from the lowest depths of Hell. It was Malik.

Malik held a large stick, and his eyes were closed. He slowly ran one palm over the crown of his great shaved head and stepped forward,

Contrition

dragging his foot, making a long scrape behind him. Then, with the wide stance and posture of the butcher who is about to begin his work, he started and his eyes jolted open, as if enmeshed in the countless threads of a terrible, savage act. He raised his eyes haughtily, and placed both palms about the top of his club. "And so . . . Tristan de Saint Germain, the *priest*—and a *friend*," he said, licking at his lower lip.

"And so," said Tristan with that perfect calm that masks fury and vengeance, "Malik, the Butcher of Medina. Bastard Son of Arabia."

Peter craned his neck to get a closer look. The moving, hulking shadow before him was like the serpent entrancing the mouse. Peter stood mesmerized, seeing himself reflected in miniature in the cold glitter of Malik's eyes. Instinctively he reached for his holster, but there nothing there to be found.

There are collapses from within, and Peter had been fiercely struggling against his since the day he had first fled the attic, since the day Little Jimmy had died, and his father—since struggling in the sea's rushing advance, and since finding the executed Placidus, but now his frame began to crumble. By degrees, he began to understand what was about to unfold.

It would be death. No, murder. A double execution. There would be no hope unless he abandoned Tristan now, or unless Tristan suddenly chose to retreat. But Peter knew the latter could not happen because even he knew that there is no man more fearless in action than a dreamer. So Peter stood there, frozen, afraid to advance, unwilling to retreat, as Malik fondly gazed at him and Tristan with the rapture of the spider that allows the moth to flutter.

"So, who is this friend you bring to the slaughterhouse, priest?" said Malik with a low, deliberate rasp, feeling the palpitation of the detective under each word.

"An ally in God," said Tristan calmly, his eyes becoming slits.

"Ha! I laugh. Like your brother then," said Malik, grasping his club firmly. Then he pointed to Peter. "And you, you've come to join your old friend hanging there? You are so impatient to die that you have followed this priest to your own execution?"

"I'll send you back to the depths of Hell," said Tristan, "you outcast. You'll howl and bay again with the other hyenas of Hell. Forever."

Malik's fixed, unblinking stare raked over Tristan a moment as he stood silent. Tristan, too, remained silent, and the attic filled with the strange, threatening stillness that precedes battle. The rope that tethered Placidus had ceased its dreadful sway, and the dull drum of the rain beating against the roof suddenly stilled, as did the wind. The whole world seemed to hold its breath as the four men, one dead, remained motionless in the confines of the attic, as if posing patiently and peacefully for a portrait while the artist paused to select his next color.

Then, in the wordless flush of consciousness, all hesitation vanished. Tristan rushed forward, hurling himself onto Malik's great chest, battering his skull and his face, clawing at him with the fury and spit of an enraged badger.

Malik stood inert, temporarily stunned, like a bear submitting to the claw of the lynx cat. The thick muscles of his throat stiffened and his neck flesh tightened as his dull eyes lit into embers. He brushed Tristan aside and sent him careening into a corner. But he was up again before Malik could focus.

"*Ecrasez l'infame!*" Tristan screamed, his voice hoarse and full of hate. "I crush this vile thing in the name of God!"

Tristan charged forward, jumped, reaching up with both hands to grip a rafter, and swung his feet forward. He caught Malik full in the face and Malik's lips burst open in a glut of flesh and blood as Tristan fell to the floor. Malik shivered violently a moment, then charged blindly forward, tripping over his attacker and collapsing.

Crushed beneath the weight of Malik's great body, Tristan felt his breath leaving him in a single rush and could suddenly find no air. He felt himself bursting from within. *Peter,* he thought, *where are you?*

Unwittingly, Malik rolled aside, grasping about blindly to strangle his enemy, thereby allowing Tristan to escape. Tristan staggered, teetered about, drunk from lack of oxygen. He did not see Malik rise, nor did he see Malik grab his stick, or smile with the knowing eye of a predator. Malik swung out with both of his huge arms, and clubbed Tristan across the knees. The crack was unmistakable. Tristan crumpled in a heap, tried to place his weight on one leg to rise, then crumpled again. "Peter, where are you?" he whispered, as a constellation of white spots flooded his vision.

Malik struck outward with the club again, delivering a vicious blow across the side of Tristan's skull. Red flesh erupted in a line from the wound as hair and skin parted, forming two horrid lips that seemed to yawn, opening a terrible river of blood and tissue.

Contrition

"Peter! *Ecrasez l'infame!*" Tristan screamed! "*Ad majorem Dei gloriam!*"

Peter was still anchored to where he had been when the fight erupted. He could feel his arteries beating and the blood rushing about his temples, but it was as if his will had been paralyzed, an unwilling witness as the angel of light and the angel of darkness grappled on a bridge over some great chasm.

"*Ad majorem Dei gloriam!*" cried Tristan, smothering below Malik's deadly blows, his knees broken, his vision lost, his consciousness waning. He could still feel Malik groping about, cackling, dragging him farther into the attic corner, holding him like an owl holding freshly killed prey in vice-like talons. "I . . . I have failed again," he whispered, unable to hear even his own voice.

"Peter!"

Chapter Thirty-Six

Peter heard this last plea, Tristan's voice faint, broken by hoarse gasping. And in the two heartbeats it took to register the horror of Tristan dying, everything suddenly fell into luminous perspective. A burning forgetfulness of everything that came before mounting the attic stairs blotted his paralysis. Reason disappeared and only instinct remained. Peter attacked.

He charged forward like a man crazed, not even aware where the courage came from, or whether it would endure. He struck Malik across the bridge of the nose with a balled, driving fist, and swept back with an elbow, catching the huge man in an eye socket. Malik stood inert, stunned, then bellowed. Peter kicked up and drove his foot into Malik's groin.

Malik crumbled, releasing Tristan in a heap to the floor. But Malik rose up quickly, regenerated somehow, and stormed forward. He caught Peter by the throat and slammed him reeling backward over the life-sized crucifix that lay on the floor. Peter rolled over and found himself on all fours, winded. Suddenly the floor creaked heavily. Malik was coming at him.

As Peter raised his head, he saw the face of Christ, staring up at him, his eyes mournful, his forehead crowned with thorns. He thought it was a vision at first, an apparition, but when he reached out, he felt a face. It was smooth, covered with the soft dust of abandonment. It was the crucifix, just inches from his face.

"God! Lord!" he cried. "Give me strength! I—"

Malik grabbed him by the head with both huge palms and slung him against the wall. "God can't help you now!" he laughed, watching Peter crash into the timbers. "You are mine!"

Peter lay in a heap on the floor, entangled in his own limbs. He tasted blood and felt its warmth trickling in rivulets from the corner of his mouth. Slowly, he rose, pushing his back against the wall for support. He saw the crucifix again, and just beyond that, Tristan, who lay motionless, staring up at the rafters with vacant eyes. It was the stare of death. It was over; they would both be dead in another few moments, thought Peter, as he watched Malik coming at him.

Suddenly, almost subconsciously, Peter's hand felt something protruding from the wall to his right at knee level. It was a nail bristling crookedly out of one of the wall timbers. And from that nail hung something. It moved in Peter's searching fingers, swiveling with his motion. It was a knife, hanging from a short string drilled through the metal handle. Peter gasped.

Malik was unaware of Peter's hand moving against the back wall. Malik was still laughing, his dark lips curled in a lewd sneer. Then he rushed forward. Peter jerked the knife from the string and his arm swung blindly in an upward arc. He caught Malik inside the thigh. They both heard fabric rip, then heard the splitting of flesh. Malik stiffened, and his eyes dilated. Stunned, he thought the pain to be someone else's at first. Or a distant memory, perhaps.

Then he roared out in agony and became a swirl of limbs, as if fighting off an aroused swarm of hornets. A swinging forearm caught Peter across the jaw, crushing it, but the blow was simultaneous with another jab of the knife, just inches above the first.

Malik crashed to the floor, writhing in pain, grasping at his thigh, cursing. Peter teetered a moment, stunned senseless as more blood began to gush from his mouth. The two men stared at each other, eyes burning with hate. For each man the necessity of eliminating the other was singular.

But Malik could not stand. His wounds were bleeding profusely, and he was like a great deadly serpent, coiled, but pinned to the floor. His striking distance was limited to the reach of his arm. He snarled and hunched on his elbows, dragging himself backward. He was looking for his club.

Nor could Peter attack. His lower jaw hung limp and broken, bleeding. His vision was blurred and he could barely keep his equilibrium. He could still feel the knife in his hand, but his grip on it was weak. It was as if his fingers had grown slack and useless. So he stood there, shivering, watching Malik gradually move about, drawing nearer to his club.

"Odo," a voice slowly murmured. "Odo . . . "

The sound shocked both men. They had thought Tristan dead. Malik swiveled his head about the room as if suddenly and rudely awakened from a dream. With difficulty, Peter raised his eyes, looking first at the crucifix, half expecting Christ to rise from his cross.

"Odo," came the voice again. Then movement. From the back of the attic, a hand slowly rose upward from the floor, fingers outstretched, tremoring. *"Dum spiro . . . spero—"*

"My *God*, he's alive," Peter whispered aloud, stunned. He wanted to rush forward, to rejoice. He wanted to stop Malik, who was still dragging his way to the corner, but he was too weak and unbalanced. His fingers trembled and he dropped the knife.

Malik heard it fall at precisely the same moment his hand seized the club. "You're finished," he bellowed, his eyes narrowing. "But first I'll finish the monk." He sat up, just feet from Tristan and raised the stick with both hands. He brought the head of the club down forcefully across Tristan's skull.

Peter winced helplessly as the cracking of bone filled the thick air, and Tristan convulsed, unable to rise, or even to scream. His whole body twitched and trembled as though a powerful electric shock has just been delivered. Malik raised the club again.

Peter cried out, knowing the next blow would deliver finality. "God!" he screamed, his throat shredding. "Where are you? In the name of mercy spare this man!"

A sudden burst of noise filled the stairway, the heavy thud of boots running up the steps. Then a voice as a huge shadow loomed into the attic entrance, casting a bulky darkness that startled Peter, and even Malik. "Peter!" the voice cried.

It was Didier LaFleur. He lumbered into the cavernous room, eyes drinking in everything, forcing assumptions out of the bloody scene that greeted him. He instantly recognized that he must move quickly, as Peter stood there quivering, his voice unintelligible, pointing at Malik who sat there, club raised over the maimed and dying Tristan.

Without a word, or even hesitation, Didier rushed, certain of purpose. He ran at Malik as though shedding decades of weathering physical abuse and wear. He charged like a young bull, full of red-blooded will and wrath. He swept aside the great club with one huge paw and delivered a smashing blow to Malik's face with the other.

Malik fell backward and the back of his head struck the floor. He quivered a moment, then his eyes floated, like raw eggs, in a glassy loss of focus.

But one of his hands reached out blindly and found the tip of his club. He sat up, moving from the waist only, as if his lower torso were nailed to the floor, and instinctively swung out with the club. He caught Didier on the side of the neck, but the old bear did not flinch. With the quickness of a cat, he grabbed the bludgeon, pulling it from Malik's grasp and reversing it, striking Malik across the bridge of the nose.

Again the great shaved head crashed against the wood flooring. Blood began to trickle from Malik's ears in thin, jagged streams. He looked up, dazed, but fully aware that Didier LaFleur was straddling his chest, holding the head of the club with both hands, firmly pressing its point into the cavity between his victim's throat and chest. "You killed my granddaughter," he said coldly.

Malik's tongue flicked out in a lizardly gesture of hate. "And so," he rasped, his eyes laughing haughtily, "what do you do now, *Christian*?" Then he spat.

"Kill him," Peter whispered hoarsely, pointing feebly at Didier's feet. "My God, Didier, do it!"

Malik sneered. "I killed a girl," he said with the wicked grin not unlike the smile of the sunning crocodile. "She was young and beautiful, large blue eyes. She said her name was Amanda. If that was your granddaughter, then, kill me . . . in the name of your *God*." He spat again. Didier's grip on the stick tightened and he pressed it deeper. Malik's flesh began to pale under the point of the club, and he sensed in Didier's expressionless eyes that there would be no quarter. This huge old bear of a man standing over him would not be confused, or faint of heart.

"I enjoyed killing her," Malik snarled with a lewd look of skulking triumph.

Didier closed his eyes, lost in a sleep-like trance. He saw his sweet Amanda, smiling, laughing, throwing herself on his lap. A lifetime of love and adoration passed through him in a span of seconds. Then he saw her pleading for mercy, crying out his name. "Grandpa!" she cried. "Oh, Grandpa! Where are you ? Help me!"

Didier shivered violently then and his eyes snapped open. He raised on his toes and with all his mighty weight, he shoved downward until he heard the crunch of bone and the tearing of flesh. Within seconds, the sharp wood of the club met the hard wood of the oak flooring and would go no further.

Malik screamed. It was the wail of the lost. The scream of the damned. He turned pallid, and his eyeballs turned scarlet with jagged veins of blood standing in high relief, as though illuminated by the fires of Hell. His head lolled to the side, and he saw Tristan, his head also turned, staring back at him emptily. They had both reached the moment when each had only time to think of his own death. Neither spoke. Neither moved.

They lay there frozen in a blank stare, just inches apart.

* * *

Didier led Peter to Tristan's side as one leads an invalid, slowly, with urging words. Peter knelt, shivering. With all the gentleness of a brother tending to his dying sibling, he gathered Tristan's head into his lap.

Tristan writhed with dull and feeble groans as he felt his crushed body being moved, thinking it was Malik again, coming for him. But he slowly raised his lids and his gaze, lethargic, rested on Peter. "I'm dying," he whispered.

Peter's face was a mask of supplication. *Lord, take him quickly*, he thought.

"Tristan's eye closed briefly. "Malik?"

"Dead," said Peter.

"You did it . . . you were strong then, in the end."

"No, it was Didier."

"Didier? Ah, of course . . . God—works—in circles."

Didier mover closer and closed his huge hand around Tristan's. "The big man, he is gone," he said, "forever."

"Ah, but Didier, there is no forever—only eternity."

Then there came a mournful calm as Tristan pulled his hands from Didier's and folded them in prayer on his chest. His eyes flared a moment, revealing the torture of his inner journeys through centuries of sorrow and despair.

"In a moment I will be gone, Peter," said Tristan, his voice beginning to gurgle with the rattle of death. "Remember, death is the entrance into great light or infinite darkness. Pray for light. *P-pax vobiscum.*"

Contrition

Peter felt a shroud of disquiet bury his heart. He raised his eyes skyward and uttered a prayer, knowing that Tristan had passed with those final words.

With his death, Peter's memory suddenly became a vague swarm of shadows beginning with the day he had first met this young man at Madame LaFontaine's.

I must heal the dry rot of my life, thought Peter. *I must gather those faint, scattered scraps of faith and knit them into conviction. I . . .*

Suddenly Peter felt a presence in the room, standing beside him even as he crouched over Tristan. "There's someone here," he said to Didier.

Didier looked about the room, puzzled. "No, just us, and the dead."

Peter closed his eyes. He felt a great warmth next to him. Then keeping his eyes tightly closed, he saw her, in his mind, and in his heart. It was Amanda LaFleur, kneeling over Tristan, taking his hand, telling him to rise.

"My God!" cried Peter. "Didier! Do you see her?"

There was no reply. But Peter felt her warmth and witnessed the pale heavenly apparition, pulling Tristan's soul from his slain body. They stood there together, then, Amanda and Tristan, smiling, gazing at Peter and Didier, hand in hand, lost in the rapture of great things coming on the wind from the heavens. And then they were gone.

The End